I0819960

Plotting History

Plotting History

The Russian Historical Novel in the Imperial Age

Dan Ungurianu

THE UNIVERSITY OF WISCONSIN PRESS

Support for this research was provided by the Susan Turner Fund
and the Emily Floyd Fund of Vassar College.

The University of Wisconsin Press
1930 Monroe Street, 3rd Floor
Madison, Wisconsin 53711-2059

www.wisc.edu/wisconsinpress/

3 Henrietta Street
London WE2E 8LU, England

5 4 3 2 1

Library of Congress Cataloging-in-Publication Data

Ungurianu, Dan.
Plotting history : the Russian historical novel in the
Imperial Age / Dan Ungurianu.
p. cm.
Includes bibliographical references and index.
ISBN 0-299-22500-3 (cloth : alk. paper)
1. Historical fiction, Russian—History and criticism. 2. Russian fiction—
19th century—History and criticism. I. Title.
PG3098.H5U54 2007
891.7′3081—dc22 2007011936

For

Lioba, Lena, *and* Nika

Contents

Illustrations

Plates

Preface and Acknowledgments

As the famous dictum goes, Pushkin is our (i.e., Russian literature's) everything. In a way, this is also true for the present study. Its initial impetus stems from my interest in *The Captain's Daughter,* the most perfect piece of Russian historical fiction, which remains elusive and enigmatic despite the appearance of tantalizing simplicity. However, the chapter on Pushkin accounts for only a small portion of this study since the past decade has produced a number of excellent works on his historical imagination. In my own pursuit of a better understanding of *The Captain's Daughter,* I had turned to its synchronic and diachronic contexts. In doing so I was struck by two perhaps somewhat naive discoveries. First, I determined that Pushkin's genius—its Shakespearean, Dantean, and Mozartian dimensions notwithstanding—can be comprehended more fully and interpreted more convincingly in the context of the literary environment contemporary with Pushkin, a consideration that requires dealing with second- and third-rate writers. Second, I realized that continuity in literary evolution is a very shaky notion, whether in positive terms (*x* gave birth to *y*) or in negative ones (*y* rebelled against *x*). Thus, if one reads Pushkin's *Captain's Daughter* and Tolstoy's *War and Peace,* it would appear that these works, separated by only three decades and written by men belonging to the same circles of the Russian aristocracy, were produced by inhabitants of different planets. In short, my focus shifted from the work of an individual genius or geniuses to broader cultural paradigms. The result is the present history of the genre in Russia, covering the period from its inception during the romantic era to the emergence of modernism on the eve of the Revolution.

In keeping with common practice, I have used a dual system of transliteration. The main body of the text and the index contain anglicized forms of Russian names (e.g., Solovyov, Merezhkovsky, Bryusov), while the bibliographical apparatus and the appendix section follow the Library of Congress guidelines (e.g., Solov'ev, Merezhkovskii, Briusov). My hope is that this will not create too much confusion and will increase the readability of the text.

Portions of the present study have appeared in modified form in the following publications: "Fact and Fiction in the Romantic Historical Novel." *Russian Review* 57 (July 1998): 364–77; "Versions and Visions of History: Veterans of 1812 on Tolstoy's *War and Peace*," *Slavic and East European Journal* 44, no. 1 (2000): 47–62; "*Ledianoi dom* Lazhechnikova i peterburgskii kanon (K voprosu o genezise peterburgskogo teksta)," *Russian Literature* 51, no. 4 (2002): 471–81; "Le Roman historique russe dans la seconde moitié du XIXe siècle," in *Histoire de la littérature russe. Le XIXe siècle: Le Temps du roman*, ed. E. Etkind et al. (Paris: Fayard, 2005), 725–43.

I would like to take this opportunity to express my gratitude to friends and colleagues who variously contributed to the shaping of this project. First and foremost, I am deeply indebted to David Bethea, Alexander Dolinin, and Alexis Klimoff. Without their generous advice and unstinting support the present study would not have been possible. I am also thankful to Vladimir Alexandrov, Gene Barabtarlo, Sergei Davydov, Caryl Emerson, Nikolai Firtich, Gerhard Gerhardi, Judith Deutsch Kornblatt, Galina Lapina, Vladimir Markovich, David McDonald, Donna Tussing Orwin, Aleksandr Ospovat, Damiano Rebecchini, Gary Rosenshield, and Yuri Shcheglov—all of whose comments were very helpful at various stages of research. I would like to thank Vanessa Bittner for translating many quotations from Russian primary sources into English and Henry Krawitz for his thoughtful and thorough editing of my manuscript. I am also grateful to Steve Salemson, Gwen Walker, and Sheila Moermond of the University of Wisconsin Press for their friendly and professional help during all stages of turning my manuscript into a book. Finally, I should mention Irina Lukka and the other staff members who service the Slavonic Library at the University of Helsinki; they guided me through their splendid collections and cheerfully provided food for my gluttonous reading appetite. The completion of this study was greatly facilitated by a generous sabbatical policy at Vassar College and additional financial support from the Susan Turner Fund and the Emily Floyd Fund of Vassar College.

Plotting History

Introduction

Fact, Fiction, and the Anxiety of Genre

The historical novel is a suspect genre. It has been compromised by a host of low-grade works that exploit the allure of history, frequently mixing two divergent trends typical of fictional renderings of bygone epochs. On the one hand, the historical record can serve as a kind of coloring book, supplying rather pedestrian writers with ready-made patterns for their narratives. On the other hand, shifting the action to the past is often seen as a carte blanche for the most unbridled fantasy, which is seasoned with varying quantities of antiquarian details. The fruit of such historical imagination can indeed be less than palatable. As Leon Feuchtwanger, himself a major historical novelist, put it in his 1935 essay "On the Sense and Nonsense of the Historical Novel": "The label 'historical novel' itself conjures for us depressing associations. We recall *Ben Hur, The Count of Monte Cristo,* and some historical films. We immediately picture to ourselves adventures, intrigues, costumes, gaudy, garish colors, bombastic chatter, a jumble of politics and love" (Feikhtvanger, 667).

More important, the very legitimacy of the historical novel has repeatedly been questioned. In Russia perhaps the most provocative and sly attack against the genre was made at the height of its popularity in 1833 by the prominent journalist Osip Senkovsky: "I don't like historical novels. I prefer morals. It offends me to take a bastard in my hands: the historical novel is, in my opinion, a bastard son without family or tribe, the fruit of history's flagrant adultery with imagination. I insist on purity of morals and would rather deal with the legitimate children of either history or imagination. The historical novel [. . .] is a false form of art. Yes! it is a false form of art" (44).

The contradiction between fact and fiction has been revisited by numerous critics and at times has frustrated even accomplished practitioners of the genre. For example, Alessandro Manzoni, the "Italian Walter Scott," whose *I Promessi Sposi* (1828) belongs to the most acclaimed works of historical fiction, arrived at the following pessimistic conclusion in 1850 in his essay "On the Historical Novel and, in General, on Works Mixing History and Invention": "[T]he historical novel is a work in which the necessary turns out to be impossible, and in which two essential conditions cannot be reconciled, or even fulfilled. It inevitably calls for a combination that is contrary to its subject matter and a division contrary to its form. Though we know it is a work in which history and fable must figure, we cannot determine or even estimate their proper measure or relation. In short, it is a work impossible to achieve satisfactorily, because its premises are inherently contradictory" (72).

It is precisely on these grounds that Harold Bloom, in his ambitious attempt to define the literary canon of the West, excludes the historical novel from the canon. "The historical novel seems to have been permanently devalued. [. . .] This subgenre is no longer available for canonization. [. . .] History writing and narrative fiction have come apart, and our sensibilities seem no longer able to accommodate them to one another" (21). Contradicting himself, however, Bloom lists among the very best "canonical" works Tolstoy's novella *Hadji Murad*, which deals with the Russian conquest of the Caucasus. Bloom's caveat that "it would be odd to regard it as historical fiction, even in the sense that *War and Peace* could be called an historical novel" (337), is hardly convincing. By combining actual and imaginary characters and events in authentic historical settings, *Hadji Murad* falls squarely within the category of historical fiction.

In general, Bloom's negative verdict cannot be applied to the Russian canon, where the historical novel is still quite prominent. Three works of the genre—Pushkin's *Captain's Daughter*, Gogol's *Taras Bulba*, and Tolstoy's *War and Peace*—form the very core of the Russian tradition. These books figure in the school curriculum and comprise the cultural legacy of the average educated Russian. A number of historical novels—including A. K. Tolstoy's *Prince Serebryany*, Lazhechnikov's *Ice Palace*, and Danilevsky's *Mirovich*—belong to the "junior" canon, being among the favorite books of Russian children and teenagers. Even more popular among Russian youngsters are historical novels by Sir Walter Scott, Alexandre Dumas, Robert Louis Stevenson, James Fenimore Cooper, and several other Western authors. At least this was the case until the mid-1980s, when the entertainment revolution began to leave its mark in Russia; as a result, both high- and lowbrow literature lost its prominence, sliding down to the humble position it holds in modern Western culture. Nevertheless, historical novels—domestic and foreign, old and new—occupy a sizable niche in the motley book market of today's Russia.

If we leave the current situation and look back at literary history, the prominence of the historical novel becomes even more obvious. In the 1830s it was by far the most important genre of romantic prose, one that produced a number of first-rate works (Pushkin's *Captain's Daughter*, Gogol's *Taras Bulba*, early novels by Zagoskin, three novels by Lazhechnikov, Veltman's *Koshchei the Deathless*) and, in a sense, laid the groundwork for the subsequent rise of the Russian novel. In the mid nineteenth century the historical novel all but disappeared from the literary scene. However, it began a gradual comeback in the 1860s with such works as A. K. Tolstoy's *Prince Serebryany* and Leo Tolstoy's monumental *War and Peace*. The second wave of the genre's popularity, which occurred in the 1870s and 1880s, is associated with the names of Danilevsky, Mordovtsev, Count Salias, and Vsevolod Solovyov, who were among the most widely read authors of their time. A steady flow of historical novels continued throughout the remainder of the imperial period. Although most of them belong to second-rate literature, the genre played a significant role in the evolution of symbolist prose (e.g., in two of Merezhkovsky's trilogies and Bryusov's *Fiery Angel* and *Altar of Victory*) and also attracted Vasily Kamensky, one of the founders of Russian futurism (e.g., *Stenka Razin*). The historical novel remained a prominent genre after 1917 as well, both in Soviet Russia and in the emigration. Also worth mentioning are works by Yury Tynyanov, Olga Forsh, Aleksei N. Tolstoy, Mark Aldanov, Roman Gul, Yury Trifonov, Yury Davydov, Vasily Yan, Valentin Ivanov, Valentin Pikul, Dmitry Balashov, Bulat Okudzhava, Natan Eidelman, Ion Drutse, Anatoly Rybakov—and, of course, Aleksandr Solzhenitsyn, with his herculean if not sisyphean *Red Wheel*. More recent contributions to the genre include Georgy Vladimov's *General and His Army*, Vasily Aksyonov's *Moscow Saga*, and Daniil Granin's *Evenings with Peter the Great*. A strong historical—or at least quasi-historical—element is also found in the immensely popular retrodetective "projects" of Boris Akunin.

Thus, although the historical novel is an important genre in Russia—both for high literature and mass culture—it is obviously understudied. Whereas in the existing scholarship there are some valuable works on individual authors and separate periods, a satisfactory general overview is lacking.[1] This study is meant to fill this gap by offering a history of the historical novel from its origins to the Revolution. While part of my effort is descriptive, the main thrust is analytical in attempting to establish the poetics of the genre that arises at the intersection of fact and fiction.

Having invoked yet again this much-abused dyad, I feel obliged to digress concerning the reevaluation in critical thought that began almost four decades ago, when the borders separating fact and fiction were subjected to vigorous assault. Among the most prominent critics were W. B. Gallie, Arthur Danto, Morton White, and Russel Nye, who in various ways questioned the nature of historical knowledge from the standpoint of an "analytical philosophy of history" and narrative theory.[2] The best-known representative of the "narratological" current is Hayden White, who concludes that historical narratives are in essence similar to fictional ones since they are informed by identical rhetorical devices and categories of emplotment. Although "narrativists" do not necessarily deny altogether the reality behind historical narratives,[3] they emphasize what White calls the "unexpungeable relativity" of historiography that is conditioned by its linguistic expression ("Historical Emplotment," 37). More radical postmodernist theoreticians—Roland Barthes being the primary example—extend the principle of relativity not only to historiographical accounts but also to the so-called historical facts, which "can only exist linguistically, as a term in discourse" (Barthes, "Historical Discourse," 153–54).

Such arguments have been engaged on both epistemological and ethical grounds, the latter being of concern even to the proponents of the narratological standpoint since—to rephrase Dostoevsky's famous dictum—if there is no fact, then everything is admissible.[4] Intentionally dodging the seriousness of philosophical questions involved in this debate, I refuse to espouse the narratological/relativist approach for a very pragmatic reason. If there is no difference between fact and fiction (with or without quotation marks), then the whole issue of the historical novel becomes irrelevant, which, aside from rendering useless the present study, does not help to elucidate an important aspect of Russian literary history. I therefore deem it unnecessary to push the similarity between the historiographer and the writer of fiction further than is done by British historian R. G. Collingwood (many of whose ideas were developed by the "narrativists"). To cite Collingwood's comparison from his *Idea of History*, the historian deals with certain "solid" points—more or less established facts, no matter how idiosyncratic the notion of historical fact may be.[5] In order to create a meaningful picture, the historian has to connect these points. In this he is akin to the writer since they both use their imagination in the process. However, they differ profoundly in the sense that for the historian the points are given, while the writer creates them all by himself. Thus, the littérateur can imagine things "happening at no place and at no date," whereas the historian's picture "must be localized in space and time" (246).

The peculiarity of the historical novel is precisely in the intersection and interaction of these two modes of narration: fictional, where the author is ultimately the sole authority, and historical, which is grounded in extraliterary reality. This creates a specific tension, which is viewed by some critics as a sign of the genre's illegitimacy. To quote Senkovsky again: "[T]he reader, constantly afraid of the unknown in this blending of truth and fantasy, wants to believe the words of the author at each step, and at each step is afraid of being betrayed, and after reading the novel either doesn't know what to think of his impressions, or good-naturedly falls for the deception" (44–45). However, such tension can be highly productive as well, adding an extra dimension to the historical novel and other "documentary fiction," aptly described by Lydia Ginzburg, who concludes: "In documentary literature the artistic symbol presupposes the reader's independent knowledge of the subject depicted. In the comparison, in the incomplete combining of the two planes—the empirical plane and its esthetic interpretation—lies the special dynamics of documentary literature" (*O literaturnom geroe*, 7).

Bearing in mind this dual nature of the genre helps to avoid what I see as two extremes in its interpretation. One should not overemphasize the continuity in the evolution of the historical novel since its poetics are not as self-contained and autonomous as in many other genres, such as those informed by intent (satire, utopia/anti-utopia) or situation (detective, picaresque, travelogue, bildungsroman). At the same time, one should not completely dissolve the historical novel in other genres of contemporary literature since its lineage includes pronouncedly nonfictional elements. The former trend is present, explicitly or implicitly, in most works dealing with the subject; the latter is carried to an extreme by the prominent Marxist critic Georg Lukács.

The term "dynamics" employed by Ginzburg is perhaps the key to the equation of fact and fiction that underlies the historical novel since there is no single "correct" formula for combining the two principles or any ideal recipe for the historical novel in general. The notions of history and fiction are historically conditioned, as is the attitude toward their combination. This presents yet another argument for avoiding the "narratological" line of reasoning. Despite its professed relativist philosophical stance, the "narratological" school ultimately claims to possess the absolute or, at least, privileged hermeneutic perspective, which tends to annul the validity of previous approaches.

My focus, however, is precisely on the change of perspectives. I therefore prefer a sliding scale rather than absolutes based on epistemological or any other criteria—Russia's alleged uniqueness included. A manifestation of the latter approach is found in Andrew Wachtel's study *An Obsession with History: Russian Writers Confront the Past,* which postulates a peculiar Russian model of "intergeneric dialogue" between historiography and literature. This model supposedly emerged in the late eighteenth and early nineteenth centuries and still exists today. Although Wachtel explicitly states that he is not concerned with the historical novel per se, he draws extensively on the works of the genre (e.g., *The Captain's Daughter, War and Peace, The Red Wheel*), which represents a prominent example of this alleged dialogue.

Wachtel's approach can be seen as the injection of a modern trend in critical theory (a modified notion of the Bakhtinian dialogue) into a time-honored tradition in Russian studies, where, for example, the names of Ivan the Terrible, Peter the Great, Joseph Stalin, and Vladmir Putin are used interchangeably; Brezhnev's detente is effortlessly likened to the temporary suspension of Moscow's isolationism under Ivan III; and Muscovy's territorial expansion is routinely projected onto the foreign policy of the Soviet Union on the authority of the notorious concept of "Moscow as the Third Rome." All of this is traced back to the enigmatic Russian soul and the mystical immutability of Mother Russia, with Russophile or Russophobe accents added according to taste. Such a notion of Russian exceptionalism has roots in both the "Slavophile" currents of Russian thought and—even more—in the lingering perception that endures in Western culture of Russia as an exotic and alien realm. Without intending to dismiss this venerable tradition, which has produced a number of classic studies, it is my belief that its hermeneutic potential is all but exhausted. In the area of theory, it has been supplanted by the semiotic approach of Lotman and Uspensky, while in practical studies its applicability is even more questionable. To accept Wachtel's claim that authors from the epochs of the Enlightenment, romanticism, realism, symbolism, and socialist realism all espoused the same model of intergeneric dialogue by virtue of being Russians is to make a leap of faith that I am not ready to accept. The notions of history, fiction, and their interrelationship underwent drastic changes over the past two centuries, and it is impossible to find a common denominator based on Russianness or any other criteria. In addition, the concept of dialogue—like any other "totalitarian" scheme—may fit neatly when applied to some periods and authors but may prove quite misleading when applied to others.

A more theoretically sound and pragmatically useful approach to the problem is outlined in the following discrete view of genres formulated by Yury Tynyanov in his essay "On Literary Evolution": "[T]he study of isolated genres apart from the properties of the genre system to which they belong is impossible. Tolstoy's historical novel is not comparable to Zagoskin's historical novel but relates to the prose of his day" (276). Lydia Ginzburg, who was among Tynyanov's students and contemplated choosing the historical novel of the 1830s as her dissertation topic, comments: "The perspective of extreme historicism gives Tynyanov the ability to subdivide the concept of the genre" ("Zapisi 1920–1930-kh godov," 14).

Needless to say, historicism should not be (and was not in Tynyanov's case) extreme and absolute. One cannot speak of a complete discontinuity in the development of a genre—the historical novel in the present case. There undeniably exists what Bakhtin terms "memory of the genre." Moreover, as we shall see, some pivotal generic features and devices can be transplanted from one epoch to another. However, being incorporated into a different system, they acquire a different meaning or—to use Tynyanov's notion again—a different function. To my mind, therefore, the most fruitful approach to the study of the genre is historical, one that does not simply follow chronology but centers on the change of literary and cultural paradigms, which, in this study's time frame, includes romanticism, realism, and early modernism in its symbolist and futurist incarnations. As I hope to demonstrate, each of these periods produced its own distinct type of historical novel, defined primarily by its contemporary context rather than by the inertia of or polemic against the genre's tradition.

On the whole, the changes in the genre's paradigm follow the overall trajectory of Russian literature, which, mutatis mutandis, parallels that of European literature. Here one can observe several scenarios: retardation and catching up with the European tradition during the romantic period; idiosyncratic developments during the realist period; and the prefiguration of several important trends in European modernism at the turn of the century, when Russian art was on the cutting edge of modernity. Nevertheless, the general tendencies in the Russian historical novel are basically similar to those in other major European literatures. In this respect there is not that much that is natively Russian about the genre, which represents a reflection upon the culture of the Petersburgian period. Russian peculiarities come to the fore in terms of subject matter and its interpretation. This, apart from the central issue of the genre's poetics, constitutes an important focus of my attention, namely, to determine what fired up the Russian historical imagination and how the various novelists in question interpreted the issue of Russian identity.

The final part of my introductory remarks concerns the scope of this book. After Tynyanov, one hardly needs to spend time proving that literary evolution cannot be adequately studied if limited to major, "canonized," writers—the so called literary generals. If one may be permitted to stretch Tynianov's military metaphor of literary hierarchy, although the generals inevitably dominate the scene, I also examine figures of lesser rank: various field and subaltern officers and even sergeants and privates, all the way down to some irregulars of the genre. Aside from the novels themselves, I focus on pertinent trends in historiography as well as on the contemporary critical reception, which is pivotal for contextualizing the genre.

As concerns the criteria for labeling this or that work a historical novel, I cannot offer any scientific formula. I define the novel rather empirically as a longer piece of prose fiction, the distinction between novel and tale (*povest'*) being quite fluid. The content criteria—the action's time span and range of characters involved—are difficult to establish, as is the length. For example, solely judged in terms of length Pushkin's *Captain's Daughter* is closer to a tale, but it is in fact a brilliantly succinct take on a full-blown Walter Scott novel. The first version of Gogol's *Taras Bulba* is clearly a novel in terms of content but may perhaps be considered a tale as far as its length is concerned; the revised edition, however, is more of a novel in terms of its length. Authorial designations are not much help either. They can get quite whimsical during the romantic period and also be influenced by mercantile considerations (the novel usually being the top-selling genre). In the second half of the nineteenth century the picture gets even more confusing since the choice of a subtitle was often the prerogative of the publisher. As a result, there are numerous works that changed their generic label in the process of republication.

The term "historical" likewise evades precise definition. To repeat, authorial labels can be quite misleading. At the height of the historical novel's popularity in the 1830s, many works belonging to other genres (e.g., gothic novels, brigand tales, love stories) were packaged as historical, but they should not be treated as such. The qualifier "historical" presupposes the presence of a more or less concrete chronotope, that is, specific events, characters, and locations placed within an authentic (or nearly authentic) chronological framework. It is, however, almost impossible to prescribe the minimum of "history" required to make a work of fiction "historical" or to fix the limits of poetic license after which history loses its "historicity." For example, although Gogol's Cossack epic telescopes two or three centuries and barely mentions real-life characters, it nevertheless clearly belongs to the historical genre since it is intended to be a summary artistic reflection on the Ukraine's medieval history.

It is equally difficult to define the upper chronological border, one that would set historical novels apart from those about contemporary life. Again, there is no exact formula—based, for example, on the time span between the moment of action and the moment of writing—that would automatically assign a novel to the ranks of the "historical." It is much more important that the action should take place in a time that is viewed by contemporaries as a different epoch. For example, World War II was for many decades—at least through the early 1980s—not perceived in Soviet art as a historical subject from a bygone age. In contrast, the Napoleonic era had already turned into "history" by the early 1830s, the first historical novels about it being written by veterans of 1812.

In short, while there are potential gray areas in terms of chronological criteria as well as sufficient "historicity," and while certain taxonomic definitions may be fairly subjective, the core of the genre can be established with sufficient credibility. According to my data, from the appearance of the first Russian historical novel in 1829 until the Revolution the genre was invoked by some 120 authors who wrote over 800 works that qualify as historical novels (or longer tales), which constitutes a very extensive corpus of texts. As much as I have striven to present an overview of the historical novel's evolution, in terms of detailed analysis I inevitably have had to be selective, leaving out many authors, works, and also aspects of the genre. Chapter 1 outlines the prehistory of the historical novel and its appearance on the scene of Russian belles lettres. Chapters 2 and 3 describe the poetics of the romantic historical novel, while chapter 4 places into this context the masterpieces of the era, namely, Gogol's *Taras Bulba* and Pushkin's *Captain's Daughter.* Chapter 5 examines the transitional period of the mid nineteenth century and the emergence of the realistic paradigm in Tolstoy's *War and Peace.* Chapter 6 is devoted to the age of positivism, while chapter 7 treats the birth of the early modernist novel. In the conclusion I return to my central idea of the genre's evolution, demonstrating—to cite Tynianov once again—how the same elements acquire a different function within another artistic system. Paying tribute to the recent tercentenary of Russia's northern capital, I analyze incarnations of the Petersburgian theme in the romantic, realist, and symbolist novel. Appendix A contains several sections: a list of all historical novels in my database, arranged according to year of first publication; the same novels arranged by subject; and statistics concerning the quantitative and thematic dynamics of the genre. Appendix B contains concise bio-bibliographical entries on virtually all practitioners of the genre in my database. As far as I know, the latter is the most comprehensive database to date of the Russian historical novel. Even if some readers may disagree with my theoretical approach, they should, to quote a poem by Joseph Brodsky, "run into something hard"—at least in the appendixes. This in itself will in my view be a satisfactory result, for—the anxiety surrounding the genre's legitimacy notwithstanding—the historical novel occupies a place of exceptional importance in Russian literary and cultural history.

I

An Overview of the Romantic Era

Roots of the Genre

The Age of History

In the 1830s Russia's newly born historical novel enjoyed enormous popularity, moving to the forefront of the country's literary scene and becoming the dominant prose genre to such a degree that the terms "novel" and "historical novel" became synonymous. In looking for the roots of this phenomenon, one should turn first to the complex of romantic historicism that emerged in the wake of the upheavals of the Napoleonic era. An obsession with history spread across Europe, manifested in art, philosophy, and historiography. As numerous contemporaries testified, Russia was no exception to this European trend. In 1830 the young thinker Ivan Kireevsky commented: "History in our day is the center of all knowledge, the science of sciences, the only condition of all development: the historical tendency embraces everything" (*Pss*, 2:19). In 1841 this was still the case, according to the bellwether critic Vissarion Belinsky: "Our age is primarily a *historical* age. *Historical contemplation* has powerfully and permanently pervaded all spheres of contemporary consciousness. History has now become a general basis and only condition for any living knowledge: without it any understanding of art of philosophy has become impossible" (*Pss*, 6:90). Perhaps the most inspired dithyramb to History comes from the Russian archromantic Aleksandr Bestuzhev-Marlinsky, who, together with his co-conspirators, felt its crushing force during the failed Decembrist uprising. In 1833 the exiled Marlinsky wrote from the Caucasus:

> We are living in a primarily historical age. History always existed. [. . .] But first it stepped unheard, like a cat, crept up unnoticed, like a thief. It would also rage, bring down kingdoms, destroy nations, cast down heroes, make princes of commoners; . . . but nations would forget their drinking bouts of yesterday after the hangover had passed, and history would become fairy tale. Now it is different. Now history is not just action but in the memory, mind, and heart of nations. We see it, hear it, sense it every moment . . . it pervades all our senses. [. . .] It is as loyal as Aubrey's dog . . . it steals like the thieving magpie . . . it is brave as a Russian soldier . . . it is shameless as a street peddler . . . it is accurate as a Breguet watch . . . it is capricious as an aristocratic lady. It is at once hero and a jester . . . it is Niebuhr and Vidocq every other line, it is the entire people, it is history, our history, created by us and living for us. Willingly or unwillingly we have gone to the altar with her and there is no divorce. History is our spouse in all the gravity of the word. (*Sochineniia,* 2:415–16)

In Russia this fascination with history was intertwined with the rediscovery of the national past, which was ushered in by the publication of Nikolai Karamzin's monumental *History of the Russian State.* Its twelve volumes appeared between 1818 and 1829, marking a major milestone in the country's cultural life. Pushkin called Karamzin the Columbus of Russian historiography (*Pss,* 8:67) and Prince Petr Vyazemsky likened him to Kutuzov, the victor over Napoleon, who "rescued Russia from the onslaught of oblivion" (quoted in Rubinshtein, 186). Not all reactions to Karamzin's *History* were positive, however. Political radicals did not accept its monarchism, while younger scholars denounced its methodology and predilection for eloquent storytelling at the expense of historical analysis. Nikolai Polevoi concluded: "It is a chronicle masterfully written by an artist of exceeding talent, inventive, but it is not a *history*" (*Literaturnaia kritika,* 44–45). Nevertheless, the very aspects criticized in Karamzin's work are responsible for its long-lasting popularity. His *History* represents a narrative of events and characters remarkable for its dynamism, force, and vividness, while the numerous notes provide a wealth of detail and extensive quotations from primary sources. Thus, Karamzin both sparked interest in the Russian past and supplied historical materials in a readily available format. It is no wonder that his *History* became a handbook for an entire generation of Russian novelists.

The "Scottish Wizard"

Some critics may dub the historical novel a "bastard," but its paternity is rightly ascribed to Sir Walter Scott. He pioneered the genre in modern

European literature. For almost two decades, beginning with the publication of *Waverley* in 1814, he was one of the most widely read authors. The first translations of Scott into French appeared in 1816, facilitating the penetration of his novels into the rest of continental Europe. Russian translations followed suit in the 1820s, with Russia quickly succumbing to the charm of the "Scottish Wizard."[1] As Bestuzhev-Marlinsky wrote in 1833: "Walter Scott met our epoch's demand for historical details; he created the historical novel that has now become a necessity throughout the reading world, from the walls of Moscow to Washington, from the study of the grandee to the shop of the petty merchant" (*Sochineniia*, 2:446).

Scott's numerous readers were fascinated by his ability to re-create the past in its intimate and living details. Pushkin commented: "The chief fascination of Walter Scott's novels lies in the fact that we grow acquainted with the past not with the *enflure* of French tragedies, or with the prudery of the novels of sentiment, or with the *dignité* of history but in a contemporary, homely manner" (*Pss*, 7:529; *Pushkin on Literature*, 275). Scott was also the first to discover a successful plot formula for historical fiction, an artistic method of interlacing fictional and historical events.[2] "The plot of the novel effortlessly fills the widest possible framework of historical events." These words, written by Pushkin about a Russian follower of Scott, are fully applicable to the "Scottish Wizard" himself (*Pss*, 7:103; *Pushkin on Literature*, 236). Scott shows the past at a dramatic point when two warring camps collide in a momentous confrontation. The main hero (a kind and noble if somewhat insipid young man) has access to both camps, going from one to the other and wavering in his loyalties and sympathies as he weighs the relative truth of both adversaries. The principal focus is on the plot line of fictional characters (usually the winning of the bride), who also participate in historical events and come into contact with historical characters; the latter play a pivotal role in their destiny. Otherwise historical figures exist in the background of the novel, although the new historical sensibility is expressed through extensive antiquarian descriptions and attention to local color. This formula is accompanied by a number of recurrent plot components, character types, and motifs, all of which create an easily adaptable template.

While the Scottian influence was formative for the romantic era, other models emerged in the 1820s and 1830s (Dolinin, *Istoriia, odetaia v roman*, 225–26).[3] One shifts the focus of attention from fictional to historical characters, as is the case in *Cinq-Mars* (1827), by Alfred de Vigny, who states his credo with obvious defiance toward Scott: "[I]t seemed to me that I ought not to imitate those foreigners who in their pictures barely show in the horizon the men who dominate their history. I placed ours in the foreground of the scene; I made them leading actors in this tragedy" (ix–x). Vigny's compatriot Victor Hugo moves in the opposite direction in his *Notre-Dame de Paris* (1831), where, despite the painstakingly precise indication of the action's time frame at the beginning ("Just three hundred and forty-eight years, six months, and nineteen days ago, today" [13]), a specific historical plot is replaced by a graphic portrayal of the mores and the general atmosphere of the "gothic" world, with its raging passions and striking contrasts. A third model is associated with the name of yet another Frenchman—Alexandre Dumas père—who in the 1840s launched his endless series of novels, where the past is used as a mere setting for breathtaking adventures and issues of historicity are of little concern. As we shall see, all of these models were actively developed by Russian novelists.

The Russian Historical Tale and the Debate Concerning the Novel

When speaking of Scott's primacy in the creation of the historical novel, one should not forget that the genre existed before him—at least since the late seventeenth century.[4] However, novels from previous epochs jarred romantic historical sensibilities. As Nikolai Polevoi formulated it in 1833: "Those Scudérys, Marmontels, Meisners, and Genlis took historical figures, dressed them as they wished, and forced them to talk in their own idiom. Scudéry had Cyrus and Horace weep over love's pains. . . . Marmontel's Peruvian caciques were freethinkers. . . . In Genlis the contemporaries of Charlemagne flirted like eighteenth-century French grandees. [. . .] Walter Scott was the first to drop the false theory of the historical novel" (*Kliatva*, 293). According to Belinsky's dictum, neoclassicist universalism translated into "characters without faces, events without space and time" (*Pss*, 7:133).

Deficiencies of this approach to history had already been pointed out by Karamzin in his preface to "A Knight of Our Time" (1802). Karamzin himself experimented with historical fiction in two tales: "Natalya, the Boyar's Daughter" (1792) and "Marfa, the Mayoress" (1803). In terms of choosing real or fictional events as the focus of narration, these tales belong to opposite ends of the spectrum. In "Natalya" we find a happy love story unfolding against a generic medieval Muscovite background that is intentionally compromised through the use of sentimental clichés. The author maintains a playful and mildly ironic tone, letting the reader feel that he or she is being treated with an elegant bagatelle *à la russe*. In contrast, "Marfa" deals with a major historical event (the fall of Novgorod) and most of the main characters (the mayoress, Ivan III, Prince Kholmsky) are historical figures. Karamzin achieves a high degree of objectivity, presenting both the cause of Moscow, in its drive to unify all the Russian lands, and that of the Novgorodians, who are fighting to preserve their ancestral freedoms. However, the writer treats historical facts and characters with great liberty, while his Novgorod, where orators make lofty speeches about civic virtue in a square adorned with a marble statue of an ancient hero, resembles Athens or Rome rather than a medieval Russian city. Raging political passions dominate the tale, supplanting the love interest, which was pivotal in "Natalya." Thus, Karamzin probed the two extremes of the genre but failed to find a middle ground, a formula for weaving a fictional love story into specific historical settings—a combination that would later fascinate readers of Scott. Nevertheless, Karamzin's tales occupy a prominent place in the genealogy of the Russian historical novel. "Marfa" is a pioneering work dealing with the struggle between Moscow and Novgorod, a topic that will be revisited numerous times in later literature. Similarly, echoes of "Natalya'" will be heard, almost four decades later, in the first Russian historical novel, Mikhail Zagoskin's *Yury Miloslavsky* (1829).[5]

During the first two decades of the nineteenth century the historical tale remained on the sidelines of Russian literature, with only several minor pieces appearing (mostly Ossianic studies set in the mythical past of the early Kievan princes). The situation changed in the 1820s, when, in the wake of Scott's popularity, Russian writers first approached the historical genre in its smaller forms, creating a number of historical tales and short stories.[6] A considerable portion of these works (especially the tales by Aleksandr Bestuzhev and his brother Nikolai, Wilhelm Kuechelbecker, and Aleksei Bochkov) are set in medieval Livonia. Although Livonia was already a part of the Russian Empire in the nineteenth century and was therefore a "legitimate" domain of Russian writers, it provided a link to European feudalism, with its knights, tournaments, and castles, which, owing to Scott's *Ivanhoe* (1820), became one of the trademarks of the historical genre. Aleksandr Bestuzhev tackled properly Russian topics as well. His "Roman and Olga" (1823) deals with the struggle between Novgorod and Moscow, and "The Traitor" (1825) is set in the Time of Troubles. Also imbued with Russian history are the stories by Aleksandr Kornilovich, who pioneered the theme of Peter the Great in Russian prose.

In the second half of the 1820s domestic subjects predominated and attempts at full-fledged historical novels were also evident. In 1824–25 Boris Fedorov published fragments from the novel *Kurbsky* (which was only completed in 1843). In 1826 Ivan Lazhechnikov began work on *The Last Page*. In 1827 Pushkin was writing *The Blackamoore of Peter the Great*, which remained unfinished; a fragment appeared in 1828 with the subtitle "Chapter IV from a Historical Novel." That same year Nikolai Polevoi published a long historical tale entitled "Simeon Kirdyapa," which thematically presages his novel *An Oath at the Holy Sepulcher.*[7]

This process was accompanied by a debate about the viability of the Russian historical novel. The most basic question was whether Russian history could provide appropriate subjects. Even Karamzin's brilliance failed to overcome the old aristocratic contempt for all things Russian. Characteristic, in this respect, is the reaction of Alexander Herzen's father, Ivan Yakovlev, a Moscow aristocrat who, like many of his peers, was a confirmed Francophile. According to Herzen's memoirs, his father—following the example of the emperor—took upon himself the arduous task of reading Karamzin's *History*. He gave up the idea, however, expressing his irritation: "Who cares about all this progeny of an Izyaslav or Oleg?" (8:88). For the younger generation of educated Russians the issue went much deeper. The historical novel, its entertainment value notwithstanding, was treated with the utmost seriousness. "In our time the novel is the highest and, consequently, the most difficult type of poetic work," wrote Nikolai Polevoi, voicing the then prevalent view (Review of *Russkii Zhil'blaz,* 230). Another contemporary theoretician, Nikolai Nadezhdin, proclaimed that the new type novel (i.e. the Scottian novel) was not a passing fashion but an expression of a "general need of the age" in all civilized countries (which, needless to say, included Europe and, mutatis mutandis, its North American offshoot) (Review of *Roslavlev,* 77). In order to meet the challenge, Russia had to join the club of civilized nations. Thus, the problem of molding the Russian past to produce the European novel was related to a much broader question: Can Russian history in general be viewed as part of European history? Ultimately the question of the historical novel must be considered in conjunction with the anxiety of historical identity experienced by Russian culture in the 1820s and 1830s. Proving that Russia is a fit subject for the historical novel would imply that she occupies a legitimate place in the history of world civilization.

The bitterest pronouncements on Russian history appeared in Pyotr Chaadaev's provocative "First Philosophical Letter," which was written in 1829 and published in 1836: "No captivating reminiscences, no graceful images in the memory of the nation, no powerful lessons in its lore. Take a look at all those ages we have lived through, all the space we occupy: you will not find a single engaging reminiscence, not a single revered monument that would bear a striking testimony of the past, that would conjure it up in a lively and picturesque manner. We live in the present alone, in its narrowest confines, without past and future, in dead stagnation" (42–43). Immersed in historical lethargy, Russia remained untouched by the intellectual and moral developments of the West. According to Chaadaev's verdict, therefore, the Russian past represents senseless commotion devoid of higher purpose or universal import. Echoes of such views are heard in the debate over the historical novel. In 1831 Nadezhdin (whose journal, *Telescope,* would be banned for publishing Chaadaev's "Letter") writes about the monotony of Russian history, which is akin to the endless plains of the country, while the nation's spirit seems to be paralyzed by the harsh climate of the north. "There is not enough average Russian life to fill even one chapter of a novel," concludes Nadezhdin (Review of *Roslavlev,* 219). However, he makes the following important observation: since Russian life only becomes meaningful during times of combat against foreign invaders, the most opportune subjects for the historical novel are to be found during periods of patriotic upsurge. Another exception was made by some Westernizers, who admitted that Russian history became more suitable for novelistic adaptations after the inoculation of European civilization through Petrine reforms. Such a distinction is found, for example, in Prince Vyazemsky's otherwise unenthusiastic appraisal of Russian history: "We doubt the wealth of material for novels along the lines of Walter Scott. In our history, at least before Peter the Great, one can find individuals, events and passions, but there are no mores, civilization, public or family life, the sources required by the novelist-observer" (*Severnaia lira,* 229)

Whereas one part of the debate addressed the issue of universality, (whether Russia belonged to European civilization), another questioned that of individuality (whether Russian history was unique enough). Given the romantic fixation on the individual, the latter consideration was perhaps of even greater importance.[8] As Orest Somov stated in his 1823 essay "On Romantic Poetry," individuality is a prerequisite for the existence of national art in general: "Convince me that the mores of our people are no different from those of other peoples, that we have no, for example, virtues and vices of *our own,* that the Russian language is entirely molded into foreign forms—only then will I agree that we do not currently have and will never have our own national poetry" (555). There were detractors of the Russian novel who answered both parts of the question in the negative: Russia was not a European nation, nor could she claim any originality. This position is voiced by the educated, socially prominent Countess O., Mikhail Pogodin's imaginary opponent in his "Letter on Russian Novels" (1827), which remains among the most famous literary manifestos of the period: "It is a pity [. . .] that we cannot have a Walter Scott. [. . .] The reason is clear: we have nothing to describe. The ancient Russians were barbarians, and the modern ones are imitators. Our character has nothing striking about it. Exhausting monotony is everywhere, almost the same as in our land, which consists of flat plain" ("Pis'mo o russkikh romanakh," 133–34). However, such a premise was hard to defend even based on simple logic since the very monotony of Russia should be recognized as a unique feature. Thus, despite or, rather, because of his frozen steppe comparisons, Nadezhdin proclaims unequivocally: "In the universal biography of the human race the Russian people have a particularly original physiognomy" (Review of *Roslavlev*, 216). The same argument paradoxically finds its way into Chaadaev's anti-Russian diatribe. On the one hand Chaadaev claims "we have nothing individual" (42). However, carrying this claim to an extreme, he arrives at the idea of Russia's uniqueness, albeit from the other end: "People are just as moral as individuals. They are raised by ages, as individuals are raised by years. But you could say that we are, in a certain sense, a special people. We belong to that group of nations that are not a part of humanity but exist only to teach the world a valuable lesson" (44).

Less negatively minded thinkers—regardless of their views on Russia's historical position, which remained a watershed for many generations of intellectuals—readily displayed the arsenal of Russia's uniqueness. "In Russia," writes Pogodin, "we have all religions. [. . .] We have many customs of which an artistic description could be of great effect. [. . .] We have all climates. [. . .] We have all settings: those of Scotland, Switzerland, and Italy." He appends this catalogue of splendid geographical settings with a long list of dramatic episodes and themes in the country's history suitable for novels ("Pis'mo o russkikh romanakh," 138–40).[9]

As the debate unfolded, proponents of the Russian historical novel became more vocal and assertive. Writing in 1829, Nikolai Polevoi proclaimed: "Not only can Russian history and Russian antiquity be a source of poetic works and historical novels, but perhaps they should be considered one of the richest sources for the poet and novelist" (*Literaturnaia kritika*, 53). That same year his brother and collaborator, Ksenofont, offered his perspective on the issue, outlining worthy subjects in all periods of Russian history:

> Not to mention our ancient history. [. . .] Boris, imposters, interregnum, the reign of the Romanovs before Peter and, finally, the Divine Reformer of Russia. . . . What a boundless expanse of events, what colors for the talented writer! No, not only the history of Scotland but probably no other single history can

> compare to the time of Peter, in which there are many unusual historical persons and events: the clash of Asian and European mores, the appearance of women in societies, the hordes of foreigners flooding in, etc., seem to await the creator of novels! ("O russkikh povestiakh i romanakh," 324–25)

Since the adaptability of the Petrine era was least doubtful, the young Vissarion Belinsky rallied to the defense of earlier periods, the significance of which was routinely misunderstood: "Russian history is an inexhaustible source for the novelist and dramatist. Many think the opposite, but this is because they do not understand Russian life and judge it by a German measure. [. . .] Russian life before Peter the Great had its forms. Understand them and then you will see that it contains for the novel and drama material just as rich as the European. . . . There would be enough for several Shakespeares and Walter Scotts" (*Pss,* 3:19).

The overall trajectory of this debate reflected the growing nationalism in Russian culture. The initial claims were rather defensive: Russian history was no less interesting than European history and also lent itself to novelistic adaptations. Gradually, however, there emerged the idea that Russia was in many ways more interesting than Europe. In 1833 Bestuzhev-Marlinsky, writing from Russia's exotic and warlike frontier in the northern Caucasus, concluded: "The personalities of princes and the people had to be more striking, more original and more decisive because in old Russia man struggled with a harsher nature and with more terrible foes than anywhere else. Old Russia, a two-faced Janus, looked simultaneously at Asia and Europe. . . . Her daily life was a link between the sedentary lifestyle of the West and the nomadic sloth of the East. What a variety of influences and relationships arise from this!" (*Sochineniia,* 2:451). Instead of being a handicap, Russia's semi-European nature was perceived as an advantage; it was a sign of uniqueness, with the country's immense diversity and location at the crossroads of civilizations providing an additional bonus to writers. The stream of novels that followed in the 1830s served as tangible proof that Russian history was fit for romantic novelistic adaptations.

The 1830s and 1840s

The Debut of the Russian Historical Novel

The first Russian historical novel, *Yury Miloslavsky, or Russians in the Year 1612,* by Mikhail Zagoskin, appeared in December 1829. Its success was immediate and widespread, embracing the entire spectrum of the reading public (which was still extremely small.)[10] A letter to Zagoskin from Prince Shakhovskoi vividly describes the impact of the novel on Russia's literary elite:

> I was already dressed to go to a meeting with our first-rate writers when, all of a sudden, your novel arrived. . . . I was glad of it and took my joy with me to Count Tolstoy. But I was met there by the same. The first actor to arrive on the scene at this dinner for authors was Pushkin, who immediately began talking about you. . . . Pushkin was enthused by the excerpts of your novel that he read in a journal. . . . Krylov came from the palace [to report] many questions about you and *smiling* approval of your novel. . . . Gnedich appeared with and expressed enthusiasm about your wonderful novel. . . . Finally Zhukovsky arrived and, after saying a couple of words, announced that he hadn't slept at all last night—and why? Because of your novel, which he received, opened, and wanted to take a look at. Then, without moving from the spot and not going to bed, he could not resist reading all three volumes (quoted in Aksakov, 3:401–2)

According to contemporary testimony, provincial readers were equally enthusiastic. One need only recall Gogol's *Inspector General* (1835), where the arch-liar Khlestakov, in the process of beguiling the small-town ladies, claims, among other things, to be the author of *Miloslavsky*.

Zagoskin's novel also penetrated to the very foundations of the reading public, becoming something of a mass-culture phenomenon. Here is how Sergei Aksakov described its impact: "We did not yet have a popular writer in the accurate and full sense of the word . . . our distance from the people and their low literacy being direct and readily apparent obstacles. [. . .] But Zagoskin more than anyone else can be called a popular writer. In addition to other classes, he has been read and is read by all merchant peasants able to read. . . . They tell about what they have read and sometimes read aloud to many other illiterate peasants. The enormous number of snuffboxes and printed kerchiefs with depictions of various scenes from *Yury Miloslavsky* carried to all corners of the Russian expanse uphold the renown of its author" (3:403).

Zagoskin's triumph was crowned by warm commendations from Emperor Nicholas I (an admirer of Scott), who granted the writer an audience and presented him with a finger ring. The novel's popularity surpassed anything produced by the great writers of the age: during Zagoskin's lifetime *Miloslavsky* went through eight editions (four of them between 1829 and 1832) and was translated into French, English, German, Italian, Dutch, and Czech.

Overall, *Miloslavsky* has been reprinted close to one hundred times and for many decades remained on the reading list shared by all classes of the population. Having followed a proven literary recipe, to create a captivating and entangled story, Zagoskin competed successfully with his mentor Scott. Equally important for the success of *Miloslavsky* was the fact that, having utilized a Western model, Zagoskin filled it with domestic content, portraying Russian types, reviving Russian history, and introducing colorful Russian folk or quasi-folk language. In the atmosphere of heated debates about *narodnost'* (nationality) in art, which reflected a growing national self-awareness in society, the conspicuous Russianness of *Miloslavsky* was greeted by many reviewers as a long overdue phenomenon in domestic literature.

The only openly hostile review of *Miloslavsky* belonged to Faddei Bulgarin, who nearly lost his newspaper, *The Northern Bee,* over this critical demarche, which angered the emperor. Bulgarin's response was prompted by jealousy; he was working on a historical novel from the Time of Troubles simultaneously with Zagoskin. Their rivalry turned into a race that was closely followed in the literary circles of both Moscow and Saint Petersburg. Zagoskin began the race with a head start since he had conceived *Miloslavsky* in 1827, whereas Bulgarin only set to work in 1829, after completing *Ivan Vyzhigin,* a highly popular picaresque novel. Spurred by the rumors of Zagoskin's progress, Bulgarin wrote at a hectic pace. The preface to his *Dimitry the Impostor* is dated August 18, 1829. Individual chapters appeared in the autumn of the same year in *The Son of the Fatherland,* and on October 13, 1829, the entire piece cleared the censor (who happened to be Osip Senkovsky). Bulgarin was obviously anxious to see his novel in print. An explanatory note in the novel's *errata* section reads: "Due to the extreme haste with which the work was copied and printed, errors crept in" (*Dimitrii Samozvanets,* 4:n.p.). In November 1829 Nikolai Polevoi's *Moscow Telegraph* heralded the forthcoming appearance of *The Impostor,* hailing Bulgarin as the first Russia historical novelist. However, Bulgarin lost the race against Zagoskin: *The Impostor* was only published at the beginning of 1830, while *Miloslavsky* appeared in December 1829. According to Mikhail Pogodin, "Zagoskin's *Miloslavsky* and Bulgarin's *Impostor* ran neck and neck for first publication. The Moscow writer won" ("Pis'ma M. P. Pogodina," 124). Zagoskin won more than the right of primogeniture. The critical reception of Bulgarin's novel was largely unfavorable, as was the case with even the best of his works, which were customarily branded as cheap reading for lackeys. The response of Pushkin's circle was especially harsh; Pushkin suspected Bulgarin of plagiarizing his unpublished drama *Boris Godunov.*[11] This may also explain Pushkin's somewhat

ЮРІЙ МИЛОСЛАВСКІЙ,

или

РУССКІЕ ВЪ 1612 ГОДУ.

Часть первая.

Соч. М. Н. Загоскина.

МОСКВА.

Въ Типографіи Н. Степанова.

При ИМПЕРАТОРСКОМЪ Театрѣ.

1829.

FIGURE 1. Title pages of Zagoskin's *Yury Miloslavsky* (vol. 1, 1829; artist V. Baranov; engraving E. Skotnikov). Between 1829 and 1832 the novel went through four printings. The main contestants in the race for the laurels of the Russian Walter Scott were Mikhail Zagoskin with his *Yury Miloslavsky* and Faddei Bulgarin with *Dimitry the Impostor*. Zagoskin won in every respect, but Bulgarin's novel became a success in its own right.

ЮРІЙ МИЛОСЛАВСКІЙ

ИЛИ

РУСКІЕ ВЪ 1612 ГОДУ.

Часть I.

МОСКВА.

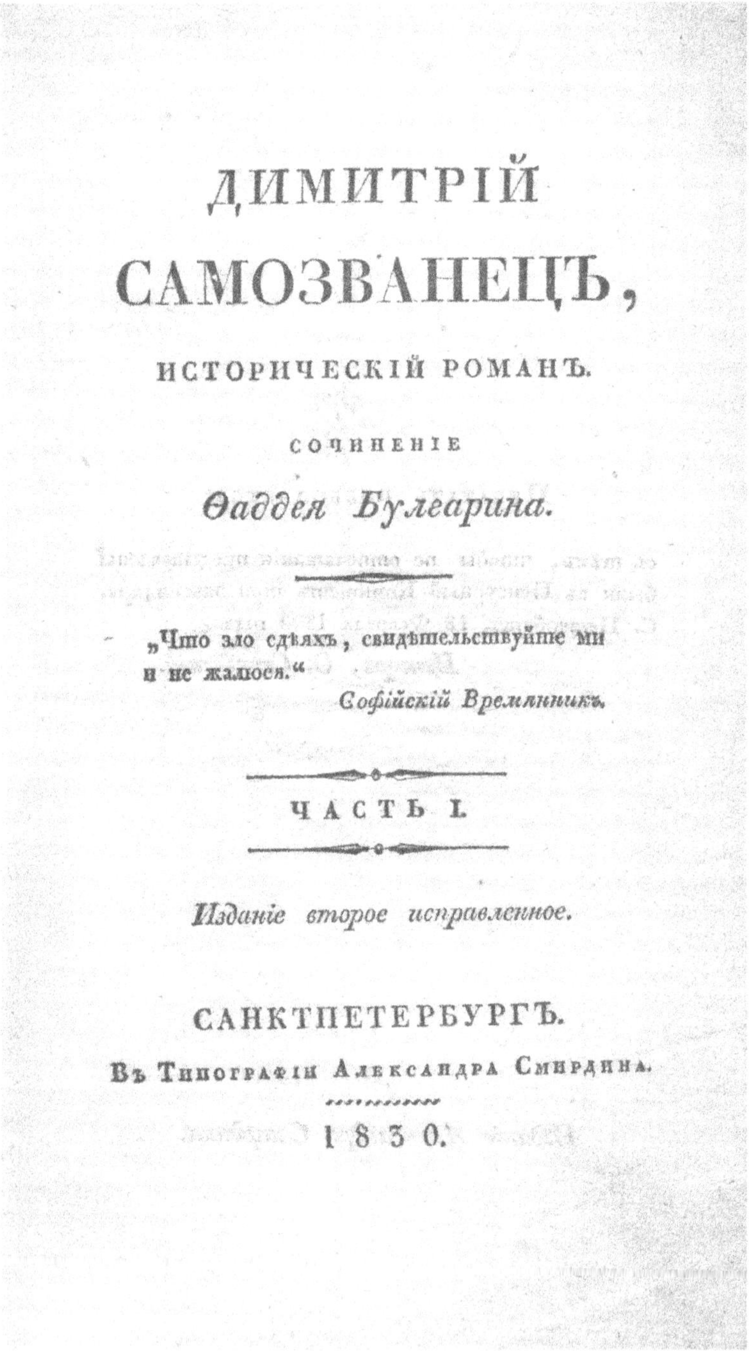

ДИМИТРІЙ

САМОЗВАНЕЦЪ,

ИСТОРИЧЕСКІЙ РОМАНЪ.

СОЧИНЕНІЕ

Ѳаддея Булгарина.

„Что зло сдѣяхъ, свидѣтельствуйте ми и не жалюся."

Софійскій Временникъ.

ЧАСТЬ I.

Изданіе второе исправленное.

САНКТПЕТЕРБУРГЪ.

Въ Типографіи Александра Смирдина.

1830.

FIGURE 2. Titles pages of Bulgarin's *Dimitry the Impostor* (vol. 1, 1830). During the first year of its publication the novel went through two printings.

ДИМИТРІЙ

САМОЗВАНЕЦЪ.

САНКТПЕТЕРБУРГЪ.

1830

exaggerated enthusiasm over *Miloslavsky*, which he saw as a preemptive strike against Bulgarin. Nevertheless, Bulgarin's novel was a success in its own right, going through two printings during its first year of publication.

Competition between the two writers continued. For their next historical novels they both turned to the War of 1812, of which they both were veterans, although Zagoskin fought on the Russian side, whereas Bulgarin served in Napoleon's Polish legions. Their novels were published practically simultaneously in 1831. Zagoskin entitled his novel *Roslavlev, or Russians in the Year 1812*, while Bulgarin created a sequel to his *Ivan Ivanovich Vyzhigin* that he entitled *Petr Ivanovich Vyzhigin*, in which the son of Ivan Ivanovich is thrown into the midst of the events of 1812. Zagoskin's novel again proved to be the more successful work. Although *Roslavlev* did not repeat the triumph of *Miloslavsky*, it went through three reprintings during Zagoskin's lifetime (which, as Aksakov points out, was actually equivalent to seven editions, given the fact that the first printing of 4,800 copies comprised four standard editions of 1,200 copies each) and was translated into French and German. Bulgarin's *Vyzhigin* sequel went through only two editions. In 1831 Zagoskin and Bulgarin were joined by numerous other writers, demonstrating that the writing of historical novels was indeed proving to be a lucrative business.[12] In 1833 Bestuzhev-Marlinsky remarked: "Dozens of writers jumped into the fray. [. . .] Moscow and Petersburg clashed. All booksellers were caught in the crossfire and novel after novel was thrown at the heads of the good Russian people" (412). The novelistic boom of the 1830s had begun in earnest, and although it subsided in the following decade, the historical novels of the 1840s also constitute a sizable group of texts.

Major Authors and Their Works

During the 1830s and 1840s over fifty authors tried their hand at the historical novel, producing well over one hundred works (see appendix A). Today the most famous of these pieces remain Pushkin's *Captain's Daughter* and Gogol's *Taras Bulba*, both of which eventually entered the high school curriculum and were read by millions of Russians. However, in their own time neither Pushkin nor Gogol were viewed as the main practitioners of the historical novel since each published only one complete work in the genre whose short length made them closer to tales than to full-fledged novels. Besides, *The Captain's Daughter*, drowned in the stream of Scottian imitations, went largely unnoticed. What follows is an overview of the other major contributors to the genre, who are ranked according to contemporary standing and retrospective assessment.

The list of major authors is headed by Mikhail Zagoskin—the first and perhaps most acclaimed novelist of the period. Although he wrote six historical novels, his fame rests on *Miloslavsky* (1829), his opus magnum, and, to a lesser extent, on *Roslavlev* (1831). Compared to their successes, Zagoskin's third novel, *Askold's Grave* (1833), which is set in Kiev during the reign of Prince Vladimir, was a failure, although it managed to secure a place in Russian culture through a popular operatic adaptation. Another leading author of the period was Ivan Lazhechnikov. All three of his novels were top-notch efforts for the 1830s, with *The Ice Palace* (1835) arguably among the best Russian historical novels ever written. Nikolai Polevoi's *Oath at the Holy Sepulcher* (1832) could never rival the popularity of either Zagoskin's or Lazhechnikov's creations, but it deserves recognition as one of the most serious programmatic novels of the period. In a league of its own is Aleksandr Veltman's *Koshchei the Deathless* (1833), which explores early Russian history through the prism of folklore, with a whimsical Sternian twist.

Although Bulgarin's *Impostor* (1830) is of the utmost importance in signaling the debut of the genre, it, as well as his other novels, ultimately belong to the second tier. Considerable popularity was enjoyed by Rafail Zotov, who wrote about a dozen adventure novels, the best of them being *Leonid, or Some Traits from the Life of Napoleon* (1832) and *A Mysterious Monk, or Some Traits from the Life of Peter I* (1834). A dependable second-rate author is Konstantin Masalsky, whose most important work is *The Strelets* (1832). The novels of Ivan Kalashnikov, a pioneer of the Siberian theme, stand out for their ethnographic interest, if not for their artistic merit. In the 1840s several novels were authored by Nestor Kukolnik, but they lagged far behind the best sellers of the previous decade and even his own historical dramas.

Into the third tier one can place the novels of Pavel Svinyin, Pyotr Golota (who specialized in Ukrainian subjects), and several others. Descending to what Belinsky dubbed "literature of the flea market," one encounters colorful figures who were best-selling authors in their specialized niche: Sergei Lyubetsky, whose most popular novels are *Sokolniki, or The Shaking of the Tatar Suzerainty over Russia* (1832) and *Tanka, the Brigandess of Rostokino* (1834); Platon Zubov, who specialized in Caucasian novels; Aleksei Moskvichin, whose *Yapancha, the Tatar Horseman* (1834) was republished throughout the nineteenth century; Ivan Glukharev, who stands out for "recycling" the names of Zagoskin's heroes for his titles; Ivan Guryanov, who labeled one of his novels as a sequel to Bulgarin's *Impostor;* and on and on, including a number of anonymous hacks.

Grouping the novels of the 1830s and 1840s thematically (see appendix

A), one notes an obvious preponderance of domestic subject matter. More than 80 percent of the novels deal with Russian history, while another 10 percent are devoted to the closely related Ukrainian history. The remaining 10 percent include three Livonian novels, three Caucasian novels (all of them by Zubov), and only four novels set entirely outside the contemporary boundaries of the Russian Empire: one in Byzantium (Polevoi's *Ioann Tsimiskhii*), one in France (Kukolnik's *Evelina de Valierol*), and one in Germany (Zotov's *Nicklas, or Some Traits from the Life of Friedrich II*).

In order not to create the illusion of cultural isolationism in historical fiction of the time, it is important to recall that foreign subjects were amply represented by numerous translations from Scott and his European followers. Moreover, the Russocentrism of the historical novel is strongly diluted by the fact that foreigners often assume prominent roles in the plot and that the action frequently alternates between Russia and the outside world. In part this can be seen as a tribute to Scott, who tends to present a collision of cultures unfolding in a borderline area, but it is also a reflection of fundamental realia of Russian history. Nevertheless, Russian subjects predominate, which is only natural given the period's preoccupation with nationality and the fact that domestic history was precisely the niche that domestic Walter Scotts were supposed to fill.

Commentators usually single out two or three subjects that dominate the historical novel of the period: the Time of Troubles, the War of 1812, and/or the rule of Peter the Great. My calculations present a different picture. There is a rather even distribution among eight major topics, each of which accounts for approximately 10 percent of the total: Early Rus (11 titles); the rise of Moscow (11 titles); Ivan the Terrible (10 titles); the Time of Troubles (13 titles); Peter the Great (11 titles); and the Napoleonic Wars (12 titles). The age of empresses accounts for 20 titles; about half of them deal with the reign of Catherine the Great. "Little Russian" novels, considered as a bloc, also constitute a major group (13 titles). The latter reflects the appeal of the Ukraine for the Russian historical imagination—a territory familiar yet distinct, with a borderline location and a turbulent past. Other prominent regional subjects include the country's eastern frontier, including Siberia (6 titles) and the medieval republics of Novgorod and Pskov (5 titles). The authors of the period thus availed themselves of various aspects of Russian history and created a diverse thematic menu. However, the Time of Troubles and the War of 1812 occupy a special place since they open the history of the genre. Their prominence is usually explained by patriotic considerations since great Russian triumphs are involved. But the appeal here can also be of a "Dionysian" nature, reflecting a fascination with the reign of chaos, disintegration, and the defeat of Russia. This is ultimately in keeping with the aspect of the historical novel akin to fairy tale or science fiction: the past serves as a magic chronotope where something unthinkable in the present is possible. In the end, however, cosmos prevails over chaos. In 1612 Holy Rus revives and gains a new tsar (rebirth of a nation and birth of the dynasty topoi). In 1812 the foreign invader is likewise expelled and Moscow rises from the ashes like the legendary phoenix, which endows these historical epochs with a powerful mythological potential.[13]

In terms of the quantitative dynamics of the genre (i.e., publication of new novels), the decade opened with a "warm-up" period when Zagoskin and Bulgarin published their first novels. This was followed by a sharp increase as new authors entered the scene. The curve peaked in the mid-1830s, after which a downward trend began, continuing into the next decade. Whereas almost one hundred new titles appeared in the 1830s, in the 1840s this figure was reduced to less than forty titles, reflecting the waning popularity of the historical novel. Moreover, in the early 1830s one could already observe signs of the inflation of the genre compromised by the proliferation of low-brow works. Nikolai Polevoi noted: "In Russia [. . .] anyone who can hold a quill undertakes the writing of a novel" (Review of *Russkii Zhil'blaz*, 230), later adding that "the novel in Russia has become not a work of Art, but a product of industry" (Review of *Ivan Mazepa*, 556). Mock recipes for concocting historical novels became a favorite topic of journalists in Europe and Russia (Zamotin, 351; Reizov, 559–60; *Kniaz' Skopin-Shuiskii* 1:vi; Rebekkini, 416–33 passim). Bestuzhev-Marlinsky, for example, advertised a samovar-propelled machine for the mass production of Russian historical novels:

> An improved steam engine [. . .] for the production of clichés for new historical novels. [. . .] Adapted to Russian mores, it is placed on a samovar and is powered by steam, so in five minutes the wordsmiths, who jot down on paper whatever enters their heads over a cup of tea, can have the pleasure of seeing the completed chapter in all its trappings, with even an epigraph tacked to the top. [. . .] Expressly for writers of Russian historical novels, Russian sayings, proverbs, and even invectives are sold by the hundreds and, when they are arranged in checkerboard fashion, yield very engrossing conversations . . . descriptions of clothing, arms, crockery, foods for feast and fast . . . as well as excerpts from ancient chronicles about processions, dinners, weddings, etc., to give the work a learned flair, and also descriptions of natural settings to fill in the gaps. [. . .] *Note:* In addition to the standard roll in the manner of Walter

FIGURE 3. Title page illustration from Zotov's *Leonid, or Some Features from the Life of Napoleon* (vol. 2, 1832; artist K. Zelentsov; engraving A. Petrov). Authors of the period draw clear parallels between two fateful confrontations with the West: the Polish intervention during the Time of Troubles and the recent invasion by Napoleon's Grande Armée. Seen as defining moments in the nation's history, these events also provided a wealth of material for Russian novelists.

> Scott, rolls for those seeking to write in the manner of other fashionable writers are also sold for this machine. ("Ob"iavlenie," 213–14)

Despite its continued proliferation, the historical novel was quickly becoming an outmoded genre. As Olimpiada Shishkina regretfully attested in the introduction to her *Prince Skopin-Shuisky* (1835): "Historical novels remained extremely popular over the course of several years. [. . .] But, as everyone knows, nothing in this world can hold the public's taste for long. This is discussed in all the societies and written about in all the journals" (*Kniaz' Skopin-Shuiskii*, 1:vi).

In the mid-1840s, the heyday of the historical novel seemed a bygone and naive era. "About fifteen years ago historical novels were all the rage," notes the young critic Valerian Maikov (b. 1823) in his 1846 review of Aleksandr Kuzmich's *Khmelnitsky*. "They were written in great quantity and according to the simplest recipe. [. . .] Who among us did not consume them in our youth at the expense of nervous strength and many hours of school time? Who did not take those fairy tales for historical novels? Who did not believe

FIGURE 4. Title page illustration from Bulgarin's *Dimitry the Impostor* (vol. 4, 1830; engraving David Weiss).

in the all-powerful genius of those Russian Walter Scotts? Oh, the golden days of childhood!" (235–36). The rise of the Natural school and the general shift to contemporary social issues removed the historical novel from mainstream literature. Stripped of its high status, the historical novel was demoted to the rank of second-rate literature, losing the educated reader and being transferred "from the living room into the children's room" (Dolinin, *Istoriia, odetaia v roman*, 236). However, even at the lowest rung many novels enjoyed exceptional longevity. The best evidence of this is found in the written record of continued republication and imitation of some of the most popular novels. To cite a few heterogeneous examples drawn from literature and personal testimony, Ivan Kalashnikov's Siberian tales were still read by commoners around the time of Maxim Gorky's childhood in the 1870s (*Russkie pisateli*, 2:444). In the mid-1880s the caustic critic Aleksandr Skabichevsky, who treated Zagoskin with the utmost contempt, nonetheless conceded: "To this day you won't find a literate soul in Rus who has not read at least *Yury Miloslavsky*" ("Nash istoricheskii roman," 684). In 1869 the cesarevich (future emperor Alexander III, b. 1845) named Zagoskin and Lazhechnikov among the best-loved authors of his childhood, whom he praised for awakening Russian national consciousness (Vengerov, cxxiii–cxxiv). A comical reflection of Lazhechnikov's popularity is found in Chekhov's short story "Failure" (1889), where the hectic parents bless a prospective couple instead of an icon by mistakenly grabbing a portrait of Lazhechnikov from the wall. In the 1930s the writer Ivan Shmelev (b. 1873) reminisced in emigration about his Moscow childhood, recalling a dog-eared volume of Lazhechnikov's *Ice Palace* and his merchant father's project to build a replica of the palace for Christmastide. Thus, having been exiled to the children's room, the novel of the 1830s maintained a constant presence in Russian culture throughout the imperial period.

Models of the Historical Novel

The 1830s in the history of the Russian novel are often described as the epoch of Walter Scott. Polevoi remarked: "Because now if you say 'historical novel' who will not immediately recall W. Scott?" (*Literaturnaia kritika*, 52). However, despite his tremendous popularity, Scott was not the only relevant influence for the authors of the period. Some of them were equally fascinated with younger and more radical French romantics or availed themselves of other possibilities for constructing a historical novel. In the most concrete terms, choosing between Scottian and non-Scottian models involved the proportion of fiction to history in the novel's plot. When Zagoskin decided to write a novel about 1812, Vasily Zhukovsky felt that this was a risky enterprise since readers vividly remembered the events and many historical figures of the epoch were still alive. Addressing Zhukovsky's concerns, Zagoskin described different recipes for historical novels: "Historical novels can be divided into two types: *some* have as their subject historical personages [while] *others* are based on a well-known epoch in history. [. . .] In them the author does not introduce a particular person but rather attempts to characterize an entire people, their spirit, customs, and mores in the epoch chosen as the basis for his novel" (2:722). In this type of novel, according to Zagoskin, historical figures can be mentioned and even appear, albeit only in the background and with great subtlety (723).

Both models appeared in Russia practically simultaneously. In his *Yury Miloslavsky* Zagoskin generally followed the example of Scott, focusing on a fictional protagonist and his love story set amid dramatic historical events. Like Scottian "camp shifters," Zagoskin's hero is torn by conflicting loyalties and comes into contact with two opposing sides. An ardent Russian patriot, he is in love with the daughter of a Polish sympathizer. In addition, Yury is bound by his oath of loyalty to the Polish prince, Wladyslaw, made in the sincere hope that the latter's ascension to the Russian throne was in the best interests of the country. Subsequently he realizes his mistake but cannot take back his word. This creates the necessary tension to move the story along and also allows the reader to "join" the protagonist during his visits with Russian patriots and their enemies. Historical figures make only brief appearances, although Avraamy Palitsyn plays a central role in the life of the protagonist.

The type of novel dominated by historical characters and events is represented by Bulgarin's *Impostor*, where the protagonist is the False Dmitry and the plot revolves around his life and the major political events of the Time of Troubles. Although very little is known about the actual life of the impostor, which leaves ample room for the author's imagination, this approach is more in line with the concept implemented in Vigny's *Cinq-Mars*. Vigny's model is also shared by Nikolai Polevoi, who in his 1829 review of *Miloslavsky* rebukes Zagoskin for not making historical events and characters more prominent: "This is not really the *Russians of 1612* announced in the title but the story of a person invented by the author. . . . A few particular *coincidences* that do not arise from the whole of the developing events, and in the distance the great events of 1612, of which the author *speaks* without showing them in tableaux vivants, without sketching the heroes participating in them, but occasionally, privately, bringing them onto the scene. [. . .] We would wish for more connections to the whole, for more of the *historical,* and fewer preliminary events" (*Literaturnaia Kritika,* 54–55). Eventually Polevoi turns against the father of the historical novel himself, becoming the most vocal Russian critic of Scott's stranglehold on the genre. In his opinion, Vigny's *Cinq-Mars* and Hugo's *Notre-Dame de Paris* "are historical novels in which the connection of truth, philosophy and poetry is accomplished to the highest degree. These are two precious pearls that exceed anything that Scott's relentless muse can offer separately" ("O romanakh Viktora Giugo," 237). Conceding that Scott is a genius and a pioneer, Polevoi claims that at present he has become an impediment on the path to innovation: "The Novel, like other works of Poetry, is a child of imagination and [. . .] the inspiration of the novelist must live in his soul, and not in the novels of some foreign old man" (Review of *Doch' kuptsa Zholobova*). In the preface to his own novel *An Oath at the Holy Sepulcher* (1832), Polevoi openly distances himself from Scott and even tries to provide a new definition of the genre, saying that his work is not a conventional novel but rather a *byl'* (true story), a kind of artistic dramatization of history: "My true stories are not at all *historical novels* in the manner of Walter Scott. . . . This [. . .] is a *history in characters* and the *life of the people in tableaux vivants*" (294). Indeed, the plot, like that of *Cinq-Mars,* is predominantly historical, focusing on the peripeties of the dynastic feud in Muscovy.[14] Further enhancement of the properly historical element leads to the creation of a "biographie romancée." The first Russian work in this genre is *Mikhail Vasil'evich Lomonosov* (1836), by Polevoi's brother Ksenofont, who speaks of the intermediate nature of his work: "I wrote neither a novel nor a history but a story about the life of Lomonosov" (2:341). Although in the following decade a number of romanticized biographies for younger audiences by Petr Furman appeared, the true blossoming of this genre would only occur in the late nineteenth and early twentieth centuries.

Other models can be found in the Russian novel of the period as well. Although Gogol, like Scott, is concerned with a clash of civilizations unfolding in a borderline area, his *Taras Bulba* is much closer to Hugo's *Notre-Dame de Paris,* with its weakening of the historical chronotope and concentration on medieval mores. Another type of deemphasis of the properly historical framework is found in the novels of Kalashnikov, which concentrated on Siberian exoticism and were often compared to the frontier novels of James Fenimore Cooper. The adventure novel, which would later become associated with the name of Alexandre Dumas père, was practiced in the 1830s by Rafail Zotov. His books abound in historical characters and events, which mainly serve as an excuse for breathtaking and improbable fictional exploits.

Thus, thanks to the whim of fate and the author's fancy the protagonist of *Leonid*, a poor nobleman from the Russian provinces, becomes a count of the French Empire, a triple agent involved in a network of conspiracies, a polygamist, a friend of Napoleon, and savior of both the French and Russian emperors. Nevertheless, Zotov retains many Scottian elements, including the situation of shifting allegiances, which is most conducive for creating a convoluted plot.

A separate niche is occupied by the so-called *lubok* novels. Here, regardless of the prominence of the historical element, the overall model is defined by the poetics, which are indeed reminiscent of *luboks* (popular print illustrations). These novels regurgitate conventions of high art in a primitivistic fashion that places them somewhere between literature and folklore. Finally, there are a number of imitative cases where—capitalizing on the latest trend—some novels falsely advertise themselves as historical. Thus, Glukharev's *Olga Miloslavskaya* (1831), misleadingly subtitled "A Historical Novel of the Nineteenth Century," contains no historical components. Other types of pseudohistorical novels are exemplified by such works as Aleksandr Protopopov's *Black Coffin, or A Bloody Star: A Legend of the Seventeenth Century* (1835) and *Pan Yagozhinsky, an Apostate and Avenger: A Novel Taken from Ancient Polish Legends* (1836). The former supposedly takes place in Kiev in 1692, but the settings are of no relevance in this tale of brigands and devilry. The latter is a society tale with supernatural elements set in Poland sometime during the 1700s, which is a meaningless generalization for one of the most dramatic centuries of Polish history. Bygone epochs are also invoked superfluously in many novels by Aleksandr Churovsky (e. g., *A Black Koshchei: A Russian Novel from the Time of Peter the Great*, 1834), Ivan Shteven (e.g., *A Ghost, or An Event of the Eighteenth Century*, 1837), as well as in some anonymous works (e.g., *A Miserable Woman: A Novel at the Beginning of the Reign of Catherine II in the Eighteenth Century*, 1839). Although such novels attest to the popularity of the genre, they cannot be treated as properly historical.

Given the wide variety of novelistic models, the Scottian one is most frequently employed by Zagoskin. He utilizes as prototypes Scott's Scottish novels in *Miloslavsky*, as well as in *The Forest of Brynsk* and in *Russians at the Beginning of the Eighteenth Century*, while Scott's medieval novels serve as the basis for *Askold's Grave*. In *Roslavlev*, however, the model is already modified: historical characters are not merely moved to the background but virtually eliminated. Besides, the principal "camp shifter" is not the male protagonist but Polina, the heroine, who betrays Vladimir, her fiancé, in the middle of the war in order to marry a captured French officer. When Napoleon advances, she and her husband join the French. Although Vladimir's loyalties never waver, he is forced to remain in occupied Moscow because of a wound. In *Miroshev* Zagoskin abandons the Scottian model altogether. Instead of a young hero buffeted by tumultuous historic events, we encounter a modest provincial landowner whose life story has little connection to the chosen epoch (the second half of the eighteenth century), with the historical element remaining insignificant.

Other authors of the time generally show even less of a purist attitude in sticking to a specific model. Characteristic in this respect is the work of Lazhechnikov, who, like Zagoskin, was crowned by his contemporaries as the Russian Walter Scott. His debut novel, *The Last Page* (1833), has a lot in common with Scott. The action is set at the border between Livland and Russia, just as many of Scott's novels are set at the border between Scotland and England. The protagonist, Vladimir, is a typical shuttle hero and "camp shifter": he is a double agent pretending to serve the Swedes while working for the Russians. Moreover, although he used to belong to Tsarevna Sofia's party and still has contacts with the opposition, he also collaborates with Peter's comrade-in-arms, Sheremetev, and yearns to join the Petrine camp. The novel, however, deviates significantly from Scott. Vladimir is not the faceless young man of the Waverley novels but a Byronic hero: a man of extraordinary passions possessed of physical force and rare beauty; an exile with a terrible and mysterious crime in his past—"a villain, fugitive, outcast," as he describes himself (*Poslednii novik,* 246). Moreover, the love story or, to be more precise, love stories—the complex plot consisting of at least three major subplots—do not involve the protagonist. Thus, the original Scottian formula is significantly contaminated and deformed.

In *The Ice Palace* (1835), his second novel, Lazhechnikov completely departs from Scott and embraces de Vigny's model, choosing his characters from among such prominent historical figures as Volynsky, Biron, and Empress Anna Ioannovna. There is also a thematic link to *Cinq-Mars* since both novels are based on the conspiracy of lofty aristocrats (Marquis Cinq-Mars / Cabinet Minister Volynsky) against powerful favorites (Cardinal Richelieu / Duke Biron) of weak monarchs (Louis XIII / Anna Ioannovna). In both novels the heroes temporarily win the monarchs over to their sides, but at the decisive moment the monarchs have second thoughts and the conspiracies fail. Both novels end with the hero's execution. Nevertheless, Lazhechnikov "dilutes" de Vigny's model. Volynsky's love for the Moldavian princess Marioritsa Lelemiko—an essential part of the plot—is entirely fictional, as is the princess herself. In addition, Marioritsa's mother—the

Gypsy woman Mariula—is an obvious reincarnation of Esmeralda's mother in Hugo's *Notre-Dame de Paris.*

In *The Infidel* (1838), his third and last completed historical novel, Lazhechnikov returns to the Scottian model in a purer form than that in *The Last Page*. The protagonist—the half-German, half-Czech physician Anton—first travels around Europe and then goes to Russia. He is noble and lofty but otherwise rather colorless. His love affair with the Russian boyar's daughter Anastasia is pivotal for the plot. However, this Scottian frame is used primarily for a graphic portrayal of the customs of medieval Muscovy—very much in Hugo's spirit. Thus, Lazhechnikov is obviously not interested in preserving the purity of the model and resorts to anything that fits his design. Similar contaminations and eclectic solutions typify the Russian historical novel during this period.

There is also a widespread misunderstanding regarding what, precisely, the Scottian model implies. For example, Zagoskin, who was hailed as the Russian Walter Scott, was simultaneously admonished for moving historical characters to the background or for choosing a somewhat passive protagonist. For example, Aksakov concludes: "We must confess that although Yury is an extremely good and noble and brave man, we cannot become too attached to him. [. . .] There is nothing glorious, strong, entertaining, or original in him. He is saved, dispatched, set free, ignored, permitted, and wed" (356). In fact, these traits are very typical of Scott. More important, in his depiction of historical conflicts Scott avoids taking sides, demonstrating the relative truth of opposing camps. Hence there is a high degree of impartiality, tolerance, and, ultimately, the sense of history's tragedy. Very few authors share Scott's ethics of history. Speaking of a clear bias found in contemporary English and French novels, a reviewer exclaims: "Which of these imitators can demonstrate [. . .] that objectiveness, that all-encompassing sympathy?" (R.B., 547). Likewise, Russian novelists rarely hide their prejudices, often presenting the past in terms of a black and white moral judgment.[15] Out of the great multitude of Russian novels of the period, perhaps the only "true" adaptation of the Scottian model is Pushkin's *Captain's Daughter.* On the one hand, the 1830s in Russia can indeed be labeled as the epoch of Walter Scott, but, on the other, it can also be viewed as the epoch of misreading, misunderstanding, or intentionally bypassing Scott. The recipe for the historical novel offered by the "Scottish Wizard" was just one among many utilized by authors during this period marked by a fascination with history.

2

Fact and Fiction in the Romantic Novel

Despite their diversity, historical novels of the period share a number of essential traits. On the most obvious level, this is reflected in recurrent formulas, narrative devices, character types, plot components, motifs, and other frequently overused commonplaces that gave rise to parodies akin to Marlinsky's samovar-propelled novel machine described in the previous chapter.[1] Beneath the surface, however, these similarities can be explained by pointing to the cardinal features of romanticism, thus enabling us to discern the general poetics of the romantic historical novel. Despite a certain consensus achieved in recent decades, the term "romantic," which can be defined both broadly and narrowly, remains elusive.[2] By applying this term to a large group of works, I do not wish to imply that each aspect of a given novel is necessarily romantic or that a given author should be described as a full-fledged romantic. However, with respect to the mode of interaction between fact and fiction, one can speak of a distinctive romantic paradigm underlying the historical novel as a genre. This paradigm emerges as a corollary to the basic binary oppositions of romanticism: (1) the binary picture of the world (romantic *dvoemirie/Doppelwelt*), with the contradiction between objective and subjective truths and the ensuing romantic irony; (2) a related opposition between the history of fact and that of legend and lore.

True/False: The Game of Self-Validation and Invalidation

By examining the ways in which novelists of the period deal with historical facts, one can discover a crucial common feature. On the one hand, these writers strive to create a world of historical verisimilitude, convincing the reader that their rendering of the past is accurate. They tend to flaunt their historical and antiquarian erudition, often describing their meticulous preparation in a preface, and frequently supply their novels with quasi-academic notes. The novelists also try to be as accurate as possible in reconstructing customs, mores, and material realia of the past. On the other hand, these writers feel themselves at liberty to alter or suppress evidence pertaining to historical events and chronology. At the same time, they interject overt or thinly disguised self-refutations and disclaimers. As a result, the novels are permeated by a contradictory drive on the part of their authors, who both validate and invalidate the historical trustworthiness of their creations.

Rather frequent are open disclaimers in a foreword, afterword, or notes, where writers confess their transgressions against history and outline how things were in reality. This device is employed extensively by Walter Scott, who pedantically points to anachronisms and other instances of historical license in his novels.[3] For instance, Scott's *Rob Roy* is supplied with a lengthy historical introduction revealing that the actual Rob Roy was less noble and romantic than his fictional counterpart. Moreover, his role in the rebellion was not as significant as that portrayed in the novel.

An overt disclaimer is found in the very first Russian historical novel, Zagoskin's *Yury Miloslavsky*, whose plot revolves around the protagonist's unfortunate oath of allegiance to Wladyslaw, the Polish crown prince. At the beginning of the novel Yury sets out for Nizhny Novgorod with the important mission of informing the city's residents that the Muscovites have recognized Wladyslaw as their tsar. According to an explicit indication in the opening chapter, this occurs in April 1612. However, as Zagoskin himself concedes in an endnote, Moscow had already sworn allegiance to Wladyslaw in 1610; by 1612 this fact was known throughout Russia. Yury's mission could therefore not have taken place in reality. Zagoskin adds: "The author confesses to these anachronisms" (283). A similar disclaimer is found in Zagoskin's second novel, *Roslavlev*, where the anachronism concerns the participation of the "Taciturn Officer" (based on Captain Figner) in the siege of Danzig (288). In the introduction to *Mazepa* Faddei Bulgarin (Zagoskin's literary foe) also acknowledgeshis sins against chronology more generally by confessing that "the exact chronological order of the events was not followed" (369). Lazhechnikov points out in a note to his *Last Page* that the attempt to stop the Swedes from fleeing at Hummelshof was made not by the novel's fictional heroes but by a historical character (295). In *Leonid* Rafail Zotov confesses that a conspiracy of Bonapartists to assassinate Alexander was afoot not in 1814 but rather in 1819 (573). Similar confessions abound in the works of the period, and although relatively minor deviations from history may be involved, they are of the utmost importance in preserving the overall integrity of the novel's historical background.

Besides open disclaimers, writers also leave more oblique, self-effacing leads, often inviting the reader to consult histories and primary sources. For example, in the introduction to his *Oath at the Holy Sepulcher* Nikolai Polevoi provides the following imaginary dialogue between the reader and the author, which ends in suggestive marks indicating an elision:

> READER: Should we believe everything you will tell us? You speak of a *true story*, but perhaps all this will turn out to be *fiction?*
> AUTHOR: What is the problem? *Double-check* me . . . (300)

Polevoi's *Oath* deals with the dynastic feud in Muscovy, in the course of which Great Prince Vasily Vasilyevich (the Blind) was challenged by his uncle Yury and Yury's sons, Vasily the Squint-Eyed and Dmitry Shemyaka. Polevoi's interpretation of the events is sharply polemical with regard to Karamzin's *History*. The latter, while speaking of the treachery and cruelty of all parties involved, ultimately asserts that historical and providential truth was behind the cause of Vasily the Blind. In Karamzin's view, his victory was a step toward consolidation of the Russian state since it prevented a relapse into the chaos of the appanage period. Polevoi, on the contrary, sides with Dmitry Shemyaka, whom he portrays as the epitome of chivalry and magnanimity. One of Polevoi's central arguments in favor of Shemyaka is that after the death of his father Shemyaka refused to recognize his own brother as the rightful heir and took an oath of allegiance to their previously deposed cousin, Vasily Vasilyevich.

In the novel Shemyaka's role in this episode is described as pivotal. After Yury's death, he stands on the Kremlin's Red Porch and proclaims Vasily Vasilyevich great prince. Everyone is moved by Shemyaka's selfless decision except his infuriated brother, who arrived too late to claim the throne. In connection with this episode, Polevoi exclaims: "O Providence! What is the man before you! Had the Squint-Eyed arrived several hours earlier, had he dispatched the troops of which he was the supreme chief, then perhaps his supporters and force could have gained him the crown of the great prince" (578).

Historians have offered conflicting explanations for Shemyaka's decision. Leaving aside the issue of motivation, one should note the factual distortions in Polevoi's story. In reality, at the time of his father's death Shemyaka was not physically present in Moscow and could therefore not make any solemn declarations in the Kremlin. His brother, who was in the city; assumed the title and actually ruled for about a month. This information can be found in Karamzin's *History* and the chronicles. Moreover, the fifth volume of Polevoi's own *History of the Russian Nation,* which deals with the feud, was published in 1833, with his *Oath* appearing in 1832, which means that Polevoi worked on both pieces virtually simultaneously. His *History* presents the same general conception of events without, however, altering established fact. Thus, Polevoi deliberately changes events in the novel and challenges the reader to verify them.

On occasion one encounters a combination of overt and covert disclaimers. In the prologue to *The Infidel* Lazhechnikov immediately lists several intentional anachronisms and invites readers to check the rest of the novel for historical accuracy. Those readers who follow his advice learn that even what is claimed by the author to be reliable historical evidence may be contaminated by deliberate fiction. The novel tells the story of the lofty and noble European physician Anton, who came to Russia during the reign of Ivan III and perished because of a conflict with a Tatar khan residing in Moscow. At the end of the novel Lazhechnikov quotes "the truthful lines of history," which consists of an excerpt from the chronicles pertaining to the incident: "The German doctor Anton came (in 1485) to the great prince. He was held in great honor by the great prince. He treated Karakacha, son of Prince Danyar, whom he poisoned with a deadly potion over an insult. The great prince gave him away to the "Tatars." . . . They brought him under the bridge on the Moscow River in the winter and slaughtered him with a knife like a sheep" (*Basurman,* 634). The actual chronicle, however, contains the following account: "The great prince gave him away to the son of Karakucha, who, having tortured him, wanted to let him go for a ransom. The great prince did not allow it but instead ordered him killed. And they brought him under the bridge on the Moscow River in the winter and slaughtered him with a knife like a sheep" (*Basurman,* 682). Lazhechnikov changes the chronicle in two significant instances. First, according to the chronicle Karakucha had an adult son. Lazhechnikov makes the khan younger in order to enhance the love plot: in the novel both the Tatar and Anton are rivals in love, so the murder of Anton's patient can seem to be motivated by jealousy. Second, in the novel the great prince pardons Anton— to no avail—since the savage Tatars hurried to kill him. In the chronicle it is the reverse situation: the Tatars are willing to accept money, but the great prince orders the doctor killed. Thus, Lazhechnikov creates the dramatic situation of the failed rescue while also underscoring the conflict between enlightenment and barbarity, which is pivotal.: The blame for Anton's death falls not on the great autocrat possessed of the vision of a new Russia but rather on the Tatars, who embody the dark Asian element of the Russian heritage. Thus, we are confronted with considerably altered facts presented as hard evidence. Identifying his source by the year given in the chronicle, the writer nevertheless leaves behind "self-incriminating" clues.

"An Interrupted Puppet Show": Authorial Presence and Narrative Frame

The game of validation and invalidation is further enhanced by elements of the narrative frame. Many novels of the period include footnotes or endnotes whose format ranges from a simple explanation of obsolete words to a quasi-academic apparatus, including quotations from primary sources, page references, and so forth. The most heavily annotated novel is Bulgarin's *Impostor,* the four volumes of which contain 218 (!) endnotes. On the most basic level, the function of notes is to demonstrate that the author had done his homework, so to speak, and can be considered an expert on the subject. As Konstantin Masalsky remarks, copious notes "reveal in the author a kind of bragging" (*Borodoliubie,* 233). Conversely, notes can also contain self-refutations. Even purely factual notes are potentially subversive since they isolate properly historical passages from fictional ones. To quote Bulgarin's own words from *The Impostor:* "From the attached notes the reader will see where history speaks and where fiction is placed" (1:vii–viii). By implication, the annotated portion of the text is historically reliable, whereas what lies outside of it is not.

A visual borderline between history and fiction is also present where passages derived from historical sources are italicized so that the reader can actually determine what is historically accurate and what represents the author's invention. Although using italics for quotations was a standard practice of the time, some writers draw special attention of their readers to this technique. As Masalsky explained: "Places in the novel printed in italics are excerpts from historical sources without any change in wording" (*Strel'tsy,* 1:18). Other writers delimited factual and fictional portions by placing historical information into markedly distinct capsules sections (the technique was widely used by Zagoskin and Zotov). The transition from one mode of narration to another could be stressed, as in Zagoskin's *Russians at the Beginning of the Eighteenth Century,* where the author says that having fulfilled the "important duty of a historian," he thankfully returns to his fictional plot and to the role of a "humble storyteller" (*Russkie v nachale,* 616). The laying bare of this device (to use the formalist term) is found in Nestor Kukolnik's *Evelina de Valierol,* which contains long digressions on Italian art of the seventeenth century. These "Roman chapters" have separate numberings and are subtitled ad libitum: the author urges uninterested readers to skip them and to proceed to the next fictional chapter, which includes a summary of relevant details. It bears repeating that such graphic contrasts between historical and fictional chapters undermines the verisimilitude of the properly novelistic part of the text.

In addition to their role in the validation/invalidation ploy, notes in romantic historical novels also disrupt the narrative flow. In the words of Masalsky himself, they "divert [. . .] in an unpleasant way the attention of the reader" (*Borodoliubie,* 4:233) and, consequently, destroy the illusion of reality. A similar effect is produced by such other framing components as subtitles (to identify the genre), forewords, afterwords, and epigraphs. The presence of a subtitle—the most frequent being "historical novel"—might seem only natural, but it is the first sign alerting us to the fact that we are being offered historical *fiction,* especially if the writer continues to refer to the genre of the work in the text itself, speaking of "my novel," "our tale," and so forth.[4] For example, Aleksandr Veltman uses this convention ad absurdum. His *Koshchei* is subtitled "an epic song of olden times." Yet in the text Veltman employs a variety of generic labels, some of which are mutually exclusive: "my long speech, word, song, tale, legend, history, true story, fiction, compendium, novel" (87).

The impression of artificiality is often enhanced by the presence of a foreword and/or afterword elaborating on the choice of subject and the author's artistic principles. (The practice was so abused that Protopopov entitled the introduction to his *Black Coffin* "One Can't Do without a Preface.") Chapter epigraphs, which, following the example of Scott, were widely used, play a similar role, depicting the action in the reflected light of other literary works. In the main text of the novel the feeling of literariness is frequently enhanced by a strong authorial presence. On many occasions the author intervenes with all sorts of digressions and asides addressed to the reader. These can take the form of simple connectors ("the reader probably recalls"; " returning to the hero of our novel"; "insisting on my right as narrator"). They can also be rhetorical questions, which at times border on parody in lowbrow works. Take, for example, Protopopov's *Pan Yagozhinsky*: "Do you know what a young gypsy woman is like? Have you known a gypsy woman? Have you experienced the love of a gypsy woman?" (55). In some instances imaginary dialogues with the reader acquire even more prominence, as in Veltman's *Koshchei.* (In Prosper Mérimée's *Chronique du temps de Charles IX* [1829] they even constitute separate chapters.)

These writers may also raise various aesthetic issues, invoke literary models, or refer to the other arts. For example, in explaining his proclivity for digressions Lazhechnikov cites as his excuse "our granddaddy Scott " (*Ledianoi dom,* 107). Speaking of a heroine's passion, he alludes to Byron, Adam Mickiewicz, and Pushkin (*Basurman,* 539). Earlier in the same novel he quotes from Gogol's *Inspector General* (456). To portray a character in *The Infidel* Lazhechnikov recalls a star singer performing in a popular opera of the day:

> Do you recall Petrov as Robert le Diable? How could you not? I saw him play that role but once . . . and ever since when I think about him I am haunted by sounds like calls from hell: "Yes, master!!"; and that gaze from whose charm your soul has not the strength to free itself, and that saffron-colored face contorted by the raging of passions, and that thicket of hair from which, it seems, a whole nest of snakes could easily emerge. Put that Petrov in traditional Russian dress and a silver belt, in a rich fox fur coat with a high boyar's fur hat, and you will immediately recognize one of those men who were riding along the banks of Neglinny Pond. (*Basurman,* 334)

A contemporary reviewer rebuked Lazhechnikov for such "comparisons taken from our modern world: you've been transported to the days of yore, you hark to an ancient tale, live among people of years long past . . . and suddenly someone is telling you about Petrov, Robert, etc. This cools you and you are unwillingly vexed with the author for having led you out of that enchantment you were in" (Mezhevich, 158). The practice, however, was widespread and penetrated to the lowest ranks of the genre. Thus, in *Pan Yagozhinsky* Protopopov likens his protagonist, Yakob, to the hero of *Evgeny Onegin* (which, as we learn from a note, is a famous novel in verse by A. S. Pushkin [24]). There follows a lengthy excerpt from *Onegin* where the original's "Evgeny" is replaced by "Yakob"— to the detriment of both rhyme and meter.

A conflicting urge concerning the creation of narrative illusion is involved in the tension between narrative and dramatic elements, the latter becoming prominent in the wake of the success of Ludovic Vitet's "historical scenes" (plays for reading). Although few "historical novels in dramatic scenes" appeared in Russia,[5] some writers strove to redefine their approach to the genre, contrasting dramatic reenactment of history with traditional novelistic discourse. As Polevoi declares in the preface to his *Oath:* "I imagine that I am living in Rus from 1433 to 1441, see the main actors, hear their conversations [. . .] record [. . .] and present everything in due order. [. . .] This is *history in personalities;* there is no novel; the plot and denouement are not mine. Let everything live, act and speak as it lived, acted, and spoke. [. . .] My task is to give the scene the necessary setting and outfit the actors" (299).[6] Indeed, Polevoi's *Oath* (as well as many other novels of the period) include long passages of dramatic dialogue normally associated with plays.[7]

There are several possible explanations for this phenomenon—from considerations of sheer convenience[8] to thoughts on the polygeneric nature of the historical novel[9]—but most relevant for the present discussion is the following statement by Zagoskin: "Ever since I started telling different kinds of stories to my dear compatriots—meaning the writing of Russian tales, novels, and stories—I have always tried to avoid long narratives, which are [. . .] extremely boring and exhausting. The pronoun "I" almost always annoys readers, but in any narrative if I am speaking not of myself, then at least I am speaking for myself and thus am like a dramatic writer who, instead of hiding in the wings, enters the stage and begins to engage the audience himself" (*Kuz'ma Petrovich Miroshev,* 804). Since dramatic dialogue delegates the right of speech only to characters, it is seen as a tool for creating an illusion of immersion. By contrast, authorial narrative is pregnant with subjective interference. The paradox here lies in the fact that this very explanation, inserted into the main text of the novel, constitutes a blatant example of such interference. Indeed, the author of the romantic historical novel generally acts very much like a *Puppenmeister,* who constantly interrupts his own show in order to address the audience in person.[10] Actualizing the process of narration, such interference demonstrates the conditional nature (*uslovnost'*) of the action. Readers are constantly reminded that the unfolding performance is the fruit of the author's imagination, that it is fiction, fabrication, make-believe. Any educated reader obviously understands that a historical novel is not pure history and contains fiction. What is important to note here is the writer's contradictory intent (*ustanovka*) simultaneously to create and dispel the mirage of history redivivus.

These devices are by no means unique to the romantic historical novel and can be found in other genres. One need only recall Pushkin's *Eugeny Onegin,* which contains epigraphs and notes and is replete with authorial digressions. Moreover, Pushkin's narrator adopts a similarly contradictory stance concerning the reality behind his narrative. On the one hand, he speaks of supposedly nonfictional characters and actual events: Onegin is his Petersburgian acquaintance; Tatyana's letter is a "document" in his possession, and so forth. On the other hand, Pushkin constantly addresses literary issues in the form of lyrical digressions, implying a process of ongoing creation of a fictional piece. The "I"s in this internal dialogue are dotted in the final digression:

> Oh, many, many days have fled
> Since young Tatyana with her lover,
> As in a misty dream at night,
> First floated dimly into sight—
> And I as yet could not uncover
> Or through the magic crystal see
> My novel's shape or what would be. (*Eugene Onegin*, 211)

This, however, is a questionable resolution since both the novel and its characters have already gained a reality of sorts, having become generators of cultural models.

Another conspicuous example of zigzagging along the axis of truth/fiction can be found in the conclusion to Gogol's "Nose." Although the story is thoroughly fantastical, at the end the narrator enters into a most serious deliberation concerning the probability of the events described. Going from one extreme to another and luring the reader into a maze of illogicality and incoherence, he concludes: "And yet, for all that, though it is certainly possible to allow for one thing, and another, and a third, perhaps even . . . And then, too, are there not incongruities everywhere? . . . And yet, once you reflect on it, there really is something to all this. Say what you like, but such incidents do happen in the world—rarely, but they do happen" (*Collected Tales*, 326). A similar ploy of saying "true" and "false" in the same breath permeates the historical novel, but there the contradictions between reality and fiction are especially acute since by definition this genre is framed by factual events that occurred in real time and space.

Two Truths: Romantic Irony

How can one explain the deliberate modification of historical facts based on divergent drives for self-validation and invalidation? Deviations from history can be the result of a number of factors, the most simple of which is the writer's desire to entertain. However, this reason alone is insufficient since many historical novels were conceived as rather serious works. An examination of the higher goals of the romantic historical novel is therefore necessary.

As Russian and European writers have stated on numerous occasions, their purpose was to portray not simply a series of events in the past but the entire epoch—or, rather, the epoch's zeitgeist (*dukh epokhi*). This implies a dichotomy of the essential and accidental, which is very much in accordance with the romantic Neoplatonic concept of the binary world, or *Doppelwelt* (*dvoemirie*). The realm of historical fact corresponds to *this* imperfect world, whereas the epoch's spirit belongs to the sphere of the ideal *other* world. Each world contains its own truth, which is sometimes called by different terms. For example, in the introduction to his famous historical novel *Cinq-Mars* entitled "Reflections on Truth in Art," Alfred de Vigny distinguishes between "le vrai" (the true) and "la vérité" (the truth).[11] The first step in attaining the truth is through an examination of the true, of historical evidence, but the goal is always to reach the higher truth.

Historical evidence, in turn, is also divided into hierarchical categories. Realia of bygone epochs—customs and costumes—are more important than events since they are more general and essential. Events belong to the realm of happenstance and should be treated as imperfect incarnations of the idea. Factual accuracy is therefore irrelevant if the spirit behind the facts is portrayed correctly. The young Vissarion Belinsky formulated this approach in 1835, defending the artist's right to poetic license: "In the higher meaning of the word [historical truth] consists not in the accurate rendering of facts but in the accurate portrayal of the development of the human spirit during this or that epoch" (*Pss*, 1:134). Echoing this widespread view, in *The Infidel* Lazhechnikov outlines the difference between a historian and a historical novelist, insisting that the historical novelist "must rather follow the poetry of history and not its chronology. He should not be the slave of data: he must be faithful only to the character of the epoch and to its mover, whom he undertook to portray. It is not his task to sort out all the melee, to recount laboriously all the links in this epoch and in the life of this mover: that is what historians and biographers are for" (302–3). Moreover, in order for their main idea to be revealed, both historical events and historical personalities should be purged of everything "accidental." According to Vigny, the muse reshapes a historical character's experiences "into conformity with the strongest idea of vice or virtue which can be conceived of him—filling the gaps, veiling the incongruities of his life, and giving him that perfect unity of conduct which we like to see represented even in evil" (*Cinq-Mars*, xvi). Vigny goes so far as to proclaim that "the names of the characters have nothing to do with the matter. The idea is everything; the proper name is only the example and the proof of the idea" (xviii).

In accordance with this approach, writers tweak and retouch recalcitrant evidence to eliminate "incongruities" and attain a higher truth. In his *Oath* Polevoi turns the medieval warlord Shemyaka into a noble loner, an exile, a rebel who refuses to follow the savage ways of his time yet also resists the onslaught of Muscovite autocracy. Similarly, in *The Ice Palace* Lazhechnikov idealizes the cunning and ruthless courtier Artemy Volynsky, whom he depicts as a selfless patriot challenging the tyranny of the "German party," which is led by Duke Biron. In order to underscore the tragedy of Volynsky's fall, Lazhechnikov transforms this man of fifty-one into a young, passionate lover who is also an astounding physical specimen.[12] Although the writer may be convinced of the truthfulness of his vision, he knows all too well that in his search for higher meaning he has deliberately altered historical fact. Can he be sure of the accuracy of his interpretation? How reliable is the method used to arrive at this interpretation? Such questions point to the issue of self-effacing leads and romantic irony. A prominent feature of romanticism is that the outside world is seen as a text, a language, someone else's (ultimately the Creator's) encoded message. History is a part of this larger text of the universe, full of "symbols" or "hieroglyphs," which must be deciphered.[13] But the scrolls of history will remain dead and dry unless they are revived through artistic imagination. As Polevoi emphatically states in his *Oath:* "Only you, the fire of imagination, only you, Poetry, inextinguishable light of the heart's truth!, can revive for us past life in its full bloom, can envelop dry bones with strength, can restore passions to decayed hearts, make them pulse with long-desiccated blood!" (542).

On a number of occasions writers have demonstrated this technique of "artificial respiration" for their readers. In his *Oath* Polevoi presents an extensive novelistic rendering of a military campaign and then quotes a laconic passage from a chronicle that served as the basis for this rendering (542–45). In the epilogue to his *Basurman* Lazhechnikov goes even further, providing a short excerpt from the annals that gave birth to his novel. As has already been mentioned, this excerpt was itself altered by Lazhechnikov. However, the chronicler's description of the Tatars slaughtering a German physician "like a sheep" on the frozen Moscow River are sufficient to spark the imagination of the writer, who expands a terse account of this obscure incident into a full-length novel. The most striking example of reviving "dead letters" is found not in Russian literature but in Hugo's *Notre-Dame de Paris* (1832).

According to the narrator, the entire novel is based upon a single word—the mysterious Greek inscription denoting "Fate"—which he allegedly spied some time ago on the walls of the cathedral and which has since been obliterated.

The romantics find it possible to revive the dead text of history only through imagination, upon which they understandably place great value. Yet while imagination is an extremely subjective category, the truth itself, the idea, the spirit that historical novelists are seeking, is believed to be objective.[14] Hence a tormenting contradiction: the truth can be attained only through subjectivity, but since the truth itself is objective, there is no guarantee that what has been attained through a subjective search is the truth since someone else's search may yield different results, and since imagination in itself is ultimately limited by the artist's earthly constraints: "After all," admits Nikolai Polevoi, "it is impossible to become detached from one's own epoch and one's own country" (Review of *Doch' kuptsa Zholobova*, 392). Therefore, as Aleksandr Herzen keenly observes, romanticism simultaneously deified and anathematized subjectivity (Gertsen, *Pss*, 3:32). Romantic irony springs from the passionate yearning for the ideal and the understanding that it is unattainable.

An example of this irony can be seen in the constant oscillation between self-validation and invalidation found in the historical novel. Although the writer asserts his artistic findings as a breakthrough to the truth, his vision may be totally false. Hence the self-effacing leads and frequent reminders to readers that they are dealing with fiction. Novelists understand that their insights are by no means definitive and represent yet another attempt to decipher a fragment of the total picture, the overall meaning of which is known only to the Creator. While the writer can perform the role of the *Puppenmeister* in his own production, he is aware that his play is but a fragment of a larger drama whose plot is beyond human comprehension. As Vigny puts it, "The acts of the human race on the world's stage have doubtless [*sic*] a coherent unity, but the meaning of the vast tragedy enacted will be visible only to the eyes of God, until the end, which will reveal it perhaps to the last man" (xi). At best artistic intuition canonly hope to uncover just one additional layer that shelters the mystery behind the hieroglyphs of the world. Accordingly, while striving to decipher the meaning of history by virtue of their imagination, the romantics also displayed an acute awareness that their attempts must remain tentative. As a result, historical novelists of the period created works based on the concept of dual truth—or, if one may be permitted a coinage, *dvoepravdie/Doppelwahrheit*—the truth of fact and the truth of the artistic imagination.

Legend and Lore: Masking the Author's Ego

While one task of the historical novelist is to convey the spirit of the epoch, another is to capture the spirit of the nation. In the words of Kseofont Polevoir: "The historical novelist does not limit himself to a historical foundation but rather explores the spirit of his nation, its former and present customs, mores, beliefs and the main elements of its nature" ("O russkikh povestiakh i romanakh," 325).

Following the general romantic preoccupation with folklore, novelists of the period filled their works with folk (or quasi-folk) elements, including songs and sayings, and drew heavily on historical lore. The latter may be divided into two overlapping areas: ancient legends dealing with the dawn of national existence and more recent popular memory. Since little or no reliable records survive, legendary times are less restrictive in terms of the author's imagination. As Zagoskin states in the preface to his early-Kievan novel *Askold's Grave:* "Let them call my story a concoction: where history is silent, where fantasy merges with truth, lore alone is sufficient" (*Askol'dova mogila,* 25). Zagoskin uses references to lore largely as an excuse for poetic license, the "folk" element being limited to stylized songs and quotations from the *Lay of Prince Igor.*[15] By contrast, folklore is essential for Veltman, an erudite archaeologist and student of mythology who—in the spirit of the early romantic scholars—is obsessed with reconstructing Germano-Slavic and Indo-Aryan prehistory. Following the familiar "hieroglyphic" logic, in *Koshchei the Deathless* Veltman declares: "Lore is a scroll rotted by time, ripped into shreds, cast out of ignorance from that high tower in which the current generation feasts, and carried by the winds to the ends of the earth. Gather these scraps of truth, put them back together, get to the meaning, compile something whole, comprehensible. [. . .] Finding the past in the present is not easy, but I found it and possess convincing proof of this" (104). One could take Veltman's assertions at face value, like Polevoi, who exclaims in his enthusiastic review of *Koshchei:* "Rus, the genuine ancient Rus, is brought to life here by the fantasy of the Russian fairy tale" (614). Deciphering lore, however, requires even more imagination than working with historical sources. Hence the familiar predicament and contradictory claims permeating *Koshchei,* such as the following: "Having examined all the chronicles, simple ones and those written on parchment, all the old narratives and musty Historical Compendia, I did not find in them a single word about the event I am retelling for posterity. [. . .] But forget the research. The reader cannot doubt the truthfulness of lore and my words" (38).[16]

Proceeding from semi-legendary times to recent history, one encounters another important romantic binary opposition between the historical memory of the educated classes and that of the common people (*narod*). The incongruity of these memories was already underscored by Karamzin in his *History of the Russian State*. In the powerful final chapter on Ivan the Terrible, Karamzin passes a historian's verdict on this tsar, whom he places among the world's most monstrous tyrants. However, he emphasizes that the commoners' memories of Ivan are positive, noting: "History is less prone to forgive than the people!" (9:280).

The dichotomous nature of historical memory gained wide currency in the 1820s and 1830s. It is summarized by Polevoi in his *History of the Russian People:* "The people have their own memory—this is indisputable. This memory does not consult history; it selects its own heroes, shrouds them in poetical inventions, and glorifies them down through the centuries" (5:74). Vigny even compares the historical memory of the people to a collectively written novel: "I will hazard the assertion that [. . .] history is a romance of which the people are the authors. [. . .] Examine closely the origin of certain deeds, of certain heroic expressions. [. . .] You will see them leap out ready-made from hearsay and the murmurs of the crowd, without having in themselves more than a shadow of truth, and, nevertheless, they will remain historical forever" (xiv–xv). In short, as the same Vigny puts it, referring to the transformation of history in the popular memory, the "voice of the people [. . .] makes every fact undergo such great changes" (xvii).

Romantic artists display a fascination with the "voice of the people" not only because understanding the spirit of the people is one of their major tasks but also because the popular imagination ultimately relates to the realm of the transcendental truth. Overcoming empirical reality, legend moves along the same trajectory as artistic imagination—with one essential difference. Whereas artistic intuition is deeply individual, legend is a collective creation and, as such, makes it possible to avoid the traps of subjectivity and introspection, which are alien to the people. (Recall Polevoi's comment: "Do the people think? Never. They only watch and live" [*Kliatva*, 400]). Hence the frequent attempts by historical novelists to hide behind the impersonal authority of folklore. However, in doing so they tweak and retouch folklore, just as they alter properly historical evidence. The anachronistic use of folkloric and legendary material is widespread. To quote a characteristic confession: "This song was not yet known at the time, but in accordance with the circumstances I decided to place it here" (Golota, *Nalivaiko*, 4:5). Often one is dealing with more or less skillful quasi-folk stylizations or totally bogus references.

The latter is the case with Veltman's novels. On the one hand, they are saturated with allusions to folklore and Old Russian literature. On the other hand, despite Veltman's repeated claims, their main stories are grounded not in Russian legends but rather in Sterne, Cervantes, and, above all, in their author's unbridled imagination, which supposedly managed to capture the spirit of folklore. Thus, we are dealing with fantasy once removed, disguised through appeals to the authority of legend.

A similar logic can be discerned in the use of other narrative masks that are widespread in the literature of the period. This may include concealing authorship (the primary example here being the protracted hide-and-seek game played by Scott with his readers), employment of a fictional narrator or multiple narrators (also practiced by Scott), and the device of a found manuscript.[17] The author's strategy here is to eliminate the appearance of subjectivity by referring to an outside text or voice independent of the author's imagination and thus more "authentic." In most instances, however, the ploy is quite transparent, often turning into a mere tribute to literary conventions. Thus, according to its preface, Dumas's *Three Musketeers* is supposedly based on the memoirs of both D'Artagnan and Athos, yet this claim is totally irrelevant both for the structure of the novel and its implied perception. Even in those instances where the author conceals his persona more consistently, it is evident that this in itself is yet another trick in the game of fact and fiction that permeates romantic literature.

3

The Changing and the Unchanged

Romantic historicism presupposes the idea of the uniqueness of the past, explaining the past within its own peculiar context, as well as the belief that the present emerges from the past in a process of organic growth and development. A corollary to historicism is the comparison between the past and the present, which can be implicit when it is left to the reader to draw conclusions or explicit when it is openly made by the author (Mann, *Poetika,* 310; Dolinin, *Istoriia, odetaia v roman,* 190–91). Numerous explicit comparisons found in the novels of the period represent yet another version of "interrupting the puppet show" by signaling the presence of the author, as well as by creating distance between the time of narration and that of the action in order to dispel the illusion of immersion into history created by exotic descriptions.

Costumes, Customs, and Mores

The romantic fixation on local color—geographical and cultural exoticism—is well known. Traveling back in time, romantics displayed an equal fascination with historical color, whose most obvious manifestation was in the material realia of bygone epochs. Starting with Scott, novelists of the period indulged in archaeological extravaganzas, which became an indispensable attribute of the genre. Heavy borrowing of antiquarian details from histories and other readily available outside sources prompted accusations of compilation as well as self-conscious responses, as in the following digression in Polevoi's *Oath:* "If we wanted to dazzle with archaeological knowledge, it would be easy for us to select from old chronicles and notes the names of various dishes that made up the diet of our ancestors. The more difficult and obscure the names, the more readers would wonder at our great erudition and expertise concerning Russian antiquities" (*Kliatva*, 419). Veltman likewise complains about abuses of antiquarian paraphernalia, although he characteristically utilizes the occasion to compile his own catalogue of exotic objects: "Let us turn to that curious time with which invention plays at will, dressing it in many-colored clothing, in a pelisse, with a quiver, in armor and breastplates, pulling a red cap over its head and an iron hat, showering it with gold, silver, pearls, precious and semiprecious stones and jewels, and ornamenting it with beads, seating it on a horse, arming it with spears, swords, *kolantyrs,* daggers, *boidans,* battle-axes, sabers, *shereshirs,* arrows, clubs, maces, cudgels, flails, etc." (104). Customs and rituals are another favorite component of historical color. As with the depiction of material culture, here the dominant attitude is sheer fascination with the exotic world of the past.

Matters get more complicated when mores are involved. A common topic is the crudeness and cruelty of bygone epochs. For example, here is how Zagoskin praises the relative humanism of his Cossack character: "Kirsha was a daring horseman, loved to brawl, drink, indulge in drunken violence . . . but even in the very heat of battle he would spare an unarmed enemy and would not amuse himself with prisoners like his mates would; in other words, he did not cut off their ears or their noses but would content himself with stealing everything from the victim but the shirt on his back and let him go" (*Iurii Miloslavskii,* 130).

Clearly the practice of mutilating prisoners—admittedly a "colorful" detail of the epoch—cannot be treated with the same antiquarian admiration as the magnificent attire of ancient warriors. To solve the problem romantic authors usually employ a "dual focus," as does Lazhechnikov, who describes the ruthless manner of waging war during the reign of Peter the Great: "The nighttime silence was broken by the cries of citizens who had been robbed, lost the roofs over their heads, and been taken captive by the thousands. That was the manner in which the Russians of the day waged war, or, to be more precise, such was their policy, namely, to turn a conquered land into a barren steppe, to strip the enemy of any means of supporting himself on this land; it was a cruel policy excused only by the time!" (*Poslednii novik,* 318).

On the one hand, Lazhechnikov uses a synchronous scale, explaining brutality in terms of the epoch. On the other, he applies a diachronic perspective, condemning brutality from the standpoint of his own time. The ratio between these two approaches varies from author to author, as does the attitude toward the idiosyncrasies of the past. Lazhechnikov is often openly critical of negative aspects of history. Thus, having described the barbaric amusements at Anna Ioannovna's court, he exclaims sarcastically: "Oh those good old days! Enviable days of yore! Alas! They don't parade people around in iron cages anymore!" (*Ledianoi dom,* 250). A comically exaggerated version of such negativism found its way into a lowbrow novel of the period: "In the seventeenth century ignorance ruled supreme in the hearts of Russians. Stupid prejudices guided the minds of all, and the dark shadow of rudeness cast itself over the Russian land" (Protopopov, *Chernyi grob,* 1:81–82).

The Russophile Zagoskin, conversely, tends to idealize the Russian past, especially in its "patriarchal" manifestations. Unlike their dissipated descendants, Russians of yore were truly religious: "In order to dispel our sad thoughts, we children of the nineteenth century set out for the theater, dash off to the promenade, go to a ball . . . but our ennui follows us; there is no escape from it! Our ancestors had a better antidote than we: when they were beset by sorrow, overcome by depression, they would pray to the Lord and their bitter cry of affliction would subside into quiet tears of tenderness" (*Brynskii les,* 255). Class barriers used to be less rigid, which Zagoskin illustrates by making the aristocratic protagonist of *Brynsky Forest* spend time conversing with his servant. "In our age," remarks Zagoskin, "this would seem quite strange, but at that time enlightenment had not yet drawn that clear line between master and servant in our country" (294). Servants, in turn, were sincerely attached to their masters. Speaking of Prokhor Kondratyevich, the protagonist's tutor in *Miroshev* (whose ancestors include Scott's Caleb and Pushkin's Savelyich in addition to the author's own real-life *dyadka*), Zagoskin laments the disappearance of servants who were true members of the household: "Whatever happened to that generation of loyal boyar servants? It disappeared along with the patriarchal mores of our ancestors. Now such altruistic love for someone else's child might seem improbable, but in the olden times it was common" (664).

More typical of the novelist's attitude toward the past, however, is a mixture of mild condescension and nostalgia. History is like our childhood and adolescence. For better or worse, we grew up and now, looking back, we smile at our naiveté while simultaneously regretting the freshness of feeling lost in our more mature age. Zagoskin tends to express sympathy for this lost "childishness": "Of course, the luxury of the old boyars was nothing compared to the present refined European luxury. [. . .] Those diversions, despite the fact that they cost very little, always achieved their goal, namely, they entertained. [. . .] But that is the way it should be: a child can be amused by a toy worth a kopeck, but we are grown-ups and if we sometimes spend money on toys, then we pay large sums but are not at all amused by them" (*Brynskii les*, 387). When describing such naiveté Lazhechnikov is more detached, as in the following remark on the crude merrymaking of yore: "There was a full-blown home-grown masquerade that only the childish art of that time could make up. Our ancestors were not artful in such pleasantries . . . but at least they were not indifferent, not affected in their merriment" (*Ledianoi dom*, 59). The underlying concept in both instances is similar: society is viewed as a living organism that passes through stages akin to those of an individual human being.

Human Nature

As a corollary to romantic historicism, authors of the period objected to modernization in the portrayal of human nature. We have already seen this in the critique of older historical fiction (described in chapter 1). Quite characteristic, in this respect, are the comments of Nikolai Polevoi, who accuses Karamzin of projecting onto the individuals of bygone epochs his own notions and values: "He is ashamed of his forebears and *embellishes* them. [. . .] He needs heroes, love of the fatherland, and he does not know that *fatherland*, *virtue*, and *heroism* do not have the same meanings for us as they did for the Varangian Svyatoslav, the resident of eleventh-century Novgorod, the twelfth-century Chernigov dweller, or the seventeenth-century subject of Tsar Fyodor—all of whom had their own notions, their own way of thinking, a peculiar goal in life and affairs" (*Literaturnaia kritika*, 50).

Various attempts to portray fundamental differences between modern Russians and their ancestors may be found in the novels of the period. One of the most frequent themes is romantic love. Many writers and critics of the day pointed out that the notion of love had been greatly modified over time and that western European courtly love was out of place in pre-Petrine Russian settings. As Bulgarin noted: "Introducing love into the seventeenth-century Russian novel ruins the entire premise of verisimilitude! In those days Russians did not know love in its modern sense, nor did they know anything about refined sentiments; they married and loved like present-day Asians" (*Dimitrii Samozvanets*, 1:xxiii). According to Zagoskin, even during the Petrine epoch the change in courtship culture came about gradually; hence his hero's clumsy wooing, which prompts the following explanation for a modern audience: "Do not laugh at my Simsky, dear female readers, for that of which I tell occurred in the year 1711, almost a century and a half ago. Back then our young men, even Guards officers, were completely inept at confessions of love" (*Russkie v nachale os'mnadtsatogo stoletiia*, 2:497).

The ban on romantic love could have proved a serious obstacle for Russian writers. After all, the historical novel was a scion of the older romance, love being a sine qua non in the novels of Scott and other leading European practitioners of the genre. One of the few consistent attempts not to make romantic love the pivot of the plot was made by Polevoi in his *Oath*, which is noted with approval by Vissarion Belinsky: "The very fact that love plays not a chief but rather a secondary role shows well enough that Mr. Polevoi has understood the poetry of Russian life better than all our novelists" (*Pss*, 1:155). Many other writers chose to ignore the problem altogether. This is Zagoskin's approach in *Iurii Miloslavsky*, where, following Karamzin's *Natalya*, Yury and Anastasia behave like perfect sentimental sweethearts, sighing and exchanging oaths of eternal love while Yury covers Anastasia's trembling hands with tender kisses (256). Even the amicable Aksakov admonishes Zagoskin, noting that, in keeping with the character of the time, it was Anastasia who should have kissed Yury's hand while bowing low before her husband and master upon parting (3:361).

Some writers tried to circumvent the obstacle by delegating romantic love only to bearers of western European culture. In *The Last Page* Lazhechnikov reserves love roles for Livonians, and in *The Impostor* Bulgarin assigns them to Poles, noting that "in Poland love existed in that day with all its refinements" (*Dimitrii Samozvanets*, 1:xxvi). Other authors find additional excuses to introduce love into their novels. Very indicative, in this respect, is the discussion of love in Pavel Svinyin's *Shemyaka's Justice:*

> Russian history [. . .] at first glance presents rich sources and striking scenes for the skilled pen of the writer, but even Walter Scott would have difficulty selecting them for reworking according to the strict rules of novel writing since he would not find there the main element—love—on which all of the interest in his works depends, and which is the soul of all good novels, as of all things under the sun. There is no doubt that in olden days beautiful Russian girls knew how to love as they do today, experienced the same passions as their delightful descendants, but they loved and suffered in the silence of their high rooms or dark towers where the male gaze did not penetrate. [. . .] They did not take any part in the affairs of society, did not decide the fates of kingdoms like heroines of the age of chivalry. (*Shemiakin sud*, 1:i–ii)

Svinyin repeats the familiar idea that love in old Russia had different manifestations and social implications, while at the same time asserting that the basic passion has remained the same. This idea is corroborated even by

FIGURE 5. Title page illustration from Svinyin's *Shemyaka's Justice, or the Last Feud of Russian Princes* (vol. 2, 1832; artist M. Lopyrevsky; engraving E. Skotnikov). The absence of romantic love in pre-Petrine Russia posed obvious difficulties in attempts to adapt domestic history to European literary models. While acknowledging the problem in theory, many Russian authors tended to disregard it in practice.

FIGURE 6. Title page illustration from Bulgarin's *Dimitry the Impostor* (vol. 3, 1830; engraving S. Galaktionov). Some writers circumvented the problem by delegating romantic love to bearers of Western European culture, such as the Poles, for example in the case of Bulgarin's *Impostor.*

Polevoi, who is much more conscious than most of his peers in his effort to avoid modernization:

> No, do not think that pleasure did not unlock the doors to women's chambers. It's true that in the days of yore there was no such thing as a modern ball and women then did not behave as queens, but did you really doubt for a moment that women in those days possessed human wit and reason as they do today? Even then love made its way to maidens through all the locks and bars, and women knew how to have pleasure . . . only the type of pleasure was different and did not resembly the present type. (*Kliatva*, 441–42)

By implication, the basic passions can overcome the conventions of the epoch, which is indeed the case in many novels filled with utterly romantic love affairs.

A similar pattern can be observed in the treatment of female beauty. It became a commonplace to emphasize the drastic difference between the modern and old Russian ideals of beauty. To quote Bulgarin's Impostor: "After all, I am a Russian and we Russians have our own ideas of beauty. We do not like gaunt charms, and the chief attribute of beauty we consider to be a full form, which is a sign of health and spiritual tranquility" (*Dimitrii Samozvanets*, 3:321). However, in most historical novels one encounters conventional romantic beauties, albeit draped in picturesque Russian costumes.[1] An explanation of this apparent contradiction can be found in Zagoskin's digression in *The Brynsky Forest:* "You probably know from the old songs that the ideal of feminine beauty of that time had little of the romantic in it. White skin, stoutness and a dark blush in the cheeks made up the chief merit of the Russian beauty. So why did Levshin gaze with such rapture at that girl with the willowy waist and almost pale cheeks? Perhaps because true, perfect beauty, despite all differences in conventions and concepts of beauty, quite simply and without any explanation captivates us with its inexplicable charm?" (*Brysnkii les*, 1:256–57) Like love, beauty is a universal, timeless quality that transcends the evanescent tastes of any given epoch or nation.

The view that the core element of the human personality remains unchanged down through the ages can be traced back to Scott. In the introduction to his first novel, *Waverley,* he speaks of "those passions common to men in all stages of society, and which have alike agitated the human heart, whether it throbbed under the steel corselet of the fifteenth century, the brocaded coat of the eighteenth, or the blue frock and white dimity waistcoat of the present day" (3). Despite the changing "state of manners," the passions or "deep-ruling impulses" involved remain the same since they constitute something given, something defined by Nature (and ultimately, God). Here is how Scott summarizes the matter in a characteristic antiquarian metaphor: "It is from the great book of Nature, the same through a thousand editions, whether of black-letter, or wire-woven and hot pressed, that I have venturously essayed to read a chapter to the public" (4). This idea was not lost on Scott's Russian readers. Pointing to the immutability of human nature in Scott's universe, Nikolay Nadezhdin does not consider this to be a modernization of history but rather a discovery of a link between past and present: "In his novels [Scott] was the first to discover in the present those very same elements, the same passions, prejudices, and delusions that troubled the past, only under other names and in other forms" (quoted in Mann, "Fakul'tety Nadezhdina," 25).

Such dynamic tensions between the changing and the unchanged play a crucial role in the poetics of the historical novel. The emphasized otherness makes the past highly exotic and exciting, while sameness provides readers with grounds for identification with bygone epochs that no longer seem to be mere collections of antiquarian oddities (Dolinin, *Istoriia, odetaia v roman,* 209–10). As Bestuzhev-Marlinsky puts it, we can "love, fight, brawl, drink and funk together with [. . .] the characters and for [. . .] the characters" (2:445–46). Although making it possible to domesticate the past, this idea also places considerable limits on romantic historicism. It largely translates into retrospective projections of romantic conflicts and heroes, which are further aggravated by clichés and commonplaces, both of which are inevitable in a popular genre.

Nation

In accordance with romantic nationalist sentiment, the historical novel was intended to reflect the spirit of a particular people. Although an understanding of nationality helps to define the poetics of the genre and to delimit the parameters of romantic historicism, it also possesses greater extraliterary significance. The 1830s was a time of heated debates concerning the meaning of Russianness and the historical destiny of Russia, which led to the three paradigmatic approaches expressed in the so-called Doctrine of Official Nationality, Slavophilism, and Westernism. It was also a time when the modern Russian self-image was formed. Given its popularity, the historical novel served as an important vehicle for this process. Russia's collective

FIGURE 7. Title page illustration from Bulgarin's *Dimitry the Impostor* (vol. 2, 1830; engraving I. Chesky). Both fictional and historical characters in the novels of the 1830s exhibit raging romantic passions, a feature that places considerable limits on the epoch's historicism.

self-portrait, as expressed in these works, proved to be remarkably enduring and, as I will argue, conspicuously romantic in nature.

A nation is viewed as a separate entity that undergoes various stages of development, in the process of which it changes while still retaining its core characteristics. In order to highlight essential traits of the national character, two sets of comparisons are commonly used, namely, between nations and within a given nation, where the comparison is between the transient and the immutable. The comparative portrayal of nations was used extensively by Scott, who in his Waverley novels portrays Scots and Englishmen side by side. In *Ivanhoe* he points out that the chosen period is particularly attractive, "affording a striking contrast betwixt the Saxons, by whom the soil was cultivated, and the Normans, who still reigned in it as conquerors, reluctant to mix with the vanquished" (4:348). Similarly, in "A Letter on Russian Novels" listing the advantages of the Russian historical novelist, Mikhail Pogodin specifically emphasizes the interaction of dramatically different peoples in the course of Russian history, starting with the earliest period: "The very beginning of our history presents a rich harvest to the writer. Here he can depict in contrast three peoples, the Normans, Slavs, and Greeks, of which each stood on its own level of education and differed greatly from the other in its character" ("Pis'mo o russkikh romanakh," 134). Developments in the twelfth and thirteenth centuries led to an increase in diversity: "Here four other peoples come into contact with the Russians: the Germans settle in the North, in Riga, the Italians in the South, in the Crimea, and the wild Lithuanians invade Russia from the West and the Mongols from the Southeast. What a vast territory is opened for the Russian novelist" (136). As Russian history progresses, this diversity grows even further, reaching its peak in the creation of the multi-ethnic Russian Empire and Russia's reentry into Europe.

Russian novelists understood well the principle of contrasting nationalities. As Lazhechnikov expressed it in the preface to his *Last Page,* which is largely set in Livland: "The Russian national physiognomy is most apparent among the foreigners, in their crowd, under the strong influence of German ways" (*Poslednii novik,* 1:37). They also took advantage of the multi-ethnic dimension of their country's history by providing colorful displays of ethnographic details so beloved by the romantics. In addition to the obvious instances of foreign wars and invasions (like the Time of Troubles or the Napoleonic wars), foreigners are present in many novels dealing with properly domestic subjects. The characters of Lazhechnikov's *Infidel,* set in the Muscovy of Ivan III, include Tatars as well as members of the motley European expatriate community, the protagonist being of Czech-German extraction. Although the action in Lazhechnikov's *Ice Palace* does not leave Saint Petersburg, it revolves around the struggle between the German and Russian parties at court. The heroine, the daughter of a Moldavian prince and a Gypsy, was brought up in a Turkish harem. Moreover, the novel unfolds against the background of a huge ethnic festival organized as a whim of the Russian empress.

The portrayal of non-Russians varies in terms of objectivity. The ultra-patriotic Zagoskin tends to caricature the enemies of Russia, be they ninth-century Vikings, seventeenth-century Poles, or nineteenth-century Frenchmen. Lazhechnikov is much more balanced. Although he confesses that his overriding emotion in *The Last Page* is patriotism, he vows to respect Russia's enemies (*Poslednii novik*, 1:37) and keeps his promise. Overall, however, very few novelists of the time rose to Scott's level of impartiality and tolerance in portraying of inter-ethnic relations or historical conflicts in general.[2] One should add that authors often tended to be openly judgmental with respect to their heroes as well, which constitutes yet another manifestation of the pervasive subjectivity described in the preceding chapter.

Aside from the multi-ethnic mosaic of Russian history, the historical novel of the time was mainly concerned with the issue of Russianness as a reflection of the constants in the Russian national character. One social class that remained largely untouched by all the perturbations of Russian history was the peasants, who in this respect differ markedly from the rest of the country's social groups. Perhaps one of the earliest statements to this effect is found in Karamzin's "Natalya": "The peasants [. . .] to this day have not changed. They dress the same, live and work the same as they lived and worked previously; in the midst of all changes and masks they still present us with the true Russian physiognomy" ("Natal'ia, boiarskaia doch'," 1:31). In the late 1820s and 1830s this idea became a commonplace. "The people's daily home life of that time hardly differs from today's," writes Zagoskin in *Miloslavsky* (*Iurii Miloslavskii*, 1:44). He repeats this thought in a later novel: "Over the past two centuries the customs of the Russian peasants have not changed at all" (*Russkie v nachale os'mnadtsatogo stoletiia*, 2:472). Zagoskin is here echoed by his archrival Bulgarin: "The court, the boyars, the noblemen and the merchants changed. Russian noblemen of the early seventeenth century seem like people from another planet when compared with present day noblemen. Their way of life, clothing, views, notions and language . . . everything was different." By contrast, "the simple folk in essence are historically no different from their seventeenth-century forebears" (*Dimitrii Samozvanets*,

1:xvii–xviii). In his review of Polevoi's *Oath* Bestuzhev-Marlinsky traces the immutability of the Russian peasants back to the Kievan period ("the people have changed little since the days of Svyatoslav" [*Sochineniia*, 2:455])—and eulogizes the Russian peasantry, who "to this day preserve their walk and idiom; their customs and look; their original character, which is founded on chance, on action without calculation; their seemingly naive shyness; their love of inebriety and brawling; their language, so picturesque, rich, brittle. . . . In short, this is a people whose every word sparkles and who spend the last kopeck in grand style. . . . But how can I name all those virgin springs hidden even today in the Russian ridges?" (456–57).

This fascination with the peasants as a repository of the national spirit stems from general romantic, nationalistic, and folkloric preoccupations. It was greatly enhanced, however, by peculiar Russian circumstances, namely, the cultural split between the educated and lower classes that resulted from Peter I's efforts at Westernization. When Russian intellectuals embarked on a search for their national identity, there emerged an understanding that they were aliens in their own land and that true Russianness was to be found in the common people. Further aggravated by the guilt complex of the exploitative classes, this notion translated into populist obsessions that were to last throughout the rest of the imperial period. Traces can already be seen in the portrayal of peasants in the historical novel of the 1830s.

Aside from the protopopulist complex, the majority of the authors in question refer to traits in the national character that transcend not only historical epochs but also class barriers. Paradigmatic in this respect are the very titles of Zagoskin's first novels: *Miloslavsky, or the Russians in 1612; Roslavlev, or Russians in 1812* (which was later expanded to *Russians at the Beginning of the Eighteenth Century*). These works constitute a kind of novelistic cycle whose core element is the Russian nation. Zagoskin himself emphasizes this overarching idea: "I wanted to prove that although the outward forms and physiognomy of the Russian nation have changed completely, what remained unchanged is . . ." (*Roslavlev*, 1:287). This remark is followed by a list of national constants. For many authors of the period what must appear at the top of this list is the triad of the nascent Doctrine of Official Nationality, namely, Orthodoxy, Autocracy, and Nationality—or, in the words of Zagoskin, "our unshakable loyalty to the throne, our devotedness to the faith of our forebears, and love for our native land" (287).[3] Whereas most illustrations of these principles are quite predictable (e.g., expulsion of the Poles, election of the Romanovs, defeat of Napoleon), others are more ingenious. For example, Bulgarin claims that the very fact that Russians initially greeted the False

Dmitry is a testimony to the monarchist instinct of the people, who accepted the supposedly legitimate ruler, although their loyalty proved to be misguided (*Dimitrii Samozvanets*, 1:xviii–xx). However, quite often these novelists are blatantly anachronistic when superimposing the triad onto the past. Russians appear to be diehard monarchists even before the institution of the absolute monarchy had come into being. This is the case in Zagoskin's *Askold's Grave*, which is set during the rule of Prince Vladimir. The novel's villain is obsessed with the idea of restoring the "legitimate" dynasty of Askold and Dir to the Kievan throne, while the positive heroes refuse to rebel against Vladimir, their current ruler (who was pagan and could thus hardly qualify as the anointed bearer of the crown). Caricatured versions of monarchism are found in lowbrow novels, as in the following remark by a certain Rudnevskii, dealing with the appanage period, which was notorious concerning the questionable legitimacy of rulers: "Despite the impetuous spirit of our forebears in those days and the coarseness of their manners, stemming from a lack of enlightenment, everyone knows of that fervent love of the people for the tsars, for their rulers, which to this day marks the Russian character; back then it often bordered on fanaticism" (*David Igorevich*, 1:2). In tune with the official ideology of Nicholas I, legitimist adoration of royalty extended to foreign monarchs as well—even to Napoleon, the arch-usurper and enemy of Russia. For instance, Zotov's Leonid, guided by the principle that the life of a monarch is sacred to a Russian, repeatedly rescues the French emperor. Similar extremes can be found regarding the issue of Russia's innate Orthodoxy. In *Askold's Grave* Zagoskin does not hesitate to use the Christian idiom "Holy Rus" when speaking of pagan times.[4]

Russian historical novels abound in declarations of passionate love for the fatherland, some of which are rather comical. For example, take Olimpiada Shishkina, who in the introduction to *Skopin-Shuisky* defines her Russianness in French: "I wanted to, because it seemed necessary, somehow a requirement, to tell everyone how my soul burns with love for my Fatherland, how zealously I wish it everlasting prosperity. [. . .] This is typical of the Russians, and it has been said of me before *que je suis Russe jusqu'au bout des ongles*" (*Kniaz' Skopin-Shuiskii*, 1:xiv). Even Lazhechnikov does not escape awkward manifestations of patriotism in his first novel. The protagonist of his *Last Page* is a patriotic Byronic hero, which is an obvious oxymoron. In the same novel a high degree of patriotic awareness is displayed by Sheremetev's jester, the dwarf Goliath, who rallies Russian soldiers for the upcoming offensive. Of all the major historical novelists, most passionate in his "Russian tendency" ("russkoe napravlenie") is Zagoskin, whose patriotism even has quasi-religious overtones with a characteristically romantic Neoplatonic twist. Having described a scene of patriotic ecstasy in Nizhny Novgorod—whose inhabitants decided to form a militia in order to put an end to the Time of Troubles—the narrator exclaims: "How many lives could one give away for that single moment of heavenly, pure ecstasy that in this solemn minute filled the hearts of all Russians! No, love of the fatherland is no earthly sentiment! It is a weak but true echo of that insurmountable love for that unknown fatherland for which we grieve and long, virtually from the day of our birth, without understanding our own longing!" (*Iurii Miloslavskii*, 1:172). The narrator's words are reiterated later in the novel by the patriotic monk Avraamy Palitsyn, who, while blessing Yury before the battle against the Poles, intones: "May you be led by the Lord's angel and may you be accompanied by the blessing of an old man who—Oh Almighty! Forgive him this transgression—loves his earthly homeland as all of us should love only our heavenly fatherland! (236).

Zagoskin's "Russian tendency" prompted charges of lowbrow patriotism. Vissarion Belinsky caustically remarks: "Zagoskin has become addicted to a strange kind of pseudopatriotic propaganda and politics and has begun [. . .] with particular pathos to praise the love of pickles and sour cabbage" (8:55–56). Among fellow writers, Zagoskin's most consistent opponent was Polevoi, who accused him of favoring primitive instincts. Referring to Zagoskin's *Miloslavsky*, he writes: "We have not yet admitted to our vain patriotism and, like children, comfort ourselves with our glory and our preeminence over other peoples of the world. The epoch of 1612 is one of the main strongholds of our national pride. [. . .] The bell ringing of national self-boasting and heroism must be pleasant. And *Yury Miloslavsky* rang this bell with all its strength" (*Literaturnaia kritika*, 92). *Roslavlev* does not fare any better in his opinion, with "the same patriotic boasting of Rus . . . the same humiliation of our enemies and depiction of them as fools and madmen" (93). The harshest attack against Zagoskin's brand of patriotism is found in Polevoi's programmatic introduction to *The Oath*: "But to praise something simply because it is *Russian* . . . to loudly proclaim our glory since the time of the Slavs . . . to think that Russian dust is better than German dust, that Russian smoke smells of roses . . . all of this I have always considered and still consider decidedly ridiculous, an unjust affront to the laws of Providence and an act worthy either of a fool or a scoundrel, a hypocrite!" (*Kliatva*, 288). Polevoi calls on the Russians not to toot their own horns but rather to examine themselves objectively in terms of their positive and negative traits.

As has been mentioned repeatedly, although objectivity is quite rare among the authors of the period, they nonetheless depict a broad array of Russian national traits that go far beyond the official Orthodoxy/Autocracy/Nationality triad. The positive aspects of Russianness are easily enumerated. First is a singular type of good-natured and open-minded intelligence. As Zagoskin describes one of his characters: "Affability, natural intelligence, alertness, tact, and Russian common sense were stamped on his expressive and open countenance" (*Roslavlev*, 1:336). Second is a "simple-hearted merriness and kindness," combined with singular wit. Zagoskin continues: "That ancient custom of giving friends and foes alike nicknames that almost always contain a touch of mocking is also one feature of the Russian national character" (*Brynskii les*, 1:319). Third is hospitality, which used to be even more gargantuan in the olden days (Vel'tman, *Koshchei bessmertnyi*, 55–56; Zagoskin, *Kuz'ma Petrovich Miroshev*, 1:890). Fourth is generosity. As Zotov remarks with respect to the behavior of Russian officers stationed in Germany: "According to the commendable custom of their nation, they always paid triple the cost for every trifle" (*Leonid*, 3:157). Fifth is faithfulness, including the extraordinary ability to endure hardship, as exemplified in Zotov's panegyrics to the Russian soldier (188, 452).

The negative qualities can be described just as easily. First is ritualism, blind prejudice, and conservatism—at least in pre-Petrine Russia. Even Zagoskin, in his description of the country's situation in 1710, admits that this stubbornness was detrimental to Russia's greatness. Characteristically, he ends up excusing autocracy: "Of all the [. . .] enemies of Russia hindering her ascendance, organization, and increasing power, there remained one, but this was the most stubborn. This enemy was an almost ever-present, instinctive predilection of Russians for all the ancient customs and prejudices of olden times. Consequences of this blind predilection were immobility, contempt for everything foreign, ignorant pride, and inveterate stubbornness. [. . .] Only the autocratic will of Peter the Great could conquer this last enemy" (*Russkie v nachale os'mnadtsatogo stoletiia*, 2:448). Second is disorder and mismanagement, which is vividly described by Polevoi in connection with Russian wedding plans (which in his view remained unchanged in the fifteenth and nineteenth centuries):

> Add to all of this the customary habit of Russians to make a fuss and bustle, and the fact that women played a key role in weddings. The Russian master can only be sure that his stewards are doing their job when they run around with their tongues hanging out, are breathless from exhaustion, and in the confusion no one can figure out what to do, how to start, and what to end with. The word

> "system" is not a Russian word and it is not in the Russian nature. We always start abruptly, lift three times more than others, but soon drop everything, perhaps because we want to do everything in one fell swoop and rapidly sap our strength when, if we were to work slowly and consistently, we would still have plenty of strength in store. And the interference of *women, Russian* women, especially when they begin to *command* in an undertaking? Empty talk, thousands of times about one and the same thing, sending ten men on the same errand, continually forgetting one or another necessity and, added to all of this, endless arguing, noise, doubts, squabbling . . . this is how any affair is carried out when women get involved. (*Kliatva,* 393)

Third is drunkenness and knavery. As Zotov ironically remarks: "Honesty and sobriety (vices of which foreigners tend to accuse all Russians)" (*Leonid,* 3:23).

Although the list of positives and negatives could be expanded, it is more interesting to examine the qualities that evade clear classification. Chief among them are Russian *udal'* (reckless courage) and *molodechestvo* (daring). "That's what the Russian is about: always ready to display his audacity in a perilous task," comments a character in *Miloslavsky* concerning a young man who died while trying to ford a river by jumping from one drifting ice floe to another (*Iurii Miloslavskii,* 1:158). In *The Oath* Polevoi describes daredevils who aggravate the already chaotic stream of traffic around the Kremlin: "The Russian impatience presented an additional obstacle: How is it possible to wait until five wagons moving at a snail's pace pass? It was considered daring to spring between the horses or climb over the wagon, and the young aristocrats would jump over the wagons on their stallions" (*Kliatva,* 364). Zagoskin also speaks about the Russian passion for reckless riding—especially while under the influence: "And if a Russian drinks one too many, you will never get him to ride German-style, that is, at a pace or easy trot. . . . He will shout, bellow songs, and race along" (*Russkie v nachale os'mnadtsatogo stoletiia,* 2:472). In *The Infidel* Lazhechnikov describes how several young men hid themselves behind a mock fortress used as a target for testing a huge cannon. Although the fortress was blown to bits, the men emerged unscathed, winning the admiration of the crowd: "What lads, aren't they brave! the people cheered them on" (*Basurman,* 2:487). Lazhechnikov continues: "They risked their lives in exchange for that praise! That's what Russians have been like since time immemorial" (487). A German interpreter, a character in the same novel, contrasts this Russian willingness to take chances with German calculatedness: "The Russian loves to go where it is most dangerous.

We Germans calculate and conjecture how to traverse a moat or a pit, but he is already on the other side, or has broken his neck" (385).

Attitudes toward such foolhardiness vary. One can emphasize the hardiness, admiring the sheer courage involved, or disapprove of the foolishness. In his "First Philosophical Letter" Pyotr Chaadaev even links the Russian disregard for danger and death to what he sees as indifference toward good and evil, truth and falsehood. Judgmental attitudes aside, the proverbial Russian daring can be treated as a paradigmatic feature since the underlying quality is immoderation and a penchant for exceeding normal limits. Closely related to this is a tendency to go from one extreme to another. In *Miloslavsky* Zagoskin speaks of mood swings from excess to asceticism: "Without a doubt the enormous amount of beer and victuals the stomach of a Russian can accommodate when he knows he is drinking and eating for free may seem astounding. But it is even more odd that the selfsame stomach that can consume in one sitting what an Italian could not eat in a week is, if necessary, prepared to make do with a piece of black bread" (*Iurii Miloslavskii*, 1:135). Elsewhere he comments: "The Russian is always like that: if there's something in the oven, then put it all on the table! If not, that's fine too! He will drink some water, follow it with a piece of dry bread, and praise the Lord for that!" (*Brynskii les*, 1:397). Polevoi describes transitions from dreary everyday existence to the unbridled merrymaking of holidays: "Moscow Shrovetide was at its height. As is the case now during holidays, nary hide nor hair were to be seen of sorrow or misery, scantness or poverty! [. . .] But Shrovetide in Rus is always a time when everyone makes merry hand over fist. If Shrovetide in our land lasted not a week but three or four, then half of Rus would go mad, and the other half would be hard put to find the means to live the remaining eleven months of the year!" (*Kliatva*, 440–41). Lazhechnikov dwells on the intermixture of servility with rudeness and unprovoked aggressiveness with selfless courage: "In the streets you will find both servile humiliation and churlish impudence. [. . .] The passerby either bows low, almost to the ground, or whistles after you with a coarse folk saying that makes you shudder. The former comes from the rule of the Tatars; the latter has been fostered by coarseness of manners and wild nature. Between them you will find our native reckless courage, hearty health, hats awry, and belts tightened, ready to mock you or pick a fight. But from the same source stems readiness to give one's life for a bosom friend, a beautiful sweetheart, for everything one holds dear—for one's mother, country, tsar, and faith" (*Basurman*, 2:399). Zagoskin even feels it necessary to emphasize sudden extreme shifts in the Russian climate: "We Russians are accustomed to rapid changes in the weather and are not astonished by sudden shifts from winter cold to spring warmth" (*Iurii Miloslavskii*, 1:142).

The Russian penchant for extremes is preserved in the very mimicking of Europe. Zagoskin exclaims: "Besides, Rus retains that which makes her different from other peoples in her very imitations. She does not like trifles, she needs room to stretch, open space; give her anything in colossal sizes, count everything in hundreds, thousands of versts!" (*Moskva i moskvichi*, 2:108). Such "extremism" is ultimately seen as a guarantee of Russia's originality (*samobytnost'*), the nature of which is one of the most hotly debated issues in the 1830s and the 1840s. Echoes of these debates are heard in the historical novel. One will not find among the corpus of texts under discussion a pronounced Slavophile position. Despite all his ardent Russophilism, Zagoskin is closer to the tenets of the Doctrine of Official Nationality and also eulogizes Peter I as "the elected of the heavens, the transformer of Russia" (*Brynskii les*, 1:238). According to Zagoskin, borrowing from Europe under Peter was justified since Russia's progress had been halted by the Tatar conquest (*Toska po rodine*, 2:782–83; *Moskva i moskvichi*, 2:700). Seeking a balance between originality and imitation, Zagoskin, through his character in *Roslavlev*, outlines three stages in every nation's journey toward enlightenment. The first is barbarism, when foreigners are hardly considered human beings and everything alien is treated with contempt. The second, a negative reflection of the first stage, is the "epoch of aping," where everything foreign is admired and everything native is despised. In the third stage the nation attains maturity, is on a par with its mentors, yet also realizes its own value: "Finally, the epoch of aping and precociousness passes. The fruit of many years, countless experiments [. . .] ripens . . . true enlightenment develops in all the land . . . we do not despise and do not deify foreigners . . . we have become equal to them. [. . .] National character and physiognomy are formed, we begin to like our language, respect our homegrown talents, and value our national glory" (1:379).

Despite such balanced declarations, Zagoskin tends to emphasize Russia's originality, often endowing it with anti-Western overtones. "Oh, my dear homeland! [. . .] You are not proud of your earthly enlightenment but you love God and His anointed, the Russian Orthodox tsars. You are reproached for lagging behind the increasingly decrepit West, but all the better: it is living out its last days and you are only beginning to feel your strength, young tsaritsa of the North, devout, original Rus!" (*Toska po rodine*, 2:916).

Zagoskin's opponent Polevoi is a consistent Westernizer—at least until the mid-1830s). He urges his compatriots to admit that, despite the sheer might of the Russian Empire, they are still in their infancy in terms of culture: "One hundred years have already passed since we were pushed into Europe, but only *materially*. We are strong and powerful; we are mighty warriors. We broke the crescent of the Turkish moon, tied the paws of the Persian lion, crossed the Alps, burned the grandeur of Napoleon in Moscow and froze his glory, chased the Swedes beyond the Bay of Bothnia, signed one peace in Paris and another at the walls of Constantinople. Despite all this (why be ashamed of the truth?) in our intellectual education we are younger than all the Europeans, we are still children" (*Kliatva*, 286). Polevoi, however, is similarly preoccupied with the search for Russianness and foresees a great destiny for his native land:

> Reveal yourself, our mother, boundless Rus, world-state, in all your fullness! Show us all your complexity, all parts of your varied composition. This is how we will learn the *elements of nationality*. Knowing the *forms of Europeanness* and the *elements of Russianness*, what will we not make of our Rus, of our people, tempered by the Asian sun in the snows of the North? We defeated Europe with the sword and will defeat it with our minds: we will create our own philosophy, our own literature, our own civilization, under the protection of the glorious reign of our great monarchs! (289–90)

Premonitions of an extraordinary future fit well into the pattern of excesses and extremes that lies at the foundation of the Russian self-image created during this period. Regardless of how grounded in reality this image may be, it is definitely shaped according to the principles of romantic poetics. Its main attribute is individuality at all cost, with the emphasis placed on intense idiosyncrasies—virtues or vices—that often complement each other, further enhancing the sense of originality in terms of contrast.

This paradigm is essential for understanding contemporary debates about Russianness. Among other things, it helps us locate a common ground in these seemingly irreconcilable positions. From this perspective, Chaadaev's nihilism can be considered a peculiar kind of negative nationalism that—alongside the positive nationalism of the Doctrine of Official Nationality—ultimately asserts Russia's uniqueness and unusual destiny.[5] A similar logic underlies the paradoxes of nationalism in Gogol, whose inspired hymn to the Rus-troika emerges from the grotesque world of *Dead Souls*. Since the 1830s and 1840s were formative years for the modern Russian self-image, the paradigm at work in the historical novel of the time has continued to influence the discourse of Russianness up to the present. In the second half of the nineteenth century it reverberates in Nekrasov's contrasting definitions of Rus in *Who Is Happy in Russia?* There is also a connection to Dostoevsky, with his "broad is the Russian" and "Russian boys." Echoes of this paradigm can be heard in Tolstoy's treatment of nationality in *War and Peace* as well as in subsequent incarnations of the historical novel.

4

Masterpieces in Context

Taras Bulba *and* The Captain's Daughter

Writing in the 1880s, Aleksandr Skabichevsky claimed that *Taras Bulba* and *The Captain's Daughter* "have nothing in common with any of the other historical novels of the thirties, which differ from them like night and day" ("Nash istoricheskii roman," 665). For a variety of reasons this idiosyncratic premise held sway for many decades. *Taras Bulba* and *The Captain's Daughter* are among the most thoroughly researched works of Russian literature; however, even nowadays, as historical novels they are mostly considered in terms of Scott's novels, whereas their links to the genre as a whole are often overlooked. In this chapter I examine them from the standpoint of a broader contemporary background, showing how Gogol and Pushkin employ elements characteristic of the historical poetics outlined previously.

Contextualizing *Taras Bulba* and *The Captain's Daughter* makes possible a better understanding of some otherwise perplexing aspects of these works (e.g., Gogol's savage patriotism; Pushkin's chronological games) and ultimately provides a more precise explanation of their uniqueness. Both of these novels are crucial for defining the parameters of the genre since they represent opposing models of the historical novel. Pushkin perfects the Scottian model by finding a balance of fictional and historical characters in highly specific historical settings. By contrast, Gogol stretches to the limits the notion of historical chronotope by combining events that occurred across two centuries and all but eliminating historical characters. Although he follows Hugo, like Scott he concentrates on the conflict between civilizations. While utilizing familiar models and numerous conventional elements, Gogol and Pushkin nevertheless achieve something unique. Gogol creates an epic meant to reflect the entirety of the Ukraine's medieval history, while

Pushkin presents an archetypal vision of Russian history in his brilliant portrayal of the Pugachev rebellion.

Taras Bulba

"Come on, son, turn around! Lord, you look funny! What sort of a priest's cassocks are you wearing?" (*Mirgorod* ed., 2:247) Although these opening remarks addressed by Taras to his sons contain no references to history, they nevertheless resonate powerfully with romantic historical poetics, setting the tone for the rest of the novel.

The most obvious device here is the lack of narrative introduction, a beginning in medias res with just a dialogue cue. Gogol shuns the convention of authorial forewords or detailed expositions, instead utilizing dialogue to create an illusion of immersion into the past. He strengthens this illusion through the use of exotic idiom (Ukrainian *synku* and *tsur tebe!* in the original) and by focusing on exotic attire. In this introductory scene historical exoticism is enhanced through description, specifically the rugged mannerisms of the Cossack colonel and antiquarian details pertaining to his dwelling. At some point, however, the authorial narrative undermines the illusion of history redivivus through the incursion of the writer's voice into the text. This happens at the opening of the novel, where Bulba's colorful diatribe against scholastic education is interrupted by the following remark: "Bulba added one more word that the censors do not allow into print—and rightly so" (2:249). Throughout the text one encounters similar interjections typical of romantic narrative conventions, such as "Now it is appropriate to say something about his sons" (2:257) or "But let us turn to our story" (2:314).

As was mentioned earlier, contemporary writers tend to raise aesthetic issues in the body of their novels by invoking artistic models or referring to specific works of art, thereby exposing the artificiality of the unfolding story. In *Taras Bulba* this device is manifested in frequent metaphors and comparisons drawn from the realm of painting, which has a direct bearing on the pictorial aspect of the romantic historical imagination. The past is represented as a series of pictures, or tableaux vivants: "and the Cossacks beheld a picturesque scene [*zhivaia kartina*]" (1842 ed., 2:99; Magarshack's translation, 109; cf. Polevoi's definition of his novel's genre: "the life of the people in tableaux vivants" [*Kliatva*, 299]). Although further animation transforms these silent and motionless scenes into a historical drama of sorts, discussions of painting techniques or interjections like "This was a picture and an artist should have grabbed a brush to paint it" (*Mirgorod* ed., 2:293) expose the presence of artistic consciousness behind the text.

In the 1842 edition of *Taras Bulba*, the episode of Andriy's journey to Dubno through an underground passage contains the following direct reference to the painter Gerrit van Honthorst, a seventeenth-century Dutch master known in Italy as Gherardo della Notte: "The light grew brighter, and as they walked together, now in the full glare of the light thrown by the candle, now hidden in the coal-black shadows, they looked like a painting by Gherardo della Notte" (2:81; Magarshack, 89). For connoisseurs of fine art, this allusion could help the reader visualize the scene. At the same time, mentioning a Dutch artist active in Italy who had nothing to do with the war waged between Poles and Cossacks in a "semi-Asiatic corner of Europe" (2:140) distracts from the action of the novel and reflects on Gogol's own Italian experience. Following a familiar contradictory pattern, this reference ultimately dispels the illusion of a bygone era.

A similar contradictory function is fulfilled by numerous explicit comparisons between the past and the present. The latter both authenticate the past and also create a distance between the time of the action and the time of narration, thus signaling the authorial presence. Applying the "now versus then" paradigm mentioned in the previous chapter, I wish to examine the particulars in *Taras Bulba*, beginning with material realia. The novel contains a number of antiquarian descriptions, appearing as early as the introductory scene, that deal with dwellings, food, weapons, and clothes. Most of them are quite predictable, but there is one prominent motif associated with clothing that should be mentioned, namely, the changing of attire and the act of masquerading.

In the very first line of the novel Taras ridicules his sons' seminary attire. The next morning the humble seminarians resemble dashing warriors: "Bulba was [. . .] picking out the best trappings for his sons himself. The students were suddenly transformed. Instead of their muddy boots, they had boots of red morocco leather with silver-shod heels; breeches as wide as the Black Sea itself, with thousands of folds and pleats drawn in with a golden cord; long straps with tassels and various appurtenances for the pipe were attached to the cord. A Cossack coat of scarlet gold, bright as fire, was girt at the waist with a gay-colored sash; a pair of chased Turkish pistols were stuck into the sash, and a saber rattled at their sides" (2:40; Magarshack, 40). After defecting to the Poles, Andriy sheds this attire and dons European-style knightly armor described by the Jewish merchant Yankel: "[He] wears gold shoulder-pieces, and his arm-guards are of gold, too, and his cuirass is of gold, and his helmet is of gold, and there's gold on his belt—everything he wears is of gold" (2:96; Magarshack, 106). This change of costume, reflecting Andriy's betrayal of his country, is prefigured by the episode where he, while still a seminarian in Kiev, surrenders his manhood, allowing a playful Polish beauty to dress him up as a maiden. Eventually even the old Taras is forced to participated in the masquerade. Appearing incognito in Warsaw, he pretends to be a German count. Thus disguised, he witnesses the execution of his eldest son, Ostap, along with other captured Cossacks. The fancy clothes of the prisoners are now in tatters, with the final change of dress occurring as the executioner disrobes his victims.

In addition to serving as important historical props, a change of clothes can symbolize a change in social status or it can contribute to twists in the plot. Although such functions of clothing are quite universal, the frequency of the topos in the contemporary historical novel suggests peculiar romantic underpinnings. Especially prominent is the motif of the masquerade. In Zagoskin's *Roslavlev* a character named Zaretsky, who is in the process of retreating from Moscow, meets a partisan commander (the "Taciturn Officer"), decked out in a bizarre uniform, who urges Zaretsky not to call him by his real name: "You can see that I am in costume, and mummers are never called by their real name" (1:469). The same "Taciturn Officer" dresses up as a muzhik when he sneaks behind French lines in Russia and as a Florentine merchant when he spies for the Russians in besieged Danzig. Heading for Moscow in search of his wounded friend Roslavlev, Zaretsky hopes the French uniform will prevent him from being exposed amid the babel of the occupied city: "There is such a mix of languages and uniforms there now" (1:486). Roslavlev also undergoes a travesty of sorts: in order to be smuggled safely out of the city, he has to put on commoner's dress. However, his masquerade does not end here. Once outside of Moscow, Roslavlev is captured by marauders, who rob him of his warm fur coat, replacing it with a French lancer's greatcoat. In the meantime Zaretsky joins the partisans of the legendary Denis Davydov. In order to avoid friendly fire, he covers his French uniform with a Russian greatcoat and dons a Russian cap. Davydov, in turn, wears "strange half-Cossack, half-peasant garb" (1:524), something that is grounded in historical fact. Speaking of himself, Davydov, and Roslavlev, Zaretsky remarks that "all three of us are wearing masquerade costumes" (1:525). Returning to their regiment, the friends create a strong impression: "It is difficult to describe the joy and amazement of Zaretsky and Roslavlev's fellow soldiers when they appeared before their mates in costume" (1:530). Napoleon's army also takes part in a masquerade. Marshal Joachim Murat, king of Naples, who is known for his eccentricity, sports dazzling and bewildering attire reflecting a "strange mixture of the Asian and European, ancient and most modern, masculine and feminine" (1:535). The retreating soldiers of the Grande Armée join the costume party out of necessity, using whatever warm clothes they can muster to shield themselves from the cold.

Travesty is also very common in Lazhechnikov's works. In *The Ice Palace* there is even a case of a double masquerade performed by Biron's spies. During Christmastide they penetrate Volynsky's house, posing as his masked friends. They thus have two layers of disguise. Volynsky himself joins the game, dressing up as a coachman. A mask can be figurative as well. For example, in the same novel Osterman is depicted as a political chameleon, "a master of the art of donning a disguise to suit the occasion" (112). In general, Lazhechnikov's novels swarm with spies and double agents, as do the novels of Zotov. The latter's Leonid, for example, finds himself at an intersection of multiple conspiracies and freely navigates between the warring camps by changing uniforms and identities.

These travesty motifs cannot be explained by applying the concept of Bakhtinian carnival since it does not necessarily include inversion or comical elements. Moreover, it is rooted not in the popular "laughter culture" but rather in the romantic masquerade complex. The latter is ultimately linked to the basic romantic topos of searching for the truth beneath various layers of disguise. To quote Vladimir Odoevsky's words from the introduction to his philosophical novel *Russian Nights:* "Do not blame the artist if under one layer he discovers yet another. [. . .] The ancient writing on the statue of Isis proclaiming 'no one has yet seen my face' is current to this day" (*Russkie nochi,* 8). Irrespective of its deeper underpinning, the motley masquerade of history provides novelists with ample opportunities for creating captivating adventures and providing sumptuous descriptions of exotic costumes.

Aside from material realia of the past, Gogol pays considerable attention to exotic customs, presenting them in a dual-focus manner familiar from other novels. On the one hand, he applies a synchronous approach, showing the value system of the chosen epoch, while, on the other, he provides a moral commentary from the point of view of his own time. The first instance of this is found in the introductory episode, where, speaking of Bulba's wife, Gogol describes the plight of women in a patriarchal society: "She was indeed pitiful, like every woman of that adventurous age. Too brief, all too brief was her experience of love; it lasted only one moment and it was gone [. . .] only one moment of the fever of youth, and her harsh lover forsook her for his saber, his comrades, his drinking bouts. She would see her husband for two or three days in a year. [. . .] She had to put up with insults, even with blows" (2:39; Magarshack, 39). The author obviously cannot condone the abuse of women, but to condemn Bulba for mistreating his wife would go against the principle of historicism since this was the common practice of the day.

Similar axiological bifurcation is especially relevant in the depiction of violence. Commenting on the Cossacks' manner of waging war, Gogol remarks: "Today the evidence of brutality which the Cossacks left behind them everywhere in that semi-savage age would make people's hair stand on end: slaughtered babes, women with breasts cut off, men set free with their skin torn from their feet and legs to their knees—in short, the Cossacks paid off old scores with interest" (2:70; Magarshack, 76). Here he also introduces the theme of mounting violence, which makes the tragedy of history inescapable. Poles commit atrocities against Cossacks, the latter respond in kind, which provokes cruel reprisals on the part of the Poles, who subject captured Cossacks to horrendous torture:

> But we will not harrow the feelings of our readers with a description of the fiendish tortures, which would make their hair stand on end. They were the product of that coarse and savage age when man's whole life seemed to be steeped in violence and blood and his heart was so hardened that he felt no pity. In vain did some people, the few who were the exception in those days, oppose those dreadful acts. In vain did the king and many nobles, enlightened in mind and heart, argue that such cruel punishments could only inflame the vengeance of the Cossack nation. For the influence of the king and those who shared his enlightened views was of no avail beside the unbridled violence and arrogant spirit of the Polish grandees whose thoughtlessness, incredible lack of foresight, childish vanity and absurd pride turned the Seym into a travesty of government. (2:144; Magarshack, 163)

In passing, Gogol pays tribute to a monarch—albeit a foreign one—and condemns the perils of decentralization. Such declarations are very much in tune with the prevalent Doctrine of Official Nationality, although—Gogol's sincere monarchism notwithstanding—this can also be seen as a ploy to counterbalance the sympathetic portrayal of the unruly Cossack democracy.

The brutal execution of prisoners, including Bulba's son Ostap, leads to another round of atrocities. In the ensuing war, Taras turns into a monomaniacal avenger ("frenzied fanatic" [2:314]), which is a common romantic type; other examples include Gudoshnik from Polevoi's *Oath,* Blud from

Zagoskin's *Askold's Grave*, and Kaleria from Bulgarin's *Impostor*.[1] Bulba's insatiable bloodthirstiness goes beyond the limits of medieval practices: "His ruthless ferocity and cruelty seemed excessive even to the Cossacks" (2:146; Magarshack, 165). This trait portends his own excruciating death at the end.

The attitude toward displays of violence varies with the historical novelists of the time. In *The Impostor* Bulgarin remarks that the gruesome details of Fyodor Godunov's murder are out of place in a novel and refers the reader to a chronicle cited in Karamzin (*Dimitrii Samozvanets*, 4:509–10 n. 31). Lazhechnikov, conversely, provides juicy descriptions of cruelty. For example, in *The Last Page* he first promises to skip Iohann von Patkul's execution but eventually succumbs to the alleged demands of his readers and provides an account of the hero's torture on the wheel and quartering (*Poslednii novik*, 481). Characteristic is the following passage, which depicts the dissection of the corpse of a young woman who died while unsuccessfully attempting to free Patkul: "My God! The body of the unfortunate Rosa lay on two benches . . . her breast was cut open . . . and a little man whose only distinguishing feature was a crimson nose busied himself with a bloodied knife and bare hand in the wide-open wound, which the uninitiated would be terrified to view. So repulsive are human innards to humans! The light of the lamp illuminated the features of the Swiss woman, which were heightened in death, fell on the long black braids whose ends twitched in the dust on the floor with the doctor's movements; on her sallow lips, the lacerated breast and the leg, as if made of wax and ringed with black blood" (484). Inspired by the French "littérature frénétique," such infatuation with ghastly details was not limited to the historical novel, although in the latter it played an especially important role, contributing to the macabre mood of the epoch. Among European authors, the most illustrious proponent of this approach was Hugo, who delighted in the portrayal of medieval brutality in *Notre-Dame de Paris*.

In his recreation of the Cossack past, Gogol also pays tribute to frenetic historicism. In the 1842 edition of *Taras Bulba* it is combined with a marked stylization of battle scenes in the spirit of Homer's *Iliad*, as well as the introduction of folk motifs. This results in frenetic passages of a polygenetic nature, as in the following scene depicting the slaying of a young Polish warrior at the hands of a Cossack adversary: "Taking his heavy broadsword in both his hands, Kukubenko drove it straight into his pale lips. The sword knocked out two teeth, white as sugar, cleft the tongue in twain, smashed the neck-bone and penetrated deep into the earth: so he pinned him there to the damp earth forever. The noble blood welled out of his body, deep red as the guelder-rose over the bank of the stream, staining his gold-embroidered coat all red" (2:103; Magarshack, 114). The contemporary French influence is evident here in the attention paid to morbid anatomical details; the epic tradition can be seen in the general situations (the death of a hero) and description of weapons and attire, while folk elements include references to the "damp earth," "teeth, white as sugar," and the guelder-rose comparison.

Folkloric references naturally lead to the issue of ethnic exoticism and nationality. Like many other key features, it is already present in the first phrase of the novel, which contains linguistic Ukrainisms (the original's *synku* and *tsur tebe*) that introduce elements of local color.[2] As Gogol's historical views evolved, the 1842 edition of *Taras Bulba* shifted the emphasis from Ukrainian uniqueness to the Russianness of the Ukraine. This was in line with the widely held notion that Great Russians, Little Russians, and White Russians are not separate peoples but branches of the common Russian nation. Bulba's language in the later edition is retouched by Gogol, who purges it of Ukrainisms, replacing the Ukrainian vocative *synku* with the standard Russian *syn*. The form *synku* will reemerge in the next paragraph, but its removal from the opening sentence softens somewhat the novel's Ukrainian accent.

Shifts of accent notwithstanding, both versions of *Taras Bulba* are preoccupied with a contrastive portrayal of nations, a favorite device since Scott. A fragment of the Orthodox Rus, dominated by the Catholic Poles, bordered by the Muslim Crimean Tatars and Ottoman Turks, and home to a large Jewish population, medieval Ukraine was at the crossroads of cultures and civilizations, constituting the frontier locus par excellence. Muslims appear only in the background of the novel, albeit in characteristically picturesque postures: the Zaporozhians "had unguarded, careless borders, in the sight of which the Tatar would show his quick head and the Turk in his green turban gazed stern and motionless" (2:268). Gogol concentrates on the Cossacks, Poles, and Jews. As far as the two latter nations are concerned, one encounters clichés familiar from other works of the period. The Polish types include lofty knights, playful beauties, arrogant potentates, and—above all—vain and stubborn braggarts (e.g., the Poles in Zagoskin's *Miloslavsky* or Zotov's *Leonid*). The Jews of *Taras Bulba* are unscrupulous profiteers: pusillanimous yet daring when it comes to moneymaking activities, which is also a common stereotype in the Russo-Ukrainian novels. Thus, the memorable character Yankel, who provides both comic relief and "camp-shifting" opportunities, appears to be not just a caricature of *Ivanhoe*'s Isaac but also a stock character of contemporary fiction (e.g., Zotov's Mozes in *Leonid* and similar personages in Golota's works).

Following the familiar paradigm of extremes in the definition of Russianness, in his portrayal of the "Cossack nation" Gogol stresses unbridled might and breadth of soul. While in the *Mirgorod* edition he speaks of the Cossacks' Slavic nature, in the final version he consistently refers to them as Russians. They represent "an expression of the boundless, reckless exuberance of the Russian character [and] an extraordinary manifestation of the Russian strength" (2:35; Magarshack, 35); they indulge "in reckless debauchery—drinking and carousing as only a Russian can" (2:37; Magarshack, 36), and so forth. One can also discern echoes of the Doctrine of Official Nationality complex in Gogol's depiction of the Cossack character. Although the "Autocracy" postulate obviously does not apply to the citizens of the "strange republic" (2:54), "Nationality" (patriotism) and "Orthodoxy" remain the pillars of their identity. The Cossacks' brand of Orthodoxy may seem somewhat bizarre. The fierce warriors, who often wage war for the sake of waging war, display very few conventional Christian values. They are not particularly keen on the ritualistic aspects of the Eastern Church either and wish to hear nothing of fasting or abstinence (2:55).[3]

In short, Cossacks in *Taras Bulba* use Orthodoxy primarily as their battle cry. Although this could be seen as yet another display of medieval local color, it is curious that Gogol, a deeply religious thinker, does not question the Christianity of his Cossacks. As recent scholars have noted, Gogol's Cossacks display a true communal spirit, which in the 1842 edition culminates in Bulba's fiery sermon on Russian camaraderie and the quasi-Eucharist administered by the old chieftain before the battle (Vaiskopf, 449). The Cossacks' organic unity is consonant with the emerging Slavophile theory of *sobornost'* (multiplicity in unity) and stands in sharp contrast to the mechanical cohesion of the Polish army, which is governed by a Western European engineer (Kornblatt, 52).

A corollary to the Cossack brotherhood is their readiness to sacrifice themselves for a common cause, which is the highest form of Christian love: "Greater love hath no man than this, that a man lay down his life for his friends" (John 15:13). This theme is reinforced by Christological motifs surrounding the deaths of Bulba and Ostap. At the height of passion Ostap calls out to his father (not suspecting that the latter might be physically present in the enemy's stronghold.). At the conclusion of the novel, Taras is actually crucified by his Polish captors. In the *Mirgorod* edition he is tied to a high log, with his right hand nailed down, while in the 1842 version he is chained to a tree, with both of his hands nailed to it. Ignoring his own torments, Bulba thinks only of guiding his fleeing comrades to safety while urging them to return in force. Thus, Christianity is again intermixed with the unforgiving rage of a medieval warrior/romantic avenger.

Like many Russian novelists of the time, Gogol openly takes sides in the historical conflict. His sympathies lie with his Cossack ancestors, whose cause is a priori just since they are defending their freedom and their faith against foreign oppression. Nevertheless, Gogol does not altogether ignore the truth of other parties involved, which—like the theme of spiraling violence—enhances the sensation of history's tragedy, especially in the reworked version of *Taras Bulba*. Indicative in this respect is Taras's amazement at Jewish resilience (2:69) and Yankel's monologue on the plight of the Jews (2:133), which are absent from the *Mirgorod* edition.

Even more significant are amendments to the Polish line, emphasizing the attractiveness of European knightly culture and Catholic civilization. Following the epic spirit of its battle scenes, the 1842 edition pays tribute to Polish warriors, who are portrayed as worthy adversaries of the Cossack heroes. Gogol also expands the episode of Andriy's defection, adding to it an impressive picture of a Catholic church with a miracle of sorts happening before the eyes of the amazed Cossack (2:82–83). As has been mentioned, Andriy's betrayal is symbolized by a change of costume. When the perplexed Bulba learns from Yankel that his younger son was seen in the besieged city sporting splendid Western armor, he asks why Andriy would wear foreign attire. "Because it is better," replies the practical Yankel, his claim remaining uncontested (2:96). In the 1842 edition Andriy's act is also more conscientious in rejecting the group mentality of patriotism: "Who says that my country is the Ukraine? Who gave it to me for my country? A man's country is what his soul most desires, what is most dear to it" (2:92; Magarshack, 100).[4] Although he behaves like a romantic rebel, even while renouncing his Cossack identity he characteristically acts like an "impetuous and indomitable Cossack" determined to "perform something which no man in the world has ever performed" (2:91; Magarshack, 100). This again underscores the connection between romantic poetics and the paradigm of Russianness (here in its Cossack incarnation) created in the 1830s and 1840s.[5]

Finally, *Taras Bulba*'s chronology or, rather, its anachronisms should be mentioned. Gogol's poetic license with respect to the time line of Ukrainian history has been noted by many commentators, but it is worth reexamining from the standpoint of the conventions of the genre. Although Gogol does not openly confess to anachronisms, they are quite obvious to attentive readers even without resorting to extratextual research. On several occasions he mentions the Union, meaning the 1596 Union of Brest-Litovsk, according to which a contingent of Ukrainian bishops recognized papal primacy. This resulted in a bitter split in the church, repressions against the Orthodox believers, and widespread unrest that fueled Cossack uprisings. In the opening scene of *Taras Bulba* we are told that the action is set in the sixteenth century, when the idea of the Union was still in its nascent phase (2:249). However, later in the novel we learn that among the goals of the uprising joined by Bulba was ridding the Ukraine of the Union (2:312). Even if they know precious little about the Union and its chronology, attentive readers cannot help but notice that the novel leaps from one period to another without any justification.

Other anachronisms can be detected with the help of conspicuous historical references placed in the text. For example, in trying to establish the age of the old Bulba, one arrives at rather perplexing results. The introductory episode suggests unequivocally that his formative years were spent in the fifteenth century: "He was one of those characters who could have only appeared during the crude fifteenth century" (2:251). Thus, he should have been born around 1480 or earlier. In the same paragraph, however, we are told that Bulba was among the first Cossack colonels created by Stefan Batory, that is, around 1580, which would have made him at least a hundred years old. Discovering this incongruity did not require particular historical erudition since Batory—Ivan the Terrible's nemesis during the Livonian war—was well known to educated Russian readers. In the final chapters of the book Bulba joins the insurrection led by Ostranitsa and Gunya, who are less famous figures. In a familiar move Gogol obliquely invites the reader to check his sources: "I will not describe [. . .] the course of the entire great campaign: this belongs to history" (2:313). Although the insurrection is indeed a historical event, it occurred not in the sixteenth century—when the action of the novel is supposed to be set—but in 1638. This adds another six decades to the already venerable age of the Cossack patriarch, who must have celebrated a sesquicentennial by the time of his final battle.

Such anachronisms do not stem from the inadequate historical preparation of the author. In the mid-1830s Gogol collected materials for a comprehensive history of Little Russia; although he eventually gave up the idea, he researched a wide range of materials, becoming sufficiently competent in the subject. Nor can one speak of inadvertent slips since the same obvious chronological incongruities are also found in the carefully revised second edition of *Taras Bulba*. We are dealing here with intentional anachronisms that figure prominently in the romantic historical novel. Even against this background, *Taras Bulba* stands out in terms of the magnitude of the author's poetic license. The revised edition widens the chronological framework of the novel even further by including Bulba's prophecy, which points to the forthcoming reunification with Russia and the demise of Poland. Thus, the novel covers virtually all of the Ukraine's medieval history (Vissarion Belinsky remarked about the revised edition that in it Gogol exhausted "the entire historical life of Little Russia" (*Pss*, 6:661) and may have served as an artistic substitute for the unrealized historiographic project.

Among the reasons for abandoning this project was Gogol's disappointment over the meager primary sources available for a student of Ukrainian history. Since his imagination could not be fired by the "chronicles," Gogol—in a characteristically romantic move—turned to folklore. In 1834 Gogol wrote the following to the young Izmail Sreznevksy, who had sent him a collection of Ukrainian historical ballads: "Lost interest in our chronicles, in which I failed to find what I was looking for. [. . .] And that is why each note of a song speaks more vividly to me of the past than our limp and brief chronicles" (*Pss*, 10:298–99). The epic element in the novel, which has been emphasized by numerous commentators, can be seen as yet another factor contributing to *Taras Bulba*'s anachronisms: unlike chronicles, oral tradition has no use for time lines.

Gogol's epic intentions are also crucial for interpreting the novel's conclusion, which describes the escape of the surviving Cossacks down the Dniester. Compared to the rest of the action-packed chapter, the closing paragraph is strangely uneventful and serene. Its most obvious function is to provide an open ending: although the old Bulba is dying, the Cossack brotherhood lives on. However, no less important is the motif of an emerging legend that sounds in the last sentence of the novel: "The Cossacks [. . .] were rhythmically plying the oars and talking of their ataman" (2:318). The talk of Bulba's feats, accompanied by rhythmic rowing, is a prelude to producing a heroic song—an epic—that the reader has just finished. This also creates an elegant circular composition by referring back to the opening scene of the novel, where the narrator remarks that "living traces" of this bygone epoch still survive in songs and folk legends (2:33). However, if one reads this passage closely, one discovers a paradox of sorts since we are told that these songs "are no longer sung in the Ukraine by the bearded blind minstrels." This is not an example of Gogol's absurdism but rather the characteristic treatment of folklore during the epoch. Indeed, any attempt to establish specific folk sources for *Taras Bulba* will prove futile since one is dealing with the spirit of folklore reinvented by the artist's imagination. This is signaled by Gogol himself in the conclusion of the 1842 edition, where the final paragraph is expanded through descriptions of the Dniester's flora and fauna, which should not be taken as a sign of the purported "realism" of Gogol's later works. Especially prominent are new ornithological details that further reinforce the song motif. Among several varieties of birds mentioned in the revised conclusion is "the proud goldeneye" (*gordyi gogol'*), which can be viewed as Gogol's playful signature. Evoking his feathered namesake, Gogol stamps the emerging Cossack song as his own creation. He also introduces a touch of irony since the goldeneye, proud though it may be, belongs to the duck family, which is not noted for its singing ability.[6]

The Captain's Daughter

This work sums up the major preoccupations of Pushkin's later works, including his experimentation with prose, fascination with history, and obsession with fate. It is Pushkin's most mature and, in many ways, most enigmatic work. Given the time of its publication, it can also be viewed as his last testament. Nevertheless, its initial reception was lukewarm at best, amounting to a dubious "succès d'honneur" (Cherniaev, 6). *The Captain's Daughter* appeared at a time when the historical novel was already becoming an outmoded genre. Besides, practically every element in *The Captain's Daughter* can be traced back to *Rob Roy, Waverley, The Heart of Midlothian, The Bride of Lammermoor, Woodstock,* or some other Waverley novel.[7] Unmistakably Scottian is the overall model of *The Captain's Daughter,* which is perhaps the only Russian novel that faithfully follows Scott both in terms of formal devices and in conveying the insoluble tragedy of history. Nevertheless, Pushkin's concentrated, dynamic, and tantalizingly "simple" novel, built around a tight grid of internal "rhymes," stands worlds apart from the unhurried narratives of the garrulous Scott.[8] Moreover, *The Captain's Daughter* ultimately departs from Scott in transforming his formula to fit the unique circumstances of Russian history.[9] In the end, the subtlety of Pushkin's literary game was lost on his contemporaries, who mistook *The Captain's Daughter* for yet another remake of Scott.

Since the Scottian connection in *The Captain's Daughter* has been well researched, I will concentrate on its Russian background, proceeding from separate motifs to Pushkin's grasp of the general poetics of the genre (bearing in mind that many stock elements in the historical novel were of a polygenetic origin). Choosing as my point of departure the snowstorm episode from *The Captain's Daughter,* one notes that it has several precedents in contemporary works. A prophetic snowstorm opens Polevoi's *Oath* (1832), where

Boyar Dmitry Ioannovich, holed up at a roadside inn, chances upon the sons of Prince Yury and begins to implement his intrigues against the great prince, plunging Muscovy into a fratricidal feud. In Zotov's *Leonid* (1832) Russian soldiers under the command of the protagonist stumble upon Napoleon during a snowstorm at Eylau. Instead of trying to kill or capture the enemy leader, who is guarded only by a small retinue, Leonid strikes up a courteous conversation with the French emperor. Although he fails to change the course of history, he lays the foundation for his own unusual friendship with Napoleon. Even more relevant for *The Captain's Daughter* is the snowstorm in the opening scene of Zagoskin's *Miloslavsky* (1829).[10] Yury and his servant are caught in a blizzard, as are Petrusha and Savelyich in the second chapter of *The Captain's Daughter*. During the snowstorms both heroes encounter strangers for whom they perform favors. Despite the grumbling of their servants, Yury saves the freezing Kirsha and Petrusha presents Pugachev with a hareskin coat. These acts of generosity trigger a disproportionate sense of gratitude: in each case the stranger overpays his debts, becoming a faithful helper, saving the benefactor's life several times, and uniting him with his sweetheart.[11]

Another complex of motifs familiar from the contemporary novel is related to the theme of travesty, which I discussed in connection with *Taras Bulba*. For Pugachev the masquerade begins when Petrusha presents him with a hairskin coat, which he pulls over his tattered *armyak*. This foreshadows further transformations in the impostor's attire. Soon after storming the Belogorskaya Fortress, he appears in the guise of a Cossack tsar seated on an improvised throne and wearing a red caftan trimmed with lace and a tall sable hat adorned with gold tassels. Later he sports travel attire consisting of a fur coat and a Kyrgyz hat, which reflects the multi-ethnic composition of his army and the frontier locale. Pugachev's "generals" also take part in the costume party. Beloborodov incongruously wears a blue ribbon (Order of St. Andrew—the highest decoration in the empire) over a gray peasant *armyak*. Klopusha is on the exotic side, mixing Cossack wide trousers, a red Russian shirt, and a Kyrgyz robe. During the storming of the fortress, Masha tries to conceal her social origin by changing into a *sarafan* dress, while the traitor Shvabrin promptly sheds his officer's uniform, replacing it with a Cossack caftan, and even manages to get an instant haircut à la Cossack. Catherine the Great, in turn, participates in the masquerade, appearing incognito before Masha in the park of Tsarskoe Selo. Later, when Masha is summoned to the palace, she finds the empress at her toilet, preparing to put on yet another mask. Inter alia, this pervasive masquerade underscores the theme of false identity that dominates the historical background of the novel, with the protagonist caught between the usurper Catherine and the impostor Pugachev.

Like Scott, Pushkin chooses a borderline setting, placing the action of his novel on Russia's eastern frontier. Although this permits him to pay tribute to ethnic exoticism in his portrayal of Cossacks and nomadic peoples of the steppe, like other contemporary Russian writers he is more preoccupied with the issue of Russianness. Pugachev, with his "broadness" of soul and penchant for extremes, embodies the Russian national character described in the previous chapter. The conspicuously inconspicuous Captain Mironov, with his Russian brand of unassuming courage, ultimately follows the same pattern. Most important, *The Captain's Daughter* is concerned with a uniquely "Russian mutiny" and, on a higher level, with peculiar paradigms of Russian history that do not fit the European mold.[12]

The narrator's general attitude toward the past recalls the double focus encountered earlier. The past is judged both in its own right and from a modern point of view. Commenting on Captain Mironov's order to torture a captured spy, Grinyov articulates this approach: "In the old days, torture was so ingrained a part of the judicial process that the beneficent order abolishing it remained a dead letter for a long time. [. . .] Even nowadays I occasionally hear old judges complaining of the abolition of the barbaric custom. At the time of which I write, nobody had any doubts as to the necessity of the torture, neither the judge nor accused" (*Kapitanskaia dochka,* 37–38; Myer's translation, 146). Pushkin's general attitude toward the "good old times" reflects a mixture of fascination and irony familiar from other works of the period.

Unlike most Russian novels, *The Captain's Daughter* is very consistent in adhering to the "found manuscript" scenario. Abandoning initial plans for an authorial introduction, Pushkin replaced it with an afterword by the "publisher," who claims that he merely selected epigraphs and changed some proper names in Grinyov's authentic memoirs. Although the ploy is transparent, it precludes explicit self-refutations so common for the poetics of the genre. However, chronological games and the alteration of historical evidence, familiar from the contemporary novel, are present in *The Captain's Daughter* as well. The most obvious example concerns the marks of omission in the opening sentence pertaining to the date Grinyov senior resigned. Judging from the historical hints provided, after refusing to accept the deposition of Peter III, in June 1762 he retired to his village and married. Thus, Petrusha is born under the star of Catherine's coup, which is pivotal for the thematic structure of the novel. However, had this been the case, Petrusha would have barely turned ten by the time of Pugachev's rebellion. The year 1762 originally figured in the manuscript explicitly, but Pushkin noticed the discrepancy and deleted the last two digits. The lacuna in the date creates a familiar tension between the chronology of history and that of the novel, threatening to undermine the supposed factual accuracy of the latter.[13]

In another important instance Pushkin suppresses historical evidence. As Aleksandr Ospovat has noted in his 1998 study of historical allusions in *The Captain's Daughter,* there is no mention of the ongoing Russo-Turkish War (1768–74) at the beginning of the novel. Andrei Grinyov dispatches his son to military service in the autumn of 1772. At this time there was a pause in combat operations, but attempts to negotiate a peace stalled, making resumption of hostilities a likely prospect. This casts a different light on Andrei Grinyov's decision not to send Petrusha to Saint Petersburg. Given the historical context, his tirade against the dissipated life awaiting a young officer in the capital does not sound particularly convincing. From Saint Petersburg Petrusha could be transferred to the front, while a posting to a remote eastern garrison would be relatively risk-free. Thus, the old Grinyov may be trying to save his only son and heir from the perils of war ("Istoricheskii material," 50–52). This detail potentially subverts the straightforward image of Grinyov senior as a stern, uncompromising old soldier.[14] However, it is also possible that allusions to the Russo-Turkish War might create unnecessary complications, thereby spoiling the "artless" opening of the novel.

Irrespective of the reasons behind Pushkin's decision to forget a major event in recent Russian history, such a handling of facts fits the romantic paradigm previously described. Given this paradigm, one can expect some kind of self-incriminating leads. Indeed, while walking through the park of Tsarskoe Selo at the conclusion of the novel, Masha sees a newly erected monument honoring the recent victories of Count Rumyantsev-Zadunaisky. This reference has several implications. First, it pays tribute to general historical poetics, with the reader being transported to a period when venerable monuments were brand-new. Second, it restores a balance in Pushkin's portrayal of Catherine's reign by invoking episodes more glorious than the bloodbath of Pugachev's rebellion. Third, it reinforces the topos of Tsarskoe Selo, which is, in turn, multifaceted and pregnant with divergent contexts (Ospovat, "Iz nabliudenii nad tsarskoesl'skim toposom"), one of them being a self-referential note. After all, the "editor" of Grinyov's manuscript dated his afterword October 19, 1836. Pushkin did indeed finish the final version of the novel on that day, but it also happens to be the day Pushkin graduated from the Lyceum at Tsarskoe Selo as well as the symbolic date of his anniversary poems. The date supplied at the end of *The Captain's Daughter* ultimately constitutes a "signature" similar to the playful markers signaling authorial presence as the flight of a *gordyi gogol'* in the concluding paragraph of *Taras Bulba*. Finally—and possibly most important for my argument—the "recent victories" of Rumyantsev-Zadunaisky were won in the Russo-Turkish War of 1768–74, which is intentionally ignored at the beginning of the novel. Bringing it up at the conclusion is tantamount to a subtle confession of conscious anachronisms.

Investigating fact and fiction in Pushkin's works inevitably leads to the issue of the relationship between *The Captain's Daughter* and *A History of Pugachev*. It is common knowledge that Pushkin worked on the novelistic and historiographic renderings of the Pugachev rebellion concurrently (Oksman, 160). It is likely that the *History* was initially conceived as a preface to the novel but later evolved into an independent historiographic project. Pushkin treated it with the utmost seriousness, conducting archival research and traveling to the scene of the rebellion. A major conceptual difference between *The Captain's Daughter* and the *History* soon becomes apparent. In the novel the revolt is somewhat poeticized and depicted as a morbidly attractive elemental force. The rebel leader Pugachev is portrayed as a complex and fascinating individual, a "remarkably attractive villain"—to use the parlance of Pyotr Tchaikovsky, who contemplated an operatic adaptation of the novel ("*Kapitanskaia dochka* v kritike," 253). By contrast, in the historical work Pugachev lacks any noble qualities, being a mere puppet in the hands of his chieftains. Pushkin characterizes him as a man "with no other merits, except for some military expertise and extraordinary audacity" (*Pss*, 9:27). The revolt he headed is described without any romantic overlay; instead, we are presented with a chilling catalogue of atrocities. Thus, two different versions of Pugachev and the *pugachevshchina* were created by the same writer virtually simultaneously.

This situation has led to a variety of solutions proposed by Pushkin scholars. Despite an obvious discrepancy between the two works, some critics (mostly in the orthodox Soviet camp) choose to ignore it altogether, projecting the "remarkably attractive villain" of the novel onto the brute of the *History* or freely combining elements of both texts in order to prove Pushkin's alleged sympathy for the popular uprising and its leader.[15] Most critics, however, do see significant differences between the novel and its source. They attempt to resolve them by applying to Pushkin's works a certain hierarchy of truths, defining one work as more "accurate" and/or convincing. Understandably, the concise and entertaining novel easily outweighs the "dry" *History*, which is overloaded with factual details of little interest to most readers.[16] Explanations vary as to why the novel appeared to be more "truthful." Some critics point to censorship, arguing that the writer could afford to take more liberties in a novel than in a work of history (Iakubovich, 196). Others point to the scarcity of sources, claiming that Pushkin had to compensate for this lack by relying on his artistic imagination and thereby transcend the truth of historical documents (Petrunina, *Proza Pushkina,* 283). Still others bluntly state that Pushkin was simply a better littérateur than a historian. In the words of Marina Tsvetaeva: "In *The Captain's Daughter* Pushkin the historian is defeated by Pushkin the poet" ("Pushkin i Pugachev," 394).[17]

Another way of addressing the problem is to assert that their differing genres situate the two works within different realms of narration and consequently make comparisons moot.[18] Some critics go even further, suggesting a complementary relationship between the two works as one between a dry text and a colored illustration.[19] More recent scholarship has expressed the view that both works are not only equally valid but also create a dialogic relationship. Andrew Wachtel has applied to them his paradigm of the "intergeneric dialogue" characteristic of Russian culture (66), while Svetlana Evdokimova has coined her own term in speaking of the "principle of complementarity" in Pushkin's historical imagination (13–14, 128).

Leaving aside subtleties of terminology, the dialogical approach to the *History* and *The Captain's Daughter* appears both warranted and productive—with two important caveats. Such dialogue is not a specifically Russian phenomenon, nor is it a peculiar creation of Pushkin's genius. One encounters here a variation on the concept of binary truth, which is a commonplace in romantic poetics (see chapter 2). Pushkin displayed a clear awareness of this dichotomy in his early poem "A Hero" (1830), which was written in connection with the scandalous memoirs of Napoleon's secretary Louis Antoine Fauvelet de Bourrienne, who refuted a number of Napoleonic myths. In Pushkin's poem the sobering revelations of "the strict historian" conflict with "the poet's reveries." Nevertheless the poet defends his stance in the oft-quoted yet highly ambiguous dictum: "The deceit that elevates us is more dear to me than a multitude of low truths," which recalls Vigny's manifesto about "le vraie du Fait" and "la vérité de l'Art."[20] The contradiction between two visions of history becomes especially poignant in Pushkin's portrayal of Pugachev's rebellion. Here he combines in one person the roles of a "strict historian" and a "poet." Allusions to the *History* in the text of the novel are oblique yet prominent. For example, Grinyov declares: "I won't describe the Orenburg siege, which belongs to history rather than to a family record"

(*Kapitanskaia docka*, 56; Myer's trans., 173). This cliché is repeated throughout numerous novels of the period, including *Taras Bulba*. In the specific context of *The Captain's Daughter*, it can be read as a direct reference to Pushkin's own recently published *History*, which contains a very different perspective on the rebellion. Especially important is the string of allusions associated with Lizaveta Kharlova, a young woman whose parents and husband were brutally executed by the rebels. She was forced to become Pugachev's concubine and was eventually murdered, together with her little brother, under pressure from the jealous Cossack chieftains. However, we do not learn this story from the novel, where her name is mentioned just once when Shvabrin threatens Masha Mironova with the destiny of Lizaveta Kharlova. Since the latter was not a well-known figure, in order to understand Shvabrin's threat the ideal reader would have had to consult historical accounts or, more specifically, Pushkin's *History*. And if one turns to the *History*, one can also fill in the story of the fall of the Nizhne-Ozernaiia Fort and the execution of the officers, whose laconic description in the novel simply reads: "The commandant and all the officers were hanged" (*Kapitanskaia dochka*, 38). Upon learning the news, Grinyov is particularly upset since he had met the commandant and his wife. The young wife, not called by name in this passage, is the same Lizaveta Kharlova. Grinyov does not know the details of her husband's death, but in the *History* it is portrayed in a very graphic manner. From the *History* one also learns about the horrible end suffered by Kharlova's mother, who was "hacked to pieces," and Kharlova's father, Colonel Elagin, an obese man whom the rebels flayed alive and whose fat was used as an ointment for their wounds (*Pss*, 9:18–19). Once a link to the *History* is established, images of violence, which are softened in the novel, acquire most gruesome overtones.[21]

Moreover, the Kharlova connection is crucial in the sense that it threatens to subvert the entire plot of the novel. The story of the colonel's daughter can be viewed as a prototype of that of the captain's daughter, Masha Mironova. The initial situation is virtually identical: the fathers of both young women are fortress commandants and their sweethearts are military officers as well. Although the opening of *The Captain's Daughter* follows the Kharlova scenario— both of Masha's parents are executed—after this point the novel differs markedly from Kharlova's somber fate, with the heroine eventually reunited with the hero and settling down to a blissful domestic life. Nevertheless, the tragic outcome of history looms over this novelistic happy ending. This becomes the pattern with respect to Pushkin's references to history: whenever the cruelty in the novel is mitigated, he invokes the most morbid details from the *History;* whenever events take a happy turn, he reminds the reader that in reality things were very different. Thus, Pushkin creates a novel that simultaneously contradicts his own *History* yet plants allusions intended to subvert the fictional rendering of history.

What are the reasons behind Pushkin's deviations from history? On the issue of portraying violence, one can cite considerations of literary taste.[22] Pushkin spoke with contempt of the frenetic school (*Pss,* 10:405). Given his characteristic minimalist prose, he includes just enough violence in the novel to portray both the cruelty of government repression and the horrors of a "Russian rebellion." Pushkin's reticence in this regard becomes especially obvious when one compares *The Captain's Daughter* to Gogol's *Taras Bulba.*

As far as the image of Pugachev is concerned, one should recall the dichotomy between historical truth and popular memory. Beginning with *Boris Godunov,* Pushkin developed an intense preoccupation with the issue of popular opinion (*mnenie naroda*). As he discovered during his trip to Orenburg, the common people retained a positive impression of Pugachev regardless of the bloodshed that accompanied the rebellion. In his "Remarks upon the Rebellion," addressed to Nicholas I, Pushkin writes: "The Ural Cossacks, especially old people, are still attached to the memory of Pugachev. 'It would be a sin to complain about him,' an eighty-year-old Cossack woman told me. 'He did us no evil . . .'—'Tell me,' I asked D. Pyanov, 'about Pugachev being your proxy father.'—'For you he is Pugachev,' answered the old man with irritation, 'and for me he was the Great Sovereign Pyotr Fyodorovich.' When I mentioned his brutalities, the old people excused him, saying: 'He didn't act of his own will . . . our drunkards stirred him up'" (*Pss,* 9:373). The ending of the *History* states that despite the passage of time and the government's attempts to commit the matter to oblivion, the memory of Pugachev lives on: "The name of the dreadful rebel still resounds throughout the parts where he raged. The people still vividly remember the bloody time to which they gave the striking name of *Pugachevshchina*" (81). Although Pushkin the historiographer paints an objective portrait of Pugachev, by evoking popular opinion in the final sentence of the *History* Pushkin implies a different perspective and an alternative "truth." That is not to say that in *The Captain's Daughter* Pushkin follows a definite folk tradition associated with Pugachev. (As we have seen, authors of the period preferred to compose their own quasi-folklore.) Rather, he releases the legendary potential of the Cossack tsar, gearing it toward the aesthetic concerns of his novel while also "reconciling Russia with Pugachev" (Cherniaev, 132). Having accomplished this feat, Pushkin fulfills the dying wish of his hero, who begged the people to absolve him of his sins before being executed: "Pugachev, having crossed himself and prostrated several times, faced the cathedrals and then, looking in haste, began to bid farewell to the people, bowing in all directions and saying with a catch in his voice: *Forgive me, Orthodox people . . . absolve my sins before you . . . forgive me, Orthodox people!*" (*Pss*, 9:80).

Ultimately it may have been Pushkin who was most in need of reconciliation with history. His findings in *The History of Pugachev* were quite unsettling. The government and the nobility, on the one hand, and most of the common people, on the other, constitute totally discrete and hostile camps drawn into a seemingly endless cycle of violence (perhaps prompting Pushkin's somewhat exaggerated fears of a looming peasant revolt in the 1830s). However, in the novel the mutual animosity is broken and the barrier dividing the two sides is breached. A nobleman and a muzhik find common ground, treat each other as human beings rather than as representatives of antagonistic social classes, and thereby transcend the cruelty of the uprising. Providence intervenes at every turn, saving the young lovers from imminent death and making both Catherine and Pugachev their benefactors and proxy parents. That is not to say that the novel idealizes history. In addition to depicting—albeit in a sanitized version—the "senseless and ruthless" Russian revolt, it also introduces the theme of pervasive impostorship, which makes the safeguarding of one's honor and dignity a daunting task.[23] It is hardly surprising, therefore, that Grinyov ultimately chooses to flee from history by opting for the timelessness of country life and peaceful procreation, a fate consonant with the mature Pushkin's own dreams of escape.

5

Tolstoy's "Book" and a New Kind of Historical Novel

The 1850s and 1860s

In the mid-nineteenth century the historical novel all but disappeared from the literary scene. The emergence of the Natural school and realism rendered the genre associated with the heyday of romanticism hopelessly outmoded, while the sociopolitical atmosphere on the eve of the Great Reforms shifted the focus of public interest to burning contemporary issues. In 1853 Ivan Turgenev expressed the prevalent attitude toward the genre while commenting on a work by Nikolai M. (pen name of Panteleimon Kulish): "I so fear Russian historical novels, I believe so little in their being possible now that I cannot force myself to read *Odnorog:* it exudes grave horror and intense ennui" (12:143). Kulish, a bilingual Russo-Ukrainian writer, is actually an interesting author, his work assuming importance in the context of Ukrainian literature. Most other novels published during the 1850s are either patently epigonic or lowbrow. In terms of quantitative output, the decade was quite meager, accounting for fewer than twenty new titles.

In the 1860s the historical novel failed to reemerge as a mass phenomenon (the yield of new titles being even smaller than in the previous decade). However, several works of major importance did appear at this time, among them Aleksei Tolstoy's *Prince Serebryany,* the last Russian tribute to Scott and one of the finest works in the "junior canon" of the genre; Nikolai Kostomarov's *Son,* a nihilist take on the romantic novel; and Leo Tolstoy's *War and Peace,* which introduced a new paradigm for historical fiction and remains by far the most famous Russian historical novel.

Conceived in the late 1840s and completed by 1861, A. K. Tolstoy's *Prince Serebryany* is conspicuously anachronistic (which is hardly surprising, given its author's staunch nonconformism). The novel's plot is rooted in the Scottian tradition, with the central love story unfolding against a dramatic historical background (the horrors of Ivan the Terrible's *oprichnina*) that owes a significant debt to Karamzin's *History*. All the major episodes and motifs are the stock-in-trade of romantic novelists, including: rendering a favor to a stranger, who becomes a faithful helper; a feast; imprisonment and escape; travesty; sorcery (with the rational explanation prevailing but the supernatural one still lingering); a trial by duel, and so forth. In addition, the novel is imbued with a mix of folkloric and antiquarian details. The characters—a lofty but bland central couple; a faithful servant; a renegade chieftain-turned-helper; a dark-haired Byronic antagonist; hellish villains, and a "God's fool"—are all very traditional. The general attitude toward history is also unmistakably romantic; in his pursuit of the epoch's spirit the author readily sacrifices factual accuracy. Like many of his predecessors, in his preface A. K. Tolstoy confesses to deliberate anachronisms in "details of no historical significance" (*Kniaz' Serebrianyi*, 3).[1]

A. K. Tolstoy differs from Scott in that he cannot maintain a sense of impartiality, openly venting his indignation both at the tyranny of Ivan the Terrible and the blind obedience of his subjects. However, as we have seen, this lack of objectivity was typical for Russian romantic novelists. In fact, *Prince Serebryany* is a quintessential example of the romantic historical novel. This is reflected in the following authorial digression, which recounts the episode where the lone protagonist rushes in to rescue Tsarevich Ioann from the notorious Malyuta Skuratov and his henchmen:

> Were you really as I imagined you, Prince Nikita Romanovich? Only the Kremlin walls and the ancient Moscow oaks can tell! But this is how you appeared to me in the hour of my peaceful dreaming, in the evening, when darkness descended on the fields, the noise of the bustling day died down in the distance, and close by all was silent but the rustle of the wind in the leaves, and only an evening beetle whizzed by. Love of the native land struck me as sad and painful, and our woeful and glorious days of yore emerged clearly from the mist, as if to replace a vision obstructed by darkness, and an inner eye opened up in me for which the centuries posed no obstacle. This is how you appeared to me, Nikita Romanovich, and I saw clearly how you flew on your mount in pursuit of Malyuta and was transported to your terrible day, those times in which nothing was impossible! (101)

The notion of history displayed here is typically romantic: the past is something to be resurrected through the imagination and artistic intuition, irrespective of factual accuracy. The author is pronouncedly patriotic, yet he sees Russian history as a mixture of horror and glory (a familiar combination of extremes). Moreover, history serves as a chronotope of adventure and fantasy. Indeed, both the description of the attempt on the tsarevich's life and even the central character of Prince Nikita Romanovich are pure fiction. Finally, the use of authorial digression, with its concomitant invalidation of the narrated story, is markedly romantic.

It is no wonder that Mikhail Saltykov-Shchedrin jumped at the opportunity to criticize the defiantly nontopical and anachronistic work. Shchedrin begins his caustic review in *The Contemporary* by saying that the journal's editorial staff was so flabbergasted by this "Byzantine opus" that they delegated the review to a retired teacher at a military academy. In the ensuing mock review, the old man cannot find enough praise for the novel and is especially thankful to the writer for transporting him back to the early 1830s: "I became young again. . . . I could not believe my eyes as I read. Dear Count, you dipped your magic brush in the miraculous water of fantasy and have made me, an old man, present in the 'deeds of days long past.' Be you praised! You should be praised all the more for having resurrected my youth and reminding me of the appearance of *Yury Miloslavsky* and *Roslavlev*, and for bringing to mind the first timid steps of Lozhechnikov [*sic*]. It was a happy time, my dear Count" (5:301).[2] Ironically, Lazhechnikov himself, who had long ago abandoned history for contemporary topics, also disapproved of the novel (Al'tshuller, 270).

Despite a negative verdict from the critics, *Prince Serebryany* was warmly received by readers and has remained one of the favorite works of Russian historical fiction. A stylistic masterpiece, it brings together the most attractive features of the Scottian tradition in a concise and purified form. Together with *The Captain's Daughter*, *Prince Serebryany* is arguably Russia's finest romantic historical novel. Paradoxically, it was created some two decades after the genre had become moribund.

Another novel from the 1860s that was conceived in the 1840s is *Adventures of Prince Gustav, Son of Eric* (1867), by Elena Veltman, who was the wife of Aleksandr Veltman. The novel traces the life of a disinherited Swedish prince and recounts the story of his failed marriage to Ksenia, the daughter of Boris Godunov. Although based on a thorough study of historical sources, Veltman's work contains factual alterations characteristic of the romantic novel. For example, the historical Gustav, who was reared by Jesuits, refused to convert to Orthodoxy—a sine qua non for marriage. In the novel, however, Gustav turns down the Russian princess because of his love for another woman. Unlike *Prince Serebryany,* this novel remained largely unnoticed.

In 1865 the famous historian Nikolai Kostomarov published a piece entitled *The Son: A Story from the Times of the Seventeenth Century,* which can be classified either as a long tale or a shorter novel. It is remarkable for its "nihilistic" treatment of Russian history and also for the transitional nature of its literary paradigm. Like many earlier authors, in the afterword Kostomarov refers to a legend that supposedly served as the basis for his work. The opening has numerous parallels in the works of Scott and Russian romantic novels. The protagonist, Osip, is a "camp shifter" caught in the whirlwind of a civil war. Although a nobleman by birth, through a whim of fate he joins the popular uprising of Stepan Razin. In terms of his literary lineage, Osip combines features of the noble yet passive Waverley hero with those of the darker and more aggressive Byronic outcast. The opening scene of the novel also contains the familiar romantic image of two horsemen sporting exotic attire (cf. the beginning of Zagoskin's *Miloslavsky*).

Generally speaking, however, *The Son* subverts the romantic paradigm, which becomes obvious when it is compared to *The Captain's Daughter.* Both novels deal with the theme of a Russian revolt (Pugachev's and Razin's, respectively). Both authors first approached these rebellions as historiographers. Pushkin did so in *A History of Pugachev,* while Kostomarov assumed this role in his monograph *The Revolt of Stenka Razin* (1858), a vivid, powerful, authoritative account that was praised by such diverse readers as Emperor Alexander II and Karl Marx (*Russkie pisateli,* 3:103). At the center of both novels we find noblemen who either engage in dubious dealings with the rebels or are outright traitors: Grinev and Shvabrin, Osip. The latter can also be seen as an incarnation of unfinished designs of Pushkin (cf. Dubrovsky and the original plans for *The Captain's Daughter*) and Lermontov (*Vadim*).

However, the way in which these situations are played out sets the two novels apart. While Pushkin's "family chronicle" redeems the horrors of the revolt, Kostomarov's novel only enhances them. Arriving home from military service, the protagonist discovers that his mother is about to be buried. As Osip learns, she was murdered by his own father, who is in love with another woman. The hero's attempts to seek justice with the *voivode* of Saransk result in his imprisonment, but he is freed by a sudden onslaught of the rebels. The storming of Saransk brings to mind the storming of Belogorskaya Fortress in *The Captain's Daughter:* the *voivode,* albeit corrupt and inept, is the only man in the garrison prepared to do his duty, following the creed of his ancestors "to die fearlessly for the faith and the tsar" (*Syn,* 132) (cf. Captain Mironov's address to his soldiers). Eventually, the *voivode,* his wife, and the beautiful young daughter are captured (cf. the Mironov family after the fall of Belogorskaya Fortress). Surpassing the Byronic villain Shvabrin, Osip assumes the role of executioner: he aims at the *voivode* but instead shoots his daughter, who has flung herself between the bullet and her father. Thus, the young hero kills the fair maiden who—according to all the rules of the genre—should become his wife. Osip nevertheless proceeds with his grisly job, smashing the old man's skull with a sword. As a chieftain of the rebels, Osip pursues his own murderous father, but is ambushed by government troops, subjected to excruciating torture, and impaled. In a mockery of poetic justice, in the epilogue Osip's father takes a young wife (whose previous husband has been eliminated by poisoning) and achieves prosperity. Needless to say, this conclusion stands in sharp contrast to the happy—and healthy—ending of *The Captain's Daughter.*

In his novel Pushkin mitigates the display of violence found in *The History of Pugachev,* whereas Kostomarov readily introduces into his novel bloody details from history, culminating in the graphic scene of Osip's impalement. Whereas Pushkin's novel redeems the "senselessness and mercilessness" of historical events, Kostomarov's novel intentionally enhances the horror of history. Also radically different is the overall perspective on the "Russian revolt." Pushkin, following in the tradition of Scott, shows the relative merits of both camps, while Kostomarov emphasizes that the ruling classes and the common people were equally corrupt. It is important to note that Kostomarov's gloomy verdict is not aimed at the human condition generally but specifically at the Russian nation and Russian history. This is underscored by means of the introduction into the novel of an "outsider," a sumptuously dressed Zaporozhian Cossack who expresses disgust with everything Russian, be it Russian vodka ("damned Muscovite wine" [105]), which he feels is inferior to the noble Ukrainian *gorilka,* or the Russian people ("Goddamn Muscovites" [141]), who are born to be slaves.

Kostomarov's Russophobia is a corollary to his ardent Ukrainophilia and has both ideological and personal roots. The illegitimate child of a Russian nobleman and a Ukrainian serf, Kostomarov chose to identify with the oppressed side of his lineage (cf. Alexander Herzen's inferiority complex, the result of his illegitimacy, which produced a revolutionary in an ancient aristocratic family related to the Romanovs). In *The Son* Russophobia resonates with the prevalent nihilism of the "democratic" intelligentsia of the late 1850s and 1860s, resulting in a work that belongs to the once popular genre of the exposé. There are, however, two peculiarities about Kostomarov's novel.

First, most exposés were concerned with contemporary topics; historical subjects usually had a vague chronotope, bringing to light the general corruption of the old ways and, in particular, the evils of serfdom.[3] The historian Kostomarov chooses a concrete period in the past—specifically the pre-Petrine past—and directs his polemical thrust against the late Slavophiles, who did not let his attack go unanswered.[4] Second, he uses recognizable romantic clichés to debunk the Russian tradition of romantic historical fiction; arguably his main weapon—a concentration of exceedingly graphic details—is also of romantic origin and can be traced to the frenetic school. Thus, Kostomarov does not create a new paradigm but rather subverts the old one through a polemical rethinking of its categories.

Tolstoy's *War and Peace*: Tradition and Innovation

The first few installments of *War and Peace* appeared in a journal in 1865–66 under the title *The Year 1805*, following which its publication was interrupted by Tolstoy himself, with the novel appearing in book form in 1867–69. The literary genealogy of *War and Peace* is complex and heterogeneous. It incorporates elements of the novels of Zagoskin and Zotov, although Tolstoy's epic is by no means a direct descendant of the historical novel of the 1830s (Eikhenbaum, *Lev Tolstoi*, 226). Employing certain elements from the romantic era, Tolstoy creates a paradigm that represents a complete rupture with the historical poetics of the 1830s. Nevertheless, we are not dealing here with intentional subversion of the old paradigm (as was the case with Kostomarov) but rather with a situation whereby older elements acquire different functions as they become part of a new system. Whereas the romantic novel is based on a dualistic outlook, with the ensuing tension between fact and fiction, Tolstoy proceeds from the monistic premises of realism, where fact and fiction supplement each other, with the novel now transformed into a synthetic genre of quasi-scientific analysis.

Echoes of the 1830s

Among the books Tolstoy used in preparation for writing *War and Peace* were Zotov's *Leonid*, Zagoskin's *Roslavlev* (*Pss*, 16:141), and possibly Bulgarin's *Petr Ivanovich Vyzhigin*. As he confesses in a letter to his wife written in November 1864, Tolstoy found Zagoskin especially fascinating: "I became engrossed in reading *Roslavlev*. [. . .] You understand how much I need it and how much it is of interest to me. [. . .] I was reading with a delight that no one but a writer can understand" (*Pss*, 83:58–59). One should not interpret these words

ТЫСЯЧА ВОСЕМЬСОТЪ ПЯТЫЙ ГОДЪ.

ВЪ ПЕТЕРБУРГѢ. [1]

I.

— Eh bien, mon prince, Gênes et Lucques ne sont plus que des apanages, des помѣстья, de la famille Buonaparte. Non, je vous préviens que si vous ne me dites pas que nous avons la guerre, vous vous permettez encore de pallier toutes les infamies, toutes les atrocités de cet Antichrist (ma parole, j'y crois) —je ne vous connais plus, vous n'êtes plus mon ami, vous n'êtes plus мой вѣрный рабъ, comme vous dites. [2] Ну, здравствуйте, здравствуйте. Je vois que je vous fais peur [3], садитесь и разказывайте.

---

[1] Чтобы сохранить колоритъ разговора дѣйствующихъ лицъ, авторъ весьма часто употребляетъ французскія фразы. Для незнающихъ французскаго языка присоединяется въ подстрочныхъ выноскахъ переводъ французскихъ выраженій текста. *Ред.*

[2] Ну что, князь, Генуя и Лукка стали не больше какъ помѣстьями фамиліи Бонапарте. Нѣтъ, я вамъ впередъ говорю, если вы мнѣ не скажете, что у насъ война, если вы позволите себѣ защищать всѣ гадости, всѣ ужасы этого Антихриста (право, я вѣрю что онъ Антихристъ),—я васъ больше не знаю, вы ужь не другъ мой, вы ужь не рабъ мой вѣрный, какъ вы говорите.

[3] Я вижу, что я васъ пугаю.

FIGURE 8. The opening page of *The Year 1805*, published in 1865 in *Russkii Vestnik*. In a provocative gesture, Tolstoy opens his Russian epic with French dialogue. This feature was already present when the beginning of *War and Peace* was first serialized under the title *The Year 1805*.

FIGURE 9. Title page illustration from Bulgarin's *Petr Ivanovich Vyzhigin* (vol. 3, 1831). "'Your people are blind,'" said Napoleon. "'They should realize that they are waging war against all of Europe. At a wave of my hand, a million soldiers will appear here. And you, what can you hope for?'" The Russian officer pointed to the sky and said: "'God and love for the fatherland will save us!'" (Bulgarin, *Petr Ivanovich Vyzhigin* 3:146–47). The enigma of 1812, when Russia was able to withstand the onslaught of a united Europe, tested the limits of historical explanation. Whereas romantics invoked Providence, Tolstoy devised an idiosyncratic historical philosophy of his own.

as praise but rather as the rapacious glee of a first-rate writer who is about to prey upon his third-rate colleague (Eikhenbaum, *Lev Tolstoi*, 237–38). It is also possible that Zagoskin and Zotov (both veterans of 1812) were important for Tolstoy in his search for the "authentic" atmosphere of the period. In any event, despite its epic and philosophical grandeur, *War and Peace* incorporates numerous elements from inferior genres, including the patriotic and adventure novels exemplified by *Roslavlev* and *Leonid*. What follows are some conspicuous instances of Tolstoy's reliance on the tradition of the 1830s (keeping in mind that some of them can be of polygenetic origin).

To begin with, in his depiction of 1812 Tolstoy employs the masquerade topos, which is extremely prominent in Zagoskin, Zotov, and Bulgarin. It surfaces in Pierre's decision to stay in occupied Moscow by disguising himself as a tradesman (like Bulgarin's Vyzhigin junior), as well as in the episode where Russian officers, having changed into French uniforms, gather intelligence in the enemy camp.

Especially numerous are parallels between *War and Peace* and Zotov's *Leonid.* The scene where a single officer, armed only with a whip and unflinching resolve, disperses a crowd of rioting commoners is found in both novels. In Zotov's novel, a Cossack colonel saves Leonid from the overly zealous patriots; in *War and Peace,* Nikolai Rostov comes to the rescue of Princess Marya, who is threatened by her own peasants.

FIGURE 10. Title page illustration from Bulgarin's *Petr Ivanovich Vyzhigin* (vol. 1, 1831; engraving S. Galaktionov). *War and Peace* relies on many stock-in-trade situations found in the novels of the 1830s. For example, Pierre Bezukhov's adventures in occupied Moscow find parallels in Bulgarin's *Vyzhigin,* whose protagonist, likewise disguised as a commoner, stays behind after the retreat of Russian troops. In broader terms, this represents a variation on the theme of masquerade prominent in the romantic period.

Alexander I's insistence on the supremacy of the law, which foils attempts to procure a pardon for brave combat officers who violated the law, can be compared with Napoleon's petition for Leonid in Tilsit and Nikolai Rostov's petition for Denisov in Tilsit. Soldiers foregoing their ration of vodka before battle is presented both by Zotov and Tolstoy as a sign of patriotism. The old drunkard Captain Zorkin abstains from vodka at Eylau and the old drunkard Captain Timokhin is impressed by the fact that his soldiers abstained from vodka at Borodino.

Tolstoy's favorite idea that the battlefield is the realm of chaos and instincts finds a parallel in Zotov's account of the conflict at Eylau: "There was no command, no leaders; each man did what he was led to do by frenzy or instinct" (*Leonid*, 134). Likewise, Tolstoy's description of Borodino's aftermath resembles Zotov's summary of Eylau both in terms of conveying the horror of the battlefield and in emphasizing the inconclusive outcome of the battle:

> This is how the battle at Eylau ended. The losses on both sides were terrible. More than ten thousand dead lay in the fields covered in snow and thirty thousand wounded filled the surrounding villages, gardens and sheds. There were not enough doctors to dress the wounds. Many died without assistance in most excruciating circumstances. The sorrowful moans of the sufferers could be heard everywhere. No one slept in either of the armies not counting the dead, laid to their eternal repose [. . .] the commanders-in-chief discussed in their military councils the undertakings of the next day. Both assumed victory, and decided to retreat in view of their enormous losses. (196)

And finally, Tolstoy's comparison of the French army after Moscow to "a deadly wounded animal" resembles Zotov's image of "a terminally sick person" (486).

Tolstoy's image of Russianness combines his own idiosyncrasies with late Slavophile overtones (Orwin, 233–34). Needless to say, Tolstoy's triad of "simplicity, kindness, truth" is a far cry from the Orthodoxy–Autocracy–Nationality prevalent in the 1830s. Nevertheless, in *War and Peace* there are discernable echoes of the nationalistic discourse of the romantic novel. Affinities can be found in Tolstoy's intense preoccupation with all things Russian, overt patriotism, and the emphatic identification of the author with one of the warring sides. In terms of specific elements, Tolstoy frequently contrasts Russian modesty with the European—mainly French—tendency for self-promotion, which is a constant theme in Zagoskin's *Roslavlev*, as in the following bit of dialogue: "You must agree that the self-conceit, presumptuousness and pride of the French are unbearable.—What can be done, my friend? All peoples have their own national weaknesses . . . and to tell the truth, at times our modesty, truly, is no better than the French swaggering" (378). The juxtaposition of national characteristics per se is a favorite romantic device. There is an obvious parallel—in form if not in content—between Tolstoy's long digression on French, English, Russian, and German varieties of arrogance (5:51) and Zotov's discussion of patriotic manifestations among the Germans, French, British, and Russians (*Leonid*, 476–77).

Most important, Tolstoy adopts the device of presenting historical information in markedly distinct inserted chapters, which figured prominently in the romantic novel. Eichenbaum traces this device to Zotov (*Lev Tolstoi*, 242–43), but it appears that the combined influence of Zotov and Zagoskin is at work. Zotov's lengthy historical capsules tend to be saturated with factual information; having authored several compilation histories, Zotov was quite knowledgeable in military and political matters of the Napoleonic era. Although Zagoskin's historical digressions are shorter, they are often sharply polemical and serve as an outlet for the author's strong opinions. Here is his commentary on Napoleon's retreat from Moscow:

> Everyone knows how Napoleon left Moscow . . . but not everyone is convinced that he was forced to retreat by the Smolensk road. What could have forced Napoleon to beat his retreat through places entirely ruined by war and, consequently, consign his troops to certain death by starvation? What? Anything you like. Napoleon did it out of stubbornness, ignorance, even out of stupidity, but certainly of his own free will. Otherwise it would have been necessary to admit that the Russians had beaten the French and that it was not us but the French who were defeated at Maly Yaroslavets. . . . And how could they agree to this when the French bulletins declared the opposite? But if we never beat the enemy, how did Napoleon's entire army perish? Oh, dear God! What is the freezing weather for? That is what Napoleon says, and what almost all the French writers say. . . . But there are people (we won't say to which nation they belong) who think that French writers always tell the truth, even when they insist that there are no nightingales in Russia . . . but there is, on the other hand, a fruit the size of a cherry called a watermelon [. . .] that the name for the Slavs comes from the French *esclaves* and that, to top it all, in 1812 the French beat the Russians when they invaded, and beat them when they retreated. . . . They beat them near Moscow, near Tarutino, near Krasnoye, near Maly Yaroslavets, near Polotsk, near Borisov and even at Vilno, in other words,

where there was no one left to beat us even if we ourselves desired this. (*Roslavlev*, 538–39)

And here are Zagoskin's remarks on the fire of Moscow:

> Despite the considerable severity of some critics, who, for God only knows what reason, cannot allow the author to speak in the first person with the reader, I intend at the conclusion of this chapter to say a few words about one unresolved issue, namely, whether it was the Russians and not the French who set fire to Moscow. . . . There was a time when, frightened by the exclamations of the Paris journalists—"Ces barbares qui ne savaient se défendre qu'en brûlant leurs propres habitations"—we were ready to swear to the contrary . . . but now, I hope, no eloquent French phrase can force us to deny what not only we but even our distant descendants will be proud of. No! We will not allow anyone to take from us the honor of the fire of Moscow. (483)

Zagoskin's digressions are quite remarkable when compared with corresponding passages in *War and Peace*. Tolstoy and Zagoskin may disagree in terms of their interpretation of events. Thus, Zagoskin advocates the "patriotic" version of the Moscow fire, claiming that the city was set ablaze by proud Muscovites, whereas Tolstoy argues that the fire in the abandoned city was the result of "natural" occurrences. Similarly, while Zagoskin stresses combative action in expelling Napoleon, Tolstoy describes an internal mechanism leading to the disintegration of the Great Army and deems all military engagements following Napoleon's retreat from Moscow senseless and even counterproductive. Despite these differences, however, Tolstoy's historical chapters display some striking similarities with Zagoskin's. Like the latter, he gives voice to the opinions of his opponents, parodies them, and ultimately undermines their credibility and their line of reasoning.[5] The categorical tone and use of absolutes ("everybody," "everything," "always," "never," "nobody," etc.) is also characteristic of both writers. As a result, some of Tolstoy's polemical digressions sound like quotations from Zagoskin. For example, consider the following caustic remarks on the purported military genius of Napoleon:

> We do not know for certain in how far his genius was genuine in Egypt—where forty centuries looked down upon his grandeur—for his great exploits there are told us by Frenchmen. We cannot accurately estimate his genius in Austria or Prussia, for we have to draw our information from French or German sources, and the incomprehensible surrender of whole corps without fighting and of

> fortresses without a siege must incline Germans to recognize his genius as the only explanation of the war carried out in Germany. But we, thank God, have no need to recognize his genius in order to hide our shame. We have paid for the right to look at the matter plainly and simply, and we will not abandon that right. (*Pss*, 6:91; *War and Peace*, 886)

Despite obvious similarities, such digressions in *War and Peace* create a very different relationship between fact and fiction.

Veterans' Critique of War and Peace: *A Clash of Cultural Paradigms*

The novelty of Tolstoy's genre can best be understood if one considers the negative reactions to *War and Peace* from several veterans of the Napoleonic era. Especially noteworthy are the "Memoirs of the Year 1812," by Prince Pyotr Vyazemsky (1792–1878), a prominent figure on the Russian cultural scene for many decades and a participant in the epic events portrayed by Tolstoy. The old prince viewed *War and Peace* as a caricature, a lampoon, a "protest against the year 1812," lumping Tolstoy with the nihilists and "killers of history" ("Vospominaniia," 187–88). Despite the outlandishness and harshness of some of Vyazemsky's remarks, it would be a mistake to treat his attack upon Tolstoy as senile grumbling or the outburst of a "born again" conservative. Expanding upon Konstantin Leontiev's idea, one could instead argue that responses from veterans reflect a clash of epochs or cultural paradigms, which in literary terms can be described as a conflict between romanticism and realism. To a considerable degree this conflict stems from differing understandings of such pivotal concepts as the hero, Providence, and legend, as well as from differing approaches to the genre of the historical novel. Presented with Tolstoy's picture of 1812 as seen through a realistic narrative prism, survivors of the romantic age refused to recognize its authenticity and questioned the legitimacy of Tolstoy's genre. Understanding the nature of the veterans' reaction may also help to define more clearly certain "hermeneutic signposts" that may facilitate interpretations of Tolstoy's novel.[6] Inter alia, the veterans' reaction strengthens the case against the "Bakhtinization" of historical aspects of *War and Peace* found in recent Tolstoy scholarship.

First and foremost, the veterans accuse Tolstoy of distorting the truly heroic atmosphere of the Patriotic War in his disparaging and irreverent tone as well as use of sensationalist details. In their eyewitness accounts the veterans attempt to refute *War and Peace*, restoring historical truth as they remembered it. On some occasions such criticism backfired and Tolstoy could feel vindicated. One such instance involved Avraam Norov (1795–1869), a young officer in 1812. He later became an amateur philologist and church historian and also had a distinguished career as the minister of education and a member of the State Council. The former warrior who had lost a leg at Borodino was insulted by the episode in which Tolstoy's Kutuzov, while assuming supreme command of the Russian army at Tsarevo-Zaimishche, is engrossed in reading a cheap French novel by Madame de Genlis. According to Norov, this was a totally improbable and inappropriate detail: "Before and after Borodino, all of us, from Kutuzov down to the last artillery lieutenant, like myself, burned with the same lofty and sacred fire of patriotism; we regarded our calling as some kind of religious rite; I do not know how comrades-in-arms would treat someone who would have among his belongings a book for light reading, especially a French one, such as a novel by Madame de Genlis" (quoted in Danilevskii, "Istoriki-ochevidtsy," 334). The same detail also irritated Parmen Demenkov, a retired officer of the elite Preobrazhensky Regiment, who participated in the War of 1812 (including Borodino) and in the European campaigns of 1813–14 (399).

Norov's negative tirade had an anecdotal dénouement related by the writer Grigory Danilevsky (a major historical novelist of the 1870s and 1880s). After Norov's death in 1869, the novel *Aventures de Roderick Random* (a French translation of Smollett's work) was found in his library. The cover of the book bears an inscription, in Norov's own hand, stating that he had read it in Moscow after being wounded and captured by the French in September 1812. Danilevsky comments that "what had happened to the artillery lieutenant in September of 1812 was forgotten by the venerable dignitary [decades later] since it did not fit the notion that he subsequently formed about the epoch of 1812" ("Istoriki-ochevidtsy," 334).

On occasion Vyazemsky becomes a victim of a similar "veteran's syndrome," the irony here being that his unconscious self-refutation is found in the same essay where he lambastes *War and Peace*.[7] While accusing Tolstoy of denigrating fatidic historical events and the glorious men of 1812, Vyazemsky saturates his own recollections with very Tolstoyan "trivial" details.

As Napoleon was advancing into Russia, Vyazemsky, like many other Moscow noblemen, joined the militia. In August 1812, while his regiment was still being formed, Vyazemsky received an invitation from General Miloradovich to join his retinue for the upcoming battle. He arrived at the army encampment right after the engagement at Shevardino, which had served as a bloody prologue to the main battle. Among his most vivid impressions of that day was an accidental pun or joke made by an officer at Kutuzov's headquarters, which connected Vyazemsky's ancient and proud family name with a brand of gingerbread (*viazemskie prianiki*) ("Vospominaniia," 03).[8] Bewildered, Vyazemsky decided not to pursue the question of whether his honor had been compromised, in which case a duel might ensue. His memories of Borodino's aftermath are even less in tune with the solemn picture of universal patriotic élan held dear by veterans. Here is what he recalls of the night following the battle: "In the log cabin ceded to me by Miloradovich I discovered a cat. I have an invincible revulsion for this animal. Before going to bed, I chased it into the stove and locked the hatch. I do not know what happened to it afterwards—whether it escaped through the chimney or died. Not infrequently ever since would my conscience remind me of this brutal faintheartedness. Back then I was not yet a member of the Animal Protection Society, and few people thought about this protection"(010–011). One of the most glorious battles of Russian history is associated in Vyazemsky's memory with a pun and violence against an innocent cat. Thus Vyazemsky unwittingly supports Tolstoy's favorite idea that great historical events are made up of the mundane concerns of ordinary men.

Vyazemsky's overall picture of Borodino is strikingly Tolstoyan as well. In fact, in his memoirs Vyazemsky appears almost as Pierre's twin. Like the latter he finds himself in the center of events. Two of his horses were killed while Vyazemsky was trying to follow Miloradovich around the battlefield (cf. Pierre's horse wounded at Borodino). And yet, again like Pierre, he remains the ultimate outsider. He does not belong to any particular unit and basically tours the battlefield out of curiosity. He is of no use to Miloradovich as an aide-de-camp. He cannot really handle weapons and looks conspicuously alien among the soldiers since he is a poor rider and wears a strange militia uniform unfamiliar to the army regulars. (A particularly bizarre part of his outfit is his unusually tall shako (cf. Pierre's white hat). This nearly gets him into serious trouble since he is mistaken for a Frenchman. Moreover, like Pierre he does not understand anything with respect to the unfolding battle, being a civilian and myopic on top of everything else (cf. Pierre's glasses). The conclusion of Vyazemsky's report on Borodino sounds almost like a quotation from Tolstoy:

> And that is my entire Iliad! Of course, following the example of others, I could have consulted dispatches and descriptions of the war in order to present a more detailed account of the positions of various units and troop movements on the Borodino field. But I never liked being a charlatan. [. . .] During the battle I was as if in a dark or, rather, burning forest. Owing to my shortsightedness I saw poorly what was before my eyes. Owing to my lack of any military

abilities or mere experience, I could not understand anything of what was going on. [. . .] And I might well be inquiring during the battle: "Are we beating them or are they beating us?" (09–010)[9]

Thus Vyazemsky again unwittingly supports his opponent, validating Tolstoy's distrust of official relations and military histories.[10]

Norov is caught in a similar predicament. Writing about Borodino, he concedes that his testimony is of limited scope: "Clouds of smoke [. . .] were hiding everything from us. What can a front-line officer see except for what happens right before his eyes?" (220). And yet his memoirs represent a compilation of military histories covering the period from 1805 to 1812. Sifting through Norov's notes in order to establish the unmediated recollections of the seventeen-year-old lieutenant in command of two cannons at Borodino, one discovers both ghastly accounts of the battlefield carnage and "trivial" details worthy of Tolstoy. For example, Norov writes that his fellow officers found time for morning tea with rye toast despite the beginning of the cannonade, with one sergeant gulping down his ration of vodka. The latter is even less "patriotic" than some soldiers of *War and Peace*, who, according to Captain Timokhin, decided to abstain from vodka on the eve of Borodino.

In other instances, however, the veterans' criticism is closer to the mark. Referring to the episode in the novel where the Russian emperor greets enthusiastic Muscovites from the balcony of the Kremlin palace while munching on a biscuit and throwing pieces to the frenzied crowd, Vyazemsky pronounces it both insulting and improbable:

> This account betrays a total lack of knowledge of Alexander I's personality. He was so measured, so careful in all his actions and slightest moves; he was so apprehensive of anything that could seem ridiculous or awkward; he was so deliberate, so proper, so imposing, so cautious and scrupulous down to the smallest detail that he would have rather jumped into the water than appear before the people *munching a biscuit*, especially on such a solemn and remarkable day. Moreover, he amuses himself by throwing biscuits into the crowd from the balcony of the Kremlin Palace—as if he were some sort of backwoods squire pitching gingerbread in order to provoke a fight among village boys on holiday! This is again a caricature, which by any rate is absolutely out of place and is out of keeping with the truth. ("Vospominaniia," 192–01)

Tolstoy was absolutely positive that he had not invented the episode, thinking that his source was Sergey Glinka's *Notes About the Year 1812*. On February

6, 1869, he wrote to his consultant, the prominent archivist Pyotr Bartenev, requesting publication of a rebuttal to Vyazemsky, with the appropriate page reference. Since Bartenev did not respond, Tolstoy appealed to him again—rather impatiently. Bartenev, however, could not satisfy Tolstoy's request for the simple reason that there was no such episode in Glinka's work. The scene emerged from a conflation of two sources: Glinka's *Notes* and the *Memoirs* by a certain A. Ryazantsev (Shklovskii, *Material i stil'*, 47–48; Kandiev, 202). Glinka attests to the enthusiasm of huge crowds gathered inside the walls of the Kremlin, while Ryazantsev writes that the emperor benevolently handed out some fruit to the people. Tolstoy combines both accounts, turning fruit into biscuits (markedly foreign, upper-class food) and adding disparaging details absent from the sources: the emperor *munches* in front of the crowd and *tosses* food to his subjects. The popular enthusiasm mentioned in Glinka's work is turned by Tolstoy into mass psychosis. In this case Vyazemsky's objections are indeed well grounded.

This brings me to the question of the factual basis for *War and Peace*. The corpus of Tolstoy's sources is well defined and includes about fifty titles of memoirs, document collections, and histories (some of which consist of multiple volumes), not to mention periodicals, private archives, and oral accounts. Two issues, however, have led to an acute controversy. The first concerns the degree of Tolstoy's historical preparation and the second his use of sources. Basing their opinions on the same evidence, commentators have arrived at diametrically opposed conclusions. Some speak of "colossal" preparatory work on the part of Tolstoy (Pokrovsky, 128; Ardens, 156; and the majority of Soviet critics), while others consider it scanty and not particularly thorough. The latter point of view is expressed most vividly in Shklovsky's iconoclastic *Material i stil'* (Material and Style, 1928), but it can be traced back to Bartenev, who in 1911 asserted: "Count Tolstoy did not study the history of that great era at all . . . just as he never engaged himself in assiduous, regular work: you could say that he was constantly choking with imagination" (385).[11] The verdict here may depend on the criteria applied, but the fact remains that Tolstoy himself was quite confident of the historical aspect of his book. In "A Few Words on *War and Peace*" he defiantly claims: "Wherever in my novel historical persons speak or act, I have invented nothing, but have used historical material of which I have accumulated a whole library during my work. I do not think it necessary to cite the titles of those books here but could cite them at any time as proof of what I say" (*Pss*, 6:521; *War and Peace*, 1094). The pronouncement is quite sincere, as can be seen from Tolstoy's attempt to deliver on his promise in countering Vyazemsky's criticism.

Examining the occasions when Tolstoy deviates from historical sources, one can establish several possible scenarios. First among these are inadvertent mistakes, usually involving minor factual details and pertaining to rank, title, designation of military units, description of military uniforms, and so forth. Such errors are virtually inevitable given the magnitude of *War and Peace*, which has more than five hundred characters, roughly two hundred of whom are historical, and describes twenty battles (Zaidenshur, 328). Second are instances of transforming or—to use Shklovsky's term—deforming historical sources. Shklovsky points to such deformative techniques as omission of details that do not fit the writer's concept, use of unreliable sources, and unscrupulous citation. Such "sins" attest primarily to the lack of academic discipline, which should hardly come as a surprise. The most serious transgression against sources revealed by Shklovsky is what he terms "perenesenie ob"ekta" (transfer of the object). As an example of this device Shklovsky uses the scene where General Balashov parts with Napoleon. In a mood of friendly familiarity Tolstoy's Napoleon nips Balashov's ear—a gesture bordering on insult for the forty-year-old Russian general and emissary of Emperor Alexander. However, according to Modest Bogdanovich, whose *History* served as the basis for this episode, Napoleon pinches his own general, Caulaincourt. Thus, Tolstoy adopts a mannerism typical of Napoleon's behavior in his own court and transfers it to a person who does not belong to this court, emphasizing the emperor's blind self-infatuation (Shklovsky, *Mater'ial i stil'*, 174). The episode of Alexander and the biscuits questioned by Vyazemsky can be seen as a combination of mistakes and deformation. Finally, there are many occasions when Tolstoy, in his revisionist portrayal of events, openly questions primary sources and disagrees with historians. But here he behaves as a historian who critically approaches both his material and its interpretation in historiography. What is essential, however, is the fact that nowhere in *War and Peace* can one find intentional anachronisms or any other major or minor "sins" against fact, which the romantics committed so routinely and to which they confessed so readily.

If one examined the nature of Vyazemsky's reaction, one discovers that he is less concerned about the alleged factual inaccuracies of the novel than the emphasis in Tolstoy's narrative. Thus, Vyazemsky comments eloquently on the scene depicting the famous assembly of Moscow nobility, whose members pledged unanimous and enthusiastic support for their sovereign and volunteered to commit huge private resources to the country's war effort. Vyazemsky is particularly appalled by Tolstoy's relish in describing the unattractive physical features of the older noblemen gathered at the Slobodskoy

Palace. Noting that Gogolian types from *Dead Souls* are out of place at this gathering, he indignantly concludes:

> "In a fit of humor (which incidentally is of dubious quality) why does he populate the meeting of July 15 (which remains a historical date) with old men who are *weak-sighted, toothless, bald,* and are either *rolling in yellow fat* or are *wrinkled and skinny?* Of course it is pleasant to keep all of one's teeth and one's hair: we old men even become envious looking at such a sight. But how are they at fault—these old men, among whom some were possibly, even probably, comrades-in-arms in Catherine the Great's time? How are they at fault and what is funny about the fact that God willed them to live until 1812 and Napoleon's invasion?" (190–91)[12]

Although Vyazemsky does not doubt that such old men were present at the meeting; he loathes the focus of Tolstoy's narrative gaze. The same scene also proved insulting to Norov and Demenkov, whereas for Tolstoy it was important and dear, as he stated in a letter to Bartenev dated December 1867 (*Pss,* 16:15).

The veterans' response to this passage is interpreted insightfully by the brilliant, albeit highly idiosyncratic, Russian thinker Konstantin Leontiev in his 1890 book *Analysis, Style, and Waft: On the Novels of Count L. N. Tolstoy.*[13] Leontiev argues that such physiological details, which dovetailed with Tolstoy's meticulous psychological analysis, are earmarks of the Natural school and contemporary (realistic) literature and are therefore incompatible with the spirit of Alexander's era: "At the time of Austerlitz and Berezina one did not delve too deeply into the *souls of others.* [. . .] If one noticed someone's pimple, one probably did not consider it one's civic duty to become immersed in its contemplation; one had not read Gogol yet; and Gogol himself [. . .] would have been writing not *The Overcoat* and *Dead Souls* but rather odes about some 'volcanoes erupting with entire nations'" (96). In other words, Tolstoy's realistic style goes against the grain of the epoch he describes, distorting what Leontiev calls its "general psychic tone" ("obshchepsikhicheskaia muzyka") and its "waft" ("veianie") or the "scent of time" ("zapakh vremeni").

Leontiev's line of reasoning was developed by Dmitry Merezhkovsky, the bellwether writer of Russian symbolism, in his famous treatise *Tolstoy and Dostoevsky* (1901–2). Merezhkovsky likewise points to "atmospheric anachronisms" in *War and Peace:* "As one reads *War and Peace* it is very difficult to get rid of the [. . .] impression that all the events depicted [. . .] take place in our own day. The air we breathe in *War and Peace* and *Anna Karenina* is one and the same; the historical scent in both epics is one and the same; both here and there we have a similar atmosphere of the second half of the nineteenth century, which is so familiar to us" (30). Merezhkovsky's verdict is not quite fair. Tolstoy was interested in the atmosphere of the epoch (hence his delight in *Roslavlev*) and included in *War and Peace* a considerable number of details meant to convey historical color—starting with the opening French dialogue in Sherer's salon. Nevertheless, Tolstoy's emphasis is not on the changing but rather on the unchanged. Scornful of the idea of progress, he counters it with the notion of private life, which constitutes the essence of human existence and remains basically unchanged throughout time. Thus, as Shklovsky and Eichenbaum noted perceptively, *War and Peace* was deeply ahistorical in terms of its design. Hence Tolstoy's stress on the constants and his favorite absolutes "always," "everything," "everyone," which were intended to bridge the gap between past, present, and eternity. The Tolstoyan idiosyncrasies notwithstanding, his "always" appears to be strongly imbued with the general worldview of the realistic era. This may indeed explain the veterans' aversion to *War and Peace*.

Aside from creating "atmospheric" distortions, Tolstoy's realism challenged some core beliefs by the survivors of the romantic age. Totally unpalatable to the old romantics was Tolstoy's philosophy of history and, in particular, his scorn of the so-called great men and heroes. Although the veterans provide commonplace, trivial details in their own recollections of the war, they do not compromise the heroism of the larger picture. As Norov notes sarcastically with reference to an episode from *War and Peace*, Kutuzov could indeed gnaw on a fried chicken at Borodino, but this did not prevent him from commanding his troops (235). Likewise Vyazemsky may relate with irony his own semicomic exploits on the battlefield, but he still pays tribute to the true heroes of 1812.

For the veterans, the debunking of heroes makes history meaningless and is tantamount to a denial of divine providence, which acts through great men.[14] Norov complains: "This is a picture without actors. [. . .] Everything occurs *by chance*, which is hardly in accordance with the high purpose given to man by God in this world. Since there are no human agents, there is no history either" (234). Vyazemsky openly brands Tolstoy an atheist: "This is no longer skepticism but rather a pure ethical and literary materialism. Atheism devastates the heavens and the afterlife. Historical freethinking and disbelief devastate the earth and life in the present by disclaiming events of the past and dismissing national heroes" ("Vospominaniia o 1812 gode,"

186). Thus, Tolstoy was mistakenly identified by his conservative critics as a proponent of nihilistic revision of the past, as in Kostomarov's *Son*.[15]

Equally unacceptable from the romantic point of view was Tolstoy's attitude toward legends and popular or national memory (*narodnaia pamiat'*). While the romantics cherished historical lore, which was seen as an expression of a higher truth, Tolstoy strove to demythologize history. As he stated explicitly in "A Few Words on *War and Peace*": "Kutuzov did not always hold a telescope, point at the enemy, and ride a white horse. Rostopchin was not always setting fire with a torch to the Voronovsky House (which in fact he never did), and the Empress Mariia Fedorovna did not always stand in an ermine cloak leaning her hand on the code of laws, but that is how popular imagination pictures them" (*Pss*, 16:10; *War and Peace*, 1091). Vyazemsky did not fail to notice this approach, writing that *War and Peace* represents "an appeal against the prevailing view" of the Year 1812 "solidified in popular memory" ("Vospominaniia o 1812 gode," 186). Whereas Tolstoy chooses to portray Kutuzov at Tsarevo-Zaimishche reading a novel by Madame de Genlis, Norov not only scorns this detail as improbable but counters it with a legend about an omen portending victory for the newly appointed commander-in-chief: an eagle allegedly flew over his head while Kutuzov was inspecting his troops (213).

A concentration of antirealistic romantic topoi is found in Vyazemsky's poem "The Battle of Borodino's Wake," which accompanies his memoirs in *The Russian Archive*. The image of Kutuzov in the poem is sharply polemical with respect to *War and Peace*, where Kutuzov is portrayed as a weary old man who realizes all too well that he has no control over the course of events. In contrast to this, Vyazemsky's Kutuzov looks almost like the Napoleon of the romantic tradition:

And Kutuzov is also before me
whenever I reminisce of Borodino:
he was wearing a white cap
and riding a white horse.

A scarf across his shoulder,
he is standing upon a hill.
And the day in its autumnal beauty
is shining brightly above the old man.

The old man's alert countenance is warlike.
He is all alone amid the troops;
he is impassive; he is enigmatic;

he is imperious like fate.
[. . .]
In his thought he soars over the battle,
and his aquiline gaze
moves the will and the power
of human masses. (175)

The spatial organization of Vyazemsky's poem is strikingly romantic as well: we see the skies, the human masses down below, and the hero, a man of fate, who is an intermediary between the sky and the earth. This vertically structured world stands in stark contrast to the "horizontal" universe of *War and Peace,* with its infinite tapestry of insignificant causes and individual wills, where the personal will of Kutuzov or Napoleon is as relevant or irrelevant as the will of the lowliest soldier in their troops.

Finally, Vyazemsky argues against the legitimacy of Tolstoy's genre with respect to its combination of fiction and history. He claims that he cannot define the genre of Tolstoy's book, calling it "a novel or a history," and makes the following pronouncement: "It is difficult to decide or merely guess where history ends and the novel begins, and vice versa. This interlacing or, rather, confusing of history with the novel undoubtedly harms the former and ultimately [. . .] does not contribute to the true merits of the latter, i.e., of the novel" ("Vospominaniia o 1812 gode," 187–88). Vyazemsky was certainly not the only critic who was puzzled by the genre question. Tolstoy himself found it difficult to choose a generic label for *War and Peace,* publishing it without a subtitle and eventually simply calling it a "book" (*Pss,* 6:514). Among other critics of the genre issue was Norov, who voiced the concern that some readers might mistake Tolstoy's book for a history. Adding that he himself treated it as a novel, he proceeded to argue against *War and Peace* as if it were a history. Other historians and military writers also subjected *War and Peace* to professional criticism within their respective fields, explicitly or implicitly treating it as a history.

For Vyazemsky Tolstoy's mixed genre is a bastardized one. Looking for positive examples, Vyazemsky turns to the historical novels of Scott and his own friend Pushkin: "In *The Captain's Daughter* there is also a contiguity of history with the novel, but a contiguity which is both natural and masterful. There history does not harm the novel and the novel does not dupe and disgrace history" ("Vospominaniia o 1812 gode," 189).

Indeed, Tolstoy departs drastically from the Scottian or—more broadly—romantic tradition of the historical novel, based on a dualistic worldview, with

FIGURE 11. Title page illustration from Zotov's *Leonid, or Some Features from the Life of Napoleon* (vol. 4, 1832; artist K. Zelentsov, engraving S. Galaktionov). The "horizontal" universe of *War and Peace* with its infinite tapestry of insignificant causes and individual wills stands in stark contrast to the vertically structured world of the romantics, whose essence is aptly captured in this engraving from Zotov's *Leonid*.

a dialogue between the truth of art and the truth of fact. By contrast, the realistic outlook in *War and Peace* is quintessentially monistic and the dichotomy of truths gives way to the concept of a single universal truth. Literary fiction ceases being an antonym to nonfiction, turning into a something of a supportive discipline in the writer's comprehensive analysis of the world.[16] Here is how the Goncourt brothers formulated it in 1864 in the preface to *Germinie Lacerteux:* "Today, when the Novel is growing broader and larger, when it is beginning to be the great and serious form [. . .] of literary study and social inquiry, when by analysis and psychological research it is becoming the moral history of our time, today when the Novel has subjected itself to the study and discipline of science, it can claim the freedom and rights of science" (16). Despite Tolstoy's well-known suspicion of "science" and the "scientific," these words fully apply to his novel. In *War and Peace* Tolstoy's historiographical findings and philosophical reflections merge with his fiction in a quasi-scientific analysis of the past, which ranges from investigations of specific problems of military history to musings about the general laws that govern human society.[17]

A prominent trend in recent Tolstoy scholarship runs counter to the latter assertion. Extending to Tolstoy the modified concepts of Bakhtinian dialogue, some scholars try to "dialogize" *War and Peace,* finding in it a tension between fiction and history. Proceeding from his theory of an "intergeneric dialogue" between history and literature in Russia, Andrew Wachtel sees in *War and Peace* the "incompatibility of the fictional and historical narratives and the clash of their perspectives, rather than their ultimate melding. That is, rather than a whole [. . .] Tolstoy succeeds in creating two equally compelling parts, each with its own truth in creative dialogue" (112). Gary Saul Morson's position is even more radical. He bases his argument on the premise that *War and Peace* is a paradoxical book, "a narrative exemplifying the falsity of all narratives" (131). According to Morson's interpretation, Tolstoy undermines not only the narratives of other historians but his own historical narrative as well. Being "an epistemic nihilist," in *War and Peace* Tolstoy stresses that "no one, including the author, can know the past" (109, 124).[18]

On a number of occasions, both in "A Few Words on *War and Peace*" and in the novel proper, Tolstoy speaks about the falsity of historiographic descriptions. This falsity derives from the historian's need to find the meaning of events and to group the "raw material of life" into a coherent story. To use Hayden White's terminology, the fictionality of historiography is conditioned by categories of emplotment inherent in the historical narrative. Morson goes so far as to name Tolstoy's narration "negative" in the sense that it primarily shows how things *did not happen.* One can indeed find numerous instances of "counternarration" in *War and Peace.* However, the point is that Tolstoy speaks about the falsity of somebody else's narratives, whereas his own narrative is supposed to be taken as truthful. While criticizing other historians and exposing the falsity of their accounts, Tolstoy offers a number of his own very assertive accounts of events, their causes, and their meaning in the broader historical picture. The most extensive example of such positive narration is found in the portrayal of the battle of Borodino. Tolstoy describes in detail how the battle unfolded—contrary to the generals' plans. He even provides a map, demonstrating the difference between the actual and the planned position of the troops, which was mistaken by historians for the actual one.[19] Tolstoy also explains why the Russians—stranded in a poorly fortified and altogether unfavorable position—were able to withstand the fierce assault of the Great Army by pointing to the unusually high morale that had been built up by the time the general battle finally took place at the approaches to Moscow. Finally, Tolstoy unambiguously defines the role of Borodino as the turning point in defeating the invasion. There is no evidence to suggest that Tolstoy is not confident of his conclusions or somehow undermines them, or that his fictional account of the battle intentionally contradicts its historical counterpart.

Morson and Wachtel, however, express the opposite opinion. Morson sees an implicit undermining in the very fact that Tolstoy, having criticized existing accounts of Borodino in historiography, "turns to fiction for his own narration of the battle," mentioning that on the morning of August 25 Pierre was leaving Mozhaisk. Morson concludes: "Obviously, the mention of a fictional character signals that what follows is not intended to represent what did happen, but only to present a model of how what did happen could have happened." Although Tolstoy considers his fictional account to be more plausible than the accounts of historians, he—in Morson's view—"appears to be saying, I responsibly present my account as fiction because there is no way of knowing whether it is true. [. . .] Fiction is used to indicate the skepticism that should accompany all attempts to reconstruct the past" (139). Although Wachtel also sees a contradiction between the historical and fictional accounts of the battle, he stresses their dialogical relationship. He supports his argument by describing what he sees as a striking difference between chapters 19 and 20 (book 3, part 2) of the novel. While the nonfictional chapter 19 contains a very schematic overview of the battle, the fictional chapter 20 portrays the extreme chaos on the ground, which precludes the possibility of any general picture. Wachtel concludes: "Thus, the perspectives of chapters 19 and 20 could not be further apart. No mental operation will allow us to combine these pictures into one. We must instead realize that fictional and historical narration present different perspectives and different truths—equal perhaps, but separate, and present here in dialogical contrast" (113).

Wachtel's conclusions seem to be based on the premise that a difference in narrative perspectives presupposes a difference in the "truths" expressed by the text in its entirety. In chapter 20 as well as other chapters involving Pierre, Borodino is viewed through the eyes of a civilian, a fictional hero whose main role is to provide maximal estrangement for a description of the war. In chapter 19 the battle is described from the standpoint of the author in his hypostasis as historian. One should not confuse the knowledge (in Bakhtinian terms, the "prospect," or *krugozor*) of a character with that of his author. The author knows more than his character. In addition, Tolstoy uses another fictional character to "brief" Pierre on the author's point of view. In chapter 21 the layman Pierre asks an expert, a fortifications officer, for an explanation of the battlefield. The officer readily satisfies Pierre's curiosity: "Our position? [. . .] I can tell you quite clearly, because I constructed nearly all our entrenchments" (*Pss,* 11:194; *War and Peace,* 679). The officer proceeds to describe succinctly the map presented to us by Tolstoy in the nonfictional chapter 19. We do not need to reconcile the two perspectives since they contain no contradiction.

Here Tolstoy's fiction is clearly meant to support his history, as is the case elsewhere in the novel. Portraying a historical event through the eyes of a fictional character—Tolstoy's favorite device—in no way undermines the historical trustworthiness of his description of these events. On the contrary, it serves as a stamp of validation since the presence of the author's "representative" signals that the event has been subjected to the peculiar brand of historical-cum-psychological criticism that Tolstoy employs in his search for truth. In addition to the Borodino chapters, there are numerous instances of a purely "positive" narration throughout the novel. For example, in book 3, part 1I, chapter 9 one finds a detailed analysis of nine factions under the command of the Russian army in the early stages of the 1812 campaign. This analysis certainly reflects Tolstoy's own opinion, is clearly nonfictional, and could easily be transposed to a nonfictional chapter or even to a historical monograph or textbook. The fact that events are viewed through Prince Andrew's eyes should not lead one to assume that the writer casts doubt on these conclusions. Likewise, in book 3, part 1, chapter 20 Alexander I's manifesto is brought from Count Rastopchin by the fictional Pierre and read out loud by the fictional Sonia, which by no means denotes the fictionality of the document.

Similarly, direct authorial incursions do not undermine the overall illusion of truth but instead support the "reality" of the fictional world (Feuer, 210). This stands in sharp contrast to the function of the authorial voice in the romantic novel, where the author behaves like a puppeteer who interrupts his own show in order to remind the audience that the unfolding performance is the fruit of artistic imagination. For Tolstoy history is not undermined but rather validated by fiction, while the historical background, in turn, helps to create the overall illusion of unconditional reality (*uslovnost' bezuslovnosti*), which is pivotal for realistic literature.

Such a blending of history and fiction is seen at all levels of *War and Peace*. It is apparent in the very names of some of the fictional characters, which represent slightly modified historical names of Russian aristocratic clans: Bolkonsky/Volkonsky, Drubetskoy/Trubetskoy, Kuragin/Kurakin, and so forth. (This onomastic mimicry irritated both Vyazemsky [188] and Demenkov [388].) It also extends to the level of Tolstoy's philosophical musings, as in the passage where, reasoning about the immense number of causes, he writes the following: "Napoleon began the war with Russia because [. . .] Alexander refused negotiations because [. . .] Barclay de Tolly tried to command his army in the best possible way because [. . .] Rostov charged the French because [. . .] and in the same way the innumerable people who took part in the war acted in accord with their personal characteristics, habits, circumstances, and aims" (*Pss*, 11:99; *War and Peace*, 607). In this passage the fictional Rostov figures on equal footing with the historical Napoleon, Alexander, and Barclay. This in no way compromises the earnestness of Tolstoy's philosophical digression, instead elevating Rostov to the status of a historical character of sorts.

In short, although attempts to "dialogize" the Tolstoy of *War and Peace* or to portray him as a modernist or even postmodernist is a stimulating intellectual exercise (which is definitely the case with Morson's intriguing study), they do little to elucidate the novel's artistic system, especially with regard to the interaction between fiction and history. Which is not to say that one can answer with finality the oft-debated question by Isaiah Berlin: Is Tolstoy a "hedgehog" or a "fox"? Can he be understood by applying a universal principle or are there multiple hermeneutic perspectives embedded in his work? It is impossible to confine all of Tolstoy to the straightjacket of realism: as a "militant archaist" he draws on some elements of the prerealist tradition and as a great artist he anticipates future developments. However, the realistic approach to history predominates in *War and Peace.* Thus, Vyazemsky's remarks about the con/fusion of fiction and history in *War and Peace* seem to be much more adroit than the "Bakhtinization" of Tolstoy. Vyazemsky discerned the essence of Tolstoy's method quite perceptively, but, having been reared in the romantic tradition, he refused to accept the new hybrid genre of the realistic novel.

As for the veterans' attempts to refute Tolstoy's novelistic tour de force with their own eyewitness accounts, they were not especially successful. Referring to Vyazemsky's poem, an anonymous reviewer for the *St. Petersburg Gazette* noted sarcastically: "Reading Prince Vyazemsky's admonitions, one cannot help but notice that, generally speaking, the pretensions of the patriots of the bygone days are rather strange. For example, the Prince eagerly allows himself to describe the Battle of Borodino in weak verse, while prohibiting Count Tolstoy from portraying it in good prose" (*L. N. Tolstoi v russkoi kritike,* 25). Echoing this opinion, Mikhail De-Pule, another contemporary critic, is forced to admit that *War and Peace* represents the best depiction of the era of 1812:

> Count Tolstoy's talented audacity has accomplished what has not yet been accomplished in history: it gave us a book about the life of Russian society in the course of an entire quarter century, presented in astonishingly vivid images. Definitely, Count Tolstoy's pronouncement on this life *is not the final one,* but he has the honor of the *first word,* even in the proper historical sense and in the sense of ethnographic sketches, irrespective of the various Memoirs and Notes or Histories by Mikhailovsky-Danilevsky and Bogdanovich. Undoubtedly not all of his sketches are irreproachable, some of them being unsuccessful and weak. But whither should we turn in search of better ones? To Prince Vyazemsky, Norov, Glinka? . . . to Zagoskin's novel *Roslavlev?* (327–28)

Thus, Tolstoy's novel was gradually perceived as more authoritative than any other contemporary accounts, which seemed biased, overly patriotic (in the "official" sense), and artistically inept. Explicit objections to *War and Peace* by the veterans were also largely ignored based on the suspicion that their recollections were distorted by the myth of 1812. In striving to demythologize history, Tolstoy paradoxically created his own myth of 1812, which was so powerful and compelling that it became firmly ingrained in the Russian national consciousness.

6

The Age of Positivism

"Historiographie Romancée"

The Second Wave of the Historical Novel

The second boom in the Russian historical novel began in the 1870s and continued until World War I. In an effort to present a coherent picture of the genre's evolution, it is tempting to ascribe these developments to the influence of *War and Peace*. Tolstoy's epic did indeed restore the status of the historical novel, elevating it from children's room back to the ranks of serious literature. It also introduced a new paradigm of historical fiction that, mutatis mutandis, would subsequently be applied throughout the realistic period. Finally, strong echoes from *War and Peace* can be discerned in such prominent novels of the period as Evgeny Salias's *Men of Pugachev*, Nikolai Chaev's *Mighty Warriors*, and Grigory Danilevsky's *Moscow Destroyed by Fire*.[1] Nevertheless, the success of *War and Peace* was just one among many factors that contributed to the flourishing of the genre.

The historical novel of the 1870s and 1880s emerged as an offshoot of Russian realism amid a renewed preoccupation with history and rapid developments in historiography. This process had already begun in the mid-1860s (which served as the background for *War and Peace*) and reached its peak during the following two decades.[2] Once again it is impossible to single out a leading author or school. Despite its lasting importance, Sergei Solovyov's monumental *History of Russia* (1851–79) did not have the same cultural repercussions as Karamzin's *History*. The new populist focus of historical research that can be traced to Nikolai Kostomarov constituted just one admittedly prominent current in Russian historiography. It is therefore more useful to point to general advances in positivist historiography, the lifting of restrictions surrounding many previously forbidden topics, and the increased publication of primary sources.

The upsurge in Russian historiography of the period was not limited to the academic community, generating intense interest in history among the wider educated public. This was manifested in a number of high-profile (and occasionally scandalous) public lectures in the 1860s by major historians and the proliferation of such historical journals as *The Russian Archive* (1863), *The Russian Antiquity* (1870), *The Historical Herald* (1880), among others. As a well-informed contemporary observer remarked: "Despite the competition [. . .] between history journals they all attracted thousands of subscribers and brought their publishers considerable profits" (Skabichevskii, *Istoriia noveishei russkoi literatury*, 343). Nonspecialist journals also addressed historical subjects on a regular basis. All this activity resulted in a wide dissemination of historical knowledge that became part of the "household culture" (Rubinshtein, 365).

Ultimately the renewed popularity of historical fiction was a corollary to the same trend of infatuation with history. According to my admittedly incomplete data, 44 new titles appeared in the 1870s and over 116 in the following decade, bringing the total to more than 160 titles in the course of two decades (see appendix A). Such a proliferation of historical fiction gave rise to complaints from literary critics. Aleksandr Skabichevsky spoke of its "monstrous" dimensions (*Istoriia noveishei russkoi literatury*, 343), while Nikolai Mikhailovsky compared historical novels to blini churned out in massive quantities during Shrovetide (4:721). Virtually all the pundits excluded the genre from the realm of serious literature.[3] Reader response was much more benevolent. Throughout the late imperial period historical novels were a staple of Russian belles lettres, their serialized editions filling many "thick" journals, magazines, and even newspapers.[4] Several historical novelists became visible figures on the literary scene, and virtually every year at least one work of the genre became a best seller. The extraordinary popularity of the historical novel alone made it an important phenomenon in the cultural life of the epoch.

Major Authors and Works

In the 1870s and through the mid-1890s some sixty authors cultivated the genre, the most prominent of them being Count E. A. Salias, G. P. Danilevsky, D. L. Mordovtsev, and Vs. S. Solovyov. Count Evgeny Salias de Turnemir was the son of a French aristocrat and the famous writer Evgenia

Tur (the sister of the playwright Aleksandr Sukhovo-Kobylin). In the 1860s Salias experimented with prose tales in various genres, but true acclaim came to him with the publication of *The Men of Pugachev* (1873–74), one of the best and most serious novels belonging to the "second wave." Reared in the atmosphere of his mother's literary salon, Salias was noted for his dynamic style, ability to create complex and captivating narratives, and extraordinary productivity. As one contemporary noted: "For Salias writing is like smiling for a pretty woman" (Izmailov, 426). He produced several dozen historical novels and tales, comprising the bulk of his collected works in thirty-three volumes. Often dubbed the "Russian Dumas," Salias was among the most widely read authors of his time—not to mention the most highly paid.[5]

Despite his tremendous popularity, Salias was treated with disdain by the dominant liberal critics, who associated him with the conservative "Moscow school" of literature, which was not fully justified. There are two distinct aspects to Salias's work. On the one hand, he depicts the historical life of the common people, with their peculiar ways and mentality. According to a reviewer from *The Russian Herald*, Salias's interest in "dark, semiconscious movements of the popular masses" echoes Tolstoy's fascination with "mysterious currents of the Russian people's life." Like Tolstoy, Salias emphasizes that history is shaped by these undercurrents and not by the whims of leaders (Anon., Review of *Pugachevtsy*, 879). This idea is embodied most vividly in *The Men of Pugachev* and secondarily in the novel *Death in Moscow* (1880), which concerns the plague mutiny.

On the other hand, Salias is attracted to the great men of the past, especially to the aristocratic eighteenth century, with its adventures, splendor, and culture of deceit, illusion, and travesty. Here his best novel is *The Petersburgian Act* (1880), which deals with the palace coup of 1762. A similar dualism is found in *War and Peace*, but whereas Tolstoy moves from the aristocratic atmosphere of the first volumes to the populist idea in the depiction of 1812, Salias's trajectory is different. Having debuted with a four-volume epic about the Pugachev revolt, later in his career he showed a predilection for subjects based on high-society intrigue and piquant anecdote, as in his novel *Breadth and Expanse* (1885), about Potemkin.

Unlike Salias, Grigory Danilevsky turned to historical fiction as a mature writer. In the 1860s he published several novels, the most successful of them being a two-part epic about peasant life in southern Russia before and after the abolition of serfdom. In his early career he occasionally treated historical subjects in short stories and tales, but in the mid-1870s he made the historical novel his main specialty. His first and perhaps most popular work in the genre is the novel *Mirovich* (written in 1875, banned by the censor in 1877, and published in 1879), which deals with the tragic fate of the deposed child-emperor Ioann Antonovich and the foiled attempt by Lieutenant Mirovich to free him from Shlisselburg. Among other important novels by Danilevsky one should mention *Princess Tarakanova* (1883), about the self-proclaimed daughter of Empress Elizabeth; *Moscow Destroyed by Fire* (1886), about Napoleon's invasion; and *The Black Year* (1888), about Pugachev.

Depicting the horrors of Russian revolt, *The Black Year* is quite tendentious. Elsewhere Danilevsky refrained from expressing strong opinions, which some critics saw as a plus, praising him for his objectivity, while others rebuked him for the lack of any "idea." The latter is more to the point. It appears at times that the writer finds himself at a loss when confronted by the immensity and complexity of the historical material. The only criterion expressed in his approach to historical figures is compassion for the victims of history. Danilevsky, however, does not rise to the heights of Scott and Pushkin and his humanism often contains suspiciously loyalist overtones. In *Mirovich* Ioann Antonovich is pitied by all the monarchs—Elizabeth, Peter III, Catherine II—who wish to alleviate his suffering, but their good intentions remain unrealized either due to adverse circumstances or because of interference from evil advisers. Here Danilevsky does not shy away from being a strict judge. Particularly noteworthy in this respect is his highly negative portrayal of Count Alexei Orlov in *Princess Tarakanova.*

The motivations of Danilevsky's heroes are often unclear. Thus, Mirovich, nurturing his desperate enterprise, first becomes inspired by civic ideals, then wants to avenge an injustice done to his family, then succumbs to the instigation of his ambitious mistress, then becomes envious of fortune's favorites, and ultimately feels pity for the royal prisoner. The end result is not multidimensional complexity in the portrayal of his character but rather blurred uncertainty. Also unclear is Danilevsky's overall concept of the Pugachev rebellion in *The Black Year.* The author unequivocally condemns the cruelty of the rebels, yet at the same time wonders how the good and religious Russian people were capable of such atrocities. The novel makes no attempt to answer this question.

Danilevsky's theory of history is inconsistent as well. On the one hand, he is quite unconventional. Contrary to the prevailing paradigm, Danilevsky stresses not the laws of historical process but rather happenstance and fatidic moments. However, unlike the romantics, Danilevsky sees no providential force behind random acts of chance; at the same time, chance does not acquire an independent existential meaning, as is the case with Mark

Aldanov and other later writers. The incongruities of Danilevsky's approach are especially obvious in *Moscow Destroyed by Fire*. Napoleon is portrayed as the instigator of the war, whose physical elimination would solve all problems. However, like Tolstoy Danilevsky frequently compares the French invasion to an attack of locusts, which implies an uncontrollable, elemental force. Likewise, in *Mirovich* the author constantly emphasizes that the success of the 1762 coup was a matter of pure chance. At the same time, Catherine's victory in the novel emerges as the logical result of widespread discontent with the unpopular Peter III. Despite their lack of conceptual and artistic integrity, Danilevsky's novels remain among the best works of historical fiction of the period, enjoying considerable success in Russia and being read in translation across Europe.

Another major novelist of the time was Daniil Mordovtsev. His literary debut dates to the mid-1850s, when he wrote several pieces in his native Ukrainian. A descendant of Zaporozhian Cossacks, Mordovtsev spent his childhood in the Sloboda Ukraine and began studying Russian in school. In the late 1860s he published two novels in Russian that dealt with the topical issues of the "New Man" and the position of young intellectuals with respect to the lower classes. During the 1860s and early 1870s Mordovtsev undertook extensive historical research and produced several monographs that—very much in the populist spirit of the times—dealt with various grassroots movements and uprisings in the seventeenth and eighteenth centuries. These works brought Mordovtsev fame, being so favorably received in academic circles that there was even serious talk of offering him the chair of Russian history at Saint Petersburg University. In the mid-1870s Mordovtsev turned to the historical novel, ultimately becoming one of the most widely read and prolific authors of the genre, creating well over thirty novels and tales.

Unlike Salias and Danilevsky, Mordovtsev is openly tendentious in his portrayal of the past, declaring that "the historical novel cannot help but serve the tasks of the present" ("K slovu ob istoricheskom romane," 649). Especially biased are his early works, beginning with his first novel *Idealists and Realists* (1876), which paints a grim picture of Petrine reforms. In his criticism of Peter, Mordovtsev does not proceed from the Slavophile premise since he admits that Russia was moving in the right direction. However, he laments the cruelty of the reformers, emphasizing that the suffering inflicted upon the common people was senseless and excessive. This reflects his core historical concept, according to which history is viewed as a field of contestation between the "centripetal" and "centrifugal" elements, the former being embodied in the state, the latter in the people. While not denying the role of centripetal forces in fostering historical progress, Mordovtsev sympathizes with the centrifugal forces since the state embodies the principle of coercion, while the potential for free historical development lies with the people. In the novel these forces are dubbed "realism" and "idealism." The "realists" may prevail, but the "idealists" have moral truth on their side. As Mordovtsev concludes: "Focused around Peter I, the realism of the early eighteenth century was confronted with equally powerful idealism. [. . .] It dwelled in the adepts of the old, in the Schism; it hid in the forests and deserts and was facing death—fearlessly, heroically—at the stake, on the executioner's block, through impalement or self-conflagration" (*Idealisty i realisty*, 25).

The "idealists" in the novel are represented by Tsarevich Alexei, numerous clergymen and common people, and the main character, Captain Vasily Levin, who is based on an actual historical figure. Crushed by a personal drama (the love of his life becomes a nun in order to avoid a forced marriage arranged by the tsar) and appalled by what he sees around him, Levin becomes a staunch opponent of Peter. Like many of his compatriots, Levin grows to believe that Peter is the Antichrist. He retires from the military, takes monastic vows, and eventually meets a martyr's death after publicly denouncing the emperor and preaching the end of the world. In contrast to the selfless and sincere "idealists," the supporters of Peter belong to a corrupt, predatory, self-seeking breed. (They also turn out to be among the spiritual ancestors of the modern Russian bourgeois.) While the "reformers" rape and pillage the country, their leader acts like a veritable sadistic monster. Such a negative treatment of Peter provoked a storm of refutations from various quarters. Mordovtsev, however, remained unfazed. In later editions he even published the novel under the title *The Shadow of Herod*, implying that the Russian tsar was an incarnation of the biblical villain.[6] Subsequently Mordovtsev altered his position, presenting an apologetic view of Peter in the novels *More Light!* (1895) and *The Royal Carpenter* (1895).[7] However, his early anti-Petrine stance set an important precedent in Russian literature. The novel *Idealists and Realists* is also noteworthy as an obvious source for Dmitry Merezhkovsky's *Antichrist: Peter and Alexis* (1904), which is discussed in the next chapter.

During his later years Mordovtsev published numerous novels covering a wide range of subjects drawn from Russian and Ukrainian history. Although Mordovtsev's views of particular figures and events could vacillate, his approach to the past was based upon the same set of principles evident in his first novel and in his previous historical studies. The writer is sympathetic to popular movements and "centrifugal" forces in general. This goes hand in hand with the ardent Ukrainian nationalism that was instilled by Mordovtsev's friend and mentor Kostomarov. Already in *Idealists and Realists* Mordovtsev has Peter making the following declaration, which praises the Ukraine and warns Russia: "The Little Russian nation is both very clever and very shrewd. Like a hard-working bee, it provides the Russian state with the best intellectual honey and the best wax for the candle of Russian enlightenment, but it has a sting as well. As long as Russians love and respect it, it will be a beast of burden and a source of light for the Russian realm; but if they encroach upon its freedom and its language, dragon's teeth will grow out of it and the Russian realm will not profit" (226). A corollary to this is Mordovtsev's pronounced anti-Moscow stance. In *Lord Novgorod the Great* (1882) he presents an unattractive portrait of Ivan III and unconditionally sides with the Novgorodians, who fight a losing battle against the "Muscovite pest" (*Gospodin Velikii Novgorod,* 3:189). In *The False Dmitry* (1879) Mordovtsev even goes against his usual "democratic" leanings, depicting the people of Moscow as a dark, blind, and cruel force that mindlessly destroys Dmitry, that "great Sphinx of history" (*Lzhedmitrii,* 244).

In his portrayal of the past Mordovtsev draws on impressive historical erudition and displays intimate familiarity with a wide range of primary sources. One should also mention his ambitious attempts at linguistic stylization in the speech of his characters. Several commentators (Panov and Ranchin) have pointed to the structural peculiarities of his novels—the multiplicity of characters and the interlacing of numerous plot lines—purportedly intended to create a stereoscopic panorama of history. However, this was quite common in the realistic epics. Moreover, this alleged architectonic complexity does not appear to be an entirely intentional device but rather a consequence of improvisation, bordering on looseness and lack of structure. A more plausible achievement lies in Mordovtsev's rendering of the formulaic and "archetypal" nature of the medieval mind. The latter, however, is undermined by instances of blatant modernization and incursions of the authorial voice with naive commentary and clumsy lyricism. Even Mordovtsev's best works are marred by verbosity and a certain sloppiness resulting from undue haste in composition.

The fourth major historical novelist of the 1870s and 1880s was Vsevolod Solovyov, elder son of historian Sergei Solovyov and brother of religious philosopher Vladimir Solovyov. Vsevolod Solovyov turned to historical fiction in 1876, debuting with *Princess Ostrozhskaya,* which explores the conflict between Catholicism and Orthodoxy in the Russian-Lithuanian state during the sixteenth century. Altogether he wrote more than a dozen novels, the most famous being the five-volume *Chronicle of the Four Generations* (1881–86), which traces the history of the fictional Gorbatov family from the reign of Catherine II to the era of the Great Reforms. Compared with the best efforts of his contemporaries, Solovyov's *Chronicle* is somewhat superficial, although this only contributed to its success among the readership of popular magazines, where it was serialized. Moreover, unlike many historical exposés reveling in the abominations of Russian history, the *Chronicle* is permeated by an atmosphere of nostalgia for the vanished age of the nobility. This helps to explain Solovyov's posthumous popularity among Russian émigrés. Interesting in their own right are also his subsequent historical novels. *The Magi* (1889) and *The Great Rosicrucian* (1890) deal with the great mystics of the late eighteenth and early nineteenth centuries, including Count Cagliostro. Although of modest artistic value, these "novels with a mystical lining," as they were dubbed by the anonymous reviewer for the *Russian Herald* (Review of *Volkhvy*, 333) reflect Russian society's fascination with the esoteric at the time. (Solovyov himself was briefly an adept of Helena Blavatsky.)

Among the multitude of prolific novelists of the period, one can also single out Evgeny Karnovich, author of historical works on various Russian and Polish subjects. Encountering a period of financial hardship during the later years of his life, he turned to historical fiction, producing eight novels. Although not endowed with artistic talent, Karnovich was nevertheless knowledgeable and thorough in his portrayal of historical backgrounds. Most other purveyors of the genre were remarkable primarily for their productivity. (See, in appendix B, entries for Nikolai Chmyrev, Ekaterina Dubrovina, Ivan Kondratyev, Petr Petrov, Petr Polezhaev, and Aleksandr Sokolov.)

There is also a separate category reserved for famous literati, historians, and others who occasionally turned to historical fiction. The prominent historian Nikolai Kostomarov authored the novel *Kudeyar* (1875) plus two novellas entitled *The Lackey* (1878) and *A Girl from Chernigov* (1881), in which he continued to debunk Russian history in the spirit of his earlier tale *The Son* (see previous chapter). *The Lackey*, arguably the best of Kostomarov's works in the genre, is set in Saint Petersburg during the reign of Catherine I and portrays the base mores of both the Russian aristocracy and their serfs. *A Girl from Chernigov* deals with the abuses of the Muscovite administration in mid-seventeenth-century Ukraine. Set in the time of Ivan the Terrible, *Kudeyar* presents an exceedingly gloomy picture of Muscovy. Kostomarov relishes descriptions of medieval torture: maidens are hanged upside down and sawed in half while their parents look on helplessly; victims are boiled alive and then fried; melted tin is poured down their throats, their hands and legs are chopped off, and the executioners make them crawl around in their own blood. All the while the sadistic tsar observes their convulsions from a throne placed in the middle of the torture chamber (*Kudeiar*, 59–65). Characteristically, as was the case in *The Son*, evil is not solely the province of the vicious ruler or even the oppressive social system: the people of Muscovy, considered as a group, are cruel, cowardly, treacherous, and devoid of any notion of justice or dignity. Individuals who rise above this base level dream of escaping abroad. The author's namesake, the nobleman Samson Kostomarov, makes the following declaration while fleeing to Lithuania: "The devil take them, all those Muscovites. I got a look at how free people live in Lithuania; it's not at all like here. [. . .] The king there would never think of playing such games as our tsar! Oh no! Not at all! In Russia even a boyar and a prince are nothing but dirt in the tsar's eyes. What good can we expect from such a land?! [. . .] I renounce once and for all the cursed land of Muscovy and her people!" (76–77).[8] While Samson Kostomarov chooses the "West," Kudeyar, whose dreams of a peaceful domestic existence on a Ukrainian farmstead are ruined by Ivan the Terrible, defects to the "East," pledging allegiance to the noble Crimean khan: "I have come to hate Moscow and the Muscovites. I reject them. I renounce them and their beliefs and will accept Islam and become one of your Tatars" (523).

Russophobic tirades aside, *Kudeyar*'s plot is so convoluted and laden with improbabilities and absurdities that it surpasses even the novels of Rafail Zotov. Combined with an exceptional lack of taste and literary ineptness, this could make Kostomarov's creation one of the worst Russian historical novels ever written. Despite all this, *Kudeyar* was serialized in the influential liberal journal *The Herald of Europe*—perhaps based on ideological considerations (it was directed against Slavophiles) and out of respect for the author, who just happened to be the associate editor of the journal. The novel was reprinted at least three times during the imperial period, and an adaptation also appeared in 1928. And "habent sua fata libelli": the fruit of the venerable historian's graphomanic passion unexpectedly resurfaced during the epoch of high Stalinism. When the filmmaker Sergei Eisenstein had to repent publicly in *Pravda* for the ideological blunders of *Ivan the Terrible Part II*, among the reasons for distorting the image of the "progressive tsar" he named an old novel about Kudeyar that he had read in childhood—undoubtedly Kostomarov's *Kudeyar*.

Kostomarov's sweeping negativism in the portrayal of the Russian past was countered by Nikolai Pavlov, a prominent figure of late Slavophilism. In his review of *The Son* he pointed to the one-sided nihilism of Kostomarov, who failed to notice the beauty and integrity of old Russian life that shines even through the writings of its main detractor, Kotoshikhin (Review of N. Kostomarov's *Syn*, 19). In 1870 Pavlov presented his own vision of seventeenth-century Russia in the tale *The Tsar's Falconer*, which is set during the reign of Aleksei Mikhailovich. Stepan Razin's rebellion appears in the tale as a dramatic albeit short episode, its horror vanishing like a bad dream.[9] The plot revolves around the love affair between scions of ancient boyar families, its happy ending brought about through the benevolent intervention of the "Quietest Tsar" Alexei Mikhailovich, whom Pavlov portrays with great sympathy.

The somber mood of Kostomarov's *Son* is epitomized by the conclusion, which describes the execution of the hero: "The pike slowly impaled his entrails as his body sank from the weight. [. . .] Osip was alone in his inexpressible agony among putrid corpses, some held erect, some hanging. He endured this torture for almost an entire day. A raven pecked out his eyes while he was still alive. Finally Osip lost consciousness. Yet he was luckier than many executed in such a fashion. Others were forced to suffer even longer, depending on how the pike pierced their bodies, and this, in turn, depended on the individual's figure and how he happened to be positioned on the pike" (204–5).

By contrast, Pavlov concentrates on the beauty of old Muscovy. *The Tsar's Falconer* opens with a winter-wonderland image of Holy Rus: "The ornate crosses of the Tikhvin church sparkled brightly in the frost, the large dome dotted with golden stars in the middle surrounded by four small domes with blue stars. Another church, this one green, could be seen nearby. [. . .] And many steeply pitched roofs, towers, monasteries, and bell towers could be seen . . . a multitude of gilded silver, checkered, shingled, and scaled roofs. . . . And in the distance the Kremlin" (*Tsarskii sokol'nik*, 4). This sets the tone for the entire tale. For example, here is a panoramic view of Moscow as glimpsed by the hero: "He thought he heard church bells ringing from afar. He locked his fervent gaze on the blue expanse before him. [. . .] In the calm spring evening Moscow itself gleamed before his very eyes like a heavenly vision. Countless churches, monasteries, and gilded Kremlin cathedrals glittered in the azure distance" (103). And here is a picture of Easter eve suffused with paschal joy: "On that day all the bells in Rus ring as one. It is the Saturday before Easter and tomorrow is the holiest day of the year. Like the life-giving spring, the Luminous Resurrection of Our Lord has come. The words 'Christ is risen!' can be heard resounding from one end of the Russian land to the other" (164). The story is full of similar affectionate descriptions of religious holidays, feasts, games, court rituals, falcon hunting, and other aspects of old Russian ways (Almost exclusively drawn from the life of the tsar and his boyars, *The Tsar's Falconer*'s Slavophilism has a distinctly aristocratic flavor.)[10]

While Kostomarov's *Son* has anticlerical overtones, the life of Pavlov's heroes literally unfolds under the watchful eye of Our Lady of Tikhvin, to whose icon their parish church is consecrated. Like Karamzin's lovers in *Natalya* and Zagoskin's lovers in *Miloslavsky*, they meet, pray to the Tikhvin icon during moments of need, and get married in the same red church. Such a happy ending stands in stark contrast to Kostomarov's *Son*, which, like the rest of his novels, closes on a note of hopelessness: the hero perishes without leaving any progeny. Pavlov not only overturns Kostomarov's gloomy conclusion but also emphasizes the living connection between Russia's past and present: "The red church still stands today. Their [the heroes'] descendants are in our midst" (228).[11]

Among celebrated writers who occasionally tried their hand at the historical novel, one should mention Vsevolod Krestovsky. His *Grandfathers* (1875) emerged as a by-product of research for an official history of the Uhlan regiment of the Guards. Krestovsky strives to reevaluate the much maligned and caricatured reign of Paul I by casting it in a more positive light. Historical subjects are also treated by Aleksei Pisemsky in his last novel *The Masons* (1880), which deals with the Masonic underground of the 1830s. Pisemsky implicitly contrasts the idealism and moral purity of the best representatives of Freemasonry with the spirit of unscrupulous profiteering that swept over post-reform Russia. The properly historical element in the book is limited to digressions on the history of the brotherhood, with long quotations from Masonic texts, detailed descriptions of rituals, and additional vignettes (e.g., the Masonic background of Archangel Gabriel's church in Moscow.) Overall, Pisemsky's novel is a borderline example of the genre. Its historical chronotope is weakened by the fact that most of the action unfolds in an unnamed provincial town, and although many historical characters appear in the novel, their role in the plot is minimal.

Semiprofessional writers who cultivated the historical novel include members of the Filippov family. Mikhail Abramovich Filippov, a lawyer and publicist, wrote the lengthy seventeenth-century saga *Patriarch Nikon* (1885). His son, Mikhail Mikhailovich, a philosopher and respected scientist, wrote several historical tales as well as a novel about the Crimean War entitled *The Besieged Sebastopol* (1888), which Tolstoy praised. As far as "dynasties" of historical novelists are concerned, one must mention Pyotr Nikolaevich Polevoi, the son of the famous romantic author. In the 1870s Polevoi Junior abandoned his academic career for that of a freelance writer. His most significant work is the once popular *History of Russian Literature in Sketches and Biographies*, but he also published a number of novels and tales dealing with various subjects drawn from Russian history.

Poetics of the Realist Novel

As was the case in the 1830s and 1840s, the vast majority (82%) of historical fiction was devoted to Russian history. Interest in closely related Ukrainian subjects also remained traditionally high (7%), with various Ukrainian subjects figuring in many other novels (such prominent practitioners of the genre as Mordovtsev, Danilevsky, and Kostomarov were either Ukrainian or part Ukrainian, based on ethnic origin). To repeat an earlier caveat intended to avoid distortion in the overall picture, in many novels classified as Russian a significant part of the action may be set outside Russia or involve foreign subjects. In addition, Russian audiences had broad access to European literature, including historical fiction, thanks to a flourishing translation industry supported by numerous periodicals, where anything of note was promptly translated into Russian.[12] Nevertheless, the properly domestic focus of Russian novelists reflected the new spirit of nationalism in art during the epoch of the Mighty Handful in music, the Wanderers in painting, and pseudo-Russian style in architecture. The wide range of attitudes toward the national past reflected the equally diverse group of authors involved. However, the predominant trend can be described as a kind of latent nationalism: an admiration for the elemental and sui generis might of the Russian people as revealed in the very turpitude of their less than idyllic history.

Although historical novels published during this period cover a broad range of Russian subjects, beginning with Early Rus, the clear favorite is the age of empresses (thirty seven novels representing nearly 30% of the total output). The eighteenth century in general is the period of choice (providing settings for almost 40% of all the novels). It was indeed a gold mine for authors of historical fiction: a period when the Empire's capital came into being; an epoch of recently "declassified" palace coups, conspiracies, and political intrigues; a century of impostors, titans, and eccentrics; an age of extremes; an era of victorious wars and popular uprisings; the golden age of the gentry and the period of serfdom's abuses—and, most important—a time when Russian and European civilizations intertwined, when the unbridled Russian nature burst forth amid the plethora of recently imported Western culture.[13]

FIGURE 12. Title page of Kelsiev's *Moscow and Tver* (1872; artist I. Panov; engraving I. Matyuishin). The novels of the 1870s and 1880s are dominated by Russian subjects, reflecting the new spirit of nationalism in art at the time of the emergence of the Mighty Handful in music, the Wanderers in painting, and pseudo-Russian style in architecture.

Another large group of novels (22 titles, roughly 14%) is set during the seventeenth century. What is new here is the fact that the popularity of the Time of Troubles subsided (only 6 titles) as authors rediscovered the reign of Aleksei Mikhailovich (13 titles), which was a very rare topic in the romantic novel. There are also completely new subjects, including the reign of Paul I (6 titles) and the Decembrist uprising (2 titles), as well as a utilization of recent events, including the Crimean War (2 titles) and various unexplored aspects of the reign of Nicholas I (see appendix sections).

As far as general historical poetics are concerned, novels of the 1870s and 1880s largely followed the paradigm of *War and Peace.* Rooted in the monistic outlook of the epoch, Tolstoy's novel stands in sharp contrast to the romantic model, which is based on a binary conception of the world. First and foremost, in the realistic novel there is no conflict between the two truths and no contradiction between the artist and historian. The author utilizes all available forms of "literary study and social inquiry" in order to describe and analyze reality (Goncourt, 19). Second, the reader encounters a different

FIGURE 13. An illustration from Sokolov's *Volga Freebooters of Stenka Razin* (1881, p. 8). In their depiction of broad popular movements, the realistic narratives of the 1870s and 1880s can be compared to the monumental historical paintings of the time. One of the fruitful subjects of the day was the reign of Alexei Mikhailovich with its massive revolts and the fateful schism in the Russian Orthodox Church.

attitude toward historical facts. Although realistic writers can reinterpret facts they consider dubious, unlike the romantics they avoid poetic license, applying their fantasy to the "gray area" beyond established evidence. Otherwise their imagination can be quite unbridled. There can also be inadvertent mistakes, but this is different from intentional anachronisms, the hallmark of the romantic novel. Third, absent from the realistic novel is the irony of self-invalidation and other narrative strategies that dispel the illusion of history redivivus. The intent of the realistic author is to create an atmosphere of unconditional reality. Finally, realists differ from romantics in their approach to such categories as providence, the hero, and legend. References to providence become rhetorical or agnostic, giving way to objective laws of history, while the so-called great men are shown to be ordinary individuals and legends are debunked. Overall, instead of romantic attempts to discern the *spirit* of the epoch, the realistic novelist analyzes its *character*, with the latter term supplanting the former in critical discourse on historical fiction.

That is not to say that the novels of the 1870s and 1880s do not have certain "birthmarks" of the romantic tradition. Occasionally one encounters

FIGURE 14. An illustration from Kelsiev and Klyushnikov's *At the Time of Peter* (1872, p. 120; artist I. Panov; engraving I. Matyuishin). Russia's formidable eighteenth century with its titanic accomplishments and titillating "secret history" was the epoch of choice for writers of historical fiction in the 1870s and 1880s.

features familiar from the novel of the 1830s: the found manuscript device;[14] epigraphs; dramatic dialogue;[15] folk divertimentos;[16] reference to lore and legend in the conclusion;[17] introductions evoking the theme of artistic imagination;[18] direct allusions to other writers;[19] and authorial incursions.[20] Extremely rare are such "subversive" elements as metadescriptions[21] and, in particular, admissions of anachronisms.[22] However, these are just isolated instances that do not support the view of two parallel worlds of fact and fiction, as was the case in the romantic novel.

Some of the romantic elements also undergo a transformation that significantly alters their function. This is most evident in authorial notes. The romantic novel's use of foot- and endnotes contributes to the contradictory drives of validation and invalidation (see chapter 2). Notes are also present in some realistic works. Their most copious use in non-Russian literature is found in the Egyptian novels of the German writer Georg Ebers, beginning with *Die Ägyptische Königstochter* (1864), which is fitted out with a lengthy commentary. In Russian novels notes are present, for example, in Danilevsky's *Mirovich*.[23] As a rule, however, these take the form of straightforward, quasi-academic footnotes devoid of romantic playfulness and do not create a dialogical tension between fiction and history.[24]

Unlike the romantics, realist writers of the period generally tend not to engage in elaborate narrative games and avoid authorial incursions in the text. The prevalent mode is objective narrative with the figure of the author absent. Whereas romantic writers are often compared to an exhibitionistic *Puppenmeister* who cannot stay behind the curtain, realist writers largely follow the "fourth wall" convention. There are some deviations from this scheme, but they are either relatively minor or serve a new purpose. This is the case with Tolstoy's authorial digressions: far from exposing the fictionality of the central action, Tolstoy's historical and philosophical digressions contribute to the overall impression of truthfulness.

In discussing the basic similarities between the historical poetics of *War and Peace* and the novels of the 1870s and 1880s, one should not portray Tolstoy as the creator of the new paradigm since it was a corollary to general realistic poetics and ultimately emerged from the prevalent worldview of the epoch. One should also recall Tolstoy's idiosyncrasies, which set *War and Peace* apart from the mainstream historical novel. Unlike Tolstoy, novelists of the 1870s and 1880s paid much more attention to the realia of the past. This can be explained by different historical concepts. Tolstoy loathed the idea of progress and supported the notion of the basic immutability of human nature, which resulted in a weakening of historical color in *War and Peace*.

Which is not to say that he is totally oblivious to the attributes of the chosen epoch. One need only recall that he deliberately opens his Russian epic with a conversation "in that refined French in which our grandfathers not only spoke but thought" (*War and Peace*, 3). This elegant French of yore, alongside Empire-style dresses with exposed shoulders and breasts, trousers of the color "cuisse de nymphe effrayée," and other details of the time are meant to emphasize Tolstoy's absolutes, the most important of which "always" pertains to human nature.

Unlike Tolstoy the "militant archaist," most authors of later historical novels were rather ordinary representatives of the age of positivism. Leaving differences in their political views aside, they shared the idea of historical progress, which is akin to the Darwinian scheme of evolution. As Mordovtsev puts it, "According to Darwin's theory, the horns and tusks of our forebears occasionally resurface many generations later, if only in a rudimentary form" ("K slovu ob istoricheskom romane," 649). By implication, the portrayal of these "tusks and horns"—the colorful signs of the past—is essential for historical narratives. This was combined with a passion for "catalogization," which these realist writers inherited from the Natural school and which was also prominent in positivist historiography. Add to this mix a general infatuation with historical exoticism, and it is understandable why these novels are often overloaded with meticulous descriptions of historical realia.

Another difference between Tolstoy and the novelists of the 1870s and 1880s lies not in the essence but in the scope of their respective goals. In addition to his role as a novelist, Tolstoy also acts in his capacity as a revisionist historian and philosopher contemplating the fundamental laws of history. Other writers are generally much less ambitious. They can reinterpret historical events, but mostly they act as popularizers of history. The latter is repeatedly emphasized by contemporary critics, who also point to the "pedagogical" advantages of historical fiction. Even such a detractor of the contemporary historical novel as N. M. Sokolov admits that "historical novels [. . .] at least are much easier to read and, moreover, mixed in with the unnecessary ballast [. . .] convey some historical information along the way, which [. . .] in such reworked form is easier to remember than, for example, when reading Ustryalov's textbook" (192). The reviewer of *The Historical Herald* praises Salias first and foremost for his dissemination of historical knowledge, paying the novelist the following dubious compliment: "The significance of Count Salias [. . .] clearly lies not in the literariness of his works. [. . .] Count Salias is extremely valuable as a popular, accessible depicter of certain historical elements of Russian life. [. . .] The historical novelist [. . .] can give [. . .]

FIGURE 15. An illustration from Sokolov's *Volga Freebooters of Stenka Razin* (1881, p. 136). The Cossack chieftain Razin with his Dionysian sacrifice of the Persian princess offered a dramatic perspective on gender issues.

FIGURE 16. An illustration from Kelsiev and Klyushnikov's *At the Time of Peter* (1872, p. 140; artist I. Panov; engraving I. Matyuishin). The "gallant" eighteenth century remained an unsurpassed source for amorous adventures.

the era such a clear conception, which no history can give, never mind the brief textbooks to which the majority of the public limits itself" (Vvedenskii, 395–96).

In the 1860s the realistic hybrid between fiction and nonfiction was a novelty, which caused much controversy in connection with *War and Peace.* In the 1870s such syncretism became a commonplace, with the result that the historical novel entered two continuums. First, contemporary critics saw little qualitative difference between the historical and nonhistorical novel since both were viewed as quasi-scientific tools for describing and analyzing reality, be it in the present or in the past. Both types of novels were perceived as literary sociology or ethnography of sorts. The reviewer from *The Russian Thought* formulated this idea in connection with Danilevsky's *Mirovich:* "Mr. Danilevsky, having drawn in *Mirovich* a grandiose historical tableau, even though he has stepped onto a new path, nevertheless remains in sync with his former mode of writing 'artistic' ethnography. [. . .] However, now the author's brush is applied not to the steppe of Novorossisk but to eighteenth-century Saint Petersburg with its plots and intrigues" (Sokal'skii, Review of *Mirovich,* 14).

The second continuum is that between historical fiction and historiography. Mordovtsev, who was both a historian and a novelist, saw the merger of historiography and belles lettres as an important trend of the modern age: "Now the higher task of science is its democratization, popularization, and accessibility. [. . .] There is no doubt that, sooner or later, the force of democratization will cause 'history' to merge with 'belles lettres' once and for all" ("Kritika i bibliografiia," 267).[25]

A vivid example of merging between historiography and historical fiction is found in the program of *The Historical Herald,* which was launched in 1880 and became one of the most successful popular historical journals: "The goal of publishing *The Historical Herald* is to acquaint [the reader] with the current state of historical science and literature in a *lively form that is accessible to all.* [. . .] On this basis the program of *The Historical Herald* will include [. . .] historical compositions, monographs, novels, tales, sketches, stories, memoirs, reminiscences, travel notes, biographies of outstanding individuals in all fields, descriptions of mores, customs, etc., a bibliography of works of Russian and foreign historical literature, obituaries, descriptions, anecdotes, news, historical publications and documents of general interest" (*Istoricheskii vestnik* 1 [1880], unpag.) Thus, many historical novels and tales appeared in the pages of this journal, surrounded by scholarly articles and publications of primary sources.[26] Such a continuum was taken for granted since the novelist, like the historian, strove to portray "the anatomy and physiology of the past" (Sokal'skii, 10).

In the 1880s this union between history and literature gave rise to the increasingly popular genre of "biographie romancée," which "colors" the factual outline with belletristic narration. Without introducing fictional characters or events, the author imagines what his hero might have seen and felt. This was also considered a type of popularized history. As Vasily Avenarius, a major practitioner of this genre, describes it in the preface to his "biographical tale" about Pushkin's youth: "The form of my story belongs to belles lettres, but as the list of materials that were in my possession appended to the end of this book shows, I tried to avoid letting slip from my sight a single fact, a single individual that might have influenced the development of the personality and talent of Pushkin the lyceum student. I preferred the belletristic form because it is more accessible and would presume a larger audience of readers and, as a result, be more useful" (iii).

Authors of historical novels, in turn, experimented with genre definitions, trying to emphasize the nonfictional element of their creations. Kostomarov, for example, labels his thoroughly improbable *Kudeyar* as "historical chronicle." Solovyov occasionally uses the subtitle "novel-chronicle." Still other authors stress the portrayal of everyday realia by introducing the term "*byt*" (everyday life) into their subtitles. Nevertheless, the time-honored "historical novel" and "historical tale" still remain the mostly widely used generic rubrics.

The properly novelistic components of historical fiction of the period—plot structure, cast of characters, their speech and descriptive portraits, psychology—fit well into the broader realistic paradigm, often in its epigonic and clichéd incarnations. General realistic features are often intertwined with peculiar cultural trends, such as proclivity for exposés and nihilism. I have already discussed Tolstoy's debunking of the "great men" and introduction of mundane details, as a result of which Vyazemsky mistook a fellow nonconformist aristocrat for a nihilist. Sometimes "lowering" can indeed be consistently nihilistic in origin, which is the case with Kostomarov.[27] Other writers succumb to this fashion only occasionally, as is the case with Vladislav Markov. Normally he pays homage to exotic realia, as in his *Frontiersmen of Kursk*, but in one instance he decides to dispel the charm of exoticism by providing disillusioning details in his portrayal of a Tatar assault: "Up close those red, blue, and yellow jackets turn out to be dirty batten rags; up close those fiercely gleaming blades on their smart handles are actually small lances, most of them old and rusted and strapped to the shaft by a rope or horsehair" (*Kurskie porubezhniki*, 144). However, such tirades are usually outnumbered by exotic descriptions, which, with very few exceptions, are essential for the poetics of historical fiction in all periods.

More frequent are attacks against the authority of great men and heroes. They can stem from the author's philosophy of history, his desire to present a shocking reevaluation of the past, his attempts to portray the past as a more "believable" fashion, or from a combination of these factors. In short, historical novelists routinely "drop many figures from their pedestals to the level of average mortals" (Rubakin, 7). We have seen this mechanism at work in *War and Peace,* but it is also found in numerous other novels. As was previously mentioned in connection with the Tolstoy versus Vyazemsky controversy, the peculiarities of the realists' approach are especially obvious when placed against the background of romantic literature. Quite indicative here is the transformation of romantic heroes in the work of Danilevsky, a sound second-rank realist writer. Among important historical characters in Zagoskin's *Roslavlev* is the Taciturn Officer (Captain Figner, the famous partisan of 1812), a ruthlessly cruel, somber, and mysterious individual, the blond counterpart of the usually dark-haired Byronic hero. Here is how Zagoskin describes him: "This taciturn officer was of average height, light-haired, round of face and generally of pleasant appearance, yet there was something odd, emotionless, and even inhuman in his gray eyes. It seemed that neither joy nor sorrow could bring to life his staring, indifferent gaze, and only a rare smile expressing a cold kind of disdain would appear on his lips" (295).

In *Moscow Destroyed by Fire* Danilevsky also mentions Figner's cruelty and steely resolve, but he portrays his appearance in a way that dispels the aura of the romantic hero: "There was something womanish in his face; the reddish strands of hair fell on his forehead and ears in straight locks, like the Finns. Widely detached eyebrows and large, pursed lips gave this face an expression of displeasure and, it seemed, fear. 'A woman,' would comment anyone who first set eyes on him, were it not for the thin sideburns passing over the face from the ears to the chin" (*Sozhennaia Moskva,* 712). Moreover, whereas in *Roslavlev* Figner is enigmatically terse, here Danilevsky makes him quite talkative and also endows him with peculiar speech mannerisms: a Baltic German-turned-Russian patriot, Figner mixes high rhetoric and Russian folk sayings, uttered with exaggerated, non-native accuracy.

Also quite striking is the contrast between the charismatic Pathfinder of *The Captain's Daughter* and Pugachev in Danilevsky's *Black Year.* Pushkin's laconic descriptions could not satisfy the realistic sensibility. This may explain Tolstoy's remark about Pushkin's novel: "*The Captain's Daughter* is somehow bare." Emerging from the blizzard, Pugachev turns into a menacing yet fascinating Russian sphinx (Bethea, "Slavic Gift-Giving"). Pushkin's Pugachev lacks biography, psychology—and physiology. Danilevsky fills in these blanks. Readers are privy to Pugachev's thoughts, dreams, and innermost urges, as in the following passage pertaining to his miserable life before the uprising: "Tossing from side to side, Yemelyan once again dwelled all night on the poverty, wretchedness, and need in which his family lived. 'How are they getting along without him? His wife, Sophia, had probably grown even thinner; his little daughters Agrafena and Christina were starving just like him, and his son Trishka was probably at his wit's end.' And Yemelya dreamed all night of aromatic and soft baked rolls, pancakes with hemp oil and onion. In his imagination he devoured a whole plate of them, chasing the food down with home-brewed mash and beer" (*Chernyi god,* 85–86).

Among the reasons why this rather ordinary—and basically good—peasant turns into a rebel are endless poverty and starvation. His dreams of gluttony could not be more different than the unbridled ambitions and Dionysian urges of Pugachev in *The Captain's Daughter.* Which is not to say that Pushkin ignores the "material" aspects of his Pugachev, including food and drink. Their function, however, is quite different[28] and has nothing to do with physiology. The latter is emphasized by Danilevsky in the scene where Pugachev, assuming a royal identity for the first time, is torn between the need to present his claim before a group of Cossacks and the desire to finish his meal, which has been interrupted by their arrival: "'Oh my children, my dear ones!' exclaimed Pugachev, breaking off from his meal, although the freshly cut and aromatic melon beckoned to him . . . 'Oh, how much I've suffered!'" (*Chernyi god,* 104). This freshly cut melon should not be mistaken for a proto-acmeist detail (the fruit's translucent white flesh encased by an amber shell) since it points not to the beauty of the fleeting moment but rather to the workings of Pugachev's digestive juices, which are superimposed on the picture of historical events. A close equivalent of this scene is found in *War and Peace,* where Kutuzov munches on chicken in the midst of the Russian armageddon. Tolstoy's chicken, however, is ultimately less degrading: unlike Danilevsky's Pugachev, who is conditioned by his physiological urges, Tolstoy's Kutuzov is endowed with higher form of historical wisdom.

In the mid-1860s objections against presenting history through a realistic narrative prism were voiced by surviving representatives of the vanished romantic era in connection with *War and Peace.* This was largely "retrograde" criticism of an innovative artistic approach. In the 1890s realistic conventions were already being attacked as clichés. Of paramount importance in the field of the historical novel are Leontiev's thoughts on *War and Peace*, which were subsequently developed by Merezhkovsky. In addition to Tolstoy, Leontiev also commented on Salias and his *Men of Pugachev*. He considered Salias to be among the more talented contemporary writers and also accepted his general view of the rebellion, which agreed with Leontiev's own pessimistic outlook. However, as with Tolstoy, he noted the incompatibility of Salias's realistic narrative with the epoch in question, contrasting it with the spirit of authenticity in *The Captain's Daughter*: "The Grinev story is fragrant with the eighteenth century, but Count Salias's *Men of Pugachev* smells more of the 1860s and 1870s. In other words, it is not fragrant but rather [exudes] an overripe stench of [. . .] the Natural school. It seems coarse from excess attentiveness, detail, and even subtlety of observation" (30). The very emergence of such criticism attested to a crisis with respect to the realist paradigm.

7

The End of Progress

Facets of the Modernist Paradigm

Turn of the Century

The second peak in the Russian historical novel, which began in the 1870s, lasted throughout the remainder of the imperial period. For obvious reasons it slowed down with the outbreak of World War I and virtually came to a standstill during the Revolution and civil war, which, among other things, disrupted the established system of literary logistics. The genre made a comeback in the 1920s and continued to prosper both in the Soviet Union and in emigration. According to my data, the quantitative dynamics for the late imperial period are as follows: 1870s (44 new titles), 1880s (116), 1890s (164), 1900s (174), 1910–17 (118). The steep rise in the 1880s and 1890s attests to the increased popularity of the genre as well as the rapid expansion of Russian readership and the overall growth of the literary "industry." Drawing on statistics from public libraries, bibliographer Nikolai Rubakin considers the historical novel to be one the most widely read genres of belles lettres at the turn of the twentieth century (5–6).

More than one hundred authors cultivated the genre during the quarter century prior to the Revolution. By far the most important was Dmitry Merezhkovsky, the groundbreaking writer of Russian symbolism and author of the two trilogies *Christ and Antichrist* (1895–1905) and *Kingdom of the Beast* (1908–18). *Christ and Antichrist*, Merezhkovsky's magnum opus, was among the paradigmatic works of the time. It enjoyed tremendous popularity in Russia and was also read in translation throughout Europe. Another founder of Russian symbolism, Valery Bryusov, published two important historical novels, *The Fiery Angel* (1907–8) and *The Altar of Victory* (1911–12). The futurist writer Vasily Kamensky published the novel *Stenka Razin* (1915), arguably

FIGURE 17. Illustrations from: (a) Altaev's *Two Queens* (1910, p. 63; artists B. V. Kashmensky and O. V. Obolyaninova); (b) Sizova's *Daughter of the Sun* (1908, cover; artist I. V. Ferster). (c) Osipov's *Three Lines* (1908, p. 123; artist K. N. Fridberg). (d) Fyodor Zarin's *At Dawn* (1911). A stylistic mélange in book illustration parallels the diversity in historical fiction during the prerevolutionary decade.

D

his most significant work. Although it could not rival Merezhkovsky's or even Bryusov's novels, its publication marked a landmark in futurist circles, representing a fascinating example of a modernist's take on history.

Among otherwise prominent authors who occasionally turned to the historical genre one should mention Vasily Nemirovich-Danchenko, a prolific writer and war correspondent who drew upon his family background and revived the Caucasian theme in Russian historical fiction. Lydia Charskaya, a phenomenally popular author of literature for young readers, chose historical subjects for some of her adventure novels. Nikolai Engelhardt, a publicist and literary historian, promoted conspiracy theories and used the historical genre to explore the workings of international secret societies and brotherhoods, which he saw as precursors of modern-day revolutionary organizations. Pavel Bezobrazov, a Byzantine scholar, was the only Russian novelist who specialized in this period, which—despite the pivotal role of Byzantium in early Russian history—was quite alien to the modern Russian historical imagination. (Other academics who dabbled in the belletristic tradition included K. Yarosh and German Genkel.) Another serious scholar, albeit not a member of the academic establishment, who tried his hand at historical fiction was Sergei Mintslov, who wrote three novels based on Russian and Lithuanian history. Finally, one should mention Pyotr Krasnov, future general in the tsarist army, White Cossack leader during the civil war, and Nazi collaborator, who was eventually executed by the Soviets. A prolific émigré writer, he began his literary career in the mid-1890s, publishing, among other things, a novel about fellow Cossack and 1812 hero Ataman Platov.

The majority of historical novels were authored by wholesale purveyors of the genre, including several old-timers (Count Salias, Mordovtsev, Avenarius) as well as writers who belonged to the younger generation. Among the latter the most noteworthy was Prince Mikhail Volkonsky. Continuing in the tradition of Salias and his own uncle, Karnovich, he wrote about twenty novels dealing mostly with the "clandestine history" of the eighteenth and early nineteenth centuries. Other prolific authors included Nikolai Geintse, N. Severin (Nadezhda Merder), Nikolai Alekseev, Dmitry Dmitriev, Aleksandr Krasnitsky, Vladimir Lebedev, the Zarin brothers, Lev Zhdanov, among others (see appendix B). Their works vary greatly in terms of literary merit and historical preparation. As usual, historical settings were often used as a mere pretext for adventure stories or as an outlet for cheap sensationalism. The latter became especially rampant with the relaxation of censorship in the wake of the Revolution of 1905, giving rise to series like "The Private Lives of the Monarchs" and "Secrets of Royalty."

In delimiting the modernist period in historical fiction, one should bear in mind that there was no visible break in the evolution of the genre comparable to the one that took place in the mid-nineteenth century, which clearly separated the tradition of the 1830s and 1840s from the emerging realistic paradigm of the 1860s. Quite the contrary: in quantitative terms, there was a steady growth from the 1870s until the Revolution. Moreover, some authors

FIGURE 18. Ilya Repin's illustration for Leskov's *Mountain* in *Zhivopisnoe obozrenie* (1890, no 1, p. 28). Turn-of-the-century novels became increasingly cosmopolitan in their subject matter. This trend was foreshadowed in the mid- and late-1880s by Nikolai Leskov, who wrote several stylized tales based on *The Prologue*, a Russo-Byzantine hagiographic collection. In *The Mountain* he brings Egyptian and Roman topics into the context of early Christianity.

who began their career during the heyday of realism remained active at the turn of the century.

However, following the general trajectory of Russian culture, in the mid-1890s the historical novel entered a new phase. The shift can already be seen in terms of subject matter. While domestic themes understandably remained dominant, there was a sharp increase in foreign topics, which accounted for a fifth of the numerical output and included Merezhkovsky's and Bryusov's masterpieces.[1] Roman and Egyptian subjects were especially popular in the 1890s.[2] In the 1900s the focus shifted to western European history (see appendix A). This process, which was paralleled in the visual arts (in the transition from the nationalist and populist preoccupations of the Wanderers to the notion of universal beauty in the World of Art), reflected the growing sense of cosmopolitism of turn-of-the-century Russia—which Osip Mandelstam retrospectively termed "nostalgia for world culture."

Such a broadening of horizons was duly noticed by critics associated with the modernist movement. Referring to the historical novels of Merezhkovsky

FIGURE 19 (left and above). Princess Lyudmila Shakhovskaya's illustrations for *Tarquinius Superbus* (1902, pp. 7, 73). A graphomaniac on the loose, Shakhovskaya published two-dozen novels from Roman history. Some of them are furnished with illustrations of her own, which could either question her sanity or qualify her as the grandmother of Russian primitivism.

and Bryusov, a reviewer for the journal *Apollo* notes: "Finally we are tackling artistic and, generally speaking, spiritual questions in the gigantic expanses of world history. This is a marvelous achievement after the total preoccupation of Dostoevsky and Tolstoy with native reality" (Chudovskii, 76). Lyubov Gurevich, however, does not see this penchant for historical exoticism as a peculiarly Russian phenomenon, linking it instead to general trends in contemporary European art: "All of our artistic modernity—not only Russian but European as well, the entire trend of the arts prevalent in the last decade of the nineteenth century and the first decade of the twentieth, not only in literature but also in painting—is colored by this love of the exotic, of the remote, the originally colorful, that which is enchanting either in its striking primitivism or stylish beauty and perfection, attractive in its inaccessibility" (143). Moreover, she interprets it not as universalism but rather as a variety of escapism. Reviewing Bryusov's *Fiery Angel,* Gurevich notes that the so-called modernists seem to be least interested in contemporary reality.

The flight from reality, however, was only temporary. Typical in this respect is the trajectory of Merezhkovsky's historical imagination: in his first trilogy he begins with the late Roman Empire in *Julian the Apostate* (1895), proceeds to Renaissance Italy in *Leonardo* (1901), and returns to domestic history in *Peter and Alexis* (1904). Starting out as a confirmed cosmopolitan, he gradually developed a keen interest in his native land. However, unlike his socially minded predecessors, he approached Russia from historiosophic and eschatological angles.

Vasily Rozanov attributes this change to Merezhkovsky's visit to the Kerzhenets Forests near Nizhny Novgorod, a territory traditionally populated by Russian Old Believers. Merezhkovsky, who made the trip in preparation for *Peter and Alexis,* was stunned to discover a rural culture uncorrupted by modern civilization and reared in a mixture of folk legend and expectations of the "final days." Such encounters, combined with Merezhkovsky's own historiosophic conclusions, conditioned his interest in Russia as the land of the Apocalypse and New Christianity. Here is how Rozanov recorded Merezhkovsky's words: "The West has already lost its faith. Russia is the new land of faith! Petersburg, with its positivism and social issues, is rotten; it is re-belching the West. . . . However, the real Russia—those women and muzhiks of Kerzhenets with their legends, and those pine forests where you can ride along and suddenly encounter an icon nailed to a tree like an ancient nymph deity in the Hellenic forests—this Russia is the world of the future, the new, risen Christ, the reconciliation of the nymphs with the winged St. John, Hellenism and Christianity, Christ and Dionysus" (71).

In reviving such mystical nationalism (which continues the tradition of the Slavophiles, Dostoevsky, and Vladimir Solovyov) Merezhkovsky presaged important trends in Russian culture. Several years later, in the period between the revolutions, a mystical interest in Russia would spread among a wide spectrum of Russian intellectuals and writers, including the younger symbolists. In his essay "On the Russian Idea" (1909) Vyacheslav Ivanov articulated the essence of this renewed attention to Russianness: "The mystics of the East and West agree that during this particular period the Slavonic peoples, and especially Russia, have been passed a certain torch. . . . Whether or not our people will be able to carry this torch is a matter of the world's destiny. It will be a tragedy not only for our people but for everyone if they drop it, and a blessing for the entire world if they manage to bear it up. We fear for humanity, and humanity is undergoing a great crisis through us" ("O russkoi idee," 318–19). Merezhkovsky's second trilogy—consisting of one play intended for reading (*Paul I* [1908]) and two novels (*Alexander I*

FIGURE 20. An illustration from Altaev's *Two Queens* (1910, p. 370; artists B. V. Kashmensky and O. V. Obolyaninova). The turn-of-the-century infatuation with mysticism found its way into many historical novels.

[1911] and *December 14* [1918])—is entirely devoted to Russian subject matter. Combining eschatological historiosophy with growing political radicalism, Merezhkovsky portrays the Russian autocracy and its union with the official church as the "kingdom of the Beast."

In terms of general poetics, the main peculiarity of the turn-of-the-century historical novel lies in the coexistence of several paradigms, which is different from the largely monoparadigmatic situation of the previous periods. Once again developments in the genre parallel those on the broader literary and cultural scene. On the one hand, there is a continuation of the realistic tradition, which approached historical fiction as a kind of entertaining historiography. Especially popular was the "biographie romancée," its most prominent practitioners being the veteran writer Vasily Avenarius and the young, prolific author Al. Altaev (Margarita Yamshchikova), who specialized in Renaissance Europe. In describing the nature of her works, Altaev displays a rather flippant attitude toward the divide between historiography and fiction. On one occasion she claims that although her piece is subtitled a "historical tale," which implies the presence of fiction, "each episode, each event, and each element is founded on fact, and only the story itself is given a lively narrative form" (*Apostol istiny*, ii). On other occasions she dismisses the issue of pedantic factuality altogether:

> The author did not at all intend to present full biographic information and avoided any kind of deliberations aimed at establishing and checking the facts. Where an issue presented controversy, the author made the decision to use that which seemed more felicitous to him and, in general, more probable as established fact, and embodied it a vivid image. [. . .] There is no pedantic reproduction of historical facts in the book, and the words the author puts into the characters' mouths, individual scenes, and pictures are not always documented by fact, but they always arise logically from the basic features of the moral makeup of each individual. (*Svetochi pravdy*, 3–4)

More factual works falling within such a genre can be classified as a "lighter" variety of historiography: they usually lack a critical apparatus and are marked by vivid, novelistic narration. Hundreds of such popular biographies appeared at the turn of the century, many of them in the famous series "Life of Remarkable People," published by Florenty Pavlenkov.[3] Still other biographical tales contain a visible element of fictionality and remain closer to the historical novel. However, it is sometimes difficult to differentiate between the two varieties of "biographie romancée."

As was the case during the 1870s and 1880s, both biographical tales and historical novels were perceived as part of the historiographical continuum. In addition, they were widely recognized for their educational value. Reacting to Mordovtsev's thoughts about the merging of history and belles lettres, in 1878 a contemporary reviewer remarked sarcastically that Russian schoolchildren would soon be required to use the novels of Count Salias and Solovyov as history textbooks (N. N., 167). This ironic prognosis almost came true. For example, lists of recommended reading for high schools included Avenarius's biographical tales about Pushkin and Gogol (*Russkie pisateli,* 1:17), while bibliographers compiled references on historical fiction geared for pedagogical use. In 1902 Avgusta Mezier published the first comprehensive index of Russian and translated historical novels arranged thematically.[4] Interpreting the notion of the historical novel very broadly, she also lists drama and poetry. Most interestingly, she often mixes modern historical novels with ancient and medieval works of literature. As a result, Homer's epics and Shakespeare's plays share equal footing with the novels of Scott, Pushkin, Flaubert, Danilevsky, Sienkiewicz, Merezhkovsky, and numerous others. Mezier's book opens with an essay by Nikolai Rubakin, another prominent bibliographer (himself the author of several historical tales), who makes an eloquent case for using historical fiction in teaching history. A younger bibliographer named Dora Zandberg compiled a systematic guide to historical novels for schoolteachers, where she outlined political, socioeconomic, and cultural issues touched upon by the works in question. Her entry on Merezhkovsky's *Leonardo,* for example, contains the following thematic breakdown: "Development of large-scale trade. [. . .] Fragmentation of Italy. [. . .] General nature and ways of political life in fifteenth-century Italy. [. . .] The teachings of Macchiavelli and his relationship to the political life of Italy in his day. [. . .] Leonardo da Vinci: considerable moral tolerance flowing from recognition that all phenomena are natural. [. . .] Italian mores in the fifteenth century (cruelty, profligacy)" (Zandberg 41–42). Reading this summary of Merezhkovsky's novel, whose thrust is above all mystical and historiosophic, one cannot help but recall Nabokov's digression in *Speak, Memory* about "librarians and bibliographers . . . good, simple souls."

At the same time, there was an erosion of the positivist approach to historical fiction connected with the general crisis of realist literature and, more broadly, with the cultural changes that occurred as core beliefs of the positivist worldview were questioned. An important symptom of this change was the spread of interest in mysticism and the occult, which had already begun in the mid-1870s and had reached new heights around the turn of the century. In the area of historical fiction, mystical themes appeared in the late 1880s in the works of Vsevolod Solovyov and other writers in the context of the "clandestine history" of the eighteenth century. Beginning in the mid-1890s, this connection was further developed by Prince Volkonsky. Belonging in a league of their own are the quasi-historical novels of Vera Kryzhanovskaya (Rochester), which began to appear in the early 1890s. Set in ancient Egypt, ancient Rome, and medieval Europe, her works represent a peculiar example of the occult novel in Russian literature. Such novels are unique in the history of the genre since the supernatural leaves no room for rational explanation. Even the romantics avoided such one-sidedness when toying with the ambiguity of miraculous occurrences. Otherworldly incursions destroy the inner logic of the realistic narrative, but otherwise the mystical novels contain nothing new in terms of artistic innovation.[5]

A new paradigm in Russian historical fiction appeared within the context of nascent modernist art. Far less coherent and uniform than romantic or realistic models, it can best be defined as *a negativo*. Reflecting contemporary philosophical trends and, more broadly, the emerging modernist weltanschauung, the turn-of-the-century historical imagination rejected the idea of continual progress that served as the basis of nineteenth-century thought.[6] As Nikolai Berdyaev would later conclude in *The End of Our Time*, historical explanation as a generator of meanings had been discredited. The idea of historical process informed by immanent forces that are describable by means of deterministic scientific analysis had been shattered. Instead, history was now perceived as a multidimensional projection of atemporal archetypes. Ultimately modernist thought took the leap from the realm of history into that of metahistory.[7] This had far-reaching implications for the genre of the historical novel since the issues of fact and fiction were transposed onto a totally different plane, now being conditioned not by a quasi-scientific approach but rather by a mythopoetic consciousness. Merezhkovsky and the Russian symbolists were among the harbingers of "neomythologism" in modern European culture.[8]

Dracula in the Summer Garden: The Multiple Realities of Merezhkovsky's Christ and Antichrist

A defining work of Russian symbolist prose, Merezhkovsky's trilogy is also one of the first examples of an extended neomythological text in modern literature. In the trilogy Merezhkovsky develops his historiosophic scheme, which revolves around the eternal conflict between two diametrically opposed elements and the ever-present yearning for their synthesis. One of these elements is the "truth of Dionysus," or "the lower abyss," while the other is the "truth of Christ," or the "upper abyss." Merezhkovsky sees both the truth and limitations in each of these principles. While paganism celebrates the beauty of the material world and the human body, it is devoid of spirituality. Christianity, conversely, attains the heights of spirituality at the expense of earthly beauty and the human body. The ideal lies in the great synthesis of Christianity and paganism, or the emergence of New Christianity, which is only attainable in the eschatological perspective.[9] Hence the main theme of the trilogy: the struggle, interaction, and interpenetration of Christianity and paganism throughout the ages. In *Death of the Gods (Julian the Apostate)* Merezhkovsky portrays the victory of Christianity over Julian's abortive attempt to restore the old religion. However, paganism returns with a vengeance during the Renaissance, which is described in *The Gods Resurrected (Leonardo da Vinci)*. The final novel of the trilogy, *The Antichrist (Peter and Alexis)*, depicts the renewed triumph of paganism, which—with Petrine reforms—invades Holy Russia. And yet the "Antichrist Tsar" fails to overcome Christianity, which finds refuge in the passionate faith of the Old Believers, who are full of eschatological expectations. The overarching dichotomy of the two abysses is refracted in numerous recurring plot components, character types, situations, and other elements that bind the novels of the trilogy together through an intricate system of symbols and correspondences.[10] The underlying code, however, can always be reduced to the primordial binary. Here is Andrei Bely's formulation:

> There is binary division in everything, between chaos and cosmos, flesh and spirit, paganism and Christianity, the unconscious and the conscious, Dionysus and Apollo, Christ and Antichrist. The contrast between the upper and lower abyss, in turn, runs through each antynomy. Thus, the spirit of Christ can be found behind the mask of the Apollonian and behind the mask of the Dionysian. . . . The same is true of the spirit of the Antichrist. This results in complex configurations, which are akin to crystallographic models. [. . .] The untutored readers of Merezhkovsky often become confused by the complex configurations of his historical counterpoint of ideas. But it is so simple: all we must do is find a principle for classification. ("Merezhkovskii," 144)

The same historiosophic scheme applies, mutatis mutandis, to all of Merezhkovsky's works in various genres throughout the balance of his life.[11] Merezhkovsky himself was fully aware of this. In the preface to the 1914 edition of his collected works he declared: "Between these books, despite their differences and even their dissonance, there does exist an indissoluble connection. These are links in a chain, parts of a whole. They are not a series of books, but one book printed in several parts purely out of convenience. One book about one theme" (*Pss,* 1:v). Merezhkovsky's oeuvre can indeed be viewed as a gigantic cycle that pushes to an extreme the symbolist penchant for cyclization and—what is most relevant for the present discussion—also resonates with his cyclical historiosophic scheme, creating yet another level of correspondences.[12]

Although Merezhkovsky's novels are mythological and metahistorical, they are the product of thorough scholarly preparation. A person of impressive erudition, with a solid background in classical and modern languages, Merezhkovsky researched a broad range of primary and secondary sources and also undertook "study trips" for *Leonardo* and *Peter and Alexis.* As a result, the trilogy contains meticulous reproductions of historical realia that link it to the positivist tradition and to the European archaeological novel in particular. In fact, the first novel of the trilogy (initially entitled *The Outcast*) was mistaken for a work in that genre. This outraged Pyotr Pertsov, a publisher and critic, who realized the uniqueness of his friend's work. He expressed his indignation in a letter to Bryusov: "I am not gladdened [. . .] by the success of this novel. I would have preferred the frank boorishness of not understanding to the traitorous compliments that, in a show of special favor, compare Merezhkovsky with . . . Ebers! They see in *The Outcast* a biography of Julian, something like a sequel to Pavlenkov's series, and in the revolt of the gods they see the archaeological digs of historical belles lettres. All of this has come about because the novel's title contains the masking word 'historical'!" (quoted in Sobolev, 3).

Although this misunderstanding did not last long, numerous critics dwelled upon Merezhkovsky's love for historical detail, often rebuking him for overindulgence in archaeological realia. Bely remarked: "Merezhkovsky tends to construct an archaeological museum out of his novels. [. . .] Everything is called by its right name, and to each utensil a label is affixed" ("Merezhkovskii," 139–41). Another reviewer was more blunt, complaining that in the trilogy "there is one flaw that is strongly detrimental to the artistic side: there is too much history" (Bogdanovich, 9). The harshest verdict on Merezhkovsky's "naturalism"—and his work in general—was handed down by Georg Lukács: "If one needs convincing of this relationship between naturalism, philistinism, and decadence, one has a particularly blatant example of it in Merezhkovsky, a typical decadent of the imperialist age who belongs with the drunken philistines. With him the historical novel really does become an organ of reactionary demagogy and hostility toward the people. If one looks a little more closely at the false profundity of these novels, one discovers remarkably naturalistic features beneath the mystical veil" (249). Lukács, however, confuses the relationship between the two elements in Merezhkovsky: it is not the mysticism that serves as a veil for naturalism but vice versa. The naturalistic surface of history is just a film—the "veil of Maya," to use the symbolists' favorite term, derived from Buddhism via Schopenhauer—an illusory shroud of the material world that is spread over its deep mystical content.

In addition to abundant archaeological details, Merezhkovsky employs an extraordinary amount of direct and indirect quotation. Contemporaries were keen to notice his citation mania—"an artillery barrage of citations and the words of others," as one reviewer stated (Ivanov-Razumnik, 133)—which often served as a target for critical attacks. For example, claiming that Merezhkovsky always hid behind somebody else's words, Leon Trotsky accused him of "spiritual cowardice," a charge that is hardly justified since Merezhkovsky never concealed his stance.[13] Moreover, whereas Merezhkovsky carefully avoids modernization in the realm of material realia, his quotations and literary allusions are boldly retouched and reshuffled; he does not hesitate to put the utterance of one historical figure into the mouth of another, thus displaying total disregard for chronological, psychological, or cultural probability. Such poetic license provoked dismayed purists like Aleksandr Amfiteatrov and Boris Sadovskoy and led to accusations of simplistic literary techniques by Victor Shklovsky.[14]

This aspect of Merezhkovsky's work has recently undergone serious reevaluation. It has been linked to essential features of modernist art in general and also to peculiar tenets of symbolist philosophy and poetics. As Zara Mints has stated: "Merezhkovsky as an artist consciously creates in the novel a peculiar poetics of quotes that becomes a kind of storehouse of symbols and, at the same time, introduces into the novel the theme of culture as a 'third reality' more important to the symbolist than the 'second' empirical reality and related to the 'first' reality, to the divine idea, as a prophecy is to its future fulfillment" ("O trilogii," 1:25). This concerns both artistic texts and texts of primary sources. Here Merezhkovsky is absolutely "omnivorous," which is quite in tune with symbolist pantheism. Since these texts exist at an intersection of several planes, Merezhkovsky takes advantage of their multidimensional nature, using them both as historical artifacts for the creation of "archaeological" color as well as symbols reflecting the ultimate meaning of history. For the latter purpose Merezhkovsky aligns the words of others in a way that releases their innermost symbolic potential. Since the issue of factual accuracy becomes irrelevant at this level of discourse, Merezhkovsky feels himself at liberty to change chronology, retouch his sources, invent quasi-documents, and otherwise alter historical evidence. After all, his own text belongs to the realm of cultural reality, entering in its own right into the maze of metahistorical reflections and correspondences.

To demonstrate the complex workings of this mechanism I wish to take as a point of departure a string of references to Bram Stoker's *Dracula* in *Peter and Alexis*. Overlooked by commentators, these allusions are especially fascinating since they represent Dracula's entrée into high Russian culture. Stoker's novel was published in Great Britain in 1897 and soon thereafter reached Russian shores. Several translations appeared at the beginning of the twentieth century, although the 1902 translation listed as its author not the obscure Stoker but the popular English writer of mystical novels Mary Corelli.[15] At this time vampire motifs, which incorporated the tradition of both romantic and folkloric vampires, penetrated various levels of Russian culture.[16] They are found in popular literature, in high literature (the most famous examples here being Blok's "Black Blood" and "The Dark Carpathians"), in the antigovernment rhetoric during the Revolution of 1905, and, finally, in the thought of such eccentrics as the Bolshevik philosopher and fiction writer Aleksandr Bogdanov. In his futuristic fantasies Bogdanov crossed Marxism with the idea of "beneficial vampirism," partially realizing his obsession after the Revolution by becoming head of the Blood Transfusion Institute.[17] However, the employment of vampire motifs in Merezhkovsky chronologically preceded all these developments. With his keen sense for new cultural trends, Merezhkovsky discerned the powerful mythological potential of *Dracula,* a work of neogothic pulp fiction, and incorporated it into the system of historiosophic symbols in the final novel of his trilogy.

Allusions to *Dracula* are introduced in *Peter and Alexis* in connection with the central pagan symbol of the trilogy, the statue of Venus of Tauria, which incorporated various feminine cults of antiquity: "It was a sculpture by Praxiteles, Aphrodite-Anadiomene, she who was born of the froth of the sea, and Urania the heavenly, the ancient Phoenician Astarte, the Babylonian Militta, protomother of the world, the great Benefactress, she who filled the sky with stars like seeds, and poured the Milky Way as milk from her breasts" (*Pss,* 4:30). In the first novel of the trilogy this statue inspires Emperor Julian to rebel against Christianity. Although he suffers a defeat and the pagan gods perish, Venus is reborn a millennium later, emerging from her grave in

Renaissance Italy. Purchased on commission for Peter the Great, the statue travels to Saint Petersburg in the early eighteenth century.

The festivities organized in honor of Venus in the Summer Garden form the center of book 1 of *Peter and Alexis,* in many ways establishing the system of reference for the entire novel. Here is Merezhkovsky's description of the goddess's arrival: "Across oceans and rivers, mountains and plains, cities and deserts, and, finally, through the poor Russian villages, dark forests and swamps, everywhere protected jealously by the will of the tsar, rocking back and forth on the waves, or to the rhythmic motion of soft springs in her dark box, as in a cradle or a coffin, the goddess made her long journey from the Eternal City to the newly founded town of Petersburg" (4:27). "Poor villages" is a quotation from Fyodor Tyutchev, who describes Rus as the land of Christ. In the balance of his description Merezhkovsky obviously alludes to the story of Dracula's voyage from Transylvania to England. Later on the vampire motifs become even more pronounced:

> The crowd made way for the strange procession. The tsar's brawny men-in-waiting and grenadiers bore the long black box that resembled a coffin on their shoulders with difficulty, bending under the weight. Judging by the size of the coffin, the corpse was of superhuman height. They placed the box on the ground. The sovereign—alone and without any assistance—undertook to open it. [. . .] He was in a hurry and pulled out the nails with such impatience that he scratched his hand so that blood flowed. [. . .] The last nails bent their way out, the wood made a cracking noise, the lid raised and the box opened. At first they saw something gray and yellow resembling the dust of crumbled bones in a grave. These were pine shavings, sawdust, felt and bits of combed wool placed in the box as cushioning. (4:28–29)

One might argue that allusions to Dracula in this passage are farfetched since what emerges from the coffin is not the foul undead with hairy palms but rather the radiant goddess of love, who brings Olympian light to the darkness of northern Hades. Nevertheless, echoes of Stoker's novel are totally appropriate in the scheme of Merezhkovsky's novel. First—and this is not ungrounded historically—adherents of the pious Christian ways saw pagan gods as creatures from hell invading the earth. As one such traditionalist explains to the tsarevich on the way to the festivities: "The gods are really demons who, driven from their temples in the name of the crucified Christ, have fled to empty, dark, abysmal places and nested there, pretending to be dead and nonexistent for a time. When early Christianity deteriorated [. . .]

these gods came to life, crawling out from their dens and—just like any base worm or bug or any other poisonous vermin that hatches from its eggs to sting people—thus did the demons emerge from these ancient idols—their cocoons—to sting and destroy Christian souls" (4:20). Thus, Venus, the "white she-devil," and vampires belong to the same category of stinging demons who emerge from under the ground. Besides, vampirism in Stoker has strong sexual connotations, which further links the Transylvanian count to the goddess of love. In addition, there is a Russian connection in Stoker's novel: both on his way to England and during his flight back to Transylvania, Dracula charters ships that fly the Russian flag. In this context, his arrival in the capital of the Russian navy can be viewed as a courtesy call of sorts. Finally, Venus and Dracula can be seen as extreme variations on the theme of carnal immortality and, as such, perfectly fit Merezhkovsky's theory of bifurcation as described by Bely.[18]

Peter and Alexis opens with an apocalyptic prophesy as one of the characters announces the coming of the Antichrist, whose way has already been paved by the arrival of lesser devils. This clearly presages the festivities in the Summer Garden and also parallels the master's arrival in *Dracula*. The chief worshiper of Venus/Dracula in Merezhkovsky's novel is Tsar Peter, likewise a figure of supernatural stature with enormous symbolic import, whose hypostases range from the Antichrist to God the Father. One of his incarnations—that of the werewolf (*oboroten'*), as the tsarevich terms it—is clearly vampiric. The blood on Peter's finger, the result of a scratch caused while removing the statue from its coffin, is the first drop in the novel's bloodbath, which will involve both historical executions and premonitions of apocalyptic cataclysms. Peter figures prominently in this sanguinary picture, often with overt vampiric connotations. "[He] cannot survive without drinking blood. Any day he drinks some blood he is merry, and on those days when he does not, he is not himself!" (4:56). Further in the novel this metaphorical invective is realized in the most gruesome fashion. Here, for example, is Peter—with his characteristic hands-on attitude—torturing one of the rebel leaders: "The [*strelets*] endures all in silence. His body already resembles a bloody carcass from which the butchers have removed the hide. But he is silent and only gazes directly into the tsar's eyes as if laughing at him. Suddenly the dying man lifts his head and spits into the tsar's eyes. 'Take that, you son of a dog, you Antichrist!' The tsar draws a dagger from its sheath and plunges it into his neck. Blood spurts onto the tsar's face" (247). In yet another bloody scene Peter personally beheads twenty mutineers during a feast in the Kremlin: "He would down a glass and chop off a head, thus, glass after glass, blow after blow. Wine and blood flowed together and wine mixed with blood" (67). This peculiar cocktail consumed by Peter also implies the black-mass travesty of the Eucharist, which both fits Merezhkovsky's concept of antithetic similarity and is also inherent in the vampire myth.

Another worshiper of Venus/Dracula present at the festivities is Pyotr Andreyevich Tolstoy, a prominent figure of the Petrine epoch and the progenitor of the Counts Tolstoy clan. His portrait also contains conspicuous vampiric features: "'He is all velvety but he has a little stinger,' they would say of him. [. . .] This 'elegant and supreme gentleman' had on his conscience more than one dark, evil, and even bloody deed" (29). Merezhkovsky depicts him as a ruthless Machiavellian, an indefatigable womanizer, a man who assimilated subtleties of the European gallant culture, and, finally, a littérateur. The latter is pure invention. Tolstoy wrote travelogues about Italy but never tried his hand at belles lettres. As Zara Mints notes in her commentary to the trilogy, although Merezhkovsky is fully aware of this, he nonetheless ascribes to Tolstoy Prince Antiokh Kantemir's verses "About Cupid," Kantemir's translation of Anacreon's "Bacchus, a Child of Zeus," Vasily Tredyakovsky's song "A Supplication to Love," and a quotation from the diary of Prince Boris Kurakin. The famous gallant verses cited by Tolstoy are permeated by images of being stung and stinging, referring to the time-honored image of sex yet also—following the familiar logic of the Merezhkovskian conceit—further underscoring vampire motifs introduced at the beginning of the episode.

As elsewhere, the anachronisms and reshufflings in this salvo of Merezhkovsky's quotations are intentional. Merezhkovsky needs them to endow Tolstoy with a very specific set of features. He serves as an embodiment of the pagan element, creating a bridge between Petrine Russia and the Italian Renaissance and—traveling farther back in time—with ancient Rome. Pyotr Andreyevich simultaneously points toward the future and can be interpreted as a symbolic prefiguration of his descendant, the great writer Leo Tolstoy.

Lest this proposition appear absurd, one should recall that Merezhkovsky postponed his work on the concluding part of the trilogy in order to write a book on Tolstoy and Dostoevsky (1901), which is likewise based on the antithesis of the two abysses. According to Merezhkovsky's oft-quoted formulation, Dostoevsky is the "seer of the spirit," while Tolstoy is the "seer of the flesh," regardless of his later moralistic sermons. Hence the link between the two Tolstoys: they belong to the same aristocratic clan, share a markedly carnal name (*tolstyi*, stout, corpulent), and are octogenarians endowed with extraordinary vitality, in a way cheating death by exceeding their allotted life span, which puts them in the same category with Dracula. Merezhkovsky enhances these similarities by introducing a fictional correspondence in making both writers.

Needless to say, this does not diminish the tremendous difference between the forefather and his scion. One Tolstoy preaches nonviolence, opposes the death penalty, and denounces the state, while the other is an unscrupulous courtier and the future head of the infamous Secret Chancellery. One speaks of carnal love with disgust in his old age, while the other "could cut the young pursuers of Venus off at the waist with his amiable approach to the women" (4:29). One is a vegetarian, opposed to shedding blood in any form, while the other joyfully greets the arrival of the vampire on Russian shores. These differences make their projection onto each other especially titillating. Thus, the shadow of the vampire in *Peter and Alexis* spreads over the sage from Yasnaya Polyana.[19]

Given the relentless antithetical trajectory of Merezhkovsky's thought, one cannot avoid the question concerning Dostoevsky, Tolstoy's antipode. Dostoevskian allusions are extremely prominent in *Peter and Alexis*. Predictably, some of them have vampiric connotations. For example, in the opening scene the tsarevich's room in infested with flies: "Flies buzzed, swarmed, and crawled everywhere in thick black legions" (4:13). They are so ubiquitous and importunate that eventually it seems to Alexis that there is "a huge sticky black fly" buzzing inside of his head (15). This recalls Dostoevskian insects signaling an evil presence (e.g., the fly heralding Svidrigailov's apparition in Raskolnikov's room). At the same time, there is an obvious link with the obsession with flies that takes hold of Renfield in anticipation of Dracula's arrival. Both of these sources resonate with the entomological imagery in the passage describing pagan gods emerging from beneath the ground like "any base worm or bug or any other poisonous vermin," culminating in the arrival of Venus in a coffin resembling Dracula's.

Another coupling of Dracula with Dostoevsky occurs in the pervasive fog enveloping Merezhkovsky's Saint Petersburg, which functions as an important symbol in the novel. Its most obvious Russian references include Gogol and Dostoevsky, who are among the chief creators of Petersburgian mythology. However, since the vampiric subtext of *Peter and Alexis* has already been established, a link to Stoker's novel should not be overlooked. There it also functions as a markedly mystical meteorological condition: the unnatural fog envelops the ship carrying the vampire to England; under the cover of fog he flees back to Transylvania, where fog conceals his castle; he enters into Mina's bedroom as a stream of fog, and so forth. Throughout Stoker's novel the mention of fog invariably signals the presence of the vampire, which adds an eerie dimension to the picture of the northern capital as portrayed by Merezhkovsky. Characteristically, the fog is also linked to Venus, as in the episode where the God seeker Tikhon, recovering from a fit of epilepsy (a markedly Dostoevskian illness), describes the following early-morning scene: "The mist turned a rosy hue as if blood had surged into the pale forms of apparitions. And the marble form of the goddess Venus in the middle gallery over the Neva turned warm and rosy, as if alive. [. . .] The body of the goddess was airy and pink like a cloud of mist, and the mist was alive and warm like the body of the goddess. The mist was her body, in her were all things, and she was everything" (4:83–84). Here the sickly Petersburgian fog seemingly changes its valence while still retaining its vampiric connotations, thus forming yet another antithetical link on the canvas of the trilogy.

Although some elements of this pattern may be quite ingenious and unexpected, its underlying algorithm is very predictable. Hence the widespread opinion that, despite Merezhkovsky's enormous erudition, his work remains overly dry, rational, and schematic. For example, Ivanov-Razumnik compares Merezhkovsky to Pushkin's Salieri, who can dissect the corpse of music but is powerless to create genuine art. "Characters without faces, without souls; walking anitheses, personified rational oppositions. [. . .] Their bifurcation, their breakup lies in D. Merezhkovsky himself, who is always trying to leap from the 'upper abyss' to the 'lower abyss' and build a bridge of words between them" (2:137). Andrei Bely likewise clearly sees the mechanics of Merezhkovsky's work: "He selects images for his schemata. Because of this living people [. . .] become dolls gussied up with archaeological rags. They become emblems of lifeless schemata" ("Merezhkovskii," 147) However, when approached from the symbolist perspective Bely discerns in the trilogy's endless reflections and correspondences a glimpse into "the labyrinthine abyss of mystery" ("O trilogii," 420) and hails it as a landmark in Russian literature.

Merezhkovsky's novels are indeed so peculiar that even such a perceptive critic as Vladislav Khodasevich found it impossible to classify them: "Merezhkovsky is apocalyptic, not historical. You'll never learn 'history' by reading his works. There have *never* been such people or events as one finds in his [novels]. 'Because they *always* exist,' Merezhovsky would say. Merezhkovsky is not about what 'happens' but about what was, is, and will be. This decidedly removes his writings from the category of the novel, whether of the historical or any other kind" (539). The latter is clearly an exaggeration. Merezhkovsky's novels definitely belong to the historical genre, but since his goal is to uncover in the flow of history the eternal principles of being he departs from the limitations of historical time and creates novels that are more mythological than historical in nature. In *Peter and Alexis,* other novels of the trilogy, and in his subsequent works he portrays history as the struggle between Christianity and anti-Christianity, reflected and refracted in various myths and intertextual and intercultural allusions. What ultimately interests Merezhkovsky is not the history of a chosen epoch in its own unique context but the enactment of timeless archetypal predicaments. Under the guise of realistic details and meticulous documentation Merezhkovsky presents a mythopoeic version of history shaped in accordance with the symbolist poetics, thus pioneering the modernist paradigm of the genre.

Barbarians at the Gates: Cyclical Visions of Valery Bryusov

Valery Bryusov's contributions to the genre include *The Fiery Angel* (1907–8), set in sixteenth-century Germany, and *The Altar of Victory* (1911–12), set in fourth-century Rome. (The sequel—*Jupiter Overthrown*—remained unfinished.) Drawing on his background in classical philology and history gained at Moscow University, Bryusov undertook intensive research in preparation for writing his novels.[20] Bryusov's broad erudition and scholarly bent had already been noted by reviewers in connection with *The Fiery Angel.* Liubov Gurevich, for example, saw it as an attempt at historical and cultural reconstruction based on painstaking research and endowed with the precision of a museum catalogue (146–48), while Sergei Solovyov spoke of an "impenetrable armor of scientific objectivity" encasing the tale (30). Some critics even rebuked Bryusov for providing too much history (it will be recalled that similar accusations were leveled at Merezhkovsky) and thereby falling into the ultimate trap awaiting a historical novelist. As Pyotr Kogan put it, *The Fiery Angel* is "academic research flawed by the technique of the novelist, and a novel flawed by the technique of a researcher" (3.2:109). Still other critics—especially those within symbolist circles—considered Bryusov's model of combining fact and fiction a major achievement. Mikhail Kuzmin even proclaimed *The Fiery Angel* to be "a Russian example for travelers on the road to the historical novel."[21]

Like Merezhkovsky, Bryusov saturates his work with historical realia while also undertaking a painstaking effort at linguistic stylization. All three of his historical novels are first-person narratives, mimicking memoirs written during their respective epochs. Although the ploy is obvious, Bryusov supports it on many levels. For example, he appends lengthy academic endnotes to both *The Fiery Angel* and *The Altar of Victory,* where he reflects in a mock-serious tone on the trustworthiness of particular details supplied by their alleged authors as if one were dealing with authentic historical texts.[22] In the preface to *The Fiery Angel* he comments on paleographic aspects of the original German manuscript and promises to publish the latter in the near future.[23] As a finishing touch in this game of stylization Bryusov provides *The Fiery Angel* with reproductions of sixteenth-century German engravings.

Several contemporary critics even proclaimed *The Fiery Angel* to be the first consistent and successful historical stylization in Russian literature, which is not quite accurate.[24] The pioneering author in this area was Nikolai Leskov, who in the late 1880s wrote a number of stylized tales based on *Prolog*, a medieval Russian collection of Byzantine hagiographic stories. One of Leskov's longer pieces—*The Mountain* (written in 1888 and published in 1890)—is labeled a historical novel. These stylizations drew praise from Merezhkovsky, who in his programmatic treatise *On the Reasons for the Decline and on the New Trends in Contemporary Russian Literature* (1893) lists them among positive exceptions in the bleak panorama of Russian letters. Although Merezhkovsky's own novels are based on the "objective" realistic narrative, they also contain conspicuous elements of stylization in terms of dialogue, the extensive use of documents, and in the introduction of alleged diaries of the characters (e.g., the diary of Giovanni Beltraffio in *Leonardo* and diaries of the tsarevich and maid of honor Arnheim in *Peter and Alexis*). His stylistic references include not only texts but also the visual arts. For instance, in *Leonardo* Bely notices refined allusions to Italian painting in Merezhkovsky's landscapes: "Merezhkovsky stylizes his sky a little à la Botticelli, Leonardo, or Filippino Lippi. He knows the works of the Italian masters too well for this" ("Merezhkovskii," 141). Additional examples of stylized historical narratives in Russian literature of the time could be mentioned.[25] With respect to similar developments in Europe—and France in particular—the earliest and most important precedent is Flaubert's *Salammbô* (1862) and, among later works, Anatole France's *Thaïs* (1890).

Such a penchant for stylization can be explained by the desire to escape the trap of modernization, which inevitably occurs when bygone epochs are rendered through a modern narrative prism. The first Russian critic who raised the problem theoretically was Konstantin Leontiev. In his book *Analysis, Style, and Waft* (written in 1890 and published in its entirety in 1911–12 [excerpts appeared in 1891]) he speaks of "atmospheric" distortions in Tolstoy's *War and Peace* and other realistic historical novels. Leontiev's argument was developed by Merezhkovsky in his *Tolstoy and Dostoevsky* (1901–2). The aerial metaphors of historical authenticity employed by Leontiev and

ОГНЕННЫЙ АНГЕЛЪ ИЛИ ПРАВДИВАЯ ПОВѢСТЬ,
ВЪ КОТОРОЙ РАЗСКАЗЫВАЕТСЯ О ДЬЯВОЛѢ, НЕ РАЗЪ
ЯВЛЯВШЕМСЯ ВЪ ОБРАЗѢ СВѢТЛАГО ДУХА ОДНОЙ ДѢВУШКѢ И СОБЛАЗ-
НИВШЕМЪ ЕЕ НА РАЗНЫЕ ГРѢХОВНЫЕ ПОСТУПКИ, О БОГОПРОТИВНЫХЪ
ЗАНЯТІЯХЪ МАГІЕЙ, АСТРОЛОГІЕЙ, ГОЕТЕЙЕЙ И НЕКРОМАНТІЕЙ,
О СУДѢ НАДЪ ОНОЙ ДѢВУШКОЙ ПОДЪ ПРЕДСѢДАТЕЛЬСТВОМЪ
ЕГО ПРЕПОДОБІЯ АРХІЕПИСКОПА ТРИРСКАГО,
А ТАКЖЕ О ВСТРѢЧАХЪ И БЕСѢДАХЪ
СЪ РЫЦАРЕМЪ И ТРИЖДЫ ДОКТОРОМЪ
АГРИППОЮ ИЗЪ НЕТТЕСГЕЙМА
И ДОКТОРОМЪ ФАУСТОМЪ,
НАПИСАННАЯ
ОЧЕВИДЦЕМЪ.

FIGURE 21. An illustration from the second edition of Bryusov's *Fiery Angel* (1909, p. viii). Abundant use of period engravings, graphic layout, and a dedication in Latin contribute to the elaborate stylization apparent in this novel. The text under the image reads "The Fiery Angel, or A Truthful Tale of the Devil who, in the guise of a Spirit of Light, appeared on many occasions to one Maiden and tempted her to commit many sinful deeds; about the ungodly practices of Magic, Astrology, Goety, and Necromancy; of the Trial of this Maiden presided by his Eminence the Archbishop of Trier, as well as of encounters and conversations with the Knight and thrice Doctor Agrippa von Nettesheim, and Doctor Faustus, composed by an Eyewitness."

NON ILLVSTRIVM CVIQVAM VIRORVM
ARTIVM LAVDE DOCTRINAEVE FAMA CLARORVM
AT TIBI
DOMINA LVCIDA DEMENS INFELIX
QVAE MVLTVM DILEXERAS
ET AMORE PERIERAS
NARRATIONEM HAVD MENDACEM
SERVVS DEVOTVS
AMATOR FIDELIS
SEMPITERNAE MEMORIAE CAVSA
DEDICAVI
SCRIPTOR

FIGURE 22. An illustration from the second edition of Bryusov's *Fiery Angel* (1909, p. ix). The text under the image reads "Not to any illustrious Men famous in Arts or Sciences, but to thee, o Woman of Light, Insanity, and Misfortune, who loved much and perished from Love, the Author, thy obedient servant and faithful lover, dedicates this truthful tale in the name of memory eternal."

FIGURE 23. An illustration from Charskaya's *A Bold Life: Feats of a Mysterious Hero* (1908, p. 176+). "I felt like running to you and throwing myself down on my knees before you . . ." Unarticulated sexual impulses and dubious gender-bending situations involving the "cavalry maiden" Nadezhda Durova create a peculiar tension in this novel pitched to teenage audiences. Grown-up literature of the "Silver Age" tends to be much more explicit. The absolute champion in this respect is Valery Bryusov, who spices up his novels with orgies, homosexuality, sex with minors, and bestiality.

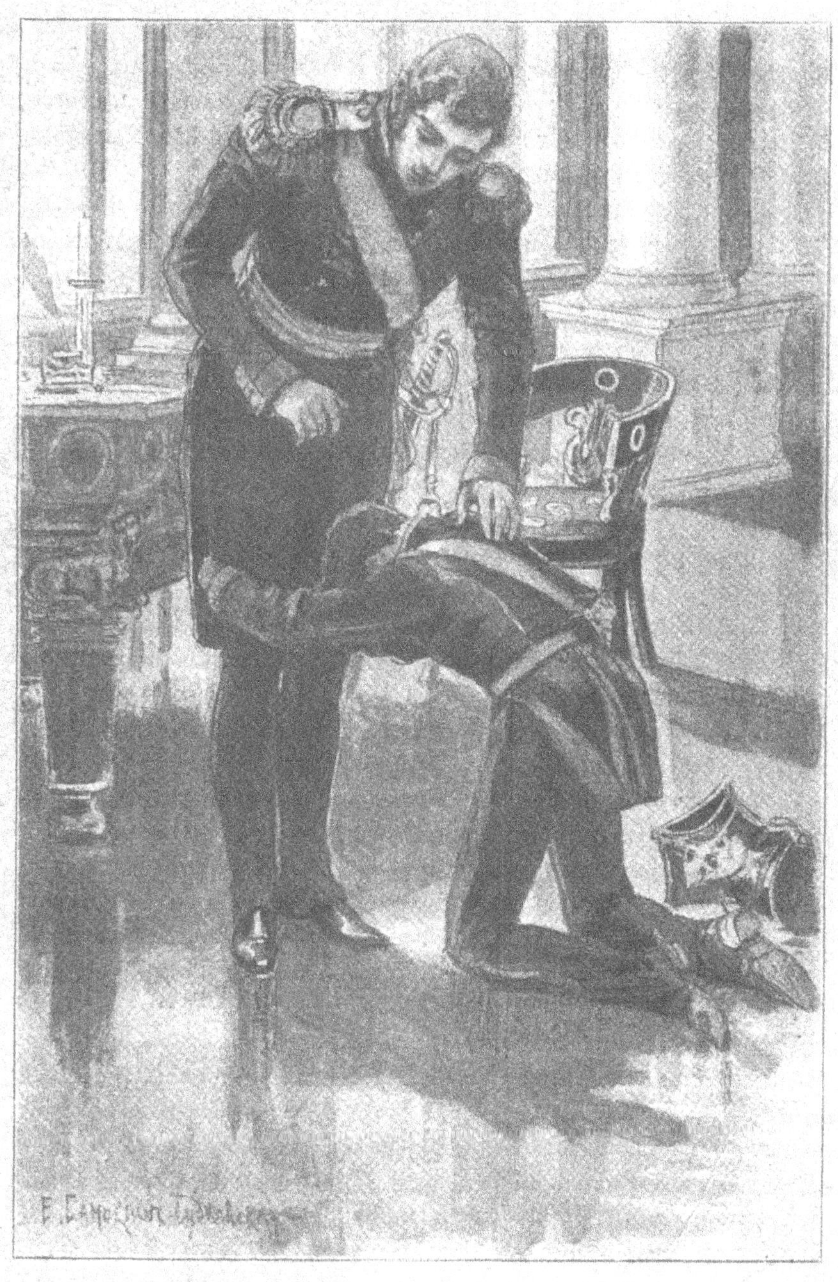

Чего же вы хотите отъ меня?—спросилъ государь...

FIGURE 24. "'So what do you want from me?'" asked the Emperor." An illustration from Charskaya's *A Bold Life* (1908, p. 206+; artist E. Samokish-Budkovskaya).

Merezhkovsky (waft/*veianie* and atmosphere, air, scent of the time/*zapakh* or *aromat vremeni*) gained wide currency in contemporary critical discourse, replacing the markedly analytical and naturalistic formula "character of the epoch" prevalent during the realistic period.

There are also specifically symbolist underpinnings for both linguistic stylization and the abundance of archaeological details. While symbolism places ultimate value on the metaphysical world and also cultivates creative subjectivity, it does not ignore the phenomenal world. The eternal symbols are not abstract notions since they exist in the multiplicity of their phenomenal manifestations. As Merezhkovsky stated in 1893: "Symbols must naturally and effortlessly emerge from the depths of reality. If the author invents them artificially to express some idea, then they become lifeless allegories that, like everything dead, are incapable of inspiring anything but revulsion" (18:216–17).[26] Vyacheslav Ivanov elaborated on this idea in 1909, postulating the concept of "realistic symbolism." According to Ivanov, the artist "should not impose his will on the surface of things (res)" but instead achieve insights into their innermost reality, which they "both conceal and signify" ("Dve stikhii," 250, 270). Hence the attention to the realia of history and to the unique "scent of time" in the works of Merezhkovsky and Bryusov.

There is, however, a significant difference between the two writers. While both strive for archaeological precision in material realia, they diverge in their approach to cultural realia and stylization. In the latter area Bryusov is much more consistent and—most important—refrains from blatant anachronisms and reshuffling of quotations, which are typical for Merezhkovsky. That is not to say that Bryusov's novels are devoid of anachronistic allusions, but these are relatively few in number and are scattered throughout the text more or less at random, whereas in Merezhkovsky they form an intricate system.[27]

The difference in attitude of Merezhkovsky and Bryusov toward cultural realia stems from their respective concepts of history. Both reject the idea of progress, sharing the mythical notion of time as eternal return characteristic of modernist thought. However, Merezhkovsky, being pronouncedly mystical and apocalyptic, is interested in atemporal similarities: the antithetical conflict between Christianity and paganism that prefigures the final Synthesis. Bryusov's concept of history is more secular and circular, lacking a clearly defined teleological perspective and emphasizing the cyclical change of relatively self-sufficient civilizations.[28] Hence there is a different attitude toward cultural realia. His attention to historical detail notwithstanding, Merezhkovsky ultimately treats culture as the realm of metaphysical prophesies. While also searching for atemporal correspondences, Bryusov conversely tends to see culture as the product of a peculiar civilization. This precludes the Merezhkovskian license in reshuffling quotations and may also account for more conscientious and meticulous stylization. Moreover, as Bryusov's notion of history evolved, his focus shifted from the universal to the unique. M. L. Gasparov has demonstrated this by analyzing translations of *The Aeneid* to which Bryusov returned throughout his life. Having begun with free renderings of Virgil, Bryusov ended up with a meticulous—and utterly unreadable—literal translation that strove to reproduce every detail of the original, including its convoluted Latin syntax, which is impossible even in such a flexible language as Russian. This is the ultimate exercise in stylization, beyond which lies only a reprinting of the original that will preserve its uniqueness without any loss en route (assuming, of course, that there is an ideal reader capable of adequately deciphering its language and the inter- and extratextual realia involved.)

In his novels, however, Bryusov still operates within the framework of the symbolist paradigm and heeds universal correspondences that shine through the plethora of historical facts. This can be seen at several levels. As has been mentioned, there are occasional anachronistic allusions, but their very scarcity and randomness seem deliberate. The intent here is not to create a system like Merezhkovsky's but rather to intersperse the exotic picture of bygone epochs with glimpses of something strikingly familiar in order to momentarily startle the reader without necessarily entailing further ramifications.

The area where the universal triumphs without reservation is the realm of passion and sexuality, which, in Bryusov's view, involves eternal impulses lying beyond history and culture. Most characteristic in this respect is *The Fiery Angel*. Its plot is based on the love triangle involving Bryusov, Bely, and Nina Petrovskaya, who figure in the novel as Ruprecht, Count Heinrich, and Renata, respectively.[29] The situation was especially piquant since the affair was still unfolding at the time of the novel's creation and Bryusov manipulated it in a way that would provide him with material for the novel. The work-in-progress, in turn, influenced the real-life romance. As Bely would recall: "Projecting the Cologne of yore onto modern Moscow, he often lost track of the line separating life from fiction and so in his mind Muscovites turned into contemporaries of the Netterheim magician, Erasmus, and Doctor Faustus; the area between Cologne and Basel became the area between the Arbat and Znamenka; the devil only knows what came out of this" (*Nachalo veka*, 306). This was one of the most striking examples of the symbolist "bioaesthetic genre" (*zhiznetvorchetvo*), as participants in this drama "attempted to transform art into life and life into art" (Khodasevich, *Konets Renaty*, 10).[30] The love plot in *The Altar of Victory*, though devoid of such titillating immediacy, in many ways reproduces that of *The Fiery Angel*.[31] In both novels Bryusov—notorious for his carefully cultivated erotomania—spices up the action with orgies, homosexuality, sex with minors, bestiality, and so forth.

Finally, the properly historical background of both novels also finds transparent parallels in the present. The atmosphere of social and religious upheaval during the Reformation in Germany in many ways resembles the situation in Russia during the Revolution of 1905. As in the case involving his love affair, life inspired Bryusov to write. He says in a private letter: "Amid the salvos of Cossack rifles, between two strolls through the unlit and barricaded streets I continued to work on my novel. The work was easy (especially since in the early chapters I had to depict the religious revolution of Germany in 1535)" (quoted in Chudetskaia, 344). Although political history is beyond the novel's main focus, certain Russian allusions are obvious. For example, the narrator remarks: "During the next two years violent popular revolts spread across the German land as if part of a satanic dance. [. . .] Fredrick, ever the dreamer, at first thought that this fiery and bloody storm would help to establish more order and justice in our land, but he soon understood that no good could be expected of the German peasants, who were still wild and ignorant" (*Ognennyi angel*, 4:19–20). One need only recall that these words were written in 1907–8, following two years of revolution, resulting in widespread despair among intellectuals. The Russian connection is also obvious in the following passage, where the narrator describes a revolutionary agitator: "Then a poorly shaven fellow sat down next to me [. . .] and embarked upon a long speech about the penurious condition of the peasant men, which was not new but also not without some truth to it. [. . .] My chance acquaintance threatened the knights and burghers with fires, pitchforks, and the gallows" (4:154).

Whereas the Revolution of 1905 finds its counterpart in the Reformation and peasant wars of sixteenth-century Germany, in Bryusov's mind the subsequent stabilization in Russia is akin to fourth-century Rome.[32] The two leading themes in *The Altar of Victory* are the grandeur of the Roman Empire and its imminent destruction (Gasparov, "Bryusov i antichnost'," 549). Bryusov emphasizes that the downfall of Rome in and of itself does not signify that Roman civilization was in decline. In his unpublished historical collection *The Golden Rome* Bryusov concludes: "The fall is not an argument (to repeat Nietzsche's expression)" (quoted in Gasparov, "Bryusov i antichnost'," 544). On the contrary, he sees the period as the apogee of Roman civilization: "The fourth century was an age during which the Roman idea was in full bloom, when the Roman world was reaping the fruits it had sown. . . . It was an era in which there was no need to conquer, organize, or set out in search of anything, but rather to hold on to what had been conquered, preserve what had been accomplished, explore in more depth discoveries in the arts and literature" (544).

Nevertheless, the empire is doomed, since it faces deadly threats from without (barbarians) and from within (Christian fanatics). The impending downfall may be hidden under a magnificent imperial facade, but it is inevitable and will take the shape of a sudden and total collapse of apocalyptic proportions. As an old patrician predicts in *The Altar of Victory:* "If Rome is fated to perish, then it should perish honorably; its past was too beautiful and magnificent to permit a humiliating end. [. . .] Our task is to preserve the grandeur of ancient Rome to the last minute. We are like the custodians of a beautiful but crumbling temple. . . . We know that the beams are rotten and the walls are threatening to collapse, but we do not allow the uninitiated to see this. Let the great building stand on in its former beauty for the eyes of all to see, and let it not crumble in parts, but rather collapse at once, covering all the world in its ruins" (*Altar' Pobedy,* 5:102).

One does not need much imagination to substitute "Rome" for "Russia" and the "Roman idea" for the "Russian idea" in order to see historical parallels. The Christian fanatics of yore are the present-day revolutionaries. The barbarians at the gates are represented by the Asiatic hordes on Russia's eastern borders: predictions of an apocalyptic invasion from the east, which are already found in Solovyov's poem "Panmongolism" and his *Three Conversations,* became especially widespread after Russia's humiliating defeat in the war with Japan. The implied result is the same as in the case of Rome: Russian civilization is destined to perish at the zenith of its glory.

Bryusov's attitude toward the looming catastrophe is far from simple. Experiencing a poignant nostalgia for the doomed civilization, Bryusov nevertheless glimpses the truth behind the cause of its enemies: barbarians will destroy culture, but they will restore vital energy and uncorrupted naiveté absent from the decadent old world. This idea is already sounded in his oft-quoted poem "The Coming Huns" (1905)—"I receive you, who will destroy me, with a hymn of salutation"—and is reiterated in *The Altar of Victory.* As these apocalyptic expectations were materializing, Bryusov, a high priest of the dying culture, fulfilled his own artistic declarations and—in an appropriately bio-aesthetic move—greeted the coming of the Bolsheviks.

The Barbarian Within: The Cossack Orpheus of Vasily Kamensky

To what degree Merezhkovsky's and Bryusov's prophecies—alongside numerous other apocalyptic manifestations in contemporary culture—contributed to conjuring up the Russian catastrophe remains an open question.[33] In terms of the present discussion, however, it is quite uncanny that Vasily Kamensky's *Stenka Razin* (1915), the most significant historical novel to appear after *The Altar of Victory*, was written about a "barbarian" (the leader of a seventeenth-century Cossack uprising) and by a "barbarian" (the futurists were often labeled "young barbarians"). Compared to Merezhkovsky or Bryusov, Kamensky is indeed a "barbarian" in terms of his historical preparation. Judging from the material used in the novel, his reading list is quite basic and includes Nikolai Kostomarov's essay, the entry on Razin in *Brockhaus*, a single chapter in the eleventh volume of Solovyov's *History*, a collection of folk songs, and possibly one or two additional articles. Even these limited resources were studied by Kamensky without much diligence.[34] The broader historical background or realia of the epoch are clearly beyond his scope.

In other respects, however, Kamensky is anything but a "barbarian." The narrative structure of his novel is complex and innovative, combining several planes: (1) the main novelistic action pertaining to the revolt; (2) historical and geographical digressions; (3) digressions about the spirit of Rus and her people; (4) lyrical digressions; and (5) interpolated poems. It is difficult to establish a clear pattern with respect to Kamensky's use of different narrative modes and their juxtapositions. In a sense, *Razin*'s narrative mosaic is reminiscent of the allogical structural principle Kamensky introduced in his scandalous "Ferro-Concrete Poems," albeit in the novel it is less radical. There is a steady chronological progression of the plot from the fictional scenes of Stenka's youth to a more or less historical canvas depicting the revolt, ending with the hero's execution. Overall, the genre of *Stenka Razin* can best be described as lyrico-epic. One could even suggest that Kamensky used *The Lay of Prince Igor* as a model, but there are no direct allusions to it in the text, nor is there extratextual evidence to support this notion.

The stylistic spectrum employed by Kamensky is extremely broad and includes the following: (1) Quasi-historical narrative (a fixture of the traditional historical novel and Kamensky's weakest point); (2) plain prose; (3) rhythmical prose; (4) occasional incursions of Church Slavonic (e.g., in Stenka's prayers); (5) excerpts from folk songs or, more frequently, quasi-folk stylizations; (6) and futurist poetry, often in the form of polylogue in mass scenes, including the use of transrational language as well as imitations of Tatar, Persian, and African speech (e.g., during their raid on Persia, Cossacks liberate thirty-three negroes, who join the rebellion and sing their songs along the banks of the Volga). To use Velimir Khlebnikov's image, Kamensky "worked deftly at his task to place in a blooming bush a hundred nightingales and larks to make Stenka Razin emerge from them" (quoted in *Russkie pisateli*, 2:457). Such stylistic polyphony, along with the lyrico-epic nature of the novel, make it a unique work in the history of the genre.

The historical concept of the novel is also unusual. The only conventional feature of Kamensky's Razin is the fact that—following the notion firmly ingrained in cultural memory—he represents Russia's archetypal quest for absolute freedom (*volia*). However, the particulars of his image are highly idiosyncratic. They cannot be fully explained by the folk and quasi-folk sources. Kamensky also goes against the historiographic tradition since he chooses to ignore the brutality of the Cossack chieftain, although factual accounts pertaining to it are incontrovertible and numerous.[35] Kamensky similarly misses the opportunity to reconstruct a peculiarly barbarous mindset of the historical Razin and his men by expanding on Solovyov's ideas:

> Doing all things in a big way, endowed with monstrous strength and monstrous power, this man exuded an enormous charisma. For him nothing mattered; he was not kept in check by anything, neither attachments nor relationships; his wild and willful antics perplexed, petrified, awed, and subdued the commoner. Such, generally speaking, are the ideas of underdeveloped societies with respect to strength and power. Just as an educated society requires a sense of measure and detests the lack of it, so an uneducated society is excited by the latter since here intelligence is silent and the imagination finds all the more room for play. Actions arising from brute force and senseless violence are most impressive to it, and here a strong man is not human at all but rather something more like lightning and thunder. (*Istoriia Rossii*,11:296)

Nor does the novel follow the populist vision subsequently inherited and enhanced by Soviet historiography, according to which Razin is seen as a protorevolutionary, a kind of Old Testament patriarch in the pantheon of revolutionary saints.[36] Kamensky lists some examples of oppression and injustice inflicted on the people, but his Razin is by no means a conscious fighter against social ills.

The novel's hero is above all a poet, a bard singing songs of his own invention to the accompaniment of his gusli, which he carries with him to the scaffold. In the novel Vaska Us, the bloodthirsty lieutenant of the historical Razin, is also transformed into an accomplished bard, hence establishing a special bond between the two men. Stenka sees himself first and foremost as a bard, with song being his most formidable tool. "Which is stronger," asks Razin of his vanquished adversary, an evil Tatar merchant, "the sword or the song? [. . .] You relied fiercely on your sword, but I triumphed with my song" (84–85). When his enemy bursts into song before being executed, Stenka pardons the Tatar and even invites him to join the Cossack brotherhood. Upon being greeted as a great leader of warriors, Razin expresses his vexation: "Forget the glory of an ataman. [. . .] I do not cherish that kind of glory; I am not a *voivode*. [. . .] I am a simple player of the *gusli* and wage war through song" (113).

Among other features repeatedly emphasized by Kamensky are his hero's childishness, purity of the soul, naiveté (recall Bryusov's imagined Huns: "You are innocent in everything, like children!"), and joyful pantheism, which he retains as his life flashes before his eyes on the scaffold:

> He loved with passion. The sand. And his children. And the grass. And wings. And songs. And youth. And the Volga. And Rus. And the Persian princess. And wine. And friends. And the expanse of the sea. And everything on earth. And everything in heaven. He loved it with all his heart.
>
> "Farewell, oh life of the *gusli* player. Bless my peace. You can see that I am light and luminous as a sucking babe at his mother's breast. I am quite small. Forgive me. Do not judge me."
>
> The domes of the churches glowed with a golden flame.
>
> Below the streltsy moved in their red caftans among the thick crowd, their sabers flashing. (193)

The novel abounds with exalted digressions on Russianness. (Some of them could have been influenced by the nationalistic propaganda that flourished during the initial phase of World War I.) The paradigmatic feature emphasized both in Stenka and Russia is a combination of extremes, which characterized the romantic period:

> Just like the Russian People, Stepan was huge, strong, talented, unexpected.
>
> Just like the Russian People, Stepan was always unsettled, always rebellious, always disheveled.
>
> Just like the Russian People, Stepan was either savagely wild or placid and magnificent in his lucidly profound wisdom.

> Just like the Russian People, Stepan believed in God, traveled to monasteries, prayed fervently, repented his sins, all the while suffering from acute loneliness, wandering along unknown, desolate roads.
>
> But, suddenly, just like the Russian People, abruptly and unexpected even by him, like an impetuous whirlwind Stepan would forsake God, the monasteries, prayers, repentance, and torment, giving himself over to a devil-may-care will, plunging into reckless debauchery. (14)[37]

On many occasions Kamensky confesses his love for Russia, seeing himself as a quintessential Russian lad, and feels a strong affinity for Stenka—a Russian lad like himself and a fellow poet.

Despite its seeming outlandishness, Kamensky's concept of Razin as Poet is well grounded in the cultural context of the period. First, it is quite likely that Kamensky was familiar with the 1907 article by a certain T. A. Martemyanov dealing with Razin-related lore, which appeared in the popular journal *Historical Herald.* Martemyanov suggested that Stenka was endowed with poetic talent and realized the importance of song in bolstering morale with respect to the rebellion. He therefore encouraged songwriting activities within the ranks of his ragtag army, perhaps drawing on a large number of professional *skomorokhs* who had been banished from Muscovy's heartland during the early years of Tsar Alexis's reign. Martemyanov concludes: "The song business was well organized and broadly implemented in Stenka's camp" (838).

Martemyanov's ideas remain pure conjecture, but for Kamensky this article would have been especially appealing since it provided him with the necessary historical authority for turning the ruthless ataman into a poet. Additional modifications of Razin's image reflect Kamensky's modernist preoccupations. The emphasis on childishness is related to the futurists' cultivation of the primitive, while Stenka's—and the author's—hymns to song follow the logocentric streak in futurist poetics: "What is a song? A song is more intoxicating than wine; a song is sharper than a sword of steel; a song is stronger than love; a song is life eternal, like a multi-colored rainbow, only brighter and more colorful than the rainbow; a song combines in one place the morning tears of joy and the evening tears of sorrow; a song is a drop of the purest dew; a song is an ocean; in a song all great beginnings sonorously bloom and all endings cease" (85–86). Kamensky's very nationalism is of a peculiar pan-poetic nature. Russia for him is not just the land of songs but also a song itself: "In every song there is great Russia and all of great Russia is a dashing, free song. The song and Russia are one and the same" (51). Similarly, "historical" reality in the novel emerges from the songs of the ingenious

FIGURE 25. Illustrations from Kamensky's *Stenka Razin* (1915) by leading futurist artists: (a) Aristarkh Lentulov (p. 5); (b) David Burlyuk (p. 71); (c) Vladimir Burlyuk (p. 103); (d) Vasily Kamensky (p. 144).

D

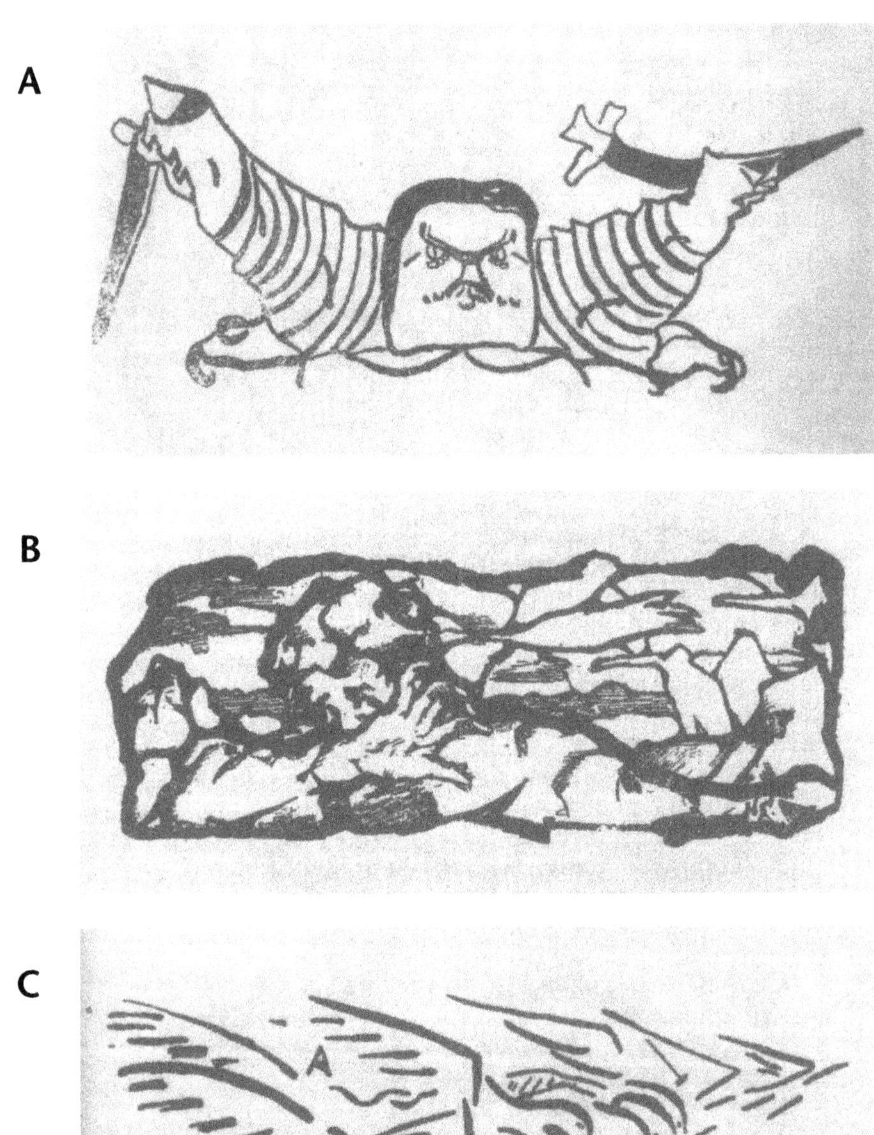

FIGURE 26. Illustrations from Kamensky's *Stenka Razin* (1915) by leading futurist artists: (a) Georgy Zolotukhin (p. 157); (b) Nikolai Gushchin (p. 175); (c) Nikolai Kulbin (p. 187); (d) Vasily Kamensky (p. 194).

bard: "Stepan never thought and never guessed that the sonorous *gusli* and his scarlet, flowing songs could weave such a marvelously wonderful life that rocked like a stormy sea, that bloomed like a rainbow-colored tale, and swirled in a magic circle" (63). Such "bio-aestheticism" in Kamensky can be traced back to the poetic doctrines of both the futurists and the symbolists.[38]

Lastly, there is an important mythological aspect present in the novel. The gusli-playing Razin is strongly reminiscent of Orpheus. Like the latter, he is a perfect "cosmic" poet who uses songs as his weapon, travels by water with great warriors, and meets a horrible death through dismemberment.[39] Kamensky—who generally avoids graphic representation of violence—provides a detailed account of Razin's torture and execution, his body being quartered. The general mood of the conclusion, however, is cathartic. Stepan retains his all-embracing love of the world and meets his end with serenity: "Righteous Lord [. . .] I submit myself to Your will and give thanks to You for

all the days of my life until my last breath" (193). In death Stepan rejoins the cosmos, while his songs live on: "Those childish eyes were lost in the sky and his childish heart was inundated by the Volga. The songs remained" (194).

The orphic dimension in the novel is likely to have come from the symbolist milieu, in particular from Vyacheslav Ivanov, who was keenly interested in the subject. In 1913 he published an essay in *The Russian Thought* entitled "On the Orphic Dionysus," a scholarly work that also contains his own philosophical commentary, which, inter alia reads like the following: "Orpheus, who personifies the mystical synthesis of both revelations, both the Dionysian and Apollonian, is that side of Dionysus in which the incarnate god, while enduring his martyrdom for the world, simultaneously relinquishes his will, subjugating it to the law of the father's will" ("O Dionise orficheskom," 75). The parallels with Kamensky's novel are quite striking. His Stepan can also be seen as an answer to Merezhkovsky's obsession with Synthesis. However, unlike Merezhkovsky's "walking antitheses," Stepan—the archetypal Russian hero—has never suffered the torments resulting from the dichotomy between spirit and flesh. The unity of the two elements in him is entirely natural and organic; in one sense he is the naive man before the Fall. He may thus be considered a "barbarian," but one whose image has been informed by a variety of impulses derived from high modernist culture.

The orphic subtext can also be extended to encompass the very genre of Kamensky's work. One the one hand, it is possible to regard *Stenka Razin* as an attempt at fulfilling Khlebnikov's dream of creating the futuristic "universal novel." On the other hand, Kamensky's stylistic and structural experimentation finds parallels in Ivanov's calls for "Dionysian Drama" and Nikolai Evreinov's ideas concerning the "theatralization of life."[40] In this sense *Stenka Razin* can be seen as a hybrid, combining features of a lyrico-epic novel and a neo-Dionysian tragedy. In terms of the present study, although *Stenka Razin* contains specific chronological and factual references, it is least concerned with the real history of a specific revolt that took place in Muscovy's southeastern frontier around 1670. Rather, it presents the mystery of a Russian Orpheus played out against somewhat stylized historical trappings. As a work dealing with mythopoeic and archetypal themes, it deserves a prominent place in the modernist metahistorical tradition.

In Lieu of a Conclusion

A Tale of Three Cities, or the Reincarnations of Saint Petersburg in the Russian Historical Novel

Rather than following a continuous linear process, the evolution of the Russian historical novel can be divided into three distinct periods—romanticism, realism, and modernism—each possessing its own poetics informed by broader literary and cultural paradigms. A concise summary of the change in the poetics of the genre may rely on the triad of consecutive formulas frequently employed during the respective periods. For the romantics it is the *spirit of the epoch,* which can be glimpsed through the writer's creative intuition and the use of legend. For the realists it is the *character of the epoch,* which emerges through artistic analysis and requires the demythologization of history. Finally, for the symbolists it is the *scent* or *atmosphere of the time,* behind which lie eternal principles embodied in symbols and myths. This discrete scheme does not preclude the existence of a certain "memory of the genre." For example, such important structural elements of Tolstoy's *War and Peace* as the alternation of fictional and historical chapters and incursions of the authorial voice can be traced back to the romantic novel of the 1830s. Merezhkovsky's and Bryusov's archaeological precision reveals their indebtedness to the positivist tradition, while their attempts at stylization can be seen as a further development of linguistic realism found in the realist novel. Even the futurist Kamensky, in his highly innovative *Stenka Razin,* pays tribute to the quasi-historiographic discourse of the positivist era. My point, however, is that once these elements are transplanted into a different system, their functions change.

This idea can be illustrated most vividly when one selects a certain element—a formal device, narrative strategy, cultural category, or specific historical topic—and traces its permutations through all three periods. Choosing as a point of departure the relationship between fact and fiction, which lies at the very core of the genre, in all periods one discovers conspicuous instances where novelists deviate from established historical facts or accepted historical accounts. A romantic does this in the belief that pedestrian facts can be sacrificed in the name of a higher artistic truth. A realist does this because he feels that his interpretation is more accurate historically and factually. Lastly, a symbolist does this because of a belief in multiple realities, the most real of which is the reality of symbols and myths. Similarly, each maintains a different stance with respect to the disparity between fiction and history. A romantic engages in an act of simultaneous self-validation and self-invalidation, which is a variety of romantic irony. A realist lacks self-doubt and is assertive, acting like a scholar in presenting his evidence. For the symbolist the problem largely disappears since his art helps to reveal yet one more reality in a multidimensional universe—a reality of a higher order, which, however, neither cancels out other planes of existence nor is itself compromised by the conflict with empirical data. Consequently, the mode of interaction between fiction and history in respective periods undergoes considerable change. Whereas in romanticism there is a dialogue between the two, realism is monological since art is perceived as yet another cognitive instrument and is not opposed to science. In symbolism there is an interweaving of history, the artist's imagination, and allusions to various cultural traditions, all of which reflect facets of mysterious and infinite meanings.

This basic difference underlies a number of apparently similar features. Thus, one can find an abundance of historical realia among romantics, realists, and symbolists alike, given the fact that savoring details of the past is among the principle impulses of the genre. However, if one examines specific artistic systems, one discovers significant differences in the functioning of antiquarianism. For the romantics realia are important because they help to create temporal distance and to present the past as a sharply etched exotic realm. Realia that reflect customs, mores, and morals are especially precious since they help to convey the epoch's spirit. In this sense, they are more valuable than "accidental" chronological or biographical facts, which are treated by the romantics with great license. For a realist, however, historical detail has a different meaning, forming a part of objective reality to be analyzed, catalogued, and labeled. While displaying a similar antiquarian thoroughness, a symbolist sees detail both as a "museum exhibit" and a symbol, a link in the chain of eternal mystical correspondences.

One can also select such a seemingly minor component of some novels as notes appended to the text. Although notes can be found in all kinds of historical novels, their role varies. In the romantic novel they serve as an element in the game of self-validation and invalidation. In the realistic novel they are devoid of self-effacing potential, fulfilling a straightforward quasi-academic function. In the symbolist novel notes can be extremely extensive and meticulous, yet this only underscores the paradoxical situation where history and reality are used as material for mythmaking and "bio-aesthetic" games, as in the case of *The Fiery Angel,* where Bryusov's own love life is projected onto sixteenth-century Germany, carefully wrapped in historical realia, and supported by pedantic endnotes.

An instance of typologically close but functionally different elements is linked to the concept of cyclization. Although novelistic cycles may be found in all three periods, their nature remains different. For example, several of Zagoskin's novels form a cycle built around manifestations of Russianness in periods of crisis, specifically the Russians in 1612, 1711, and 1812. This cyclization is clearly based upon the romantic notion of the nation as an organic entity that retains essential core characteristics while changing outwardly during periods of historical growth. Cyclization can also be found in the 1880s in Solovyov's chronicle of the Gorbatovs. Despite the mystical inclinations of its author, this cycle is realistic in the sense that it portrays the "Darwinian" evolution of a genteel family set against the country's history. Finally, one can point to Merezhkovsky's trilogies, where cyclization reflects the very essence of the symbolist philosophy, serving as yet another projection of the mythical time of eternal return.

Another conspicuous example is found in the treatment of historical heroes. For the romantics, heroes are "men of fate"—conduits of the providential design of history. The Scottian manner of showing great men not on a solemn pedestal but in an intimate fashion amid the details of everyday life is not tantamount to a lowering in esteem. On the contrary, it ultimately underscores their extraordinary stature (cf. Catherine and Pugachev in *The Captain's Daughter*). Genuine debunking occurs in realistic prose, where so-called heroes are indeed portrayed as ordinary men both in terms of their demeanor (including physiology) and the humble place they occupy within the historical process, which is governed by impersonal laws. Heroes regain their elevated status in early modernist fiction. Here they no longer serve as mere conduits between heaven and earth, as was the case for the romantics, but rather as incarnations of eternal mystical and mythical principles, be it Kamensky's Russian Orpheus in the person of Razin or Merezhkovsky's Peter the Great, who is vampire, biblical Abraham, Demiurge, God the Father, and the Antichrist rolled into one. Although the figure of Napoleon in *War and*

Peace is also associated with the Antichrist, for Tolstoy this serves as a historical detail (i.e., reference to the epoch's frame of mind) as well as an excuse for caricaturing Napoleon by highlighting the chasm separating the grandeur of myth from the puny reality of history. Characteristically, although both novels evoke the Antichrist in their very first paragraphs, the implications are quite dissimilar. Whereas Anna Scherer's salon chatter—"Buonaparte, cet Antichrist (ma parole, j'y crois)"—sets the tone for the satirical depiction of high society in *War and Peace,* the opening sentence of Merezhkovsky's novel—"The Antichrist wants to come"—points to the overarching historiosophic theme of the trilogy, which is appropriately titled *Christ and Antichrist.*

Similar transformations occur with respect to the notion of myth and legend. For the romantics legend is either the product of the collective unconscious (lore/folklore) or a creation of the individual imagination—the Truth of Art. Although both types of legends represent a higher form of truth and are closer to the absolute than ordinary reality, their truth is not complete and cannot cancel out the material truth of facts. For the realists legends are fables, long tales, and fictions that obscure the objective truth, which is to be discerned by means of quasi-scientific analysis; hence the widespread debunking of legends and demythologization of history. In modernism one can observe the opposite tendency, with history being re-mythologized. However, unlike the romantic legend, the modernist myth has nothing to do with lore. Although it is linked to individual artistic insights, myth for the modernists (especially the symbolists) is the "objective truth about reality" (Ivanov, "Dve stikhii," 278)—a type of universal explanation and a key to the codes of the world.[1]

As a final illustration of this ternary scheme and also to pay tribute to the recent anniversary of Russia's northern capital, I wish to contrast the portrayal of Saint Petersburg in the romantic, realist, and symbolist novel. Although in all instances one and the same subject is involved, the perspectives on it change so drastically that it might appear that we are dealing with descriptions of three different cities.

My thesis seemingly contradicts the well-established academic tradition that postulates the existence of a relatively unified, semantically coherent, and internally consistent "Petersburgian text" of Russian literature.[2] However, this is not the case. To begin with, not every literary work involving the theme of Saint Petersburg qualifies as a "Petersburgian text" (Toporov, 279–80). Of the historical novels under consideration, only Lazhechnikov's *Ice Palace* and Merezhkovsky's *Peter and Alexis* are full-fledged Petersburgian texts, the others being about Saint Petersburg. Furthermore, looking at the properly Petersburgian paradigm, it is possible to single out several components: First is the set of ur-impulses created by the city's geographical location and the circumstances surrounding its founding. Second is the influence of literary and cultural tradition. Third is the influence of contemporary sociopolitical circumstances. Fourth is the influence of contemporary poetics. For the purpose of my argument, I will focus on the last aspect. This approach is especially warranted since the understanding of the Petersburgian text as a cultural entity only emerged at the turn of the twentieth century and was inevitably colored by the symbolist mythopoeic outlook. That is not to say that the myth of Saint Petersburg is a symbolist creation. Starting with Pushkin's *Bronze Horseman*, Russian literature produced a number of genuinely mythological Petersburgian texts. In general, however—at least in the historical novel—one can observe the familiar triad: (1) the legend of Saint Petersburg during the romantic period; (2) its demythologization (or at least decidedly nonmythological picture) in realistic fiction; and (3) the reinvention of the high Petersburgian myth by the symbolists.

The most extensive treatment of Saint Petersburg in romantic historical fiction is found in Lazhechnikov's *Ice Palace*. The novel has been overlooked by students of the Petersburgian tradition, yet it remains one of the ur-texts of the canon both chronologically and thematically, containing virtually all the features that would later become associated with the Petersburgian paradigm.[3] This is immediately obvious from the physical characteristics of the city emphasized by Lazhechnikov. A prominent role is played by Saint Petersburg's aquatic "frame"—the Neva and the Gulf of Finland. The climate is markedly strange (e.g., severe frosts combined with sudden fog; bizarre snowfalls; eerie sunsets). The city, still under construction, is full of yawning gaps—empty squares and vacant vistas intended for future thoroughfares—which creates an impression that the center of the empire is situated in a wasteland. This is echoed in other pairings that abound in Saint Petersburg (luxurious palaces/wretched huts, imperial capital/ Finnish village), contrast being the organizing principle in Lazhechnikov's portrayal of a city that blends aspects of Europe, Russia, and the Orient: "It is Holland and Siberia combined [. . .] meeting curiously on the Gulf of Finland." Like representatives of the warring German and Russian parties at court, "they look askance at one another and strive to chase the other out" amid the somber snow-covered desert, which is enlivened only by the boisterous spirit of the Russian crowd (*Ledianoi dom*, 83). The heroine of the novel is a Moldavian princess (actually half-Moldavian, half-Gypsy) who mixes Orthodox Christianity with

FIGURE 27. Title page illustration from Lazhechnikov's *Ice Palace* (vol. 1, 1837). Portraying the Northern Capital as a glacial inferno, the novel reflects the negative metaphysics of the emerging Petersburgian myth.

Islamic fatalism. This exotic beauty lives at the court of the Russian empress and is in love with a Russian boyar. As if this were not enough, exoticism runs rampant during the ethnic festival that functions as background scenery.

The existential attributes of the city are also strikingly familiar from other works of the Petersburgian canon. The Petersburg of *The Ice Palace* is a gigantic theatrical set, its reality both unreliable and illusory. This feeling is first created by the Petersburgian climate. The setting sun casts a "phantasmagoric hue" over everything, while "snow threads shuttle between sky and earth as if falling down and fleeing up," as a result of which the sight is troubled and all things seem to "dance" (182). The very air of the city seems to induce hallucinations. "Is there not a disease in the air that causes everyone to rave?" inquires Volynsky (147). The unreal feeling created by nature is further enhanced by human undertakings. Life in Saint Petersburg unfolds like a theatrical show, culminating in the ethnic festival and wedding of jesters in the frozen mirage of a palace where everything is made of ice: the foundation, walls, statues, furniture, utensils, ornaments, cannons, and even the sauna and fireplaces, where logs composed of ice burn from the petroleum poured on them, illuminating the phantasmagoric edifice.

The sense of uncertainty is also created by the convoluted political intrigue entangling the novel's characters. The city teems with all sorts of informers, spies, and double agents. Part of the game involves provocation and the changing of masks not only metaphorically but also literally. Remarkable is the scene involving a double masquerade, discussed earlier in connection with the romantic masquerade topos. During Christmastide Volynsky is visited by a group of carnival guests wearing a double disguise. Pretending to be the cabinet minister's friends, they are actually agents of Biron, his archenemy. Their cunning plan is foiled when Volynsky is tipped off by a secret sympathizer among Biron's spies, thereby creating a triple masquerade.

Saint Petersburg's unreliability has a metaphysical dimension of a decidedly negative cast, which is very much in tune with the Petersburgian canon from the 1830s onward. Saint Petersburg is portrayed as a doom-laden, mystical city that exerts a pernicious influence over men. Some kind of ominous devilish act is being played out on the snowy expanses of the northern capital, with the otherworldly abyss breaking through the imperial facade. The threat of death and destruction constantly hovers over the city and its residents, who feel threatened by apocalyptic premonitions.

The sinister metaphysics is reflected in the very climate of Saint Petersburg. The severe frost of December 1739–January 1740 is not just a meteorological fact but a symbol of Biron's cruel rule. The cosmic cold "suffocates," "grabs at the heart," "seizes all living things with its burning claws; people have difficulty breathing; the flight of birds is slowed; and the sun itself, like a fiery cannonball, makes its way with difficulty from behind the frosty darkness" (25, 30, 52). From the first pages of the novel the picture of the somber, frozen city is imbued with infernal overtones. Local residents perceive preparations for court festivities as "Satan's Sabbath," "a demonic entertainment" (8, 97). The political intrigue unfolding in Saint Petersburg also reeks of infernal qualities. For example, when Biron's henchman, Lipman, smiles sadistically, Lazhechnikov remarks: "In hell, of course, a host of onlookers applauded at that [. . .] arch-demonic smile, that is, if the onlookers down there are able to see the work of their fellow demon-actors" (93).

Lazhechnikov's Saint Petersburg often appears as an accursed spot, an evil and dangerous space where a human being is constantly threatened by death. Describing Biron's residence, he remarks: "Dread surrounds that dwelling," adding that all the passersby avoid it like "a labyrinth in which, if you wind up there, you will be devoured by the Minotaur instantly" (29). Even more eerie is the picture of the nocturnal Neva into which Biron's servants intend to dump the body of their victim: "Holes had been drilled in many places in the river's ice, which, thanks to the water's waves, resembled live maws moving as if to swallow up the victims brought to them." "What a cemetery!" notes one of the servants. "There's no need to dig graves!" (78).

A prominent role in the novel is given over to graveyard episodes. Wishing to punish the disguised spies, Volynsky abandons them at the Volkovo cemetery in the middle of the night, on which occasion the narrator exclaims: "Masquerading on a moonlit night at a cemetery—and what a cemetery at that, my dear Lord!, where corpses were not interred. The Inca, Semiramis, a Capuchin monk, a little demon, and all of this company fighting with the dead, who, it seemed to them, gripped the living in their frigid embrace, grabbed at them with their claws and loomed up in the sky" (67). The epilogue also unfolds at a cemetery—a churchyard at Saint Samson's, where the body of the executed Volynsky is buried. It is as if the entire city has been transformed into one gigantic cemetery: The wind "whines plaintively" through the empty paths of the Summer Garden and the frames of the statues are "wrapped in winding cloths like togas" (29). Dark palaces "are silent as sarcophaguses" (25) and the city dwellers, petrified by frost and fear, resemble "moving coffins" (49).

The funerary theme enhances the eschatological motifs introduced in the first chapter. When, amid noisy preparations for the festivities, Volynsky is overcome by a fit of melancholy, the life around him comes to a standstill:

"Everything fell silent in the room as if afraid to make a move. It seemed that everything had turned to stone at that moment, like the Pompeians under the lava that overcame them" (15).[4] Similar imagery appears in the episode where the noisy marketplace is disrupted by the appearance of a convicted criminal wearing a "tongue" mask, who can point to any passerby as his accomplice: "All of a sudden the call of a sentry rings out. It sounds like the voice of a herald bringing tidings of the end of the world. Thereafter all falls silent, all movement ceases, and the pulse stops beating, as if life has been extinguished in one fell stamp of an angry god's heel. Scales, measuring sticks, legs, arms, mouths all freeze in the same position in which they were caught by that call" (84). In addition, the city is full of ominous rumors about sinister apparitions and the coming of the end. The ethnic festival itself, for which paired beasts had been assembled from all four corners of the empire, acquires a pre-deluge connotation.

The meeting point of all Petersburgian topoi is the ice palace of the title. The palace functions as a kind of microcosm of the city of Saint Petersburg: a miniature artificial city enclosed within another artificial city, a theatrical set within a larger theatrical setting. Whereas Saint Petersburg is composed of stone and built on a swampy foundation, that is, land resting on water, the ice palace is even more precarious, being composed of water resting on water. According to popular myth, Saint Petersburg was built atop the bones of its builders. Similarly, the idea of the ice palace's construction occurs to the empress when she sees a strange block of ice in the courtyard of Biron's stables. The duke's henchmen insist that this is an ice statue, but in reality it is the body of an enemy who was frozen alive. Thus, at the foundation of the ice palace there is also a corpse, casting an otherworldly light on the entire edifice. Here is how Lazhechnikov describes the empress's visit to the newly erected structure: "The ice palace presented a magical attraction. [. . .] Along with the tsaritsa, who seemed asleep for all eternity in her winter carriage, those horses, warriors, the court, the onlookers on the snowy canvas, all made white by the frost and all of them seemed as if shrouded, motionless, dumb, dead" (162). The eerie immobility soon becomes a scene of confusion as the court train is enveloped in a sudden fog:

> A thick mist fell over the earth so that it was impossible to see anything a few steps ahead. Occasionally could be seen a horse's head or tail, or a warrior seemingly floating in the air, or a sled without horses impelled by a magical force, or a broadsword gleaming momentarily in its glide. Large, fiery splotches (the light shining from houses), like the terrible eyes of a ghost, stood disembodied

> in the air; erratic lights (from lanterns carried along the street) glimmered here and there. Invisible horses snorted and whinnied; unseen whips snapped. In the twilight mist sleds attempting to take on passengers collided with other sleds; horses bolted. [. . .] The bustle of police, the yelling of coachmen, the groans of crushed pedestrians, and the whirring of carriages merged into complete and utter chaos. (164)

When the empress's sled finally pulls up to the palace entrance, it is surrounded by torchbearers. The superstitious Anna Ioannovna exclaims in fear: "But it's a coffin! This is a funeral! . . . They want to bury me alive!" and begs her retinue: "get me out of this hell!" (164). In a final melodramatic flourish to the funerary theme, the first and only coitus between Volynsky and Marioritsa occurs in the abandoned ice palace after the Moldavian princess has been poisoned and her lover is destined for the scaffold. Thus, the ice palace represents the quintessential symbol of Saint Petersburg, an abstract city, splendid yet murderous, merciless, and infernal. It is also the symbol of the city's ephemeral nature since it is doomed to melt, which indeed happens at the conclusion. Turning into water can be interpreted as a variation of being swallowed by water, which is a sine qua non of Petersburgian eschatology.

Although Lazhechnikov's novel possesses a very strong mythological dimension, it is important to note that his Saint Petersburg is created according to the poetics of romantic freneticism. Moreover, the Petersburgian myth is of a limited nature, being explicitly associated with a specific historical episode. This unfortunate period, during which a weak-willed empress falls under the influence of a ruthless and self-seeking German favorite, is preceded by the vibrant and joyful atmosphere of the city's founding years, reflecting the charismatic personality of "Peter the Unparalleled," who is eulogized by Lazhechnikov as the greatest Russian ruler and a true embodiment of Russianness. When Biron falls, Peter's spirit reclaims the throne during the reign of his daughter, Elizabeth. Thus, the sinister metaphysics of Saint Petersburg in the novel represent not a universal myth, as is the case with Merezhkovsky, but rather a symbol of Biron's "winter," as well as serving as a dramatic background for the legend of Volynsky the patriot and his doomed love affair with the exotic beauty Marioritsa.

Eschatology and mystical overtones are generally absent from the portrayal of the northern capital in the realist historical novel. In *War and Peace* Saint Petersburg is first and foremost the city of officialdom and high society, which is totally divorced from the vital concerns of the country—even as

Napoleon invades Russia: "But the calm, luxurious life of Petersburg, concerned only about phantoms and reflections of real life, went on in its old way and made it hard, except by great effort, to realize the danger and the difficult position of the Russian people" (827). "Phantoms" and "reflections" here should not be mistaken for protosymbolist vocabulary since the sole intention of this passage is to emphasize the falsity of the Petersburgian way of life. For Tolstoy Saint Petersburg, as well as its antipode, Moscow, are merely kinds of social environments that condition human behavior and also attract certain character types. Tolstoy himself openly prefers Moscow, which is more natural, spontaneous, and genuinely Russian. The quintessential Muscovites in the novel are the Rostovs, while Saint Petersburg is the locus of the depraved beauty Hélène and the calculating careerist Boris Drubetskoy, a renegade Muscovite who loves Saint Petersburg and despises Moscow. As for the physical appearance of the northern capital, it is clearly beyond Tolstoy's scope.[5] Nor is he interested in the archaeology of Saint Petersburg, which is very much in line with his general handling of historical detail.

Archaeological portrayals of the city abound in the second wave of the historical novel. Danilevsky's *Mirovich* (written in 1875 and published in 1879) contains a long descriptive digression about Saint Petersburg during the reigns of Elizabeth and Peter III. It is not directly related to the novel's action and represents an inserted "physiological sketch," touching upon such subjects as buildings, streets, climate, sanitary (or, rather, unsanitary) conditions, mores, the prominence of foreigners and ethnic minorities, crime, prices, fashions, cosmetics, hairstyles, drinking establishments, Petersburgian types, class structure, billboards, teachers, diseases, military parades, and so forth. Danilevsky even permits himself pronouncements like the following: "Refined Europe and wild, unwashed Asia coexisted together" (54). This, however, has nothing to do with the romantic poetics of contrast one observed in Lazhechnikov, instead representing a kind of exposé often encountered in realistic narratives. A similarly mixed impulse (archaeological precision plus debunking) is found in Count Salias's novel *The Petersburgian Act* (1880)[6] and, perhaps most vividly, in Kostomarov's *Lackey* (1878). Kostomarov the historian meticulously describes various aspects of the capital's life in the mid-1720s (e.g., urban planning, demographic profile, transportation, commercial activities), especially those pertaining to Vasilyevsky Island, which figures prominently in the novel. Nevertheless, the main thrust of the novel remains "nihilistic," as elsewhere in Kostomarov, who openly declares his position in the introductory chapter: "No matter how hard Tsar Peter tried to make the Russians love Petersburg, the Russians could not love it. [. . .] After his death it also inspired disgust and hatred, and to this day the people of Rus are not particularly fond of Petersburg" (*Kholui*, 7–8). However, it is important to emphasize that Kostomarov's negativism vis-à-vis Saint Petersburg is of a moral and social nature and is devoid of metaphysical connotations.

Matters get more complicated in Mordovtsev's *Idealists and Realists* (1876). Given its eschatology, specifically its emphasis on the city's infernal nature and cosmic and mythological dimensions, it might outwardly appear that the novel falls within the metaphysical tradition of the Petersburgian text. However, a closer examination reveals a realistic foundation. For example, Saint Petersburg is often compared to Babylon, while its founding father is dubbed the Antichrist, which reflects the mind of religious conservatives opposed to Peter's reform and also adds a shocking "dissident" note. However, authorial discourse in the novel does not operate within this biblical frame of reference, instead preferring emphatically modern, quasi-scientific, "progressive" categories. This clearly distances the author from the apocalyptic pronouncements of his characters.[7] For example, Captain Vasily Levin, the protagonist, is overwhelmed with eschatological premonitions like the following while roaming the streets of the capital: "Everything should fly to bits, end, vanish, disappear. . . . This is the end of the world" (161).[8] However, the author explicitly states that such thoughts were the result of Levin's delirium and a consequence of the epoch's backwardness. Although he was appalled by the injustices of Petrine Russia, Levin had no notion of proper social ideals (implicitly the populist and liberal ideals of the 1870s) and expressed his frustrations in religious terms. Consider the following apocalyptic passage: "'What will happen to this new Babylon?' wonder Russian people. 'Will it not become deserted after the tsar's death?' [. . .] Those wide streets and open squares will be overgrown with grass, the granite hills will turn green with moss, the canals will bloom with river weeds and water lilies. . . . And the white-eyed Finnish night will laugh in the skies above the ruins of the abandoned city" (82–83). Here the designation of Saint Petersburg as a new Babylon belongs to the people of the Petrine epoch, while the apocalyptic vision is of a less radical nature since it does not involve cosmic cataclysms but rather physical abandonment of the city in case Russia veers away from the trajectory charted by Peter.

In the novel Saint Petersburg appears as the kingdom of the dead, as in the following passage, where Levin stumbles upon decaying remnants of a mass execution: "Something is attached to the posts [. . .] something covered with hoarfrost like bunches of gray wool. . . . On some posts hang wheels with spikes. . . . Something flattened and formless is lying on the wheels. . . . White bones are jutting out. [. . .] There are people on the wheels! Human corpses. . . . The white bones are legs, arms, exposed ribs. . . . Birds have pecked away most of the flesh. . . . Levin was overcome with dread. He stood there and could not move. . . . What if these half-devoured dead would pursue him?" (161–62). However, the major emphasis in this episode is on Peter's brutality and should be considered primarily within the poetics of historical exposés.

The portrayal of the Petersburgian climate in Mordovtsev can by no means be reduced to straightforward meteorology. Its strangeness has definite cosmic overtones, as in the following description of the white nights: "Again the staring, whitish summer night is upon Petersburg. It is neither night nor day, neither dawn nor dusk, but something indescribable, as if unfinished and disturbing to anyone not accustomed to it, capable of wrecking the nerves and causing insomnia. It seems that the sun is about to appear from over the horizon, albeit not where God intended for it to appear but rather [. . .] in the North" (205). Once again the mythological potential here is undermined by physiological references to nervous disorders. "Nervous illness" is Mordovtsev's diagnosis for the condition of his protagonist, a man possessed of a gentle soul who is crushed by the cruelty of his time, becomes deranged, and publicly denounces Peter as the Antichrist.

Mordovtsev also makes direct mythological references regarding the creation of Saint Petersburg: "Piles of timber, sand, clay, stones and huge granite slabs—as if titans are building their mythical dwelling. But these titans are Russian men erecting the hated Petersburg" (82). However, mythology is here used as a mere rhetorical embellishment for the novel's populist ideology, which includes both a positive element (admiration for the common people) and a negative one (condemnation of the unjust social system that keeps them poor and oppressed):

> And all of this has been done by the gray peasant coats with their gray faces, threadbare elbows, worn and dirty bast shoes, all of them constantly starved and beaten. [. . .] They have managed to pile such a multitude of granite slabs, whole cliffs, stones, rubble, houses, chambers, palaces, churches, prisons, bridges. . . . They have done so much, they have built all of Russia, conquered entire nations, captured Siberia, beaten Swedes, gained control of new seas, built armadas of ships. . . . They have done so much and it seems they could have earned so much, yet they are still hungry, still poor, still needy. (159–60)

The mythological plane in the novel is invariably undermined by the aesthetics and ideology of the topical 1870s. Nevertheless, the very presence of this plane in Mordovtsev's novel is quite remarkable and sets him apart from other historical novelists of the time, linking him to Dostoevsky's visions of Saint Petersburg.[9] Without a doubt, *The Idealists and Realists* figured among several important sources for Merezhkovsky's *Peter and Alexis,* one of the most openly mythological works of the Petersburgian canon.[10]

Merezhkovsky was arguably the first writer to realize the unity of the Petersburgian theme in Russian literature, which is very much in line with his concept of culture as a "third reality" (Mints, "O trilogii"). His *Peter and Alexis* represents a sui generis encyclopedic compilation of the "Petersburgian text" that summarizes all of its main motifs, from Pushkin to Dostoevsky. Although most of these motifs were previously encountered in Lazhechnikov's *Ice Palace,* Merezhkovsky presents them in a much more concentrated and deliberate fashion—to such a degree that, to paraphrase Dostoevsky's famous dictum, his novel is in a way the most artificial text about the most artificial city. Merezhkovsky's Saint Petersburg is constructed of carefully interwoven literary and historical reminiscences, quotations, and allusions that maximize the semantic charge of his cityscapes. As elsewhere in the novel, Merezhkovsky combines archaeological precision with blatant anachronisms, which is in the following passage, where the city is viewed through the eyes of the young God seeker Tikhon:

> Petersburg shocked Tikhon with its appearance, which was so unlike Moscow's. He walked the streets for days on end, looked and marveled: the endless canals, prospects, houses on piles driven into the unsteady deep of the swamps, built in a "linear fashion" by decree "so that no building could be built behind or beyond the line," the poor mud-wall huts in the forests and wastelands, covered with sod and birch bark in the Finnish manner, the palaces of elaborate architecture "in the Prussian manner," the cheerless military magazines, armories, barns, churches with Dutch spires and ringing clock towers—everything was flat, trite [*poshlo*], dull, and, at the same time, as if in a dream. Sometimes on overcast mornings, in the haze of dirty yellow fog, it seemed to him that the entire city would float up with the fog and vanish like a dream. [. . .] And once again he succumbed to that dreadful feeling [. . .] the feeling of the end. (4:80–81)

Thematically we are presented in this short passage with almost a full catalogue of Petersburgian topoi: the contrast between Saint Petersburg and Moscow; contrasts within Saint Petersburg (Europe/Finnish village, palaces/huts, modern urban life/rural wastelands and forests, stone/swamp); surreal spatial organization (unnatural regularity, endless vistas, strange emptiness); the artificiality of the city; and the city as an illusion. We also encounter pronounced eschatological motifs. There is the risk of the city being swallowed by the abyss of the swamps, being dispelled like a mirage, and finally becoming part of the universal apocalypse anticipated by Tikhon and numerous other characters in the novel and, most important, its author.

As far as Merezhkovsky's sources are concerned, the beginning of the passage contains quotations from Peter's decrees regarding urban planning,

FIGURE 28. An illustration from Osipov's *Three Lines* (1908, p. 237; artist K. N. Fridberg). "He began to speak slowly."

which adds a touch of stylization and also agrees with the historical details of the cityscape. However, immediately thereafter Merezhkovsky has Tikhon—who is purportedly roaming the streets of Saint Petersburg in the year 1715—utter the famous words concerning the oneiric qualities of Saint Petersburg and the city disappearing like fog, both of which are borrowed from Dostoevsky's *Raw Youth,* which was written in 1875 (*Pss,* 13:112–13). There is a difference in the color of the fog, which is "milky" in *The Raw Youth* and "dirty yellow" in *Peter and Alexis.* This change in hue can be taken as a reference to the dominant color of Dostoevsky's city in general and specifically to the yellow fog in the opening scene of *The Idiot.*[11] The fog motif can also be found in Gogol's *Nevsky Prospect,* where it has explicit demonic connotations. The Gogolian connection is further enhanced by the mention of Saint Petersburg's "triteness" (*poshlost'*), which, as Merezhkovsky notices in his *Gogol and the Devil* (1906), serves as a quasi-realistic substitute for devilry in Gogol's late works. As was mentioned in the preceding chapter, fog in Merezhkovsky can be traced to Bram Stoker's *Dracula,* where it signifies the presence of the vampire. Lastly, fog can also be a reference to Lazhechnikov's *Ice Palace,* where it serves as one of the attributes of Saint Petersburg's glacial inferno.[12] Thus, Merezhkovsky inserts into a seemingly historical description of the city a string of anachronistic and polygenetic allusions that introduce the theme of Saint Petersburg's sinister metaphysics.

Saint Petersburg also figures prominently in Merezhkovsky's historiosophic scheme, which follows the familiar pattern of continuous antithetic bifurcation with the promise of synthesis, usually in the apocalyptic perspective, since any synthesis achieved in historical time is incomplete and imperfect. Among the many antipodes in the novel are Europe and Russia, which—all mutual distrust and animosity notwithstanding—need each other since Europe can offer its "barbaric," semi-Asian neighbor the fruits of sophisticated civilization, while Russia can revive the corrupt Old World with the force of its spirituality. (In the novel this conspicuously Dostoevskian theory is ascribed to Leibniz, which constitutes yet another obvious anachronism.) Saint Petersburg, erected on the border separating the two worlds, seems to be their ideal meeting place. However, the synthesis that occurs in Saint Petersburg is a false one, since Peter borrows only the external attributes of European civilization and combines them with Russian despotism. Instead of compromising the idea of a true synthesis, this imperfect union of the two elements serves as its prefiguration.

In many other respects Saint Petersburg is also an "inside out" phenomenon. Instead of being a paradise (as Peter stubbornly calls his creation), it is an inferno. Instead of being the City of Saint Peter, it is the City of the Beast. However, in a familiar Merezhkovskian logical twist, one "abyss" does not cancel out the other. Both are projected onto each other to create a maze of reflections and correspondences in anticipation of their synthesis and the ultimate communion of the New Christianity. For example, there are unexpected similarities between Peter's New Babylon and the legendary Kitezh, the city of the righteous that became invisible when the Tatars approached it. According to the Old believers, in Kitezh holy elders spend their time incessantly praying to God, and "when night descends their prayers become visible, rising like fiery columns with sparks. And this light is so strong that it is possible to read and write without a candle" (Merezhkovsky, *Pss*, 4:69). Much to his amazement, Tikhon, who ardently believes these legends and dreams of finding the way to Kitezh, discovers similar nights without darkness in the godless Saint Petersburg. Ultimately the relationship between the two cities follows the pattern of Merezhkovsky's reverse conceit: "In the city of Kitezh the existing is invisible, but here in Petersburg it is the other way around and we see that which does not exist; both cities are equally illusory" (81). Saint Petersburg for Merezhkovsky once again appears as a mythical city, straddling the abyss between the realms of Christ and Antichrist.

As was stated in the preceding chapter, Merezhkovsky's apocalyptic vision was not the only mythological model present in the novel of the period. Bryusov's cyclical concepts in *The Fiery Angel* and his Roman novels and Kamensky's archetypal orphic act in *Stenka Razin* present two distinct models. Further refinements of these modernistic metahistorical paradigms occurred in the decades following the Revolution. One prominent trend in the Russian historical imagination developed the idea of cycles. In *The Cursed Days*, a diary he kept during the civil war, Ivan Bunin underscored the evil repetitiveness of Russian history, drawing parallels between contemporary events and mutinies of the past, including Razin's revolt. Evgeny Zamyatin raised the cyclical theory to the cosmic level, postulating the law of energy and entropy, according to which an outburst of energy is inevitably followed by a period of entropy. From this perspective he predicted an imminent fossilization of the Revolution in his anti-utopian novel *We*. Toward the late 1920s, when Russian history was about to take yet another turn and the decade of revolutionary aspirations was giving way to a reincarnated empire, this sensation was reflected in Yury Tynyanov's *Death of Vazir-Mukhtar*.[13] Among émigré writers, many of whom shared the cyclical vision, the emphasis is on the senselessness and arbitrariness of history. It is expressed most vividly in Mark Aldanov's philosophy of chance and in Vladimir Nabokov's defiant denial of history's reality, which represents, at best, "an arbitrary gyration of multicolored spots."[14]

Another prominent trend is found among socialist realist writers whose teleological scheme draws on the Christian apocalyptic tradition, a variety of which appears in Merezhkovsky's historiosophy. According to such a vision, history is geared toward a grand finale, which achieves a leap into an atemporal dimension and retrospectively endows with meaning all previous developments. The most immediate implication of this is that all historical manifestations of class struggle, no matter how "senseless and merciless," become prefigurations of the coming Revolution. After the mid-1930s, following the sanctioned return of certain aspects of Russian national history, the spectrum of correspondences grew wider, now including the great rulers of yore (most notably Ivan the Terrible and Peter the Great) as prefigurations of Stalin. Thus, regardless of the avowed historical materialism and historicism of Soviet artists, their concept of history is deeply mythological and, in this respect, no less metahistorical than that of their émigré colleagues. If one were to look for a catchphrase to describe the conception of history in the 1920s and 1930s, Osip Mandelstam's "noise of time" or Yury Olesha's "rumble of time" might be appropriate. However, this period clearly falls outside the chronological framework of the current study. Instead of trying to define the common thread between metahistorical visions of high modernism and socialist realism, it would be more appropriate to recall autometadescriptional devices of the romantic tradition and to conclude with a typical line from the epilogue to one of Rafail Zotov's novels: "Regarding the rest of them, try to concoct something yourself, and for me it's time to head to the shore, from which I respectfully bid you farewell" (*Shapka iurodivogo,* 651).

Appendix A:
Chronological and Thematic Distribution of Works

Appendix B:
Annotated List of Authors

Notes

Works Cited

Index

Appendix A

Chronological and Thematic Distribution of Works

In addition to the novels I read or examined *de visu*, this appendix is based on the following major reference sources:

Card catalog of the Russian National Library in Saint Petersburg.

Chentsov, N. M. *Vosstanie dekabristov. Bibliografiia*. Ed. N. K. Piksanov. Moscow and Leningrad: Gos.izd, 1929.

Ezhov, I. S. *Khudozhestvenno-istoricheskaia literatura. Ukazatel' literatury*. Ed. N. M. Korobkov. Moscow: Vsesoiuznaia knizhnaia palata, 1943.

Handbook of Russian Literature. Ed. Victor Terras. New Haven, Conn.: Yale University Press, 1985.

Istoriia russkoi literatury XIX veka:Bibliograficheskii ukazatel'. Ed. K. D. Muratova. Moscow and Leningrad: AN SSSR, 1962.

Istoriia russkoi literatury kontsa XIX—nachala XX veka: Bibliograficheskii ukazatel'. Ed. K. D. Muratova. Moscow and Leningrad: AN SSSR, 1963.

Mezier, A. V. *Russkaia slovesnost' s XI po XIX stoletiia vkliuchitel'no. Bibliograficheskii ukazatel' proizvedenii russkoi slovesnosti v sviazi s istoriei literatury i kritikoi*. St. Petersburg: A. Porokhovshchikov, 1899.

Rebekkini, Damiano. "Russkie istoricheskie romany 30-kh godov XIX veka (Bibliograficheskii ukazatel')." *Novoe literaturnoe obozrenie* 34 (1998): 416–33.

Russkie pisateli (1800—1917). Biograficheskii slovar'. 4 vols. Moscow: Bol'shaia rossiiskaia entsiklopedia-Fianit, 1992–99.

Ukazatel' zaglavii proizvedenii khudozhestvennoi literatury, 1801–1975. 7 vols. Moscow: RGB, 1985–95.

Zandberg, D. G. *Istoricheskaia belletristika v shkole. Opyt sistematicheskogo kriticheskogo ukazatelia. Part I. Vseobshchaia istoriia*. Ed. D. N. Egorov. Moscow: A. A. Levenson, 1912.

List of Works by Date of Publication

As was mentioned in the introduction, there is no "scientific" formula for labeling a work of literature as a historical novel. It is difficult to distinguish between a novel and a longer tale (*povest'*), while the required degree of historicity is an even more elusive issue. I have therefore included both novels and longer tales that contain a more or less specific historical chronotope—or at the very least display a historical intent. The inclusion of some works and exclusion of others can be disputed, but ultimately this involves borderline cases.

No such listing is ever totally complete—and this one is no exception. Particularly challenging is the period spanning the late nineteenth and early twentieth centuries, which saw an unprecedented proliferation of periodicals, with many novels being serialized in magazines and even newspapers. However, the current list is the most comprehensive one to date and, despite inevitable lacunae, offers a representative picture of the genre's dynamics.

Wherever possible I have cited the earliest date of publication, which can be problematic if a work initially appeared in a periodical. I have also tried to provide the original title and subtitle, noting subsequent alterations parenthetically. If a work was published in the course of two or more calendar years, it is usually listed under the first year. Brackets around an author's name mean that the work initially appeared anonymously or with just initials. Parentheses indicate pseudonyms or, conversely, the author's real name if he mainly published under a pseudonym. In those instances where a work only appeared in a periodical and was not republished in book form, I provide a reference to the periodical.

1829 Zagoskin, M. N. *Iurii Miloslavskii, ili Russkie v 1612 g. I. r.*

1830 Bulgarin, F. V. *Dimitrii Samozvanets. I. r.*

1831 Bulgarin, F. V. *Petr Ivanovich Vyzhigin. Nravopisatel'no-istoricheskii roman XIX st.*

Ertel', V. *Garal'd i Elizaveta, ili Vek Ioanna Groznogo. I. r.*

[Gur'ianov, I. G.] *Marina Mnishekh, kniazhna Sendomirskaia, zhena Dimitriia Samozvantsa. I. r., otnosiashchiisia ko vremeni tsaria Borisa Godunova, Lzhe-Dimitriia, tsaria Vasiliia Shuiskogo i mezhdutsarstviia, sluzhashchii dopolneniem romana Dimitrii Samozvanets.*

Kalashnikov, I. T. *Doch' kuptsa Zhelobova. Roman, izvlechennyi iz irkutskikh predanii.*

Lazhechnikov, I. I. *Poslednii Novik, ili Zavoevanie Lifliandii v tsarstvovanie Petra Velikogo. I. r.*

Zagoskin, M. N. *Roslavlev, ili Russkie v 1812 g.*

1832 [Glukharev, I. N.] *Grafinia Roslavleva, ili Supruga-geroinia, otlichivshaiasia v znamenituiu voinu 1812 g. Istoriko-opisatel'naia povest' XIX st., sluzhashchaia prodolzheniem romana "Ol'ga Miloslavskaia."*

Golota, P. I. *Ivan Mazepa. I. r., vziatyi iz narodnykh predanii.*

De Sanglen, Ia. I. *Rytsarskaia kliatva na grobe. Russkii roman iz vremen `mechenostcev.*

[Kornilovich, A. O.] *Andrei Bezymianyi. Starinnaia povest'.*

[Liubetskii, S. M.] *Sokol'niki, ili Pokolebanie vladychestva tatar nad Rossieiu. I. r. XIV v. Epizod iz kniazheniia Dimitriia Donskogo.*

Masal'skii, K. P. *Strel'tsy. I. r.*

Polevoi, N. A. *Kliatva pri Grobe Gospodnem. Russkaia byl' XV v.*

Svin'in, P. P. *Shemiakin sud, ili Poslednee mezhduusobie kniazei russkikh. I. r. XV v.*

Zotov, R. M. *Leonid, ili Nekotorye cherty iz zhizni Napoleona.*

1833 Anon. (Sh. S.). *Vasilii Delinskii, ili Novgorodtsy v XIV stoletii. I. r.*

[Bantysh-Kamenskii, D. N.] *Kniazhna Menshikova. I. r.*

Bulgarin, F. V. *Mazepa.*

Glukharev, I. N. *Bratoubiitsa, ili Sviatopolk Okaiannyi* [banned; publication halted].

Golota, P. I. *Nalivaiko, ili Vremena bedstvii Malorossii. I. r. XVI v.*

Kalashnikov, I. T. *Kamchadalka.*

[Kurbatov, A. D.] *Poslednii god vlasti gertsoga Birona. Povest', vziataia iz starinnoi arkhivy moego dedushki.*

[Kuryshev, I.] *Maliuta Skuratov, ili Trinadtsat' let tsarstvovaniia tsaria Ioanna Vasil'evicha Groznogo. I. r. XVI stoletiia.*

[Liubetskii, S. M.] *Padenie Velikogo Novgoroda. I. r. XV v., iz kniazheniia Ioanna Vasil'evicha III Velikogo.*

Vel'tman, A. F. *Koshchei bessmertnyi. Bylina starogo vremeni.*

Zagoskin, M. N. *Askol'dova mogila. Povest' iz vremeni Vladimira Pervogo.*

1834 [Andreev, A.] *Ioann Groznyi i Stefan Batorii. I. r.*

Glukharev, I. N. *Inoki, ili Vtorichnoe pokorenie Sibiri.*

Golota, P. I. *Khmel'nitskie, ili Prisoedinenie Malorossii. I. r. XVII v.*

[Iablochkova, E. N.] *Shigony. Russkaia povest' XVI stoletiia. S tochnym opisaniem zhit'ia-byt'ia russkikh boiar, ikh pribytiia v otchiny, pokornost' zhen, piry vel'mozhei i, nakonets, tsarskaia vecherinka. Mimokhodom zamecheny monakhi togo vremeni, ikh poklonnitsy, ne zabyty i istinno sviatye muzhi, kak-to startsy Simeon Kurbskii, Vassian Patrikeev i Maksim Grek v dostovernuiu epokhu vtorichnogo braka tsaria Vasiliia Ioannovicha. Vybrano iz rukopisei izdatel'nitseiu "Suprug Vladimira."*

Kalashnikov, I. T. *Izgnanniki. Povest'.*

Konshin, N. M. *Graf Oboianskii, ili Smolensk v 1812 godu. Rasskaz invalida.*

[Liubetskii, S. M.] *Rozhdenie blagolsovennogo doma Romanovykh na Rossiiskom prestole. Romanicheskie kartiny istoricheskikh sobytii.*

[Liubetskii, S. M.] *Tan'ka, razboinitsa Rostokinskaia, ili Tsarskie terema. I. p. XVIII stoletiia. S pesniami, obriadami i prazdnestvami togdashnego byta. Iz predanii russkoi stariny.*

Masal'skii, K. P. *Regenstvo Birona. Povest'.*

Moskvichin, A. (A. A. Pavlov) *Iapancha, tatarskii naezdnik, ili Zavoevanie Kazani tsarem Ioannom Groznym. Roman XVI v.*

Rudnevskii. *David Igorevich kniaz' Vladimirskii, ili 1097 god. I. r. XI veka.*

Svin'in, P. P. *Ermak, ili Pokorenie Sibiri. I. r. XVI stoletiia.*

Zotov, R. M. *Tainstvennyi monakh, ili Nekotorye cherty iz zhizni Petra I. I. r.*

Zubov, P. P. *Karabakhskii astrolog, ili Osnovanie kreposti Shushi v 1752 g. Istoricheskii zakavkazskii roman.*

Zubov, P. P. *Prekrasnaia gruzinka, ili Nashestvie Ali Magmet Khana na Tiflis v 1795 g. Istoricheskii gruzinskii roman.*

1835 Andreev, A. *Dovmont, kniaz' pskovskii. I. r. XIII veka.*

[Churovskii, A. I.] *Ataman Buria, ili Vol'nitsa zavolzhskaia. Russkii roman iz predanii stariny.*

Gogol, N. V. *Taras Bul'ba* (*Mirgorod* edition).

[Kuryshev, I.] *Osnovanie Moskvy, ili Smert' boiarina Stepana Ivanovicha Kuchki. I. r., vziatyi iz vremen kniazheniia Iziaslava Mstislavicha.*

Lazhechnikov, I. I. *Ledianoi dom. Roman.*

Shishkina, O. P. *Kniaz' Skopin-Shuiskii, ili Rossiia v nachale XVII stoletiia. I. r.*

Vel'tman, A. F. *Sviatoslavich vrazhii pitomets. Divo vremen Krasnogo Solntsa Vladimira.*

1836 Fomin, N. *Sten'ka Razin.*

Griboedov, I. *Sof'ia Kuchko, ili Liubov' i mshchenie. I. r. XII stoletiia.*

Kislov, A. S. *Padenie Shuiskikh, ili Vremena bedstvii Rossii. I. r. XVII v.*

l'vov, V. V. *Seryi armiak, ili Ispolnennoe obeshchunie.*

[Pavlov, A. A.] *Brat Viacheslav, ili Podzemel'e bliz Kasimova. Povest' XVI stoletiia.*

Polevoi, K. A. *Lomonosov* (rpt. as *roman*).

Protopopov, A. *Smert' Napoleona, ili Rasstreliannyi shpion. I. r. v dramaticheskikh kartinakh.*

Pushkin, A.S. *Kapitanskaia dochka.*

1837 Anon. (D—— M——) *Dimitrii Donskoi. I. r.*

Anon. *Zaraisk, ili Nachalo vladychestva tatar nad Rossieiu. I. p. XIII stoletiia.*

[Churovskii, A. I.] *Zaporozhskie naezdy. Ukrainskaia byl' iz vremen getmanshchiny.*

Masal'skii, K. P. *Borodoliubie.*

[Merkli, M. M.] *Boris Godunov i Rossiia v XVII stoletii. Roman poluistoricheskii* (rpt. as *Kniaz' Vasilii Sitskii*).

[Pavlov, A. A.] *Russkii bogatyr'. Povest' vremen davno minuvshikh.*

Shteven, I. P. *Providenie, ili Sobytie XVIII veka.*

[Veidemeier, A. I.] *Epizod iz vladychestva Bironova. I. p.*

Zarnitsin, M. *Sten'ka Razin. I. r.*

Zotov, R. M. *Niklas, Medvezh'ia Lapa, ataman kontrabandistov, ili Nekotorye cherty iz zhizni Fridrikha II. I. r.*

Zriakhov, N. I. *Mikhail Novgorodskii, ili Narushennaia kliatva. Rossiisko-istoricheskii roman.*

1838 Lazhechnikov, I. I. *Basurman.*

[Pavlov, A. A.] *Kramol'niki. I. r. iz vremen Petra Velikogo.*

Shteven, I. P. *Tsygan, ili Uzhasnaia mest'. Proisshestvie minuvshego stoletiia.*

Zotov, R. M. *Fra-Diavolo, ili Poslednie dni Venetsii. I. r.*

Zotov, R. M. *Student i kniazhna, ili Vozvrashchenie Napoleona s ostrova El'by. I. p.*

1839 Anon. *Ermak, pokoritel' Sibiri. I. r.*

Anon. *Vechevoi kolokol. Russkii roman XV stoletiia.*

Anon. *Borodinskoe pole, ili Smert' za chest'.*

Gur'ianov, I. G. *Dmitrii Ioannovich Donskoi, ili Uzhasnoe Mamaevo poboishche. Povest'.*

Dmitrevskii, M. *Ivan Susanin, ili Smert' za tsaria. I. r.*

[Salmanov, P. A.] *Chernoe vremia, ili Stseny iz zhizni Emel'ki Pugacheva. I. r. XVIII v.*

Zotov, R. M. *Shapka iurodivogo, ili Trilistvennik. I. r. iz vremen Elisavety i Ekateriny.*

1840 Glukharev, I. N. *Kniaz' Pozharskii i nizhegorodskii grazhdanin Minin.*

Pavlov, A. A. *Rytsar' Kresta. Nekotorye cherty iz dostopamiatnogo goda.*

1841 Anon. (D——rii S——ov). *Izgnannik. Roman vremeni Ioanna Groznogo.*

Korf, F. F., Baron. *Sud v revel'skom magistrate. Roman iz istorii Estliandii XVI st.*

Kukol'nik, N. V. *Evelina de Val'erol'.*

Polevoi, N. A. *Ioann Tsimiskhii.*

Zagoskin, M. N. *Kuz'ma Petrovich Miroshev. Russkaia byl' vremen Ekateriny II.*

1842 Gogol, N. V. *Taras Bul'ba* (rev. ed.).

Kukol'nik, N. V. *Al'f i Al'dona.*

Masal'skii, K. P. *Nevesta Petra Vtorogo* [unfinished].

1843 Grebenka, E. P. *Chaikovskii. Roman.*

Fedorov, B. *Kniaz' Kurbskii. I.r. iz sobytii XVI v.*

Kuz'mich, A. P. *Kazaki.*

Protopopov, A. P. (Slavin). *Osada Troitse-Sergievskoi lavry, ili Russkie v 1608 g.*

Vel'tman, A. F. *Raina, korolevna Bolgarskaia.*

1844 Kukol'nik, N. V. *Dva Ivana, dva Stepanycha, dva Kostyl'kova.*

Zotov, R. M. *Borodinskoe iadro i Berezinskaia pereprava. Poluistoricheskii roman.*

1845 Potapov, V. F. *Marfa Vasil'evna, tret'ia supruga Ioanna Groznogo. I. r. XVI v.*

Sementovskii, N. M. *Kochubei, general'nyi sud'ia. I. p.*

Shishkina, O. P. *Prokopii Liapunov, ili Mezhdutsarstvie v Rossii.*

1846 Gessel', N. P. *Mstislavlev, ili Sdacha goroda Mogileva. Iz tsarstvovaniia Alekseia Mikhailovicha 1654 g.* (rpt. as *Vladimir Mstislavskii* and *Vladimir, russkoe serdtse*).

Korenevskii, V. *Getman Ostrianitsa. Iz epokhi smut i bedstvii Malorossii. I. r. XVII v.*

Kulish, P. A. *Kievskie bogomol'tsy XVII v.*

Kuz'mich, A. P. *Zinovii-Bogdan Khmel'nitskii.*

Potapov, V. F. *Ivan Velikoi. I. r. vremen Borisa Godunova, Lzhedimitriia i tsaria Vasiliia Shuiskogo.*

Potapov, V. F. *Raskol'niki, ili Khizhina v Chernom boru* (rpt. as *Charodei, ili Khizhina v Cherom boru and Chernyi bor, ili Tainstvennaia khizhina*).

Pospelov, A. *Matiushka Verevkin, buntovshchik i samozvanets, iavivshiisia v Rossii v tsarstvovanie Vasiliia Ioannovicha Shuiskogo. I. r.*

Zagoskin, M. N. *Brynskii les. I. r. iz pervykh godov tsarstvovaniia Petra I.*

1847 Furman, P. R. *Aleksandr Danilovich Menshikov.*

Zubov, P. P. *Talisman, ili Kavkaz v poslednie gody Ekateriny II.*

1848 Furman, P. R. *Aleksandr-Vasil'evich Suvorov-Rymnikskii.*

Furman, P. R. *Blizhnii boiarin Artamon Matveev.*

Furman, P. R. *Doch' shuta.*

Masal'skii, K. P. *Leitenant i poruchik. Byl' vremen Petra Velikogo.*

Zagoskin, M. N. *Russkie v nachale XVIII stoletiia. Rasskaz iz vremen edinoderzhaviia Petra Velikogo.*

1849 Skal'kovskii, A. *Porubezhniki. Kanva dlia romanov.* (includes tales: *Kagal'nichanka, Khrustal'naia balka, Brat'ia-iskupiteli*).

1850 Zotov, R. M. *Dva brata, ili Moskva v 1812 g.*

1851 Potapov, V. F. *Andrei Besstrashnyi, invalid Petra Velikogo, ili Za Bogom molitva, a za tsarem sluzhba ne propadaiut! Russkaia byl'.*

Sementovskii, N. M. *Potemkin kak kazak Voiska zaporozhskogo.*

1852 Balashevich, Iu. *Iezuity. V nachale XVII stoletiia.*

1853 Kukol'nik, N. V. *Tonni, ili Revel' pri Petre Velikom.*

Kulish, P. A. (M. Nikolai). *Aleksei Odnorog. I. r.*

Nikolaevich, I. *Bitva russkikh s cherkesami, ili Pastukh chernoi doliny. I. r.*

Nikolaevich, I. *Chigirinskii les, ili Vera sil'nee liubvi. Nravstvenno-istoricheskii roman.*

Nikolaevich I. *Nishchii, ili Izbavlennaia zhertva. Iz vremen kniazia Pozharskogo.*

1854 Nikolaevich, I. *Brilliantovaia luna. Iz poslednikh vremen vladeniia genueztsev v Tavrii. Rasskaz balaklavskogo otstavnogo shkol'nogo storozha.*

[Potapov, V. F.] *Eretik. Istoricheskii roman XIII stoletiia.*

Savinov, V. I. *Znakhari. I. r.*

1856 Furman, P. R. *Natal'ia Borisovna Dolgorukova.*

1857 Golota, P. I. *Zarutskii, getman voiska Zaporozhskogo* [written in 1844].

Kulish, P. A. *Chernaia rada. Khronika 1663 g.*

1858 Anon. *Oleg veshchii, velikii knaz' Kievskii.*

Shmitanovskii, V. Ia. *Ermak, ili Pokorenie Sibirskogo tsarstva. I. p.*

1859 Zotov, R. M. *Tainstvennye sily, ili Nekotorye cherty iz tsarstvovania imperatora Pavla I.*

1860 Zotov, R. M. *Dve sestry, ili Smolensk v 1812 g.*

1861 Anon. *Chertovo razdol'e, ili Mest' zhidovki. Istoricheskii roman iz vremen Borisa Godunova i Dimitriia Samozvantsa.*

1862 Tolstoi, Count A. K. *Kniaz' Serebrianyi. Povest' vremen Ioanna Groznogo.*

1864 Kulish, P. A. *Porubezhniki. Istoricheskii rasskaz.*

1865 Kostomarov, N. I. *Syn. Rasskaz iz vremen XVII v.*

1865–66 Tolstoi, Count L. N. *Tysiacha vosem'sot piaty god*

1867–69 Tolstoi, Count L. N. *Voina i mir.*

1867 Vel'tman, E. I. *Prikliucheniia korolevicha Gustava Irikovicha, zhenikha tsarevny Ksenii Goduovoi.*

1870 Bulkin (S. A. Ladyzhenskii) *Syshchiki. I. p. iz bironovskogo vremeni.*

Kel'siev, V. P. *Moskva i Tver'.*

Pavlov, N. M. *Tsarskii sokol'nik. I. p. iz vremen Alekseia Mikhailovicha.*

1871 Averkiev, D. V. *Khmelevaia noch'. Povest'* (rpt. as *I.r*).

Kel'siev, V. P. *Na vse ruki master.*

Kel'siev, V. P. and V. P. Kliushnikov. *Pri Petre. I. p. vremen preobrazovaniia Rossii.*

1872 Chaev, N. A. *Bogatyri. Roman iz vremen imp. Pavla I.*

Miliukov, A. P. *Tsarskaia svad'ba. Bylina o gosudare Ivane Vasil'eviche Groznom.*

Petrov, P. N., and V. P. Kliushnikov. *Sem'ia vol'nodumtsev. I. p. vremeni Ekateriny Velikoi.*

Zotov, R. M. *Poslednii potomok Chingis-Khana.*

1873 Markov, V. L. *Kurskie porubezhniki. I. r.*

Salias, Count E. A. *Pugachevtsy. R.*

1874 Golitsyn, Prince S. V. *Byloe vremechko.* (pt. 1. Pt. 2 published in 1876).

Petrov, P. N. (completion of novel begun by N. V. Kukol'nik), *IoannIII, sobiratel' Zemli Russkoi. I. r., nachatyi N. V. Kukol'nikom, a so 2-i gl. II-i chasti prodolzhennyi i zakonchennnyi Petrovym.*

1875 Kostomarov, N. I. *Kudeiar. Istoricheskaia khronika.*

Krestovskii, V. V. *Dedy. I. p.*

1876 Bogrov, G. I. *Evreiskii manuskript. Pered dramoi. I. p.*

Danilevskii, G. P. *Potemkin na Dunae.*

Mordovtsev, D. L. *Idealisty i realisty. I. r.* (rpt. as *Ten' Iroda*).

Solov'ev, V. S. *Kniazhna Ostrozhskaia.*

1877 Karnovich, E. P. *Mal'tiiskie rytsari v Rossii. Povest' iz vremen imperatora Pavla I.*

Petrov, P. N. *Tsarskii sud. I. p.*

Salias, Count E. A. *Madonna (Iz odnoi semeinoi khroniki).*

Solov'ev, V. S. *Iunyi imperator.*

1878 Karnovich, E. P. *Samozvannye deti. (Iz skazanii XVIII stoletia)* (rpt. as *I. p. iz vremen Ekateriny II*).

Kondrat'ev, I. K. *Drama na Lubianke. I. r. iz epokhi krovavykh dram i velikikh smiatenii* (rpt. as *Velikii razgrom and Kazn' Vereshchagina, ili Moskvichi v 1812 g*).

Kondrat'ev, I. K. *Gunny. Epoha velikogo pereseleniia narodov. I. r. iz zhizni slavian IV i V st.* (rpt. as *Bich Bozhii*).

Kostomarov, N. I. *Kholui. Epizod iz istoriko-bytovoi russkoi zhizni pervoi poloviny XVIII stoletiia.*

Petrov, P. N. *Dva uzla odnoi verevki (Kharakteristika vremen Petra I).*

Polezhaev, P. V. *Prestol i monastyr'. Letopis' 1682 i 1689 g.*

Solov'ev, V. S. *Kapitan grenaderskoi roty. Roman-khronika iz XVIII v.*

Solov'ev, V. S. *Tsar'-Devitsa. Roman-khronika XVII v.*

1879 Averkiev, D. V. *Likho. I. p.*

Danilevskii, G. P. *Mirovich. I. r.* (written in 1875).

Karnovich, E. P. *Liubov' i korona. I. r iz vremen imp. Anny Ioannovny i v regentstva printsessy Anny Leopol'dovny.*

Karnovich, E. P. *Na vysote i na dole. Iz skazanii XVII v (Tsarevna Sof'ia Alekseevna).*

Mordovtsev, D. L. *Dvenadtsatyi god (Kavalerist-devitsa). I. r.*

Mordovtsev, D. L. *Lzhedimitrii.*

Mordovtsev, D. L. *Nanosnaia beda. Istoricheskaia povest' vremeni chumy na Moskve.*

Mordovtsev, D. L. *Tsar' i getman.*

Politkovskii, V. *Novgorodskii pogrom. I. p. iz russkoi zhini XV st.*

Salias, Count E. A. *Graf Taitin Baltiiskii. I. r.*

Sokolov, A. A. *Tsar'-baba. I. r.*

Solov'ev, V. S. *Kasimovskaia nevesta. I. r.*

1880 Bogoslavskii, N. G. *Starye poriadki. I. p. iz byta voennykh poselenii* (rpt. in 1882 as *Arakcheevshchina as Onofrei i Osip Kuz'miny, konets voennykh poselenii*).

Chmyrev, N. A. *Raskol'nich'i muchenitsy. I. r. iz epokhi tserkovnykh smut.*

Chmyrev, N. A. *Razvenchannaia tsarevna.*

Danilevskii, G. P. *Na Indiiu pri Petre.*

Mordovtsev, D. L. *Solovetskoe sidenie* (also published as *Sidenie raskol'nikov v Solovkakh*).

Mordovtsev, D. L. *Velikii raskol. I. p. XVII v.*

Petrov, P. N. *Balakirev. I. r. iz vremen Petra I.*

Pisemskii, A. F. *Masony.*

Politkovskaia, M. E. *Ivon Moldavskii. I. p. iz bor'by za svobodu slavian v XVI v.*

Politkovskii, V. *Tsarskaia nevesta. I. p. (1613–1624)* [*Istoricheskaia biblioteka* 1–2].

Salias, Count E. A. *Brigadirskaia vnuchka. Moskovskaia byl'.*

Salias, Count E. A. *Mor na Moskve I. r. iz vremen chumy 1771* g. (rpt. as *Na Moskve*).

Salias, Count E. A. *Peterburgskoe deistvo (1762 g.) I. r.*

Salmanov, P. A. *Kniaz' Boris Shegliatev. I. r. XIII v., iz vremen nashestviia Batyia na Rossiiu.*

Shardin, A. (P. P. Sukhonin) *Rod kniazei Zatsepinykh, ili Bor'ba nachal. I. r.*

Sokolov, A. A. *Ponizovaia vol'nitsa atamana Sten'ki Razina. I. r.*

1881 Eval'd, A. V. *Imperator Vizantii. I. r. epokhi tsarstvovaniia imp. Aleksandra I.*

Kostomarov, N. I. *Chernigovka. Byl' vtoroi poloviny XVII v.*

Mordovtsev, D. L. *Mamaevo poboishche. I. p.*

Kazantsev, N. V. *Protiv techeniia. I. r. vremen Sten'ki Razina.*

Salias, Count E. A. *Printsessa Volodimirskaia (Samozvanka).*

Shakhovskaia, Princess L. D. *Karfagen i Rim. I. r.*

Shakhovskaia, Princess L. D. *Sivilla, volshebnitsa Kumskogo grota. I. r.*

Shardin, A. (P. P. Sukhonin). *Kniazhna Vladimirskaia (Tarakanova), ili Zatsepinskie kapitaly. I. r.*

Solov'ev, V. S. *Sergei Gorbatov. I. r. kontsa XVIII v. (pt. 1 of Khronika chetyrekh pokolenii).*

1882 Markov, V. L. *Likholet'e (Smutnoe vremia). I. r.*

Mordovtsev, D. L. *Gospodin velikii Novgorod.*

Mordovtsev, D. L. *Sagaidachnyi.*

Polezhaev, P. V. *Lopukhinskoe delo. I. p. vremen Elizavety Petrovny.*

Salias, Count E. A. *Kamer-iungefa.*

Shakhovskaia, Princess L. D. *Nad bezdnoi. I. r. epokhi Tsitserona.*

Solov'ev, V. S. *Vol'ter'ianets. I. r. kontsa XVIII v.* (pt. 2 of *Khronika chetyrekh pokolenii*).

1883 Chmyrev, N. *Vo sviatoi obiteli. Istoricheskii roman iz vremeni Petra Velikogo.*

Danilevskii, G. P. Kniazhna Tarakanova. I. r.

Danilevskii, G. P. *Vosem'sot dvadtsat' piatyi god* (1821–25) (unfinished) [*Istoricheskii vestnik*].

Karnovich, E. P. *Pridvornoe kruzhevo. I. r.*

Polezhaev, P. V. 150 *let nazad. Biron i Volynskii.*

Salias, Count E.A. *Naidenysh (Prodolzhenie romana "Pugachevtsy").*

Shardin, A. (P. P. Sukhonin). *Na rubezhe dvukh stoletii.*

Solov'ev, V. S. Staryi dom. I. r. nachala tsarstvovaniia imp. Nikolaia I (pt. 3 of *Khronika chetyrekh pokolenii*).

Zaguliaev, M. A. *Russkii iakobinets. Strannaia istoriia.*

1884 Chmyrev, N. A. *Ataman volzhskikh razboinikov Ermak, kniaz' Sibirskii* (also rpt. as *Ermak, pokoritel' Sibiri*).

Chmyrev, N. A. *Ivan Mazepa. I. r.*

Karnovich, E. P. *Paguba. I. r.*

Petrov, P. N. *Kozyri ne v ruke. I. r. 1725–1727 gg.* (rpt. as *Belye i chernye*).

Shakhovskaia, Princess L. D. *Zhrebii broshen. I. r. epokhi Iuliia Tsezaria.*

Sokolov, A. A. *Sestra miloserdiia. Roman. I. r.*

Solov'ev, V. S. *Izgnannik. I. r.* (pt. 4 of *Khronika chetyrekh pokolenii*).

Sysoeva, E. A. *Aktea. Povest' iz drevnei rimskoi i grecheskoi zhizni.*

Tolycheva, T. *Kniaz' Ivan Kalita—Solnecnyi luch.*

1885 Avenarius, V. P. *Otrocheskie gody Pushkina. Biograficheskaia povest'.*

Chmyrev, N. A. *Aleksandr Nevskii i novgorodskaia vol'nitsa. I. r.*

Filippov, M. A. *Patriarkh Nikon.*

Karatygin, P. P. *Chernoknizhniki. R. iz vremeni tsarstvovaniia Pavla I.*

Khrushchov-Sokol'nikov, G. A. *Sten'ka Razin. I. r.* (rpt. as *Pri Sten'ke Razine. Byl' na Volge*).

Mordovtsev, D. L. *Avantiuristy.*

Mordovtsev, D. L. *Pokhorony. I. r.*

Mordovtsev, D. L. *Tsar' Petr i pravitel'nitsa Sof'ia.*

Pazukhin, N. M. *Ermak—pokoritel' Sibiri.*

Polezhaev, P. V. *Tsarevich Aleksei Petrovich.*

Salias, Count E. A. *Ataman Ustia (Povolzhskaia byl').*

Salias, Count E. A. *Kudesnik (Graf Kaliostro) I. r.*

Salias, Count E. A. *Shir' i makh (Million). I. r.*

Salias, Count E. A. *V staroi Moskve (Samokrutka) I. p.*

Solov'ev, V. S. *Poslednie Gorbatovy.* (pt. 5 of *Khronika chetyrekh pokolenii*).

Tolycheva, T. (E. V. Novosil'tseva) *Krest patriarkha Filareta. Roman.*

1886 Danilevskii, G. P. *Sozhzhennaia Moskva. I. r.*

Filippov, M. M. *Ostap. I. p. iz vremen Khmel'nitskogo.*

Karatygin, P. P. *Zakoldovannoe zerkalo.*

Karnovich, E. P. *Smelaia zhizn'. Roman iz moskovskoi zhizni na iskhode XVII st.*

Khrushchov-Sokol'nikov, G. A. *Chudo-bogatyr' (Suvorov). I. r.*

Makarova, S. M. *Groznaia tucha. I. p. dlia iunoshestva iz vremen Otechestvennoi voiny.*

Salias, Count E. A. *Svadebnyi bunt (1705 g.). I. r.*

Shakhovskaia, Princess L. D. *Molodost' tsezaria Oktaviana Avgusta, triumvira rimskogo. I. r.*

Shchepkina, A. V. *Na zare. Ocherk iz byta vremen Elisavety.*

1887 Abaza, V. A. *Markitantka (Istoricheskii eskiz vremen revoliutsii, konsul'stva i imperii).*

Chmyrev, N. A. *Boiarin Petr Basmanov.*

Filippov, M. A. *Pod nebom Ukrainy.*

Karnovich, E. P. *Perepolokh v Peterburge.*

Makarova, S. M. *Sueta suet. I. p. dlia iunoshestva iz russkoi zhizni proshlogo stoletiia.*

Mordovtsev, D. L. *Beglyi korol'. I. p.*

Pazukhin, N. M. *Kniaz' Skopin-Shuiskii. I. r. XVI stoletiia.*

Polezhaev, P. V. *Favor i opala. I. r. vremen Petra II.*

Pazukhin, A. M. *Egor Urvan—ataman zaporozhskogo voiska. I. p.*

Salias, Count E. A. *Iaun-Kundze.*

Shakhovskaia, Princess L. D. *Pod vlast'iu Tiveriia. I. r.*

Sokolov, A. A. *Borodino. I. r. s portretami deiatelei 1812 g.*

1888 Avenarius, V. P. *Iunosheskie gody Pushkina. Biograficheskaia povest'.*

Danilevskii, G. P. *Chernyi god.*

Dobrov, F. V. (Dombrovskii). *Vladimir Krasnoe Solnyshko, ili 900 let nazad. I. r.*

Dubrovina, E. O. *Mertvetsy-mstiteli.*

Filippov, M. M. *Osazhdennyi Sevastopol'.*

Karatygin, P. P. *Dela davno minuvshikh dnei (1818–1825). I. r.*

Khitrov, M. I. *Evstafii Plakida. Povest' iz istorii khristianskoi tserkvi kontsa I i nachala II stoletiia.*

Kondrat'ev, I. K. *Saltychikha. Iz ugolovnykh khronik XVIII v.*

Kondrat'ev, I. K. *Tserkovnaia kramol'nitsa. I. r. iz epokh staroobriadcheskikh smut.*

Polevoi, P. N. *Brat'ia-soperniki I. r. iz vremen pravleniia Sofii.*

Rogova, O. I. *Bogdan Khmel'nitskii. I. p. dlia iunoshestva.*

Salias, Count E. A. *Arakcheevskii synok. I. r.* [*Istoricheskii vestnik* 1–12].

Salias, Count E. A. *Brigadirskaia vnuchka. Moskovskaia byl'.*

Sokolov, A. A. *Belyi general. I. r.*

Sokolov, A. A. *Ustin'ia Fedorovna (Ustia), ataman volzhskikh golovorezov. I. r.*

Sokolov, A. A. *Za chest' i svobodu. I. r. iz vremen osvobozhdeniia Malorossii.*

Sokolov, A. A. *Zinovii Bogdan Khmel'nitski—osvoboditel' Malorossii. I. r.*

Solov'ev, V. S. *Volkhvy. Roman XVIII v.*

1889 Dmitriev, D. S. *Samoszhigateli, ili Za staruiu veru. I. p. iz vremen Petra I.*

Dmitriev, D. S. *V proshlom veke. I. p.*

Dubrovina, E. O. *Rukhnuvshii velikan. I. r. iz XV veka.*

Khovanskii, M. A. *Nevestka Petra Velikogo (Tsarevna Sharlota). I. r.*

Khrushchev-Sokol'nikov, G. A. *Griunval'dskii boi, ili Slaviane i nemtsy. Roman-khronika.*

Mikhailov, A. (A. K. Sheller). *Iz-za vlasti. I. r.—khronika.*

Nikolaev, N. *Raby vrazhdy. Roman iz vremen pol'skikh zagovorov i miatezha 1863 g.*

Salias, Count E. A. *Arakcheevskii podkidysh.* (Prodolzhenie romana *Arakcheevskii synok*) [*Istoricheskii vestnik* 1–10].

Salias, Count E.A. *Baryni-krest'ianki. I. r.*

Shakhovskaia, Princess L. D. *Neron. I. r.*

Solov'ev, V. S. *Velikii Rozenkreitser. Roman XVIII veka.*

1890 Avenarius, V. P. *Tri ventsa* (1 ch. trilogii *Za tsarevicha!*).

Bykov, A. A. *Sedaia starina. Original'nyi roman iz drevneegipetskoi zhizni* [*Nabliudatel'* 7–12].

Dmitriev, K. *Ne v sile Bog, a v pravde. I. r. iz vremen Ioanna III* (also published as *Sobrat' Rus'!*).

Dubrovina, E. O. *Opal'nyi. I. r.*

Leskov, N. S. *Gora. Roman iz egipetskoi zhizni.*

Mikhailov, A. (A. K. Sheller). *Dvorets i monastyr'. I. r.—khronika vremen velikogo kniazia Vasiliia Ivanovicha i tsaria Ioanna Groznogo.*

Mordovtsev, D. L. *Za ch'i grekhi? Povest' iz vremen bunta Razina.*

Mordovtsev, D. L. *Zamurovannaia tsaritsa. Roman iz zhizni drevnego Egipta.*

Nikolaeva, E. *Ot plakhi k pochesti. I. r. iz epokhi zavoevaniia Sibiri.*

Salias, Count E. A. *Pan Krul'. I. r.*

Salias, Count E. A. *Zaira. Roman.*

Shakhovskaia, Princess L. D. *Vestalka.*

Sokolov, A. A. *Krov'iu, ognem i zhelezom* (Prodolzhenie rom. *Za chest' i svobodu*). *I. r.*

Solov'ev, V. S. *Tsarskoe posol'stvo. I. r. XVII v.*

1891 Bezobrazov, P. V. *Imperator Mikhail.*

Dmitriev, D. S. *Russkie orly. I. p. iz epokhi 1812, 1813 i 1814 g.*

Dubrovina, E. O. *Zasluzhennaia kara. I. r. vremen Arakcheeva* (Prodolzhenie romana *Opal'nyi*).

Geintse, N. E. *Maliuta Skuratov. I. r.*

Markov, E. L. *Razboinitsa Orlikha. Iz mestnykh predanii XVIII v.*

Mordovtsev, D. L. *Tsar' bez tsarstva. Roman iz poslednikh dnei tsarstva Imeretinskogo.*

Mordovtsev, D. L. *Za vsemirnoe vladychestvo. I. r. vremen Mariia (Bor'ba pontiiskogo tsaria Mitridata).*

Mordovtsev, D. L. *Zhertvy vulkana. I. r. iz posldnikh dnei zhizni Pompei.*

Pazukhin, A. M. *Opolchennaia Rossiia.*

Polevoi, P. N. *Koren' zla. I. r.*

Polevoi, P. N. *Tal'ianskaia chertovka. I. p.*

Salias, Count E. A. *Filozof. I. p.*

Salias, Count E. A. *Vedun'ia. I. r.*

Severin, N. (Merder). *Vorotyntsevy (Famil'naia khronika)* (rpt. as *Famil'naia khronika orotyntsevykh*).

Shakhovskaia, Princess L. D. *Iuvenal.*

Volkonskii, Prince M. N. *Kniaz' Nikita Feodorovich. I. r.*

Volkonskii, Prince M. N. *Mal'tiiskaia tsep'.*

1892 Arsen'ev, A. V. *Kniaz' Dmitrii Ioannovich Donskoi (Iz epokhi groznogo veka). I. r.*

Avenarius, V. P. *Vampir. Byl' ekateriniskikh vremen* [*Knizhki "Nedeli"* 1–4].

Danilevskii, G. P. *Tsarevich Aleksei. I. r.* (unfinished).

Dubrovina, E. O. *Iz t'my vekov.*

Kassirov, I. S. *Strashnaia smert' bez viny. I. p. vremen Ioanna Vasil'evicha III* (remake of Lazhechnikov's *Basurman*).

Mamin-Sibiriak, D. N. *Okhoniny brovi.*

Nemirovich-Danchenko, V. I. *Gornye orly. I. r.* [*Sever*].

Pavlova, N. I. *V smutnye gody. Roman* [*Russkii vestnik* 1892: 10–11; 1893: 1–4, 8–12].

Polevoi, P. N. *Gde Bog i pravda? I. p.*

Salias, Count E. A. *Novaia Sandril'ona. R.* [*Russkoe obozrenie* 1892–93].

Severin, N. (Merder). *Poslednii iz Vorotyntsevykh. I. r.*

Shakhovskaia, Princess L. D. *Liubimets kesaria. I. r. epokhi pervykh vekov khristianstva.*

Shreknik, E. F. *Soperniki. I r. iz vremen tsarstvovaniia Vasiliia Shuiskogo.*

1893 Arsen'ev, A. V. *Frantsuzinka. Istoricheskaia povest' iz epokhi Otechestvennoi voiny.*

Bezobrazov, P. V. *Ded i vnuk. I.r.* [*Trud* 7–12].

Geintse, N. E. *Arakcheev. I. r. XIX st.*

Kryzhanovskaia, V. I. (Rochester) *Gerkulanum* (originally published in French 1889).

Kryzhanovskaia, V. I. (Rochester) *Sim pobedishi!* (Hoc signo vinces!).

Nemirovich-Danchenko, V. I. *Gore zabytoi kreposti. Roman* [*Sever*].

Polevoi, P. N. *Marinka-bezbozhnitsa. I. r. XVII-go st.*

Polevoi, P. N. *Pod neotrazimoi desnitsei. I. r.*

Ryskin, S. F. *Kuplennyi mitropolit, ili Rogozhskie milliony. R. iz istorii raskola.*

Salias, Count E. A. *Krutoiarskaia tsarevna. I. p. (1773 g.).*

Shakhovskaia, Princess L. D. *Po pravu sil'nogo. I. r. epokhi pervykh vekov khristianstva.*

Shelonskii, N. N. *Za krest i rodinu. Roman iz epokhi bor'by za osvobozhdenie Gretsii.*

Shreknik, E. F. *Khristofor Kolumb. Original'nyi i. r. iz epokhi otkrytiia Ameriki.*

Sokolov, A. A. *S zhivogo kozhu. I. r.* (Prodolzhenie rom. *Krov'iu ognem i zhelezom*).

Solov'ev, V. S. *Zhenikh tsarevny. Roman-khronika XVII v.*

Tiumenev, I. F. (Privol'ev). *Khaldei. Povest' iz novgorodskogo byta XV v.*

Vasil'ev, P. S. *Van'ka-Kain. I. p.*

Volkonskii, Prince M. N. *Volia sud'by.*

Volkonskii, Prince M. N. *Zabytye khoromy.*

1894 Aksakov, N. P. *Deti krestonostsy. I. p.*

Arsen'ev, A. V. *Zhestokoe ispytanie. I. r.*

Bezobrazov, P. V. *Zhenikh dvukh nevest.*

Dubrovina, E. O. *Beskrovnaia mest'* [sequel to *Iz t'my vekov*].

Grinev, S. A. *Povstantsy. Roman iz vremeni pol'skogo vosstaniia 1863 g.*

Kryzhanovskaia, V. I. (Rochester) *Tsaritsa Khatasu.*

Mordovtsev, D. L. *Zhelezom i krov'iu. Roman iz zavoevaniia Kavkaza pri Ermolove.*

Pavlova, N. I. *Razviazka. Roman* (Prodolzhenie romana *Smutnye gody*). [*Russkii vestnik* 1894: 1, 2, 4].

Salias, Count E. A. *General Makhov. I. p.* [*Russkoe obozrenie* 1–3].

Salias, Count E. A. *Via facti. I. r. (1771–1773)* [*Istoricheskii vestnik*].

Shakhovskaia, Princess L. D. *Potomki geroev. I. r.*

Shreknik, E. F. *Gutenbeg i Sheffer. I. r. iz epokhi vozrozhdeniia nauk i iskusstv.*

Sokolov, A. A. *Priviazannyi k boiryshne. I. r.* (Prodolzhenie rom. *S zhivogo kozhu*).

1895 Avenarius, V. P. *Vo l'vinoi pasti. I. p. dlia iunosheshstva iz epokhi osnovaniia Peterburga.*

Geintse, N. E. *Kniaz' Tavridy. I. r.*

Geintse, N. E. *Koronovannyi rytsar' (Tainy Tavricheskogo sada). I. r. iz tsarstvovaniia imp. Pavla I.*

Geintse, N. E. *Novgorodskaia vol'nitsa. I. r. iz vremen Ioanna III.*

Krasnitskii, A. I. *V tumane tysiacheletiia. I. r. iz epokhi obrazovaniia russkogo gosudarstva.*

Merezhkovskii, D. S. *Otverzhennyi* (rpt. as *Smert'bogov Iulian Otstupnik*).

Mordovtsev, D. L. *Derzhavnyi plotnik.*

Mordovtsev, D. L. *Mest' zhretsov.*

Mordovtsev, D. L. *Svetu bol'she! I. r.*

Orlovskii, S. N. (S. N. Shil'). *Ziriub. Povest' iz zhizni arabov v deviatom veke.*

Salias, E. A. Count. *Puteshestvenniki. I. p.*

Salias, E. A. Count. *Sluzhitel' Boga. I. r.*

Severin, N. (Merder). *V poiskakh istiny* [*Istoricheskii vestnik* 1–12].

Shakhovskaia, Princess L. D. *Serebrianyi vek. I. r. epokhi pervykh vremen khristianstva.*

Volkonskii, Prince M. N. *Brat gertsoga.*

1896 Alekseev, N. N. *Tatarskii otprysk.*

Anichkova, I. A. *Ringil'da. Istoricheskii roman XIII st.* (also published as *Dominus Eilard*).

Dmitriev, D. S. *Dva imperatora. I. p. iz epokhi srazhenii imp. Aleksandra I s Napoleonom I.*

Dmitriev, D. S. *Zachalo Moskvy i boiarin Kuchka. I. p.*

Geintse, N. E. *Generalissimus Suvorov. I. r. XVIII st.*

Karasev, A. A. *Polkovnik Gruzinov. I. p. vremen imp. Pavla I.*

Kondrat'ev, I. K. *Raskol'nich'i gnezda (khlysty, skoptsy, beguny). I. r.—khronika.*

Krasnitskii, A. I. *Matsmaiskie plenniki. I. r. (1811–1813 gg.).*

Krasnov, P. N. *Ataman Platov. I. r. iz vremen Otechetvenoi voiny.* [*Domashniia biblioteka* 8–9].

Kryzhanovskaia, V. I. *Varfolomeevskaia noch'.*

Mordovtsev, D. L. *Prometeevo potomstvo. Roman is poslednikh dnei nezavisimosti Abkhazii.*

Popov, N. A. *Iuzia Chaplinskaia. I. r. XVII stoletiia.*

Shakhovskaia, Princess L. D. *Kesar' Adrian. I. r.*

Shakhovskaia, Princess L. D. *Konets rimskoi doblesti.*

Svetlov, V. Ia. *Belye tsvety. Original'nyi roman iz vremen frantsuzskoi revoliutsii.*

Volkonskii, Prince M. N. *Kol'tso imperatritsy. I. r. iz epokhi XVIII stoletiia.*

1897 Alekseev, N. N. *Sredi bed. I. r. (1395–1407).*

Alekseev, N. N. *Volia sud'by.*

Avenarius, V. P. *Gogol'-gimnazist.* Pervaia povest' iz biograficheskoi trilogii *Uchenicheskie gody Gogolia.*

Dmitriev, D. S. *Velikolepnyi kniaz' Tavridy. I. p.*

Dubrovina, E. O. *Zhertva trekh chestoliubii. I. r.*

Geintse, N. E. *Liudoedka. I. r. XVIII v.*

Geintse, N. E. *Pervyi russkii samoderzhets.*

Gorbachevskii, I. D. *Starina starodavniaia. I. p. X veka.*

Mordovtsev, D. L. *Irod.*

Mordovtsev, D. L. *Padenie Ierusalima I. p.* (rpt. as *Poslednie dni Ierusalima*).

Radich, V. A. *V dymu pozharov. I. r.*

Severin, N. (Merder). *Tsarskii prikaz. I. p.* (1800).

Shchepkina, A. V. *Boiare Starodubskie. I. r. iz vremen tsaria Alekseia Mikhailovicha.*

Shakhovskaia, Princess L. D. *Rimliane v Afrike. I. r.*

Volkonskii, Prince M. N. *Zapiski pradeda.*

1898 Alekseev, N. N. *Rozy i ternii.*

Avenarius, V. P. *Gogol'-student.* Vtoraia povest' iz biograficheskoi trilogii *Uchenicheskie gody Gogolia.*

Averkiev, D. V. *Vechu ne byt'.*

Beliaev, I. S. *Iskushenie. I. r. XVIII v. Iz vremen "Slova i dela".*

Dmitriev, D. S. *Kavalerist-devitsa (I. p. iz epokhi voin imp. Aleksandra I s Napoleonom I).*

Filippov, M. M. *Dvorianskaia chest' (Byl' proshlogo stoletiia).*

Geintse, N. E. *Doch Petra Velikogo.*

Geintse, N. E. *V chadu izmeny. I. r. kontsa XVII st.*

Kondrat'ev, I. K. *Trifon-sokol'nik. Istoricheskaia byl' XVI st.*

Krasnitskii, A. I. *Groza Vizantii.*

Lebedev, M. N. *Za Bogom molitva, a za tsarem sluzhba ne propadaiut. I. r.—khronika iz epokhi Otechestvennoi voiny (1812 g.).*

Mikheev, V. M. *Otrok muchenik. Uglitskoe predanie.*

Nemirovich-Danchenko, V. I. *Podnebesnyj aul. I. p. iz starykh kavkazskikh bylei.*

Polevoi, P. N. *Na rokovom prostore. I. r.*

Potapenko, I. N. *Slovo i delo.*

Rubakin, N. A. *Velikii inkvizitor (Pod gnetom vremeni). Istoricheskaia khronika XIII veka o langedokskikh eretikakh.*

Severin, N. (Merder). *Korzhunskie korshuny* [*Istoricheskii vestnik* 1–12].

Sizova, A. K. *Kseniia Godunova. I. r.*

Shakhovskaia, Princess L. D. *Lev pobeditel'. Pervyi v russkoi literature i. r. iz abissinskoi zhizni.*

Shelonskii, N. N. *Sevastopol' v osade. Roman-khronika.*

Svetlov, V. Ia. *Zvezda liubvi (1692–1695). Florentiiskaia novella (*rpt. as *Nedostroennyi khram. Florentiiskii roman).*

Alekseev, N. N. *Raby i vladyki. I. r. iz vremen tsaria Fedora Ioannovicha.*

1899 Avenarius, V. P. *Shkola zhizni velikogo iumorista. Biograficheskaia povest'* (3-ia ch. biografichesko trilogii *Uchenicheskie gody Gogolia*).

Alekseev, N. N. *Lzhetsarevich. I. r.* (Prodolzhenie romana *Rozy i ternii*).

Dmitriev, D. S. *Chudo-bogatyr'. I. r.*

Dmitriev, D. S. *Gosudareva nevesta.*

Dmitriev, D. S. *Ivan Mazepa. I. r. vremen Petra I.*

Dmitriev, D. S. *Kniaginia Elena Glinskaia. I. p.*

Dmitriev, D. S. *Kniaz' Vladimir Krasnoe solnyshko. Povest' iz pervykh vremen khristianstva na Rusi.*

Geintse, N. E. *Opolchenskii krest. I. r.*

Kryzhanovskaia, V. I. (Rochester) *Zheleznyi kantsler drevnego Egipta.*

Mikheev, V. M. *Koldun'ia Marina. I. p.*

Nashchekina, V. *Prokliatie. Povest' iz vremen tsaria Alekseia Mikhailovicha.*

Polevoi, P. N. *Izbrannik Bozhii. I. p. nachala XVII v.*

Osipov, A. A. *Namestnik. I. r. iz vremen XVI veka* [*Russkii vestnik* 1–6].

Radich, V. A. *Stepnye orly. I. r.*

Rubakin, N. A. *Vechnaia slava. Istoricheskaia khronika XVI v., izvlechennaia iz gollandskikh arkhivov Knizhnym Cherviakom i izlozhennaia N. A. Rubakinym.*

Salias, Count. E. A. *Frantsuz. I. p. (1812 g.).*

Salias, Count E. A. *Vladimirskie Monomakhi. I. r.—khronika.*

Shakhovskaia, Princess L. D. *Po geroiskim sledam! Romanticheskaia greza iz byta drevnikh rimlian.*

Sokolov, A. A. *Sozhzhennye stepi. I. r.* (Prodolzhenie rom. *Priviazannyi k boiaryshne*).

Staritskie (father and daughter). *Pered burei. I. r. iz vremen khmel'nyshchiny.*

1900 Alekseev, N. N. *Zamorskii vykhodets.*

Altaev, A. *Miguel' Servantes* [Prilozh. k zhurnalu *Vskhody*, no. 22].

Avenarius, V. P. *Syn atamana. Povest' dlia iunushestva iz byta zaporozhtsev* (2 ch. trilogii *Za tsarevicha!*).

Dmitriev, D. S. *Tushinskii vor. I.p. iz epokhi Smutnogo vremeni.*

Geintse, N. E. *Do liasu. I. r. XIX st.*

Geintse, N. E. *Ermak Timofeevich. I. r.*

Krasnitskii, A. I. *Chudo-bogatyr'. I. r.—khronika.*

Kryzhanovskaia, V. I. (Rochester). *Dva sfinksa.*

Lebedev, V. P. *Kniaz'-muchenik. I. r.*

Lebedev, V. P. *Za sviatuiu obitel'. I. r. iz smutnogo vremeni.*

Merezhkovskii, D. S. *Voskresshie bogi (Leonardo da Vinchi).*

Salias, E. A. *Geroi svoego vremeni. I. r.*

Severin, N. (Merder). *V godinu bedstvii. I. r.*

Shakhovskaia, Princess L. D. *Na beregakh Al'buneia.*

Svetlov, V. Ia. *Dar slez.*

Vasil'ev, P. S. *Suvorov. R.-khronika.*

Volkonskii, Prince M. N. *Viaznikovskii samodur.*

1901 Dmitriev, D. S. *Boiarynia Morozova. I. p. iz vremen "Tishaishego" tsaria.*

Dmitriev, D. S. *Bol'shoi boiarin. I. p. iz vremen tsaria Petra I.*

Dmitriev, D. S. *Ermak i Sibir'. I.p. iz vremen Ioanna Groznogo.*

Dmitriev, D. S. *Tainstvennyi dom. I. r. iz epokhi imp. Ekateriny II.*

Iarosh, K. N. 1611 god. *I. p.* [*Russkii vestnik* 6–9].

Krasnitskii, A. I. (Lavrov). *Nebesami pobezhdennye. I. p.*

Krasnitskii, A. I. (Lavrov). *V dali vekov. I. p.*

Kryzhanovskaia, V. I. (Rochester). *Na rubezhe (Narvskoe predanie).*

Lebedev, V. P. *Tsarskii dukhovnik. I. p.*

Lebedev, V. P. *Velikii stradalets. (Patriarkh Germogen).*

Mintslov, S. R. *Na zare veka. I. p. iz epokhi Smutnogo vremeni* (also rpt. as *Volki*).

Nemirovich-Danchenko, V. I. *Tsaritsa Tamara (Iz rasskazov starogo maiora).*

Osipov, A. A. *Bobyl'. I. p. (XVI v.).*

Pavlov, A. P. *U stupenei trona. I. r.*

Pavlov, A. P. *V setiakh vlastoliubtsev (Pod sen'iu korony). I. p.*

Salias, Count E. A.. *Nazvanets. I. r.* (1740 g.).

Shakhovskaia, Princess L. D. *Dal'she ot Zevsa! Bytovye kartiny epokhi rimskikh tsarei.*

Shakhovskaia, Princess L. D. *Pri tsare Servii. Bytovye kartiny semeinoi i religioznoi zhizni drevnikh rimlian.*

Smirnov, A. *Sklirena.*

Sokolov, A. A. *Pugachevskaia smuta. I. r.*

Volkonskii, Prince M. N. *Chernyi chelovek* [sequel to the novel *Viaznikovskii samodur*].

Zarin, A. E. *Krovavyi pir (1669–1672). Bunt Sten'ki Razina.*

Zarin, A. E. *Na izlome. Kartiny iz vremeni tsarstvovaniia tsaria Alekseia Mikhailovicha (1653–1673). I. r.*

Zenchenko, M. V. *Poteshnye, ili Ozorniki i koniukhi Velikogo Petra. I. r.*

1902 Alekseev, N. N. *V grozu narodnuiu. Roman XVII v.*

Avenarius, V. P. *Na Moskvu!* (3 ch. trilogii *Za tsarevicha!i).*

Dmitriev, D. S. *Zolotoi vek. I. r. iz tsarstvovaniia imp. Ekateriny II.*

Krasnitskii, A. I. *Dva bogatyria. Roman-khronika.*

Krasnitskii, A. I. (Lavrov) *Krasnoe Solnyshko.*

Krasnitskii, A. I. *Po stopam Velikogo Petra. I. r. iz epokhi prosoedineniia Gruzii i pervykh russkikh voin s Persiei.*

Krasnitskii, A. I. *Pod russkim znamenem. Povest'-khronika osvoboditel'noi voiny 1877–1878 gg.*

Krasnitskii, A. I. (Lavrov). *Pred rassvetom. I. p. (Prodolzhenie romana "Krasnoe solnyshko").*

Krasnitskii, A. I., and V. A. Pinchuk. *Za krest i veru. I. p.*

Lebedev, M. N. *Bur-An'. Povest' iz drevne-zyrianskoi zhizni.*

Lebedev, V. P. *Dovmontov mech. I. p.*

Lebedev, V. P. *Putem neispovedimym. I. p. iz zhizni patriarkha Filareta.*

Nazar'eva, K. V. *Potomki titanov. I. r. iz epokhi Ekateriny Velikoi.*

Osipov, A. A. *Variag. I. p.*

Pavlov, A. P. *Bozh'ia volia. I. r. iz vremeni Petra II* (simultaneously published as *Torzhestvo liubvi*).

Pavlov, A. P. *Likhaia pora. I. r. iz epokhi 1606–12 gg.*

Polevoi, P. N. *Kudesnik. I. p. dlia iunoshestva.*

Radich, V. A. *Pered burei. I. r.*

Rossiev, P. A. *Sviatitel' Aleksii. I. p.*

Shakhovskaia, Princess L. D. *Nabeg etruskov. Bytovye kartiny epokhi rimskikh tsarei.*

Shakhovskaia, Princess L. D. *Tarkvinii Gordyi. Bytovye kartiny epokhi rimskikh tsarei.*

Solov'ev-Nesmelov, N. A. *Mirnyi zavoevatel'.*

Svetlov, V. Ia. *Avantiuristka. I. r.*

Volkonskii, Prince M. N. *Dva maga. Roman iz epokhi XVIII stoletiia.*

1903 Alekseev, N. N. *Fedoseevskii vladyka. P. iz istorii raskola XVIII v.*

Altaev, A. *Kostry pokaianiia. I. p.*

Altaev, A. *Pod gnetom inkvizitsii. I. p.*

Avenarius, V. P. *Sozdatel' russkoi opery, Mikhail Ivanovich Glinka. Biograficheskaia povest' dlia iunoshestva.*

Iakimov, V. L. *Komediinoe deistvo. I. p. XVII v.*

Kryzhanovskaia, V. I. (Rochester). *Svetochi Chekhii. I. r. iz vremen probuzhdeniia cheshskogo natsional'nogo samosoznaniia.*

Lebedev, M. N. *Son velikogo khana. I. p.*

Likharev, N. O. (Streshnev). *Adskii god (Iezuity v Rossii). Tserkovno-istoricheskaia khronika.*

Likharev, N. O. (Streshnev). *Pod gnetom Unii. I. p. iz byta Belorussii XVII v.*

Lunin, A. V. (under Kukel'). *Novgorodskaia vol'nitsa, ili Bashnia smerti. Roman XV st.*

Lunin, A. V. *V lesakh dremuchikh. Roman iz vremen tsaria Petra Velikogo.*

l'vova, L. P. *Iarko Khabarov. Amurskii geroi. Istorichesskii rasskaz XVII st.*

Markov, V. L. *Rassvet (Predki v trudnoe vremia).*

Mintslov, S. R. *V grozu. I. p. iz epokhi Petra Velikogo.*

Mordovtsev, D. L. *Vel'mozhnaia panna* (rpt. as *Iasnovel'mozhnaia panna. Elena Masal'skaia. 1771–1815*).

Nemirovich-Danchenko, V. I. *Vol'nyi Shamkhar. I. r.*

Osetrov, Z. B. *Shut Balakirev. Povest' iz vremen tsarstvovaniia Petra Velikogo. K 200-letiiu S.-Peterburga.*

Radich, V. A. *Na strazhe pravoslaviia. Povest' iz zhizni ukrainskogo dukhovenstva XVIII v.*

Salias, Count E. A. *Petrovskie dni. I. r.*

Salias, Count E. A. *Shemiakin sud. Istoriko-bytovoi roman.*

Salias, Count E. A. *Voennye muzhiki. Roman* [*Istoricheskii vestnik*].

Shakhovskaia, Princess L. D. *Sila dukha.*

Staniukovich, K. M. *Sevastopol'skii mal'chik. Povest' iz vremen Krymskoi voiny.*

Stroev-Pollin, I. A. *Dekabrist. I. r. iz pervoi poloviny nikolaevskikh vremen.*

Tiutchev, F. F. *Na skalakh i dolinakh Dagestana. Roman iz vremen bor'by s Shamilem za vladychestvo na Kavkaze.*

Volkonskii, Prince M. N. *Gamlet XVIII veka. Roman iz vremeni Pavla I.*

Volkonskii, Prince N. M. *Sirena. I. r. iz epokhi imp. Pavla I.*

Volkova, E. *Petr Basmanov.*

1904 Alekseev-Kungurtsev, N. A. (N. N. Alekseev). *Brat na brata. I. p.—khronika.*

Altaev, A. *Benvenuto Chellini. I. p.*

Altaev, A. *Ian Gus iz Gusintsa. I. p.*

Charskaia, L. A. *Evfimiia Staritskaia. I. r.*

Dmitriev, D. S. *Zmei ognennyi (Ponizovaia vol'ntsa) Istoricheskii illiustrirovannyi roman iz vremen tsaria Alekseia Mikhailovicha.*

Krasnitskii, A. I. *Belyi general. Povest' khronika iz zhizni gen. M. D. Skobeleva.*

Krasnitskii, A. I. (A. I. Lavintsev). *Pod shchitom Sevastopolia. I. r. (Po povodu 50-letiia Krymskoi kampanii 1853–56).*

Kryzhanovskaia, V. I. (Rochester). *Tampliery.*

Lebedev, V. P. *Prel'shchenie litovskoe.*

Levitskii, M. *Moskovskii navigator (Povest' nachala XVIII veka.* [*Nabliudatel'* 1–2].

Likharev, N. O. (Streshnev). *Russkii Savonarola. I. p.*

Merezhkovskii, D. S. *Antikhrist (Petr i Aleksei).*

Mintslov, S. R. *V lesakh Litvy. I. p.* (rpt. as *i. r.*).

Oks, V. B. *Obitel' v osade. I. p.*

Rossiev, P. A. *Na severe dikom. Tserkovno-istoricheskaia povest'.*

Severin, N. (Merder). *Pered razgromom (Epizod iz semeinoi khroniki). I. r. epokhi XVIII v.*

Severtsev-Polilov, G. T. *Boiarynia Morozova. Povest' iz istorii russkogo raskola.*

Sizova, A. K. *Krym-Girei khan i Dalira Bikech. I. r. XVIII v.*

Sizova, A. K. *Novgorodskie povol'niki. XIII v.*

Volkonskii, Prince M. N. *Ishchite i naidete. Roman iz epokhi XVIII veka.*

Volkova, E. F. *Sed'maia zhena. Istoricheskii ocherk.*

Zhdanov, L. G. *Tsar' Ioann Groznyi. Istoricheskaia khronika.*

1905 Alekseev, N. N. *Ognevoi eretik. Tserkovno-istoricheskaia p. iz XVII v.*

Altaev, A. *Chernaia smert'. Povest' iz florentiiskoi zhizni XV v.*

Altaev, A. *V novyi mir. I. p.*

Avenarius, V. P. *Opal'nye. I. p. dlia iunoshestva iz vremen tsaria Alekseia Mikhailovicha.*

Dmitriev, D. S. *Poluderzhavnyi vlastelin. I. r.*

Dmitriev, D. S. *Zaria. Ot mraka k svetu. I.p. iz epokhi Smutnogo vremeni.*

Kisnemskii, S. P. *Predskazaniia vorozhei. I. r. iz vremen pravlenia Sofii.*

Lebedev, V. P. *Sviataia kniaginia.*

Likharev, N. O. (Streshnev). *Voronograi. I. p. iz XV v.*

Likharev, N. O. (Streshnev). *Zhidovskoe plenenie. Istoricheskie kartiny iz byta Rusi kontsa XV v.*

Severtsev-Polilov, G. T. *Kniazhoi otrok. I. p. iz predanii XIII v.*

Sokolov, A. A. *Sevastopol' i sevastopol'tsy. Istoricheskaia khronika-roman.*

Zhdanov, L. G. *Zakat. I. r.*

1906 Altaev, A. *Pod znamenem bashmaka. Krest'ianskaia voina v Germanii. I. p. XVI v.*

Altaev, A. *Razorennye gnezda. I. p. iz russkoi zhizni XVII v.*

Altaev, A. *Svetoch Kampo di Fiori. I. p. iz zhizni Dzhiordano Bruno.*

Altaev, A. *Syn rudokopa. Kartiny iz zhizni Martina Liutera.*

Bebutova, Princess O. M. *Dekabristy.*

Charskaia, L. A. *Gazavat. Tridtsat' let bor'by gortsev za svobodu.*

Krasnitskii, A. I. *Pskovitianka. Svet istiny. I. p.*

Lebedev, V. P. *Mitropolit Filipp. I. p.*

Liubich-Koshurov, A. I. *Rytsari zemli. Povest' iz epokhi krest'ianskoi voiny v Germanii.*

Mintslov, S. R. *Na krestakh. I. p.*

Mordovtsev, D. L. *Bulava i bunchuk. Iuras (syn getmana) i Sirko. I. r. iz smutnogo vremeni getmanstva. I. r. iz smutnogo vremeni getmanstva i Sechi. S opisaniem istoricheskogo otveta kazakov turetskomu sultanu Makhmudu IV.* (2nd ed.)

Oks, V. B. *Vol'nye dni Velikogo Novgoroda. I. p.*

Osipov, A. A. *Pop Ivan Okulov. Istoricheskaia khronika (1679–1703). I. p.*

Radich, V. *Maksim zheleznìak. I. r.*

Severin, N. *Zvezda tsesarevny. I. r. iz epokhi 1710–1734 gg.*

Zarin, A. E. *Kniaz' Teriaev-Raspoiakhin. I. r.*

1907 Alekseev, N. N. *Tsar'-rabotnik.*

Avenarius, V. P. *Pod nemetskim iarmom. Dve i. p.: I. Bironovshchina (1739–1740 gg.) II. Dva regentstva (1740–1741 gg.).*

Briusov, V. Ia. *Ognennyi angel. Povest' XVI veka.*

Engel'gardt, N. A. *Okrovavlennyi tron. I. r. iz epokhi imperatora Pavla I.* [*Istoricheskii vestnik*].

Kryzhanovskaia, V. I. (Rochester). *Faraon Mernefta* (originally published in French in 1888).

Lebedev, M. N. *Poslednie dni Permi Velikoi. I. p.*

Opochnin, E. N. *Korolevskaia nevesta. I. r. iz poslednikh let tsarstvovaniia imp. Ekateriny II.*

Osipov, A. A. *Chernets Feodosii. Istoricheskii ocherk iz tserkovno-obshchestvennoi zhizni XVIII v.*

Osipov, A. A. *Na vysote. I. r. (1785 g.).*

Radich, V. A., and L. G. Zhdanov (Gel'man). *Na Malakhavom kurgane. I. p. dlia iunoshestva.*

Volkonskii, Prince M. N. *Tainye sily.*

Volkova, E. F. *Prints-lekar'. Istoricheski rasskaz iz vremen tsaria Borisa Godunova.*

Zhdanov, L. G. *Venchannye zatvornitsy. I. p.—khronika o zhenakh Ivana Groznogo* (also published as *Piat' zhen tsaria Ivana*).

1908 Alekseev, N. N. *Izmennik. I. r.*

Altaev, A. *Apostol istiny. I. p. o zhizni odnogo iz velikikh geroev nauki.*

Altaev, A. *Trotsnovskii pan. Istoricheskii roman iz vremen gusitskikh voin.*

Altaev, A. *Vniz po Volge reke. I. p. iz russkoi zhizni XVII v.*

Charskaia, L. A. *Pazh tsesarevny.*

Charskaia, L. A. *Smelaia zhizn'. Podvigi zagadochnogo geroia.*

Charskaia, L. A. *Svetlyi voin—kniaz' Mikhail Vasil'evich Skopin-Shuiskii. I. p. vremen tsarstvovaniia Borisa Godunova, Lzhedimitriia i Vasiliia Shuiskogo.*

Danilevskii, M. G. *Rassvet. I. r. (1853–1856 gg.). Po neizdannym dokumentam.*

Engel'gardt, N. A. *Ekaterininskii koloss. I. r.*

Genkel', G. G. *Pod nebom Ellady. I. p. VI v. do R. Khr.*

Kryzhanovskaia, V. I. (Rochester). *Benedektinskoe abbatstvo.*

Osipov, A. A. *Tri stroki. I. p. dlia iunoshestva iz vremen tsarstvovanii Elizavety Petrovny, Petra III i Ekateriny II.*

Zhdanov, L. G. *Rus' na perelome. I. p. kontsa tsarstvovaniia Alekseia Mikhailovicha.*

Merezhkovskii, D. S. *Pavel I.* (play).

1909 Engel'gardt, N. A. *Graf Feniks. I. r. iz epokhi Ekateriny Velikoi.* [*Istoricheskii vestnik*].

Severtsev-Polilov, G. T. *Pod udel'noi vlast'iu.*

Zarin, F. E. *Skopin-Shuiskii. I. p.*

Zhdanov, L. G. *Otrok-vlastelin. I. p. iz zhizni Petra Velikogo* (also published as *Strel'tsy u trona*).

1910 Altaev, A. *Dve korolevy. (Mariia Stiuart i Elizaveta Angliiskaia). I. p. dlia iunoshestva.*

Altaev, A. *Vperedi vekov. I. p. iz zhizni Leonardo da Vinchi.*

Erzin, M. (M. M. Teben'kov) *Za krest Gospoden'. I. p. iz srednevekovoi vizantiiskoi zhizni.*

Krasnitskii, A. I. Tron i liubov'.

Okreits, S. S. *Drama 11 marta 1801 g. I. r.*

Severtsev-Polilov, G. T. *Brat na brata. I. p. dlia iunoshestva.*

Volkonskii, Prince M. N. *Zhanna de Lamott.*

Volkova, E. F. *Vozhd' muzhikov. Kniaz' Mikhail Vasil'evich Skopin-Shuiskii. Istoricheskii rasskaz iz vremen tsaria Vasiliia Ivanovicha Shuiskogo (1601–1610).*

1911 Altaev, A. *Osvoboditel' chernykh rabov. (Povest' iz zhizni Linkol'na).*

Altaev, A. *Sumerki Vozrozhdeniia. I. p.*

Altaev, A. *Za svobodu Rodiny. Istoricheskii roman dlia iunoshestva iz vremen padeniia Chekhii.*

Briusov, V. Ia. *Altar' Pobedy.*

Kostritskii, M. D. *Zaporozhtsy v Saragosse. I. r. dlia iunoshestva.*

Krasnitskii, A. I. (Lavintsev). *Oberegatel'. I. r.*

Krasnitskii, A. I. *Tsaritsa-poliachka.*

Liubich-Koshurov, I. A. *Partizany 1812 g.*

Liubich-Koshurov, I. A. *Pozhar Moskvy v 1812 g. Roman.*

Maurin, E. I. *Liudovik i Elizaveta.*

Maurin, E. I. *Mogil'nyi tsvetok.* (1-i roman iz serii *Prikliucheniia devitsy Gius*).

Maurin, E. I. *V chadu naslazhdenii. I. r.*

Maurin, E. I. *Vozliublennaia favorita* (2-i roman serii *Prikliucheniia devitsy Gius*).

Merezhkovskii, D. S. *Aleksandr I.*

Nemirovich-Danchenko, V. I. *Rytsari gor. I. r. iz Kavkazskoi voiny. Dlia starshego vozrasta.*

Okreits, S. S. *Voskresshaia Rossiia (I. r. iz epokhi smutnogo vremeni).*

Opochnin, E. N. *Krovavoe nasledstvo* [*Moskovskii listok*].

Opochnin, E. N. *Vremenshchiki i samoderzhcy* [*Moskovskii listok*].

Sadovskoi, B. A. *Dvukhglavyi orel.*

Sokolova, A. I. *Svetlyi luch na prestole.*

Sokolova, A. I. *Taina tsarskosel'skogo dvora. I. r. iz epokhi imp. Anny Ioannovny.*

Zarin, A. E. *Zakharka-stremiannyi. I. p.*

Zarin, F. E. *Letaiushchii ponomar'. I. r. iz vremen tsarstvovaniia imp. Anny Ioannovny* (also published as *Taina popovskogo syna*).

Zarin, F. E. *Na zare. I. r.*

Zhdanov, L. G. *Poslednii favorit. (Ekaterina II i Zubov). Roman-khronika (1789–1796 gg.).*

Zhdanov, L. G. *Tsar' i oprichniki.*

1912 Altaev, A. *Streloi i arkanom. I. r. iz russkoi zhizni XIII v.*

Avenarius, V. P. *Doch' posadnich'ia. Povest' dlia iunoshestva iz vremen Velikogo Novgoroda i Ganzy.*

Avenarius, V. P. *Sredi vragov. Dnevnik iunoshi, ochevidtsa voiny 1812 g.*

Briusov, V. Ia. *Iupiter poverzhennyi* (unfinished).

Dmitriev, D. S. *Russki amerikanets. I. r. iz epokhi Aleksanra I.*

Fedorov-Davydov, A. A. *Basurmanskii pogrom. I. p.*

Krasnitskii, A. I. *Poslednie orly. I. r. (Iz sobytii vengerskoi voiny 1848–1849 gg.).*

Lebedev, V. P. *V boiakh 12-go goda (Iz zapisok sovremennika.) I. p.*

Liubuch-Koshurov, A. I. *Pozhar Moskvy v 1812 g. I. r.*

Nemirovich-Danchenko, V. I. *Razzhalovannyi. I. r.*

Nikol'skii, M. E. *Po sledam velikogo Napoleona. I. r.*

Ordyntsev, M. D. (Kostritskii). *Za tron moskovskii.*

Sokolov, A. A. *Lzhe-Petr.*

Sokolova, A. I. *Na vsiu zhizn'. I. r. iz zhizni imp. Aleksandra I.*

Volkonskii, Prince M. N. *Taina gertsoga.*

Zarin, A. E. *Dvoevlastie. I. r.* (Prodolzhenie romana *Vlast' zemli*).

Zarin, A. E. *Vlast' zemli. I. r.*

Zarin, A. E. *Zhivoi mertvets. I. r. vremen imperatora Pavla.*

Zhdanov, L. G. *V setiakh intrigi (Dva potoka). I. r. epokhi Ekateriny II.*

Zhdanov, L. G. *V stenakh Varshavy (Tsesarevich Konstantin). I. r.—khronika (1824–1831).*

1913 Altaev, A. *V velikuiu buriu. I. r. iz vremen angliiskogo korolia Karla I i Olivera Kromvelia dlia detei starshego vozrasta.*

Altaev, A. *Zaria zanialas'. I. p.*

Avenarius, V. P. *Za nevedomyi okean. I. p. dlia iunoshestva ob otkrytii Novogo Sveta.*

Charskaia, L. A. *Zhelannyi tsar'. I. p.*

Dmitriev, D. S. *Osirotevshee tsarstvo (I.r. iz epokhi tsarstvovaniia Petra II).*

Dmitriev, D. S. *Razrushennaia nevesta (Prodolzhenie romana Osirotevshee tsarstvo).*

Il'ina-Pozharskaia, E. D. *Vtroem na Bonaparta! I. p. dlia detei srednego vozrasta.*

Liubich-Koshurov, I. A. *Tushinskie volki. I. r.*

Nikol'skii, M. E. *Bogom dannyi tsar'. I. r.*

Nikol'skii, M. E. *Na zare russkoi slavy. I. r. iz vremen Sviatoslava Igorevicha.*

Okreits, S. S. *Strashnoe vremia. I. r. iz epokhi 1812 g.*

Opochnin, E. N. *Lesnaia tsarevna* [*Moskovskii listok*].

Opochnin, E. N. *Ten' imperatora* [*Moskovskii listok*].

Orlovskii, S. (S. N. Shil'). *Pevets-izgnannik. I. r. dlia iunoshestva* (2nd ed.).

Sergievskii, N. N. *Na zare tsarstva. I. r.*

Sokolova, A. I. *Mertvye iz groba ne vstaiut. I. r. iz epokhi Nikolaia I.*

Sokolova, A. I. *Tsarskoe gadan'e. I. r. iz vremen tsarstvovaniia Nikolaia I.*

Svetlov, V. Ia. *Pri dvore Tishaishego. I. r. iz vremen tsaria Alekseia Mikhailovicha.*

Volkonskii, Prince M. N. *Mne zhal' tebia, gertsog!*

Zarin, A. E. *Severnyi bogatyr'. I. r.*

Zarin, A. E. *Temnoe delo. I. r.*

Zarin-Nesvitskii, F. E. *Bor'ba u prestola.*

Zhdanov, L. G. *Bylye dni Sibiri. Roman-khronika (1711–1721)* (also published as *Po vole Petra Velikogo*).

Zhdanov, L. G. *Nasledie Groznogo. I. p. iz epokhi samozvanchestva.*

Zhdanov, L. G. *Osazhdennaia Varshava. Roman-khronika (1830–1831 gg.).*

Zhdanov, L. G. *Sgibla Pol'sha! (Finis Poloniae!).*

Zhdanov, L. G. *Vo dni smuty (1610–1613 gg.) I. p.*

1914 Altaev, A. *Groza na Moskve. I. r. iz epkhi Ioanna Groznogo.*

Altaev, A. *Syny Solntsa. I. p.*

Avenarius, V. P. *Na Parizh! Dnevnik iunoshi, uchastnika kampanii 1813–1814 gg.*

Brusianin, V. V. *Toska po vlasti* (pt. 1 of *Tragediia mikhailovskogo zamka. Roman-khronika iz epokhi tsarstvovaniia Pavla I*).

Dmitriev, D. S. *Avantiuristka.*

Iakimov, V. L. *Za rubezhom i na Moskve. I. r.*

Kostomarova, A. K. *Muraveinik. I. r.*

Lebedev, V. P. *Zamorskii zhenikh. I. p.*

Maurin, E. I. *Krovavyi pir.*

Maurin, E. I. *Pastushka korolevskogo dvora. I. r.*

Maurin, E. I. *Shakh koroeleve. I. r. iz epokhi tsarstvovaniia Liudovika XIV.*

Ordyntsev, M. D. (Kostritskii). *Opal'nyi kniaz'.*

Ordyntsev, M. D. (Kostritskii). *Koroleva zemli frankov*

Severtsev-Polilov, G. T. *Storoha zamorskogo puti. Povest' iz epokhi "imenitykh gostei" Stroganovykh.*

Sokolova, A. I. *Veshchee slovo. I. r.*

Volkonskii, Prince M. N. *Dve zhizni.*

Zarin, F. E. *Naslednitsa Vizantii. I. p.*

Zhdanov, L. G. *Groznoe vremia (1552–1584 gg.).*

Zhdanov, L. G. *Tretii Rim. Roman-khronika (1526–1532 gg.).*

1915 Altaev, A. *Korol' i infant. I. p. iz vremen Filippa II.*

Altaev, A. *V lesakh dneprovskikh. I. p. iz russkoi zhizni X v.*

Brusianin, V. V. *Gatchinskii pomeshchik* (pt. 2 of *Tragediia Mikhailovskogo zamka*).

Kamenskii, V. V. *Sten'ka Razin. Roman.*

Maurin, E. I. *Na oblomkakh trona.*

Opochnin, E. N. *Slovo i delo* [*Moskovskii listok*].

Severin, N. *Avantiuristy. I. p.*

Timofeev, V. I. *V vek Ekateriny. I. r.* [*Nasha starina* 6–12].

Zarin-Nesvitskii, F. E. *Za chuzhuiu svobodu. I. r.* [*Istoricheskii vestnik* 5–12].

Zhdanov, L. G. *Novaia Rus'. Roman-khronika kontsa XVII v.*

Zhdanov, L. G. *Petr i Sof'ia.*

1916 Engel'gardt, N. A. *Ognennaia kupel'. I. p.*

Sokolova, A. I. *Tsarskii kapriz. I. r. iz vremen tsarstvovaniia Nikolaia I.*

Timofeev, V. I. *Tsarstvo vlasti. I. r.* [*Nasha starina*].

Zhdanov, L. G. (Gel'man). *Pod vlast'iu favorita. Roman.*

Zhdanov, L. G. (Gel'man). *Ubiistvo posla. I. r.—khronika.*

1917 Brusianin, V. V. *Koronovannyi Gamlet* (pt. 3 of *Tragediia Mikhailovskogo zamka*).

Zhdanov, L. G. (Gel'man). *Shlissel'burgskaia tragediia. I. r.* [*Istoricheskii vestnik* 2–6].

List of Works by Subject

Russia and the Russian Empire

EARLY RUSSIAN HISTORY (9TH–13TH CEN.)

Glukharev, I. N. *Bratoubiitsa, ili Sviatopolk Okaiannyi* [banned; publication not completed] (1833); Vel'tman, A. F. *Koshchei bessmertnyi. Bylina starogo vremeni* (1833); Zagoskin, M. N. *Askol'dova mogila. Povest' iz vremeni Vladimira Pervogo* (1833); Rudnevskii. *David Igorevich kniaz' Vladimirskii, ili 1097 god. I. r. XI veka* (1834); Andreev, A. *Dovmont, kniaz' pskovskii. I. r. XIII veka* (1835); [Kuryshev, I.] *Osnovanie Moskvy, ili Smert' boiarina Stepana Ivanovicha Kuchki. I. r., vziatyi iz vremen kniazheniia Iziaslava Mstislavicha* (1835); Vel'tman, A. F. *Sviatoslavich vrazhii pitomets. Divo vremen Krasnogo Solntsa Vladimira* (1835); Griboedov, I. *Sof'ia Kuchko, ili Liubov' i mshchenie. I. r. XII stoletiia* (1836); Anon. *Zaraisk, ili Nachalo vladychestva tatar nad Rossieiu. I. p. XIII stoletiia* (1837); [Pavlov, A. A.] *Russkii bogatyr'. Povest' vremen davno minuvshikh* (1837); Vel'tman, A. F. *Raina, korolevna Bolgarskaia* (1843);

Anon. *Oleg veshchii, velikii knaz' Kievskii* (1858); Salmanov, P. A. *Kniaz' Boris Shegliatev. Istoricheskii roman XIII v., iz vremen nashestviia Batyia na Rossiiu* (1880); Chmyrev, N. A. *Aleksandr Nevskii i novgorodskaia vol'nitsa. I. r.* (1885); Dobrov, F. V. (Dombrovskii). *Vladimir Krasnoe Solnyshko, ili 900 let nazad. I. r.* (1888); Krasnitskii, A. I. *V tumane tysiacheletiia. I. r. iz epokhi obrazovaniia russkogo gosudarstva* (1895); Dmitriev, D. S. *Zachalo Moskvy i boiarin Kuchka. I. p.* (1896); Gorbachevskii, I. D. *Starina starodavniaia. I. p. X veka* (1897); Dmitriev, D. S. *Kniaz' Vladimir Krasnoe solnyshko. Povest' iz pervykh vremen khristianstva na Rusi* (1899); Lebedev, V. P. *Kniaz'-muchenik. I. r.* (1900); Krasnitskii, A. I. (Lavrov). *Nebesami pobezhdennye. I. p.* (1901); Krasnitskii, A. I. (Lavrov). *V dali vekov. I. p.* (1901); Krasnitskii, A. I. (Lavrov). *Krasnoe Solnyshko* (1902); Krasnitskii, A. I. (Lavrov). *Pred rassvetom. I. p. (Prodolzhenie romana "Krasnoe solnyshko")* (1902); Lebedev, V. P. *Dovmontov mech. I. p.* (1902); Osipov, A. A. *Variag. I. p.* (1902); Sizova, A. K. *Novgorodskie povol'niki. XIII v.* (1904); Lebedev, V. P. *Sviataia kniaginia* (1905); Severtsev-Polilov, G. T. *Kniazhoi otrok. I. p. iz predanii XIII v.* (1905); Krasnitskii, A. I. *Pskovitianka. Svet istiny. I. p.* (1906); Severtsev-Polilov, G. T. *Pod udel'noi vlast'iu.* (1909); Severtsev-Polilov, G. T. *Brat na brata. I. p. dlia iunoshestva* (1910); Altaev, A. *Streloi i arkanom. Istorichesskii roman iz russkoi zhizni XIII v.* (1912); Nikol'skii, M. E. *Na zare russkoi slavy. I. r. iz vremen Sviatoslava Igorevicha* (1913); Altaev, A. *V lesakh dneprovskikh. I. p. iz russkoi zhizni X v.* (1915).

THE RISE OF MOSCOW (14TH–MID-15TH CEN.)

[Liubetskii, S. M.] *Sokol'niki, ili Pokolebanie vladychestva tatar nad Rossieiu. I. r. XIV v. Epizod iz kniazheniia Dimitriia Donskogo* (1832); Polevoi, N. A. *Kliatva pri Grobe Gospodnem. Russkaia byl' XV v.* (1832); Svin'in, P. P. *Shemiakin sud, ili Poslednee mezhduusobie kniazei russkikh. I. r. XV v.* (1832); Anon. (Sh. S.). *Vasilii Delinskii, ili Novgorodtsy v XIV stoletii. I. r.* (1833); [Liubetskii, S. M.] *Padenie Velikogo Novgoroda. I. r. XV v., iz kniazheniia Ioanna Vasil'evicha III Velikogo* (1833); Anon. (M——D——). *Dimitrii Donskoi. I. r.* (1837); Zriakhov, N. I. *Mikhail Novgorodskii, ili Narushennaia kliatva. Rossiisko-istoricheskii roman* (1837); Lazhechnikov, I. I. *Basurman* (1838); Gur'ianov, I. G. *Dmitrii Ioannovich Donskoi, ili Uzhasnoe Mamaevo poboishche. Povest'* (1839); Anon. *Vechevoi kolokol. Russkii roman XV stoletiia* (1839); Potapov, V. F. *Raskol'niki*, ili *Khizhina v Chernom boru* (rpt. as *Charodei, ili Khizhina v Chernom boru* and *Chernyi bor, ili Tainstvennaia khizhina*) (1846); Kel'siev, V. P. *Moskva i Tver'* (1870); Petrov, P. N. (completion of novel begun by N. V. Kukol'nik). *Ioann III, sobiratel' Zemli Russkoi. I. r., nachatyi N. V. Kukol'nikom, a so 2-i gl. II-i chasti prodolzhennyi i zakonchennnyi Petrovym* (1874); Politkovskii, V. *Novgorodskii pogrom. I. p. iz russkoi zhini XV st.* (1879); Mordovtsev, D. L. *Mamaevo poboishche. I. p.* (1881); Mordovtsev, D. L. *Gospodin velikii Novgorod* (1882); Tolycheva, T. *Kniaz' Ivan Kalita—Solnecnyi luch* (1884); Dubrovina, E. O. *Rukhnuvshii velikan. I. r. iz XV veka* (1889); Dmitriev, K. *Ne v sile Bog, a v pravde. I. r. iz vremen Ioanna III* (also published as *Sobrat' Rus'!*) (1890); Arsen'ev, A. V. *Kniaz' Dmitrii Ioannovich Donskoi (Iz epokhi groznogo veka). I. r.* (1892); Dubrovina, E. O. *Iz t'my vekov* (1892); Kassirov, I. S. *Strashnaia smert' bez viny. I. p. vremen Ioanna Vasil'evicha III* (remake of

Lazhechnikov's *Basurman*) (1892); Tiumenev, I. F. (Privol'ev). *Khaldei. Povest' iz novgorodskogo byta XV v.* (1893); Dubrovina, E. O. *Beskrovnaia mest'.* (sequel to *Iz t'my vekov*) (1894); Geintse, N. E. *Novgorodskaia vol'nitsa. I. r. iz remen Ioanna III* (1895); Alekseev, N. N. *Sredi bed. I. r. (1395–1407)* (1897); Geintse, N. E. *Pervyi russkii samoderzhets* (1897); Averkiev, D. V. *Vechu ne byt'* (1898); Rossiev, P. A. *Sviatitel' Aleksii. I. p.* (1902); Lunin, A. V. (Kukel') *Novgorodskaia vol'nitsa, ili Bashnia smerti. Roman XV st.* (1903); Alekseev-Kungurtsev, N. A. (N. N. Alekseev) *Brat na brata. I. p.—khronika* (1904); Lebedev, V. P. *Prel'shchenie litovskoe* (1904); Likharev, N. O. (Streshnev). *Zhidovskoe plenenie. Istoricheskie kartiny iz byta Rusi kontsa XV v.* (1905); Mintslov, S. R. *Na krestakh. I. p.* (1906); Oks, V. B. *Vol'nye dni Velikogo Novgoroda. I. p.* (1906); Zarin, A. E. *Zakharka-tremiannyi. I. p. (*1911); Avenarius, V. P. *Doch' posadnich'ia. Povest' dlia iunoshestva iz vremen Velikogo Novgoroda i Ganzy* (1912).

IVAN THE TERRIBLE

Ertel', V. *Garal'd i Elizaveta, ili Vek Ioanna Groznogo. I. r.* (1831); [Kuryshev, I.] *Maliuta Skuratov, ili Trinadtsat' let tsarstvovaniia tsaria Ioanna Vasil'evicha Groznogo. I. r. XVI stoletiia* (1833); [Andreev, A.] *Ioann Groznyi i Stefan Batorii. I. r.* (1834); [Iablochkova, E. N.] *Shigony. Russkaia povest' XVI stoletiia* (1834); Moskvichin A. [A. A. Pavlov] *Iapancha, tatarskii naezdnik, ili Zavoevanie Kazani tsarem Ioannom Groznym. Roman XVI v.* (1834); Svin'in, P. P. *Ermak, ili Pokorenie Sibiri. I. r. XVI stoletiia* (1834); [Pavlov, A. A.] *Brat Viacheslav, ili Podzemel'e bliz Kasimova. Povest' XVI stoletiia* (1836); Anon. *Ermak, pokoritel' Sibiri. I. r.* (1839); Anon. (S——ov, D——rii). *Izgnannik. Roman vremeni Ioanna Groznogo* (1841); Fedorov, B. *Kniaz' Kurbskii. I.r. iz sobytii XVI v.* (1843); Potapov, V. F. *Marfa Vasil'evna, tret'ia supruga Ioanna Groznogo. I. r. XVI v.* (1845); Shmitanovskii, V. Ia. *Ermak, ili Pokorenie Sibirskogo tsarstva. I. p.* (1858); Tolstoi, Count A. K. *Kniaz' Serebrianyi. Povest' vremen Ioanna Groznogo* (1862); Miliukov, A. P. *Tsarskaia svad'ba. Bylina o gosudare Ivane Vasil'eviche Groznom* (1872); Kostomarov, N. I. *Kudeiar. Istoricheskaia khronika* (1875); Petrov, P. N. *Tsarskii sud. I. p.* (1877); Chmyrev, N. A. *Ataman volzhskikh razboinikov Ermak, kniaz' Sibirskii.* (also published as *Ermak, pokoritel' Sibiri*) (1884); Pazukhin, N. M. *Ermak—pokoritel' Sibiri* (1885); Nikolaeva, E. *Ot plakhi k pochesti. I. r. iz epokhi zavoevaniia Sibiri* (1890); Geintse, N. E. *Maliuta Skuratov. I. r.* (1891); Alekseev, N. N. *Tatarskii otprysk* (1896); Alekseev, N. N. *Volia sud'by* (1897); Kondrat'ev, I. K. *Trifon-sokol'nik. Istoricheskaia byl' XVI st.* (1898); Osipov, A. A. *Namestnik. I. r. iz vremen XVI veka* (1899); Alekseev, N. N. *Zamorskii vykhodets* (1900); Geintse, N. E. *Ermak Timofeevich. I. r.* (1900); Dmitriev, D. S. *Ermak i Sibir'. I.p. iz vremen Ioanna Groznogo* (1901); Lebedev, V. P. *Tsarskii dukhovnik. I. p.* (1901); Osipov, A. A. *Bobyl'. I. p. (XVI v.)* (1901); Charskaia, L. A. *Evfimiia Staritskaia. I. r.* (1904); Volkova, E. F. *Sed'muia zhena. Istoricheski ocherk* (1904); Zhdanov, L. G. *Tsar' Ioann Groznyi. Istoricheskaia khronika* (1904); Zhdanov, L. G. *Zakat. I. r.* (1905); Lebedev, V. P. *Mitropolit Filipp. I. p.* (1906); Zhdanov, L. G. *Venchannye zatvornitsy. I. p.—khronika o zhenakh Ivana Groznogo* (also published as *Piat' zhen tsaria Ivana*) (1907); Zhdanov, L. G. *Tsar' i oprichniki* (1911); Altaev, A. *Groza na Moskve. I. r. iz epkhi Ioanna Groznogo* (1914); Severtsev-Polilov, G. T. *Storoha zamorskogo puti. Povest' iz epokhi "imenitykh gostei" Stroganovykh* (1914); Zhdanov, L. G. *Groznoe vremia (1552–1584 gg.)* (1914).

MISCELLANEOUS SIXTEENTH-CENTURY SUBJECTS

Mikhailov, A. (A. K. Sheller). *Dvorets i monastyr'. I. r. -khronika vremen velikogo kniazia Vasiliia Ivanovicha i tsaria Ioanna Groznogo* (1890); Polevoi, P. N. *Na rokovom prostore. I. r.* (Russian frontier under Fedor Ioannovich) (1898); Dmitriev, D. S. *Kniaginia Elena Glinskaia. I. p.* (1899); Likharev, N. O. (Streshnev). *Russkii Savonarola. I. p.* (Maxim the Greek) (1904); Rossiev, P. A. *Na severe dikom. Tserkovno-istoricheskuia povest'* (St. Trifon of Pechenga) (1904); Zhdanov, L. G. *Tretii Rim. Roman-khronika (1526–1532 gg.)* (1914).

THE TIME OF TROUBLES

Zagoskin, M. N. *Iurii Miloslavskii, ili Russkie v 1612 g.* (1829); Bulgarin, F. V. *Dimitrii Samozvanets. I. r.* (1830); [Gur'ianov, I. G.] *Marina Mnishekh, kniazhna Sendomirskaia, zhena Dimitriia Samozvantsa. I. r., otnosiashchiisia ko vremeni tsaria Borisa Godunova, Lzhe-Dimitriia, tsaria Vasiliia Shuiskogo i mezhdutsarstviia, sluzhashchii dopolneniem romana Dimitrii Samozvanets* (1831); [Liubetskii, S. M.] *Rozhdenie blagolsovennogo doma Romanovykh na Rossiiskom prestole. Romanicheskie kartiny istoricheskikh sobytii* (1834); Shishkina, O. P. *Kniaz' Skopin-Shuiskii, ili Rossiia v nachale XVII stoletiia. I. r.* (1835); Kislov, A. S. *Padenie Shuiskikh, ili Vremena bedstvii Rossii. I. r. XVII v.* (1836); [Merkli, M. M.] *Boris Godunov i Rossiia v XVII stoletii. Roman poluistoricheskii* (rpt. as *Kniaz' Vasilii Sitskii*) (1837); Dmitrevskii, M. *Ivan Susanin, ili Smert' za tsaria. I. r.* (1839); Glukharev, I. N. *Kniaz' Pozharskii i nizhegorodskii grazhdanin Minin* (1840); Protopopov, A. P. (Slavin) *Osada Troitse-Sergievskoi lavry, ili Russkie v 1608 g.* (1843); Shishkina, O. P. *Prokopii Liapunov, ili Mezhdutsarstvie v Rossii* (1845); Potapov, V. F. *Ivan Velikoi. I. r. vremen Borisa Godunova, Lzhedimitriia i tsaria Vasiliia Shuiskogo* (1846); Pospelov, A. *Matiushka Verevkin, buntovshchik i samozvanets, iavivshiisia v Rossii v tsratsvovanie Vasiliia Ioannovicha Shuiskogo. I. r.* (1846); Kulish, P. A. (M. Nikolai) *Aleksei Odnorog. I. r.* (1853); Nikolaevich, I. *Nishchii, ili Izbavlennaia zhertva. Iz vremen kniazia Pozharskogo* (1853); Anon. *Chertovo razdol'e, ili Mest' zhidovki. Istoricheskii roman iz vremen Borisa Godunova i Dimitriia Samozvantsa* (1861); Kulish, P. A. *Porubezhniki. Istoricheskii rasskaz* (1864); Vel'tman, E. I. *Prikliucheniia korolevicha Gustava Irikovicha, zhenikha tsarevny Ksenii Godunovoi* (1867); Markov, V. L. *Kurskie porubezhniki. I. r.* (1873); Mordovtsev, D. L. *Lzhedimitrii* (1879); Markov, V. L. *Likholet'e. (Smutnoe vremia). I. r.* (1882); Chmyrev, N. A. *Boiarin Petr Basmanov* (1887); Pazukhin, N. M. *Kniaz' Skopin-Shuiskii. I. r. XVI stoletiia* (1887); Mikhailov, A. (A. K. Sheller). *Iz-za vlasti. I. r.-khronika* (1889); Avenarius, V. P. *Tri ventsa.* (1 ch. trilogii *Za tsarevicha!*) (1890); Polevoi, P. N. *Koren' zla. I. r.* (1891); Pavlova, N. I. *V smutnye gody. Roman* [*Russkii vestnik*, 1892:10–11. 1893:1–4, 8–12]; Polevoi, P. N. *Gde Bog i pravda? I. p.* (1892); Shreknik, E. F. *Soperniki. I r. iz vremen tsarstvovaniia Vasiliia Shuiskogo* (1892); Polevoi, P. N. *Marinka-bezbozhnitsa. I. r. XVII-go st.* (1893); Solov'ev, V. S. *Zhenikh tsarevny. Roman-khronika XVII v.* (1893); Pavlova, N. I. *Razviazka. Roman* (Prodolzhenie romana *Smutnye gody*) [*Russkii vestnik* 1894: 1, 2, 4]; Dubrovina, E. O. *Zhertva trekh chestoliubii. I. r.* (1897); Mikheev, V. M. *Otrok muchenik. Uglitskoe predanie* (1898); Sizova, A. K. *Kseniia Godunova. I. r.* (1898); Alekseev, N. N. *Raby i vladyki. I. r. iz vremen tsaria Fedora Ioannovicha* (1898); Alekseev, N. N. *Lzhetsarevich. I. r.* (Prodolzhenie romana *Rozy i ternii*) (1899); Mikheev, V. M. *Koldun'ia Marina. I. p.* (1899); Polevoi, P. N. *Izbrannik Bozhii. I. p. nachala XVII v.* (1899); Dmitriev, D. S. *Tushinskii vor. I.p. iz epokhi Smutnogo vremeni* (1900); Lebedev, V. P. *Za sviatuiu obitel'. I. r. iz smutnogo vremeni* (1900); Iarosh, K. N. 1611 god. *I. p.* [Russkii vestnik 6–9] (1901); Lebedev, V. P. *Velikii stradalets (Patriarkh Germogen)* (1901); Mintslov, S. R. *Na zare veka. I. p. iz epokhi Smutnogo vremeni* (also published as *Volki*) (1901); Alekseev, N. N. *V grozu narodnuiu. Roman XVII v.* (1902); Avenarius, V. P. *Na Moskvu!* (3 ch. trilogii *Za tsarevicha!)* (1902); Lebedev, V. P. *Putem neispovedimym. I. p. iz zhizni patriarkha Filareta* (1902); Pavlov, A. P. *Likhaia pora. I. r. iz epokhi 1606–12 gg.* (1902); Volkova, E. *Petr Basmanov* (1903); Oks, V. B. *Obitel' v osade. I. p.* (1904); Dmitriev, D. S. *Zaria. Ot mraka k svetu. I.p. iz epokhi Smutnogo vremeni* (1905); Volkova, E. F. *Prints-lekar'. Istoricheski rasskaz iz vremen tsaria Borisa Godunova* (1907); Charskaia, L. A. *Svetlyi voin—kniaz' Mikhail Vasil'evich Skopin-Shuiskii. I. p. vremen tsarstvovaniia Borisa Godunova, Lzhedimitriia i Vasiliia Shuiskogo* (1908); Zarin, F. E. *Skopin-Shuiskii. I. p.* (1909); Volkova, E. F. *Vozhd' Muzhikov. Kniaz' Mikhail Vasil'evich Skopin-Shuiskii. Istoricheskii rasskaz iz vremen tsaria Vasiliia Ivanovicha Shuiskogo (1601–1610)* (1910); Krasnitskii, A. I. *Tsaritsa-poliachka* (1911); Okreits, S. S. *Voskresshaia Rossiia (I. r. iz epokhi smutnogo vremeni)* (1911); Ordyntsev, M. D. (Kostritskii). *Za tron moskovskii* (1912); Zarin, A. E. *Vlast' zemli. I. r.* (1912); Charskaia, L. A. *Zhelannyi tsar'. I. p.* (1913); Liubich-Koshurov, I. A. *Tushinskie volki. I. r.* (1913); Nikol'skii, M. E. *Bogom dannyi tsar'. I. r.* (1913); Sergievskii, N. N. *Na zare tsarstva. I. r.* (1913); Zhdanov, L. G. *Nasledie Groznogo. I. p. iz epokhi samozvanchestva* (1913); Zhdanov, L. G. *Vo dni smuty (1610–1613 gg.) I. p.* (1913); Lebedev, V. P. *Zamorskii zhenikh. I. p.* (1914).

THE REIGN OF ALEKSEI MIKHAILOVICH

Gessel', N. P. *Mstislavlev, ili Sdacha goroda Mogileva. Iz tsarstvovaniia Alekseia Mikhailovicha 1654 g.* (rpt. as *Vladimir Mstislavskii* and *Vladimir, russkoe serdtse)* (1846); Nikolaevich, I. *Chigirinskii les, ili Vera sil'nee liubvi. Nravstvenno-istoricheskii roman* (1853); Pavlov, N. M. *Tsarskii sokol'nik. I. p. iz vremen Alekseia Mikhailovicha* (1870); Averkiev, D. V. *Khmelevaia noch'. Povest'.* (rpt. as *I.r.*) (1871); Solov'ev, V. S. *Kasimovskaia nevesta. I. r.* (1879); Chmyrev, N. A. *Raskol'nich'i muchenitsy. Istoricheskii roman iz epokhi tserkovnykh smut* (1880); Mordovtsev, D. L. *Solovetskoe sidenie* (also published as *Sidenie raskol'nikov v Solovkakh*) (1880); Mordovtsev, D. L. *Velikii raskol. I. p. XVII v.* (1880); Filippov, M. A. *Patriarkh Nikon* (1885); Tolycheva, T. (E. V. Novosil'tseva) *Krest patriarkha Filareta. Roman* (1885); Karnovich, E. P. *Smelaia zhizn'. Roman iz moskovskoi zhizni na iskhode XVII st.* (1886); Kondrat'ev, I. K. *Tserkovnaia kramol'nitsa. I. r. iz epokh staroobriadcheskikh smut* (1888); Solov'ev, V. S. *Tsarskoe posol'stvo. I. r. XVII v.* (1890); Shchepkina, A. V. *Boiare Starodubskie. I.*

r. iz vremen tsaria Alekseia Mikhailovicha (1897); Alekseev, N. N. *Rozy i ternii* (1898); Nashchekina, V. *Prokliatie. Povest' iz vremen tsaria Alekseia Mikhailovicha* (1899); Dmitriev, D. S. *Boiarynia Morozova. I. p. iz vremen "Tishaishego" tsaria* (1901); Zarin, A. E. *Na izlome. Kartiny iz vremeni tsarstvovaniia tsaria Alekseia Mikhailovicha (1653–1673). I. r.* (1901); Iakimov, V. L. *Komediinoe deistvo. I. p. XVII v.* (1903); l'vova, L. P. *Iarko Khabarov. Amurskii geroi. Istorichesskii rasskaz XVII st.* (1903); Severtsev-Polilov, G. T. *Boiarynia Morozova. Povest' iz istorii russkogo raskola* (1904); Alekseev, N. N. *Ognevoi eretik. Tserkovno-istoricheskaia p. iz XVII v.* (1905); Avenarius, V. P. *Opal'nye. I. p. dlia iunoshestva iz vremen tsaria Alekseia Mikhailovicha* (1905); Altaev, A. *Razorennye gnezda. I. p. iz russkoi zhizni XVII v.* (1906); Zhdanov, L. G. *Rus' na perelome. I. p. kontsa tsarstvovaniia Alekseia Mikhailovicha* (1908); Altaev, A. *Zaria zanialas'. I. p.* (1913); Svetlov, V. Ia. *Pri dvore Tishaishego. I. r. iz vremen tsaria Alekseia Mikhailovicha* (1913); Iakimov, V. L. *Za rubezhom i na Moskve. I. r.* (1914); Sokolova, A. I. *Veshchee slovo. I. r.* (1914).

THE RAZIN REBELLION

Fomin, N. *Sten'ka Razin* (1836); Zarnitsin, M. *Sten'ka Razin. I. r.* (1837); Kostomarov, N. I. *Syn. Rasskaz iz vremen XVII v.* (1865); Sokolov, A. A. *Ponizovaia vol'nitsa atamana Sten'ki Razina. I. r.* (1880); Kazantsev, N. V. *Protiv techeniia. I. r. vremen Sten'ki Razina* (1881); Khrushchov-Sokol'nikov, G. A. *Sten'ka Razin. I. r.* (rpt. as *Pri Sten'ke Razine. Byl' na Volge*) (1885); Mordovtsev, D. L. *Za ch'i grekhi? Povest' iz vremen bunta Razina* (1890); Zarin, A. E. *Krovavyi pir (1669–1672). Bunt Sten'ki Razina* (1901); Dmitriev, D. S. *Zmei ognennyi (Ponizovaia vol'ntsa) Istoricheskii illiustrirovannyi roman iz vremen tsaria Alekseia Mikhailovicha* (1904); Altaev, A. *Vniz po Volge reke. I. p. iz russkoi zhizni XVII v.* (1908); Kamenskii, V. V. *Sten'ka Razin. Roman* (1915).

OTHER SUBJECTS DURING THE SEVENTEENTH CENTURY

Furman, P. R. *Blizhnii boiarin Artamon Matveev* (1848); Averkiev, D. V. *Likho. I. p.* (set in the 1630s) (1879); Chmyrev, N. A. *Razvenchannaia tsarevna* (about the first bride of Mikhail Romanov) (1880); Politkovskii, V. *Tsarskaia nevesta. I. p. (1613–1624)* [*Istoricheskaia biblioteka* 1–2] (1880); Zarin, A. E. *Kniaz' Teriaev-Raspoiakhin. I. r.* (1906); Zarin, A. E. *Dvoevlastie. I. r.* (Prodolzhenie romana *Vlast' zemli*) (1912).

PETER THE GREAT

Lazhechnikov, I. I. *Poslednii Novik, ili Zavoevanie Lifliandii v tsarstvovanie Petra Velikogo. I. r.* (1831); [Kornilovich, A. O.] *Andrei Bezymianyi. Starinnaia povest'* (1832); Masal'skii, K. P. *Strel'tsy. I. r.* (1832); Zotov, R. M. *Tainstvennyi monakh, ili Nekotorye cherty iz zhizni Petra I. I. r.* (1834); Masal'skii, K. P. *Borodoliubie* (1837); [Pavlov, A. A.] *Kramol'niki. I. r. iz vremen Petra Velikogo* (1838); Kukol'nik, N. V. *Dva Ivana, dva Stepanycha, dva Kostyl'kova* (1844); Zagoskin, M. N. *Brynskii les. Istoricheskii roman iz pervykh godov tsarstvovaniia Petra Pervogo* (1846); Furman, P. R. *Aleksandr Danilovich Menshikov* (1847); Masal'skii, K. P. *Leitenant i poruchik. Byl' vremen Petra Velikogo* (1848); Zagoskin, M. N. *Russkie v nachale XVIII stoletiia.*

Rasskaz iz vremen edinoderzhaviia Petra Velikogo (1848); Potapov, V. F. *Andrei Besstrashnyi, invalid Petra Velikogo, ili Za Bogom molitva, a za tsarem sluzhba ne propadaiut! Russkaia byl'* (1851); Kel'siev, V. P. and V. P. Kliushnikov. *Pri Petre. I. p. vremen preobrazovaniia Rossii* (1871); Mordovtsev, D. L. *Idealisty i realisty. I. r.* (rpt. as *Ten' Iroda*) (1876); Petrov, P. N. *Dva uzla odnoi verevki (Kharakteristika vremen Petra I)* (1878); Polezhaev, P. V. *Prestol i monastyr'. Letopis' 1682 i 1689 g.* (1878); Solov'ev, V. S. *Tsar'-Devitsa. Roman-khronika XVII v.* (1878); Karnovich, E. P. *Na vysote i na dole. Iz skazanii XVII v. (Tsarevna Sof'ia Alekseevna)* (1879); Danilevskii, G. P. *Na Indiiu pri Petre* (1880); Petrov, P. N. *Balakirev. I. r. iz vremen Petra I* (1880); Chmyrev, N. *Vo sviatoi obiteli. Istoricheskii roman iz vremeni Petra Velikogo* (1883); Mordovtsev, D. L. *Pokhorony. I. r.* (1885); Mordovtsev, D. L. *Tsar' Petr i pravitel'nitsa Sof'ia* (1885); Polezhaev, P. V. *Tsarevich Aleksei Petrovich* (1885); Salias, Count E.A. *Svadebnyi bunt (1705 g.) I. r.* (1886); Polevoi, P. N. *Brat'ia-soperniki I. r. iz vremen pravleniia Sofii* (1888); Dmitriev, D. S. *Samoszhigateli, ili Za staruiu veru. I. p. iz vremen Petra I* (1889); Khovanskii, M. A. *Nevestka Petra Velikogo (Tsarevna Sharlota). I. r.* (1889); Danilevskii, G. P. *Tsarevich Aleksei. I. r.* (unfinished) (1892); Polevoi, P. N. *Pod neotrazimoi desnitsei. I. r.* (1893); Avenarius, V. P. *Vo l'vinoi pasti. I. p. dlia iunosheshstva iz epokhi osnovaiia Peterburga* (1895); Mordovtsev, D. L. *Derzhavnyi plotni?* (1895); Mordovtsev, D. L. *Svetu bol'she! I. r.* (1895); Beliaev, I. S. *Iskushenie. I. r. XVIII v. Iz vremen "Slova i dela"* (1898); Geintse, N. E. *V chadu izmeny. I. r. kontsa XVII st.* (1898); Potapenko, I. N. *Slovo i delo* (1898); Dmitriev, D. S. *Bol'shoi boiarin. I. p. iz vremen tsaria Petra I* (1901); Zenchenko, M. V. *Poteshnye, ili Ozorniki i koniukhi Velikogo Petra. I. r.* (1901); Krasnitskii, A. I. *Dva bogatyria. Roman-khronika* (1902); Polevoi, P. N. *Kudesnik. I. p. dlia iunoshestva* (1902); Svetlov, V. Ia. *Avantiuristka. I. r.* (1902); Lunin, A. V. *V lesakh dremuchikh. Roman iz vremen tsaria Petra Velikogo* (1903); Markov, V. L. *Rassvet (Predki v trudnoe vremia)* (1903); Mintslov, S. R. *V grozu. I. p. iz epokhi Petra Velikogo* (1903); Osetrov, Z. B. *Shut Balakirev. Povest' iz vremen tsarstvovaniia Petra Velikogo. K 200-letiiu S.-Peterburga* (1903); Levitskii, M. *Moskovskii navigator (Povest' nachala XVIII veka)* [*Nabliudatel'* 1–2] (1904); Merezhkovskii, D. S. *Antikhrist (Petr i Aleksei)* (1904); Dmitriev, D. S. *Poluderzhavnyi vlastelin. I. r.* (1905); Kisnemskii, S. P. *Predskazaniia vorozhei. I. r. iz vremen pravlenia Sofii* (1905); Osipov, A. A. *Pop Ivan Okulov. Istoricheskaia khronika (1679–1703). I. p.* (1906); Alekseev, N. N. *Tsar'-rabotnik* (1907); Osipov, A. A. *Chernets Feodosii. Istoricheskii ocherk iz tserkovno-obshchestvenoi zhizni XVIII v.* (1907); Zhdanov, L. G. *Otrok-vlastelin. I. p. iz zhizni Petra Velikogo* (also published as *Strel'tsy u trona*) (1909); Krasnitskii, A. I. (Lavintsev). *Oberegatel'. I. r.* (1911); Zarin, F. E. *Na zare. I. r.* (1911); Zarin, A. E. *Severnyi bogatyr'. I. r.* (1913); Zhdanov, L. G. *Bylye dni Sibiri. Roman-khronika (1711–1721)* (also published as *Po vole Petra Velikogo*) (1913); Zhdanov, L. G. *Novaia Rus'. Roman-khronika kontsa XVII v.* (1915); Zhdanov, L. G. *Petr i Sof'ia* (1915).

FROM CATHERINE I TO ELIZABETH

Kalashnikov, I. T. *Doch' kuptsa Zhelobova. Roman, izvlechennyi iz irkutskikh predanii* (1831); [Bantysh-Kamenskii, D. N.] *Kniazhna Menshikova. I. r.* (1833); [Kurbatov,

A. D.] *Poslednii god vlasti gertsoga Birona. Povest', vziataia iz starinnoi arkhivy moego dedushki* (1833); Kalashnikov, I. T. *Izgnanniki. Povest'* (1834); [Liubetskii, S. M.] *Tan'ka, razboinitsa Rostokinskaia, ili Tsarskie terema. I. p. XVIII stoletiia* (1834); Masal'skii, K. P. *Regenstvo Birona. Povest'* (1834); Lazhechnikov, I. I. *Ledianoi dom. Roman* (1835); [Veidemeier, A. I.] *Epizod iz vladychestva Bironova. I. p.* (1837); Masal'skii, K. P. *Nevesta Petra Vtorogo* (unfinished) (1842); Furman, P. R. *Doch' shuta* (1848); Furman, P. R. *Natal'ia Borisovna Dolgorukova* (1856); Bulkin (S. A. Ladyzhenskii) *Syshchiki. I. p. iz bironovskogo vremeni* (1870); Solov'ev, V. S. *Iunyi imperator* (1877); Kostomarov, N. I. *Kholui. Epizod iz istoriko-bytovoi russkoi zhizni pervoi poloviny XVIII stoletiia* (1878); Solov'ev, V. S. *Kapitan grenaderskoi roty. Roman-khronika iz XVIII v.* (1878); Karnovich, E. P. *Liubov' i korona. I. r iz vremen imp. Anny Ioannovny i regentstva printsessy Anny Leopol'dovny* (1879); Shardin, A. (P. P. Sukhonin) *Rod kniazei Zatsepinykh, ili Bor'ba nachal. I. r.* (1880); Polezhaev, P. V. *Lopukhinskoe delo. I. p. vremen Elizavety Petrovny* (1882); Salias, Count E. A. *Kamer-iungefa* (1882); Karnovich, E. P. *Pridvornoe kruzhevo. I. r.* (1883); Polezhaev, P. V. *150 let nazad. Biron i Volynskii* (1883); Karnovich, E. P. *Paguba. I. r.* (1884); Petrov, P. N. *Kozyri ne v ruke. I. r. 1725–1727 gg.* (rpt. as *Belye i chernye*) (1884); Shchepkina, A. V. *Na zare. Ocherk iz byta vremen Elisavety* (1886); Karnovich, E. P. *Perepolokh v Peterburge* (1887); Makarova, S. M. *Sueta suet. I. p. dlia iunoshestva iz russkoi zhizni proshlogo stoletiia* (1887); Polezhaev, P. V. *Favor i opala. I. r. vremen Petra II* (1887); Salias, Count E. A. *Iaun-Kundze* (1887); Polevoi, P. N. *Tal'ianskaia chertovka. I. p.* (1891); Volkonskii, Prince M. N. *Kniaz' Nikita Feodorovich. I. r.* (1891); Volkonskii, Prince M. N. *Volia sud'by* (1893); Volkonskii, Prince M. N. *Brat gertsoga* (1895); Kondrat'ev, I. K. *Raskol'nich'i gnezda (khlysty, skoptsy, beguny). I. r.-khronika* (1896); Volkonskii, Prince M. N. *Kol'tso imperatritsy. I. r. iz epokhi XVIII stoletiia* (1896); Geintse, N. E. *Doch Petra Velikogo* (1898); Pavlov, A. P. *V setiakh vlastoliubtsev (Pod sen'iu korony). I. p.* (1901); Pavlov, A. P. *U stupenei trona. I. r.* (1901); Salias, Count. E. A. *Nazvanets. I. r.* (1740 g.) (1901); Pavlov, A. P. *Bozh'ia volia. I. r. iz vremeni Petra II.* (simultaneously published as *Torzhestvo liubvi*) (1902); Alekseev, N. N. *Fedoseevskii vladyka. P. iz istorii raskola XVIII v.* (1903); Mordovtsev, D. L. *Vel'mozhnaia panna* (rpt. as *Iasnovel'mozhnaia panna. Elena Masal'skaia. 1771–1815*) (1903); Severin, N. *Zvezda tsesarevny. I. r. iz epokhi 1710–1734 gg.* (1906); Avenarius, V. P. *Pod nemetskim iarmom. Dve i. p.: I. Bironovshchina (1739–1740 gg.) II. Dva regentstva (1740–1741 gg.)* (1907); Charskaia, L. A. *Pazh tsesarevny* (1908); Sadovskoi, B. A. *Dvukhglavyi orel* (1911); Sokolova, A. I. *Taina tsarskosel'skogo dvora. I. r. iz epokhi imp. Anny Ioannovny* (1911); Zarin, F. E. *Letaiushchii ponomar'. I. r. iz vremen tsarstvovaniia imp. Anny Ioannovny* (also published as *Taina popovskogo syna*) (1911); Volkonskii, Prince M. N. *Taina gertsoga* (1912); Volkonskii, Prince M. N. *Mne zhal' tebia, gertsog!* (1913); Dmitriev, D. S. *Osirotevshee tsarstvo (I.r. iz epokhi tsarstvovaniia Petra II)* (1913); Dmitriev, D. S. *Razrushennaia nevesta (Prodolzhenie romana Osirotevshee tsarstvo)* (1913); Zarin-Nesvitskii, F. E. *Bor'ba u prestola* (1913); Severin, N. *Avantiuristy. I. p.* (1915); Zhdanov, L. G. (Gel'man). *Pod vlast'iu favorita. Roman* (1916); Zhdanov, L. G. (Gel'man). *Ubiistvo posla. I. r.—khronika* (1916).

CATHERINE THE GREAT

Kalashnikov, I. T. *Kamchadalka* (1833); Shteven, I. P. *Providenie, ili Sobytie XVIII veka* (1837); Shteven, I. P. *Tsygan, ili Uzhasnaia mest'. Proisshestvie minuvshego stoletiia* (1838); Zagoskin, M. N. *Kuz'ma Petrovich Miroshev. Russkaia byl' vremen Ekateriny II* (1841); Furman, P. R. *Aleksandr-Vasil'evich Suvorov-Rymnikskii* (1848); Skal'kovskii, A. *Porubezhniki. Kanva dlia romanov* (includes tales: *Kagal'nichanka, Khrustal'naia balka, Brat'ia-iskupiteli)* (1849); Petrov, P. N., and V. P. Kliushnikov. *Sem'ia vol'nodumtsev. I. p. vremeni Ekateriny Velikoi.* (1872); Danilevskii, G. P. *Potemkin na Dunae* (1876); Karnovich, E. P. *Samozvannye deti (Iz skazanii XVIII stoletia)* (rpt. as *I. p. iz vremen Ekateriny II*) (1878); Danilevskii, G. P. *Mirovich. I. r.* (written in 1875) (1879); Mordovtsev, D. L. *Nanosnaia beda. Istoricheskaia povest' vremeni chumy na Moskve* (1879); Salias, Count E. A. *Graf Taitin Baltiiskii. I. r.* (1879); Sokolov, A. A. *Tsar'-baba. I. r.* (1879); Salias, Count E. A. *Brigadirskaia vnuchka. Moskovskaia byl'* (1880); Salias, Count E. A. *Mor na Moskve* (rpt. as *Na Moskve*). *I. r. iz vremen chumy 1771 g.* (1880); Salias, Count E. A. *Peterburgskoe deistvo (1762 g.). I. r.* (1880); Salias, Count E. A. *Printsessa Volodimirskaia* (*Samozvanka*) (1881); Shardin, A. (P. P. Sukhonin). *Kniazhna Vladimirskaia (Tarakanova), ili Zatsepinskie kapitaly. I. r.* (1881); Solov'ev, V. S. *Sergei Gorbatov. I. r. kontsa XVIII v.* (pt. 1 of *Khronika chetyrekh pokolenii*) (1881); Solov'ev, V. S. *Vol'ter'ianets. I. r. kontsa XVIII v.* (pt. 2 of *Khronika chetyrekh pokolenii*) (1882); Danilevskii, G. P. *Kniazhna Tarakanova. I. r.* (1883); Salias, Count E. A. *Naidenysh (Prodolzhenie romana "Pugachevtsy")* (1883); Shardin, A. (P. P. Sukhonin). *Na rubezhe dvukh stoletii* (1883); Mordovtsev, D. L. *Avantiuristy* (1885); Salias, Count E. A. *Shir' i makh (Million). I. r.* (1885); Salias, Count E. A. *Kudesnik (Graf Kaliostro). I. r.* (1885); Salias, Count E. A. *V staroi Moskve (Samokrutka). I. p.* (1885); Mordovtsev, D. L. *Beglyi korol'. I. p.* (1887); Salias, Count E. A. *Brigadirskaia vnuchka. Moskovskaia byl'* (1888); Kondrat'ev, I. K. *Saltychikha. Iz ugolovnykh khronik XVIII v.* (1888); Solov'ev, V. S. *Volkhvy. Roman XVIII v.* (1888); Solov'ev, V. S. *Velikii Rozenkreitser. Roman XVIII veka* (1889); Markov, E. L. *Razboinitsa Orlikha. Iz mestnykh predanii XVIII v.* (1891); Salias, Count E. A. *Filozof. I. p.* (1891); Salias, Count E. A. *Vedun'ia. I. r.* (1891); Avenarius, V. P. *Vampir. Byl' ekateriniskikh vremen* [*Knizhki "Nedeli"* 1–4] (1892); Volkonskii, Prince M. N. *Zabytye khoromy* (1893); Geintse, N. E. *Kniaz' Tavridy. I. r.* (1895); Geintse, N. E. *Generalissimus Suvorov. I. r. XVIII st.* (1896); Dmitriev, D. S. *Velikolepnyi kniaz' Tavridy. I. p.* (1897); Geintse, N. E. *Liudoedka. I. r. XVIII v.* (1897); Filippov, M. M. *Dvorianskaia chest' (Byl' proshlogo stoletiia)* (1898); Salias, Count E. A. *Vladimirskie Monomakhi. I. r.—khronika* (1899); Vasil'ev, P. S. *Suvorov. R.—khronika* (1900); Krasnitskii, A. I. *Chudo-bogatyr'. I. r.—khronika* (1900); Dmitriev, D. S. *Tainstvennyi dom. I. r. iz epokhi imp. Ekateriny II* (1901); Dmitriev, D. S. *Zolotoi vek. I. r. iz tsarstvovaniia imp. Ekateriny II* (1902); Nazar'eva, K. V. *Potomki titanov. I. r. iz epokhi Ekateriny Velikoi* (1902); Volkonskii, Prince M. N. *Dva maga. Roman iz epokhi XVIII stoletiia* (1902); Salias, Count E. A. *Petrovskie dni. I. r.* (1903); Opochnin, E. N. *Korolevskaia nevesta. I. r. iz poslednikh let tsarstvovaniia imp. Ekateriny II* (1907); Osipov, A. A. *Na vysote. I. r. (1785 g.)* (1907); Engel'gardt, N. A. *Ekaterininskii koloss.*

I. r. (1908); Osipov, A. A. *Tri stroki. I. p. dlia iunoshestva iz vremen tsarstvovanii Elizavety Petrovny, Petra III i Ekateriny II* (1908); Engel'gardt, N. A. *Graf Feniks. I. r. iz epokhi Ekateriny Velikoi* [*Istoricheskii vestnik*] (1909); Zhdanov, L. G. *Poslednii favorit (Ekaterina II i Zubov). Roman-khronika (1789–1796 gg.)* (1911); Zhdanov, L. G. *V setiakh intrigi (Dva potoka). I. r. epokhi Ekateriny II* (1912); Timofeev, V. I. *V vek Ekateriny. I. r.* [*Nasha starina* 6–12] (1915); Zhdanov, L. G. (Gel'man). *Shlissel'burgskaia tragediia. I. r.* [*Istoricheskii vestnik* 2–6] (1917).

THE PUGACHEV REBELLION

Pushkin, A. S. *Kapitanskaia dochka* (1836); [Salmanov, P. A.] *Chernoe vremia, ili Stseny iz zhizni Emel'ki Pugacheva. I. r. XVIII v.* (1839); Savinov, V. I. *Znakhari. I. r.* (1854); Salias, Count E. A. *Pugachevtsy. Roman* (1873); Salias, Count E. A. *Ataman Ustia (Povolzhskaia byl')* (1885); Danilevskii, G. P. *Chernyi god* (1888); Mamin-Sibiriak, D. N. *Okhoniny brovi* (1892); Salias, Count E. A. *Krutoiarskaia tsarevna. I. p. (1773 g.)* (1893); Sokolov, A. A. *Pugachevskaia smuta. I. r.* (1901); Sokolov, A. A. *Lzhe-Petr* (1912).

PAUL I

I have excluded several novelistic renderings of Suvorov's biography, which are listed under Catherine the Great.

Zotov, R. M. *Tainstvennye sily, ili Nekotorye cherty iz tsarstvovania imperatora Pavla I* (1859); Chaev, N. A. *Bogatyri. Roman iz vremen imp. Pavla I* (1872); Krestovskii, V. V. *Dedy. I. p.* (1875); Karnovich, E. P. *Mal'tiiskie rytsari v Rossii. Povest' iz vremen imperatora Pavla I* (1877); Karatygin, P. P. *Chernoknizhniki. R. iz vremeni tsarstvovaniia Pavla I* (1885); Khrushchov-Sokol'nikov, G. A. *Chudo-bogatyr' (Suvorov). I. r.* (1886); Salias, Count E. A. *Baryni-krest'ianki. I. r.* (1889); Volkonskii, Prince M. N. *Mal'tiiskaia tsep'* (1891); Geintse, N. E. *Koronovannyi rytsar' (Tainy Tavricheskogo sada). I. r. iz tsarstvovaniia imp. Pavla I.* (1895); Salias, Count E. A. *Sluzhitel' Boga. I. r.* (1895); Severin, N. (Merder). *V poiskakh istiny.* [*Istoricheskii vestnik* 1–12] (1895); Karasev, A. A. *Polkovnik Gruzinov. I. p. vremen imp. Pavla I* (1896); Severin, N. (Merder). *Tsarskii prikaz. I. p. (1800)* (1897); Dmitriev, D. S. *Chudo-bogatyr'. I. r.* (1899); Volkonskii, Prince M. N. *Viaznikovskii samodur* (1900); Volkonskii, Prince M. N. *Chernyi chelovek* (sequel to the novel *Viaznikovskii samodur*]) (1901); Likharev, N. O. (Streshnev). *Adskii god (Iezuity v Rossii). Tserkovno-istoricheskaia khronika* (1903); Salias, Count E. A. *Shemiakin sud. Istoriko-bytovoi roman* (1903); Volkonskii, Prince M. N. *Gamlet XVIII veka. Roman iz vremeni Pavla I* (1903); Volkonskii, Prince M. N. *Sirena. I. r. iz epokhi imp. Pavla I* (1903); Volkonskii, Prince M. N. *Ishchite i naidete. Roman iz epokhi XVIII* veka (1904); Engel'gardt, N. A. *Okrovavlennyi tron. I. r. iz epokhi imperatora Pavla I.* [*Istoricheskii vestnik*] (1907); Merezhkovskii, D. S. *Pavel I* (play) (1908); Okreits, S. S. *Drama 11 marta 1801 g. I. r.* (1910); Zarin, A. E. *Zhivoi mertvets. I. r. vremen imperatora Pavla* (1912); Zarin, A. E. *Temnoe delo. I. r.* (1913); Brusianin, V. V. *Toska po vlasti* (pt. 1 of *Tragediia mikhailovskogo zamka. Roman-khronika iz epokhi tsarstvovaniia Pavla I*) (1914); Brusianin, V. V. *Gatchinskii pomeshchik* (pt. 2 of *Tragediia Mikhailovskogo zamka*) (1915); Timofeev, V. I. *Tsarstvo vlasti. I. r.* [*Nasha starina*] (1916); Brusianin, V. V. *Koronovannyi Gamlet.* (pt. 3 of *Tragediia Mikhailovskogo zamka*) (1917).

THE NAPOLEONIC WARS

Bulgarin, F. V. *Petr Ivanovich Vyzhigin. Nravopisatel'no-istoricheskii roman XIX st.* (1831); Zagoskin, M. N. *Roslavlev, ili Russkie v 1812 g.* (1831); [Glukharev, I. N.] *Grafinia Roslavleva, ili Supruga-geroinia, otlichivshaiasia v znamenituiu voinu 1812 g. Istoriko-opisatel'naia povest' XIX st., sluzhashchaia prodolzheniem romana "Ol'ga Miloslavskaia"* (1832); Zotov, R. M. *Leonid, ili Nekotorye cherty iz zhizni Napoleona* (1832); Konshin, N. M. *Graf Oboianskii, ili Smolensk v 1812 godu Rasskaz invalida* (1834); l'vov, V. V. *Seryi armiak, ili Ispolnennoe obeshchanie* (1836); Protopopov, A. *Smert' Napoleona, ili Rasstreliannyi shpion. I. r. v dramaticheskikh kartinakh* (1836); Zotov, R. M. *Fra-Diavolo, ili Poslednie dni Venetsii. I. r.* (1838); Zotov, R. M. *Student i kniazhna, ili Vozvrashchenie Napoleona s ostrova El'by. I. p.* (1838); Anon. *Borodinskoe pole, ili Smert' za chest'* (1839); Pavlov, A. A. *Rytsar' Kresta. Nekotorye cherty iz dostopamiatnogo goda* (1840); Zotov, R. M. *Borodinskoe iadro i Berezinskaia pereprava. Poluistoricheskii roman* (1844); Zotov, R. M. *Dva brata, ili Moskva v 1812 g.* (1850); Zotov, R. M. *Dve sestry, ili Smolensk v 1812 g.* (1860); Tolstoi, Count L. N. *Tysiacha vosem'sot piaty god* (1865–66); Tolstoi, Count L. N. *Voina i mir* (1867–69); Kondrat'ev, I. K. *Drama na Lubianke. I. r. iz epokhi krovavykh dram i velikikh smiatenii* (rpt. as *Velikii razgrom* and *Kazn' Vereshchagina, ili Moskvichi v 1812 g.*) (1878); Mordovtsev, D. L. *Dvenadtsatyi god. (Kavalerist-devitsa). I. r.* (1879); Danilevskii, G. P. *Sozhzhennaia Moskva. I. r.* (1886); Makarova, S. M. *Groznaia tucha. I. p. dlia iunoshestva iz vremen Otechestvennoi voiny* (1886); Sokolov, A. A. *Borodino. I. r. s portretami deiatelei 1812 g.* (1887); Dmitriev, D. S. *Russkie orly. I. p. iz epokhi 1812, 1813 i 1814 g.* (1891); Arsen'ev, A. V. *Frantsuzinka. Istoricheskaia povest' iz epokhi Otechestvennoi voiny* (1893); Salias, Count E. A. *Puteshestvenniki. I. p.* (1895); Dmitriev, D. S. *Dva imperatora. I. p. iz epokhi srazhenii imp. Aleksandra I s Napoleonom I* (1896); Krasnov, P. N. *Ataman Platov. I. r. iz vremen Otechetvenoi voiny* [*Domashniia biblioteka* 8–9] (1896); Dmitriev, D. S. *Kavalerist-devitsa (I. p. iz epokhi voin imp. Aleksandra I s Napoleonom I)* (1898); Lebedev, M. N. *Za Bogom molitva, a za tsarem sluzhba ne propadaiut. I. r.—khronika iz epokhi Otechestvennoi voiny (1812 g.)* (1898); Salias, Count. E. A. *Frantsuz. I. p. (1812 g.)* (1899); Severin, N. (Merder). *V godinu bedstvii. I. r.* (1900); Alekseev, N. N. *Izmennik. I. r.* (1908); Charskaia, L. A. *Smelaia zhizn'. Podvigi zagadochnogo geroia* (1908); Liubich-Koshurov, I. A. *Partizany 1812 g.* (1911); Liubich-Koshurov, I. A. *Pozhar Moskvy v 1812 g. Roman* (1911); Avenarius, V. P. *Sredi vragov. Dnevnik iunoshi, ochevidtsa voiny 1812 g.* (1912); Lebedev, V. P. *V boiakh 12-go goda (Iz zapisok sovremennika). I. p.* (1912); Liubuch-Koshurov, A. I. *Pozhar Moskvy v 1812 g. I. r.* (1912); Nikol'skii, M. E. *Po sledam velikogo Napoleona. I. r.* (1912); Il'ina-Pozharskaia, E. D. *Vtroem na Bonaparta! I. p. dlia detei srednego vozrasta* (1913); Okreits, S. S. *Strashnoe vremia. I. r. iz epokhi 1812 g.* (1913); Avenarius, V. P. *Na Parizh! Dnevnik iunoshi, uchastnika kampanii 1813–1814 gg.* (1914); Zarin-Nesvitskii, F. E. *Za chuzhuiu svobodu. I. r.* [*Istoricheskii vestnik* 5–12] (1915); Engel'gardt, N. A. *Ognennaia kupel'. I. p.* (1916).

THE DECEMBRIST REVOLT

Danilevskii, G. P. *Vosem'sot dvadtsat' piatyi god* (1821–25) (unfinished) [*Istoricheskii vestnik*] (1883); Karatygin, P. P. *Dela davno minuvshikh dnei (1818–1825). I. r.* (1888); Bebutova, Princess O. M. *Dekabristy* (1906).

OTHER SUBJECTS DURING THE RULE OF ALEXANDER I

Salias, Count E. A. *Madonna (Iz odnoi semeinoi khroniki)* (1877); Bogoslavskii, N. G. *Starye poriadki. I. p. iz byta voennykh poselenii* (rpt. in 1882 as *Arakcheevshchina* as *Onofrei i Osip Kuz'miny, konets voennykh poselenii*) (1880); Eval'd, A. V. *Imperator Vizantii. I. r. epokhi tsarstvovaniia imp. Aleksandra I* (1881); Avenarius, V. P. *Otrocheskie gody Pushkina. Biograficheskaia povest'* (1885); Karatygin, P. P. *Zakoldovannoe zerkalo* (1886); Avenarius, V. P. *Iunosheskie gody Pushkina. Biograficheskaia povest'* (1888); Dubrovina, E. O. *Opal'nyi. I. r.* (1890); Salias, Count E. A. *Zaira. Roman* (1890); Dubrovina, E. O. *Zasluzhennaia kara. I. r. vremen Arakcheeva* (Prodolzhenie romana *Opal'nyi*) (1891); Severin, N. (Merder). *Vorotyntsevy (Famil'naia khronika)* (rpt. as *Famil'naia khronika Vorotyntsevykh*) (1891); Geintse, N. E. *Arakcheev. I. r. XIX st.* (1893); Severin, N. (Merder). *Korzhunskie korshuny* [*Istoricheskii vestnik* 1–12] (1898); Salias, Count E. A. *Geroi svoego vremeni. I. r.* (1900); Merezhkovskii, D. S. *Aleksandr I* (1911); Opochnin, E. N. *Krovavoe nasledstvo* [*Moskovskii listok*] (1911); Dmitriev, D. S. *Russki amerikanets. I. r. iz epokhi Aleksanra I* (1912); Sokolova, A. I. *Na vsiu zhizn'. I. r. iz zhizni imp. Aleksandra I* (1912).

THE CRIMEAN WAR

Sokolov, A. A. *Sestra miloserdiia. Roman. I. r.* (1884); Filippov, M. M. *Osazhdennyi Sevastopol'* (1888); Pazukhin, A. M. *Opolchennaia Rossiia* (1891); Shelonskii, N. N. *Sevastopol' v osade. Roman-khronika* (1898); Geintse, N. E. *Opolchenskii krest. I. r.* (1899); Staniukovich, K. M. *Sevastopol'skii mal'chik. Povest' iz vremenn Krymskoi voiny* (1903); Krasnitskii, A. I. (A. I. Lavintsev) *Pod shchitom Sevastopolia. I. r. (Po povodu 50-letiia Krymskoi kampanii 1853–56)* (1904); Sokolov, A. A. *Sevastopol' i sevastopol'tsy. Istoricheskaia khronika-roman* (1905); Radich, V. A., and L. G. Zhdanov (Gel'man). *Na Malakhavom kurgane. I. p. dlia iunoshestva* (1907); Danilevskii, M. G. *Rassvet. I. r. (1853–1856 gg.) Po neizdannym dokumentam* (1908).

OTHER SUBJECTS DURING THE REIGN OF NICHOLAS I

Solov'ev, V. S. *Staryi dom. I. r. nachala tsarstvovaniia imp. Nikolaia I* (pt. 3 of *Khronika chetyrekh pokolenii*) (1883); Solov'ev, V. S. *Izgnannik. I. r.* (pt. 4 of *Khronika chetyrekh pokolenii*) (1884); Salias, Count E. A. *Arakcheevskii synok. I. r.* [*Istoricheskii vestnik* 1–12] (1888); Salias, Count E. A. *Arakcheevskii podkidysh* (Prodolzhenie romana *Arakcheevskii synok*) [*Istoricheskii vestnik* 1–10] (1889); Severin, N. (Merder). *Poslednii iz Vorotyntsevykh. I. r.* (1892); Arsen'ev, A. V. *Zhestokoe ispytanie. I. r.* (1894); Avenarius, V. P. *Gogol'-student.* Vtoraia povest' iz biograficheskoi trilogii *Uchenicheskie gody Gogolia* (1898); Avenarius, V. P. *Shkola zhizni velikogo iumorista. Biograficheskaia povest'* (3-ia ch. biograficheskoi trilogii *Uchenicheskie gody Gogolia*)

(1899); Avenarius, V. P. *Sozdatel' russkoi opery, Mikhail Ivanovich Glinka. Biograficheskaia povest' dlia iunoshestva* (1903); Salias, Count E. A. *Voennye muzhiki. Roman [Istoricheskii vestnik]* (1903); Stroev-Pollin, I. A. *Dekabrist. I. r. iz pervoi poloviny nikolaevskikh vremen* (1903); Sokolova, A. I. *Mertvye iz groba ne vstaiut. I. r. iz epokhi Nikolaia I* (1913); Sokolova, A. I. *Tsarskoe gadan'e I. r. iz vremen tsarstvovaniia Nikolaia I* (1913); Sokolova, A. I. *Tsarskii kapriz. I. r. iz vremen tsarstvovaniia Nikolaia I* (1916).

RUSSIA'S FOREIGN WARS (MID-19TH–EARLY 20TH CEN.)

Sokolov, A. A. *Belyi general. I. r.* (1888); Krasnitskii, A. I. *Pod russkim znamenem. Povest'-khronika osvoboditel'noi voiny 1877–1878 gg.* (1902); Krasnitskii, A. I. *Belyi general. Povest' khronika iz zhizni gen. M. D. Skobeleva* (1904); Krasnitskii, A. I. *Poslednie orly. I. r. (Iz sobytii vengerskoi voiny 1848–1849 gg.)* (1912); Kostomarova, A. K. *Muraveink* (1914) [The Russo-Japanese War].

NOVGOROD AND PSKOV

These novels are also listed under the appropriate chronological rubrics.

[Liubetskii, S. M.] *Padenie Velikogo Novgoroda. I. r. XV v., iz kniazheniia Ioanna Vasil'evicha III Velikogo* (1833); Anon. (Sh. S.). *Vasilii Delinskii, ili Novgorodtsy v XIV stoletii. I. r.* (1833); Andreev, A. *Dovmont, kniaz' pskovskii. I. r. XIII veka* (1835); Zriakhov, N. I. *Mikhail Novgorodskii, ili Narushennaia kliatva. Rossiisko-istoricheskii roman* (1837); Anon.. *Vechevoi kolokol. Russkii roman XV stoletiia* (1839); Potapov, V. F. *Raskol'niki, ili Khizhina v Chernom boru* (rpt. as *Charodei, ili Khizhina v Cherom boru* and *Chernyi bor, ili Tainstvennaia khizhina*) (1846); Politkovskii, V. *Novgorodskii pogrom. I. p. iz russkoi zhini XV st.* (1879); Mordovtsev, D. L. *Gospodin velikii Novgorod* (1882); Chmyrev, N. A. *Aleksandr Nevskii i novgorodskaia vol'nitsa. I. r.* (1885); Dubrovina, E. O. *Rukhnuvshii velikan. I. r. iz XV veka* (1889); Dubrovina, E. O. *Iz t'my vekov* (1892); Tiumenev, I. F. (Privol'ev). *Khaldei. Povest' iz novgorodskogo byta XV v.* (1893); Dubrovina, E. O. *Beskrovnaia mest'.* (sequel to *Iz t'my vekov*) (1894); Geintse, N. E. *Novgorodskaia vol'nitsa. I. r. iz remen Ioanna III* (1895); Averkiev, D. V. *Vechu ne byt'* (1898); Krasnitskii, A. I. (Lavrov) *V dali vekov. I. p.* (1901); Lebedev, V. P. *Dovmontov mech. I. p.* (1902); Lunin, A. V. (Kukel') *Novgorodskaia vol'nitsa, ili Bashnia smerti. Roman XV st.* (1903); Lebedev, V. P. *Prel'shchenie litovskoe* (1904); Sizova, A. K. *Novgorodskie povol'niki. XIII v.* (1904); Likharev, N. O. (Streshnev). *Zhidovskoe plenenie. Istoricheskie kartiny iz byta Rusi kontsa XV v.* (1905); Oks, V. B. *Vol'nye dni Velikogo Novgoroda. I. p.* (1906); Avenarius, V. P. *Doch' posadnich'ia. Povest' dlia iunoshestva iz vremen Velikogo Novgoroda i Ganzy* (1912).

SIBERIA, THE FAR EAST, AND THE NORTH

These novels are also listed under the appropriate chronological rubrics.

Kalashnikov, I. T. *Doch' kuptsa Zhelobova. Roman, izvlechennyi iz irkutskikh predanii* (1831); Kalashnikov, I. T. *Kamchadalka* (1833); Glukharev, I. N. *Inoki, ili Vtorichnoe pokorenie Sibiri* (1834); Svin'in, P. P. *Ermak, ili Pokorenie Sibiri. I. r. XVI stoletiia*

(1834); Anon. *Ermak, pokoritel' Sibiri. I. r.* (1839); Shmitanovskii, V. Ia. *Ermak, ili Pokorenie Sibirskogo tsarstva. I. p.* (1858); Chmyrev, N. A. *Ataman volzhskikh razboinikov Ermak, kniaz' Sibirskii* (also published as *Ermak, pokoritel' Sibiri*) (1884); Pazukhin, N. M. *Ermak—pokoritel' Sibiri* (1885); Nikolaeva, E. *Ot plakhi k pochesti. I. r. iz epokhi zavoevaniia Sibiri* (1890); Geintse, N. E. *Ermak Timofeevich. I. r.* (1900); Dmitriev, D. S. *Ermak i Sibir'. I.p. iz vremen Ioanna Groznogo* (1901); Lebedev, M. N. *Bur-An'. Povest' iz drevne-zyrianskoi zhizni* (1902); l'vova, L. P. *Iarko Khabarov. Amurskii geroi. Istorichesskii rasskaz XVII st.* (1903); Rossiev, P. A. *Na severe dikom. Tserkovno-istoricheskaia povest'* (1904); Lebedev, M. N. *Poslednie dni Permi Velikoi. I. p.* (1907); Zhdanov, L. G. *Bylye dni Sibiri. Roman khronika (1711–1721)* (also published as *Po vole Petra Velikogo*) (1913); Severtsev-Polilov, G. T. *Storoha zamorskogo puti. Povest' iz epokhi "imenitykh gostei" Stroganovykh* (1914).

THE SCHISM

These novels are also listed under the appropriate chronological rubrics.

[Pavlov, A. A.] *Kramol'niki. I. r. iz vremen Petra Velikogo* (1838); Zagoskin, M. N. *Brynskii les. Istoricheskii roman iz pervykh godov tsrastvovaniia Petra Pervogo* (1846); Petrov, P. N., and V. P. Kliushnikov. *Sem'ia vol'nodumtsev. I. p. vremeni Ekateriny Velikoi* (1872); Chmyrev, N. A. *Raskol'nich'i muchenitsy. Istoricheskii roman iz epokhi tserkovnykh smut* (1880); Mordovtsev, D. L. *Solovetskoe sidenie* (also published as *Sidenie raskol'nikov v Solovkakh*) (1880); Mordovtsev, D. L. *Velikii raskol. I. p. XVII v.* (1880); Chmyrev, N. *Vo sviatoi obiteli. Istoricheskii roman iz vremeni Petra Velikogo* (1883); Filippov, M. A. *Patriarkh Nikon* (1885); Kondrat'ev, I. K. *Tserkovnaia kramol'nitsa. I. r. iz epokh staroobriadcheskikh smut* (1888); Dmitriev, D. S. *Samoszhigateli, ili Za staruiu veru. I. p. iz vremen Petra I* (1889); Ryskin, S. F. *Kuplennyi mitropolit, ili Rogozhskie milliony. Roman iz istorii raskola* (1893); Mordovtsev, D. L. *Svetu bol'she! I. r.* (1895); Kondrat'ev, I. K. *Raskol'nich'i gnezda (khlysty, skoptsy, beguny). I. r.—khronika* (1896); Dmitriev, D. S. *Boiarynia Morozova. I. p. iz vremen "Tishaishego" tsaria* (1901); Alekseev, N. N. *Fedoseevskii vladyka. P. iz istorii raskola XVIII v.* (1903); Severtsev-Polilov, G. T. *Boiarynia Morozova. Povest' iz istorii russkogo raskola* (1904); Alekseev, N. N. *Ognevoi eretik. Tserkovno-istoricheskaia p. iz XVII v.* (1905); Altaev, A. *Razorennye gnezda. I. p. iz russkoi zhizni XVII v.* (1906).

UKRAINIAN HISTORY

Golota, P. I. *Ivan Mazepa. I. r., vziutyl iz narodnykh predanii* (1832); Bulgarin, F. V. *Mazepa* (1833); Golota, P. I. *Nalivaiko, ili Vremena bedstvii Malorossii. I. r. XVI v.* (1833); Golota, P. I. *Khmel'nitskie ili Prisoedinenie Malorossii. I. r. XVII v.* (1834); Gogol, N. V. *Taras Bul'ba* (*Mirgorod* ed.) (1835); [Churovskii, A. I.] Zaporozhskie naezdy. Ukrainskaia byl' iz vremen getmanshchiny (1837); Gogol, N. V. *Taras Bul'ba* (rev. ed.) (1842); Grebenka, E. P. *Chaikovskii. Roman* (1843); Kuz'mich, A. P. *Kazaki* (1843); Sementovskii, N. M. *Kochubei, general'nyi sud'ia. I. p.* (1845); Korenevskii, V. *Getman Ostrianitsa. Iz epokhi smut i bedstvii Malorossii. I. r. XVII v.* (1846); Kulish, P. A. *Kievskie bogomol'tsy XVII v.* (1846); Kuz'mich, A. P. *Zinovii-Bogdan*

Khmel'nitskii (1846); Sementovskii, N. M. *Potemkin kak kazak Voiska zaporozhskogo* (1851); Golota, P. I. *Zarutskii, getman voiska Zaporozhskogo* (written in 1844) (1857); Kulish, P. A. *Chernaia rada. Khronika 1663 g.* (1857); Bogrov, G. I. *Evreiskii manuskript. Pered dramoi. I. p.* (1876); Mordovtsev, D. L. *Tsar' i getman* (1879); Kostomarov, N. I. *Chernigovka. Byl' vtoroi polovony XVII v.* (1881); Mordovtsev, D. L. *Sagaidachnyi* (1882); Chmyrev, N. A. *Ivan Mazepa. I. r* (1884); Filippov, M. M. *Ostap. I. p. iz vremen Khmel'nitskogo* (1886); Filippov, M. A. *Pod nebom Ukrainy* (1887); Pazukhin, A. M. *Egor Urvan—ataman zaporozhskogo voiska. I. p.* (1887); Rogova, O. I. *Bogdan Khmel'nitskii. I. p. dlia iunoshestva* (1888); Sokolov, A. A. *Za chest' i svobodu. I. r. iz vremen osvobozhdeniia Malorossii* (1888); Sokolov, A. A. *Zinovii Bogdan Khmel'nitski—osvoboditel' Malorossii. I. r.* (1888); Sokolov, A. A. *Krov'iu, ognem i zhelezom* (Prodolzhenie rom. *Za chest' i svobodu*). *I. r* (1890); Sokolov, A. A. *S zhivogo kozhu. I. r.* (Prodolzhenie rom. *Krov'iu ognem i zhelezom*) (1893); Sokolov, A. A. *Priviazannyi k boiryshne. I. r.* (Prodolzhenie rom. *S zhivogo kozhu*) (1894); Popov, N. A. *Iuzia Chaplinskaia. I. r. XVII stoletiia* (1896); Avenarius, V. P. *Gogol'-gimnazist.* Pervaia povest' iz biograficheskoi trilogii *Uchenicheskie gody Gogolia* (1897); Radich, V. A. *V dymu pozharov. I. r.* (1897); Dmitriev, D. S. *Ivan Mazepa. I. r. vremen Petra I* (1899); Radich, V. A. *Stepnye orly. I. r.* (1899); Sokolov, A. A. *Sozhzhennye stepi. I. r.* (Prodolzhenie rom. *Priviazannyi k boiaryshne*) (1899); Staritskie [father and daughter]. *Pered burei. I. r. iz vremen khmel'nyshchiny* (1899); Avenarius, V. P. *Syn atamana. Povest' dlia iunushestva iz byta zaporozhtsev* (2 ch. trilogii *Za tsarevicha!*) (1900); Radich, V. A. *Pered burei. I. r.* (1902); Radich, V. A. *Na strazhe pravoslaviia. Povest' iz zhizni ukrainskogo dukhovenstva XVIII v.* (1903); Mordovtsev, D. L. *Bulava i bunchuk. Iuras (syn getmana) i Sirko. I. r. iz smutnogo vremeni getmanstva. I. r. iz smutnogo vremeni getmanstva i Sechi. S opisaniem istoricheskogo otveta kazakov turetskomu sultanu Makhmudu IV* (2nd ed.) (1906); Radich, V. *Maksim zhelezniak. I. r.* (1906); Kostritskii, M. D. *Zaporozhtsy v Saragosse. I. r. dlia iunoshestva* (1911).

POLAND AND LITHUANIA

Kukol'nik, N. V. *Al'f i Al'dona* (1842); Balashevich, Iu. *Iezuity. V nachale XVII stoletiia* (1852); Solov'ev, V. S. *Kniazhna Ostrozhskaia* (1876); Khrushchev-Sokol'nikov, G. A. *Griunval'dskii boi, ili Slaviane i nemtsy. Roman-khronika* (1889); Nikolaev, N. *Raby vrazhdy. Roman iz vremen pol'skikh zagovorov i miatezha 1863 g.* (1889); Salias, Count E. A. *Pan Krul'. I. r.* (1890); Grinev, S. A. *Povstantsy. Roman iz vremeni pol'skogo vosstaniia 1863 g.* (1894); Salias, Count E. A. *Via facti. I. r. (1771–1773)* [*Istoricheskii vestnik*] (1894); Geintse, N. E. *Do liasu. I. r. XIX st.* (1900); Likharev, N. O. (Streshnev). *Pod gnetom Unii. I. p. iz byta Belorussii XVII v.* (1903); Mintslov, S. R. *V lesakh Litvy. I. p.* (rpt. as *i. r.*) (1904); Severin, N. (Merder). *Pered razgromom (Epizod iz semeinoi khroniki). I. r. epokhi XVIII v.* (1904); Zhdanov, L. G. *V stenakh Varshavy (Tsesarevich Konstantin). I. r.—khronika (1824–1831)* (1912); Zhdanov, L. G. *Osazhdennaia Varshava. Roman-khronika (1830–1831 gg.)* (1913); Zhdanov, L. G. *Sgibla Pol'sha! (Finis Poloniae!)* (1913); Ordyntsev, M. D. (Kostritskii). *Opal'nyi kniaz'* (1914).

LIVONIA

De Sanglen, Ia. I. *Rytsarskaia kliatva na grobe. Russkii roman iz vremen mechenostsev* (1832); Lazhechnikov, I. I. *Poslednii Novik, ili Zavoevanie Lifliandii v tsarstvovanie Petra Velikogo. I. r.* (1831); Korf, Baron. F. F. *Sud v revel'skom magistrate. Roman iz istorii Estliandii XVI st.* (1841); Kukol'nik, N. V. *Tonni, ili Revel' pri Petre Velikom* (1853); Kryzhanovskaia, V. I. (Rochester). *Na rubezhe (Narvskoe predanie)* (1901).

THE CAUCASUS

Zubov, P. P. *Prekrasnaia gruzinka, ili Nashestvie Ali Magmet Khana na Tiflis v 1795 g. Istoricheskii gruzinskii roman* (1834); Zubov, P. P. *Talisman, ili Kavkaz v poslednie gody Ekateriny II* (1847); Nikolaevich, I. *Bitva russkikh s cherkesami, ili Pastukh chernoi doliny. I. r.* (1853); Mordovtsev, D. L. *Tsar' bez tsarstva. Roman iz poslednikh dnei tsarstva Imeretinskogo* (1891); Nemirovich-Danchenko, V. I. *Gornye orly. I. r.* [*Sever*] (1892); Nemirovich-Danchenko, V. I. *Gore zabytoi kreposti. Roman* [*Sever*] (1893); Mordovtsev, D. L. *Zhelezom i krov'iu. Roman iz zavoevaniia Kavkaza pri Ermolove* (1894); Mordovtsev, D. L. *Prometeevo potomstvo. Roman is poslednikh dnei nezavisimosti Abkhazii* (1896); Nemirovich-Danchenko, V. I. *Podnebesnyi aul. I. p. iz starykh kavkazskikh bylei* (1898); Nemirovich-Danchenko, V. I. *Tsaritsa Tamara (Iz rasskazov starogo maiora)* (1901); Krasnitskii, A. I. *Po stopam Velikogo Petra. I. r. iz epokhi prosoedineniia Gruzii i pervykh russkikh voin s Persiei* (1902); Krasnitskii, A. I., and V. A. Pinchuk. *Za krest i veru. I. p.* (1902); Nemirovich-Danchenko, V. I. *Vol'nyi Shamkhar. I. r.* (1903); Tiutchev, F. F. *Na skalakh i dolinakh Dagestana. Roman iz vremen bor'by s Shamilem za vladychestvo na Kavkaze* (1903); Charskaia, L. A. *Gazavat. Tridtsat' let bor'by gortsev za svobodu* (1906); Nemirovich-Danchenko, V. I. *Rytsari gor. I. r. iz Kavkazskoi voiny. Dlia starshego vozrasta* (1911); Nemirovich-Danchenko, V. I. *Razzhalovannyi. I. r.* (1912).

MISCELLANEOUS

Nikolaevich, I. *Brilliantovaia luna. Iz poslednikh vremen vladeniia genueztsev v Tavrii. Rasskaz balaklavskogo otstavnogo shkol'nogo storozha* (1854); Politkovskaia, M. E. *Ivon Moldavskii. I. p. iz bor'by za svobodu slavian v XVI v.* (1880); Sizova, A. K. *Krym-Girei khan i Dalira Bikech. I. r. XVIII v.* (1904).

Outside the Russian Empire

ANCIENT EGYPT

Bykov, A. A. *Sedaia starina. Original'nyi roman iz drevneegipetskoi zhizni.* [*Nabliudatel'* 7–12] (1890): Mordovtsev, D. L. *Zamurovannaia tsaritsa. Roman iz zhizni drevnego Egipta* (1890); Kryzhanovskaia, V. I. (Rochester). *Tsaritsa Khatasu* (1894); Mordovtsev, D. L. *Mest' zhretsov* (1895); Kryzhanovskaia, V. I. (Rochester). *Zheleznyi kantsler drevnego Egipta* (1899); Kryzhanovskaia, V. I. (Rochester). *Dva sfinksa* (1900); Kryzhanovskaia, V. I. (Rochester). *Faraon Mernefta* (originally published in French in 1888) (1907).

ANCIENT GREECE

Genkel', G. G. *Pod nebom Ellady. I. p. VI v. do R. Khr.* (1908).

ANCIENT ROME AND THE ROMAN EMPIRE (INCLUDING EARLY CHRISTIANITY)

Shakhovskaia, Princess L. D. *Sivilla, volshebnitsa Kumskogo grota. I. r.* (1881); Shakhovskaia, Princess L. D. *Karfagen i Rim. I. r.* (1881); Shakhovskaia, Princess L. D. *Nad bezdnoi. I. r. epokhi Tsitserona* (1882); Shakhovskaia, Princess L. D. *Zhrebii broshen. I. r. epokhi Iuliia Tsezaria* (1884); Sysoeva, E. A. *Aktea. Povest' iz drevnei rimskoi i grecheskoi zhizni* (1884); Shakhovskaia, Princess L. D. *Molodost' tsezaria Oktaviana Avgusta, triumvira rimskogo. I. r.* (1886); Shakhovskaia, Princess L. D. *Pod vlast'iu Tiveriia. I. r.* (1887); Khitrov, M. I. *Evstafii Plakida. Povest' iz istorii khristianskoi tserkvi kontsa I i nachala II stoletiia* (1888); Shakhovskaia, Princess L. D. *Neron. I. r.* (1889); Leskov, N. S. *Gora. Roman iz egipetskoi zhizni* (1890); Shakhovskaia, Princess L. D. *Vestalka* (1890); Mordovtsev, D. L. *Za vsemirnoe vladychestvo. I. r. vremen Mariia (Bor'ba pontiiskogo tsaria Mitridata)* (1891); Mordovtsev, D. L. *Zhertvy vulkana. I. r. iz poslednikh dnei zhizni Pompei* (1891); Shakhovskaia, Princess L. D. *Iuvenal* (1891); Shakhovskaia, Princess L. D. *Liubimets kesaria. I. r. epokhi pervykh vekov khristianstva* (1892); Kryzhanovskaia, V. I. (Rochester). *Sim pobedishi! (Hoc signo vinces!)* (1893); Shakhovskaia, Princess L. D. *Po pravu sil'nogo. I. r. epokhi pervykh vekov khristianstva* (1893); Kryzhanovskaia, V. I. (Rochester). *Gerkulanum* (originally published in French in 1889) (1893); Shakhovskaia, Princess L. D. *Potomki geroev. I. r.* (1894); Merezhkovskii, D. S. *Otverzhennyi* (rpt. as *Smert' bogov. Iulian Otstupnik*) (1895); Shakhovskaia, Princess L. D. *Serebrianyi vek. I. r. epokhi pervykh vremen khristianstva* (1895); Shakhovskaia, Princess L. D. *Kesar' Adrian. I. r.* (1896); Shakhovskaia, Princess L. D. *Konets rimskoi doblesti* (1896); Mordovtsev, D. L. *Irod* (1897); Mordovtsev, D. L. *Padenie Ierusalima* (rpt. as *Poslednie dni Ierusalima*). *I. p.* (1897); Shakhovskaia, Princess L. D. *Rimliane v Afrike. I. r.* (1897); Shakhovskaia, Princess L. D. *Po geroiskim sledam! Romanticheskaia greza iz byta drevnikh rimlian* (1899); Shakhovskaia, Princess L. D. *Na beregakh Al'buneia* (1900); Svetlov, V. Ia. *Dar slez* (1900); Shakhovskaia, Princess L. D. *Dal'she ot Zevsa! Bytovye kartiny epokhi rimskikh tsarei* (1901); Shakhovskaia, Princess L. D. *Pri tsare Servii. Bytovye kartiny semeinoi i religioznoi zhizni drevnikh rimlian* (1901); Shakhovskaia, Princess L. D. *Nabeg etruskov. Bytovye kartiny epokhi rimskikh tsarei* (1902); Shakhovskaia, Princess L. D. *Tarkvinii Gordyi. Bytovye kartiny epokhi rimskikh tsarei* (1902); Shakhovskaia, Princess L. D. *Sila dukha* (1903); Briusov, V. Ia. *Altar' Pobedy* (1911); Briusov, V. Ia. *Iupiter poverzhennyi* (unfinished) (1912).

THE BYZANTINE EMPIRE

Polevoi, N. A. *Ioann Tsimiskhii* (1841); Bezobrazov, P. V. *Imperator Mikhail* (1891); Bezobrazov, P. V. *Ded i vnuk. I.r.* [*Trud* 7–12] (1893); Bezobrazov, P. V. *Zhenikh dvukh nevest* (1894); Krasnitskii, A. I. *Groza Vizantii* (1898); Smirnov, A. *Sklirena* (1901); Erzin, M. (M. M. Teben'kov) *Za krest Gospoden'. I. p. iz srednevekovoi vizantiiskoi zhizni* (1910).

MEDIEVAL EUROPE

[Potapov, V. F.] *Eretik. Istoricheskii roman XIII stoletiia* (1854); Anichkova, I. A. *Ringil'da. Istoricheskii roman XIII st.* (also published as *Dominus Eilard*) (1896); Rubakin, N. A. *Velikii inkvizitor (Pod gnetom vremeni). Istoricheskaia khronika XIII veka o langedokskikh eretikakh* (1898); Kryzhanovskaia, V. I. (Rochester). *Tampliery* (1904); Kryzhanovskaia, V. I. (Rochester). *Benedektinskoe abbatstvo* (1908); Ordyntsev, M. D. (Kostritskii). *Koroleva zemli frankov* (1914).

RENAISSANCE EUROPE

Shreknik, E. F. *Gutenbeg i Sheffer. I. r. iz epokhi vozrozhdeniia nauk i iskusstv* (1894); Kryzhanovskaia, V. I. *Varfolomeevskaia noch'* (1896); Rubakin, N. A. *Vechnaia slava. Istoricheskaia khronika XVI v., izvlechennaia iz gollandskikh arkhivov Knizhnym Cherviakom i izlozhennaia N. A. Rubakinym* (1899); Altaev, A. *Miguel' Servantes* [Prilozh. k zhurnalu *Vskhody*, no. 22] (1900); Merezhkovskii, D. S. *Voskresshie bogi (Leonardo da Vinchi)* (1900); Solov'ev-Nesmelov, N. A. *Mirnyi zavoevatel'* (1902); Altaev, A. *Kostry pokaianiia. I. p.* (1903); Altaev, A. *Pod gnetom inkvizitsii. I. p.* (1903); Kryzhanovskaia, V. I. (Rochester). *Svetochi Chekhii. I. r. iz vremen probuzhdeniia cheshskogo natsional'nogo samosoznaniia* (1903); Altaev, A. *Benvenuto Chellini. I. p.* (1904); Altaev, A. *Ian Gus iz Gusintsa. I. p.* (1904); Altaev, A. *Chernaia smert'. Povest' iz florentiiskoi zhizni XV v.* (1905); Altaev, A. *Pod znamenem bashmaka. Krest'ianskaia voina v Germanii. I. p. XVI v.* (1906); Altaev, A. *Syn rudokopa. Kartiny iz zhizni Martina Liutera* (1906); Liubich-Koshurov, A. I. *Rytsari zemli. Povest' iz epokhi krest'ianskoi voiny v Germanii.* (1906); Briusov, V. Ia. *Ognennyi angel. Povest' XVI veka* (1907); Altaev, A. *Apostol istiny. I. p. o zhizni odnogo iz velikikh geroev nauki* (1908); Altaev, A. *Trotsnovskii pan. Istoricheskii roman iz vremen gusitskikh voin* (1908); Altaev, A. *Dve korolevy. (Mariia Stiuart i Elizaveta Angliiskaia). I. p. dlia iunoshestva.* (1910); Altaev, A. *Vperedi vekov. I. p. iz zhizni Leonardo da Vinchi* (1910); Altaev, A. *Sumerki vozrozhdeniia. I. p.* (1911); Altaev, A. *Za svobodu Rodiny. Istoricheskii roman dlia iunoshestva iz vremen padeniia Chekhii* (1911); Altaev, A. *Korol' i infant. I. p. iz vremen Filippa II* (1915).

MODERN EUROPEAN HISTORY

Zotov, R. M. *Niklas, Medvezh'ia Lapa, ataman kontrabandistov, ili Nekotorye cherty iz zhizni Fridrikha II. I. r.* (1837); Kukol'nik, N. V. *Evelina de Val'erol'* (1841); Zaguliaev, M. A. *Russkii iakobinets. Strannaia istoriia* (1883); Abaza, V. A. *Markitantka (Istoricheskii eskiz vremen revoliutsii, konsul'stva i imperii)* (1887); Svetlov, V. Ia. *Belye tsvety. Original'nyi roman iz vremen frantsuzskoi revoliutsii* (1896); Svetlov, V. Ia. *Zvezda liubvi (1692–1695). Florentiiskaia novella* (rpt. as *Nedostroennyi khram. Florentiiskii roman*) (1898); Maurin, E. I. *Liudovik i Elizaveta* (1911); Maurin, E. I. *Mogil'nyi tsvetok* (1-i roman iz serii *Prikliucheniia devitsy Gius*) (1911); Maurin, E. I. *V chadu naslazhdenii. I. r.* (1911); Maurin, E. I. *Vozliublennaia favorita* (2-i roman serii *Prikliucheniia devitsy Gius*) (1911); Altaev, A. *V velikuiu buriu. I. r. iz vremen angliiskogo korolia Karla I i Olivera Kromvelia dlia detei starshego vozrasta* (1913);

Maurin, E. I. *Krovavyi pir* (1914); Maurin, E. I. *Pastushka korolevskogo dvora. I. r.* (1914); Maurin, E. I. *Shakh koroeleve. I. r. iz epokhi tsarstvovaniia Liudovika XIV* (1914); Maurin, E. I. *Na oblomkakh trona* (1915).

AMERICAN HISTORY

Shreknik, E. F. *Khristofor Kolumb. Original'nyi i. r. iz epokhi otkrytiia Ameriki* (1893); Altaev, A. *V novyi mir. I. p.* (1905); Altaev, A. *Osvoboditel' chernykh rabov (Povest' iz zhizni Linkol'na)* (1911); Avenarius, V. P. *Za nevedomyi okean. I. p. dlia iunoshestva ob otkrytii Novogo Sveta* (1913); Altaev, A. *Syny Solntsa. I. p.* (1914).

MISCELLANEOUS

Kondrat'ev, I. K. *Gunny. Epokha velikogo pereseleniia narodov. I. r. iz zhizni slavian IV i V st.* (rpt. as *Bich Bozhii*) (1878); Shelonskii, N. N. *Za krest i rodinu. Roman iz epokhi bor'by za osvobozhdenie Gretsii* (1893); Orlovskii, S. N. (S. N. Shil') *Ziriab. Povest' iz zhizni arabov v deviatom veke* (1895); Krasnitskii, A. I. *Matsmaiskie plenniki. I. r. (1811–1813 gg.)* (V. M. Golovin's travel to the Far East) (1896); Shakhovskaia, Princess L. D. *Lev pobeditel'. Pervyi v russkoi literature i. r. iz abissinskoi zhizni* (1898).

Statistics (Quantitative Dynamics and Subject-Matter Distribution)

The following tables and charts are based on the first section of this appendix, which takes into account the publication of over 750 new novels by Russian authors. Using new titles as the principal statistical unit requires several caveats. First and foremost, this method does not account for subsequent editions or the overall circulation of a given novel. As a result, a best seller "weighs" as much as a third-rate work.

Grouping by subject matter also poses a number of problems, beginning with the general issue of periodization. Here I either opted for clearly definable categories (e.g., the reign of Ivan the Terrible, the Time of Troubles, the reign of Peter the Great) or for larger periods that, in turn, tend to be perceived as one topos (e.g., the Early Rus or the rise of Moscow). I am aware that some of my rubrics are questionable. For example, I define most of the post-Petrine eighteenth century as the "Age of Empresses," although one could argue that the reign of Catherine the Great deserves a separate rubric. I merged it with the previous reigns in order to avoid chronological overlaps found in a number of novels. Conversely, I singled out the epoch of Paul I because of its transitional character (straddling the eighteenth and nineteenth centuries) and because the publication of some thirty novels devoted to the short reign of this quixotic emperor represents a phenomenon worth registering.

Even more problematic are instances of thematic overlap. In a bibliography one novel can often be listed under several rubrics. For example, Lazhechnikov's *Last Page* can be classified as a novel belonging to the reign of Peter the Great, a

Livonian novel, and, to a limited degree, a novel dealing with the Schism. In terms of statistical calculations, this creates an obvious problem: either one novel has to be counted several times or its thematic components have to be ranked and "weighted." I have avoided both of these awkward solutions by designating a single predominant subject for each novel at the expense of any secondary subjects. Thus, I list *The Last Page* as a novel belonging to the reign of Peter the Great. Following a similar logic, I have eliminated some subject headings altogether. For example, works dealing with Novgorod, Siberia, or the Schism are placed under appropriate chronological rubrics, which necessarily narrows the scope of thematic statistics.

The need to avoid cross-listing also increases the share of novels devoted to Russian subjects by eliminating their foreign component. For example, the abovementioned *Last Page* is not classified as a Livonian novel. This admittedly questionable decision (most of the action takes part in Swedish Livonia) is justified since the plot is rooted in collisions occurring in Petrine Russia. Such "Russification," carried out for the sole purpose of statistical convenience, should not distort the overall focus of the Russian historical imagination. This consideration is especially relevant if one recalls the numerous translations of European historical novels that also fall outside the scope of my statistics. According to my calculations, 88 percent of Russian novels published in the 1830s dealt with domestic subjects. However, one should bear in mind that this concerns only the works of Russian authors, whereas Russia in general was still under the sway of Walter Scott. Mutatis mutandis, the same can be said concerning other periods since my calculations tend to favor domestic subject matter. Despite the above limitations, the following data are useful for a student of the genre since they provide some relatively "hard evidence" for analyzing important trends in the Russian historical imagination.

Publication of New Titles

CHART 1. New Titles by Year

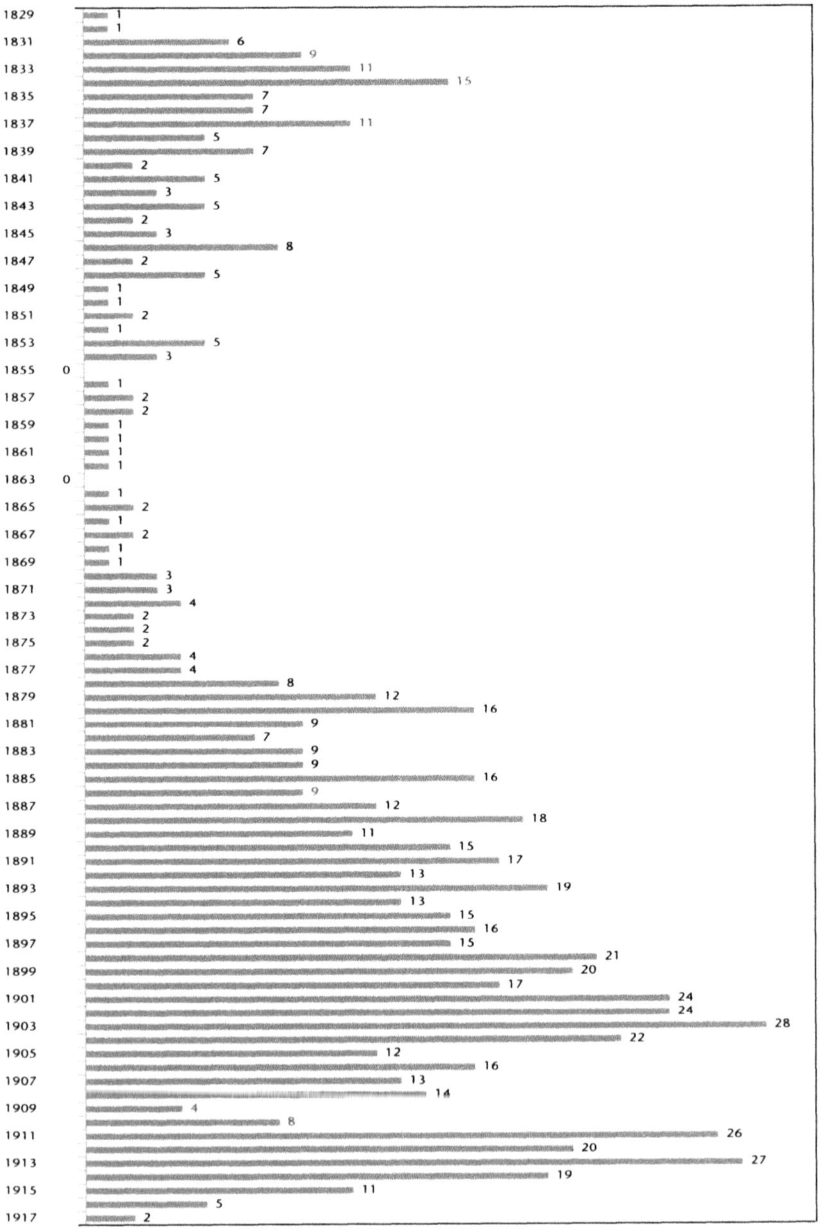

Year	New titles
1829	1
	1
1831	6
	9
1833	11
	15
1835	7
	7
1837	11
	5
1839	7
	2
1841	5
	3
1843	5
	2
1845	3
	8
1847	2
	5
1849	1
	1
1851	2
	1
1853	5
	3
1855	0
	1
1857	2
	2
1859	1
	1
1861	1
	1
1863	0
	1
1865	2
	1
1867	2
	1
1869	1
	3
1871	3
	4
1873	2
	2
1875	2
	4
1877	4
	8
1879	12
	16
1881	9
	7
1883	9
	9
1885	16
	9
1887	12
	18
1889	11
	15
1891	17
	13
1893	19
	13
1895	15
	16
1897	15
	21
1899	20
	17
1901	24
	24
1903	28
	22
1905	12
	16
1907	13
	14
1909	4
	8
1911	26
	20
1913	27
	19
1915	11
	5
1917	2

CHART 2. New Titles by Decade

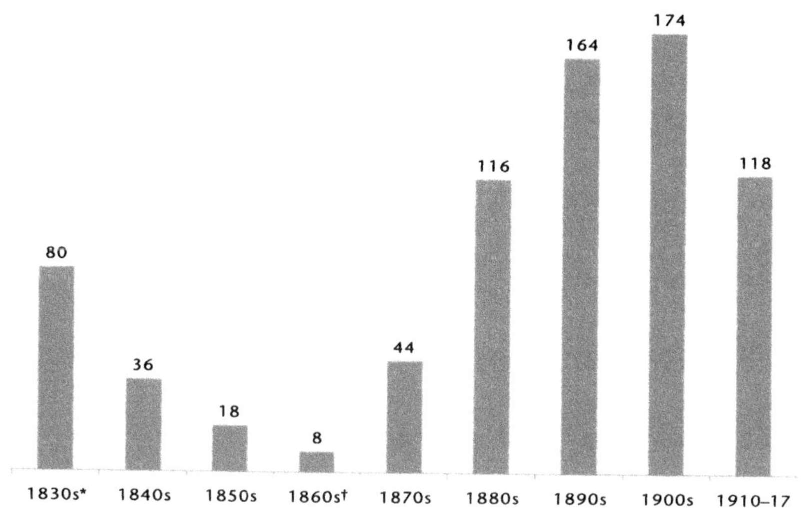

* including 1829

† I normally list serialized novels by the first year of publication. However, chart 1 registers as separate units the installments of Tolstoy's *The Year 1805* (an early version of *War and Peace*) and also of *War and Peace* proper. This exception was made in order to avoid distortion of the literary process. Otherwise the yearly chart would create the false impression that no historical novels appeared in 1866, 1868, and 1869. In the overview by decade, I count these works as only two new titles.

TABLE 1. Subjects by Decade

	1830s		1840s		1870s		1880s		1890s		1900s		1910–17	
	new titles	%	new titles	%	new titles	%	new titles	%	new titles	%	new titles	%	new titles	%
RUSSIAN	71	88	24	67	40	91	92	79	104	63	123	70	83	70
Early Russian	10	12	1	3			3	3	4	2	12	7	4	3
"Gathering of Lands"	10	12	1	3	3	7	4	4	10	6	9	5	2	2
Ivan the Terrible	7	9	3	8	3	7	2	2	6	4	10	6	4	3
Time of Troubles	8	10	5	14	2	5	4	4	15	9	15	9	12	10
First Romanovs	2	3	2	6	4	9	12	10	5	3	13	7	6	5
Peter the Great	6	7	5	14	6	14	10	9	8	5	16	9	6	5
Age of Empresses	15	19	5	14	14	32	33	28	20	12	21	12	15	13
Paul I					3	7	3	3	7	4	9	5	7	6
1812	10	12	2	6	2	5	3	3	8	5	3	2	11	9
Balance of 19th century					1	2	16	14	13	8	12	7	7	6
Miscellaneous Russian	3	4			2	5	2	2	8	5	3	2	9	8
BROADER EMPIRE	9	11	10	28	3	7	12	10	19	12	20	11	8	7
Ukraine	6	7	7	19	2	5	9	8	10	6	5	3	1	1
Poland and Lithuania			1	3	1	2	2	2	3	2	4	2	4	3
Livonia	1	1	1	3							1	<1		
Caucasus	2	3	1	3					6	4	6	3	3	3
Other							1	1			4	2		
NON-RUSSIAN	1	1	2	6	1	2	11	10	39	24	30	17	22	19
Ancient Egypt									5	3	1			
Rome							9	8	18	11	7	4	2	2
Byzantium			1	3					4	2	1	<1	1	1
Western and Central Europe	1	1	1	3			2	2	7	4	18	10	16	14
Misc. non-Russian					1	2			5	3	3	2	3	3
Unknown							1	1	2	1	2	1	5	4
TOTAL	81		36		44		116		164		175		118	

NOTE: The 1850s and 1860s have been omitted as statistically unrepresentative.

CHART 3. Russian vs. Non-Russian Subjects (% of total)

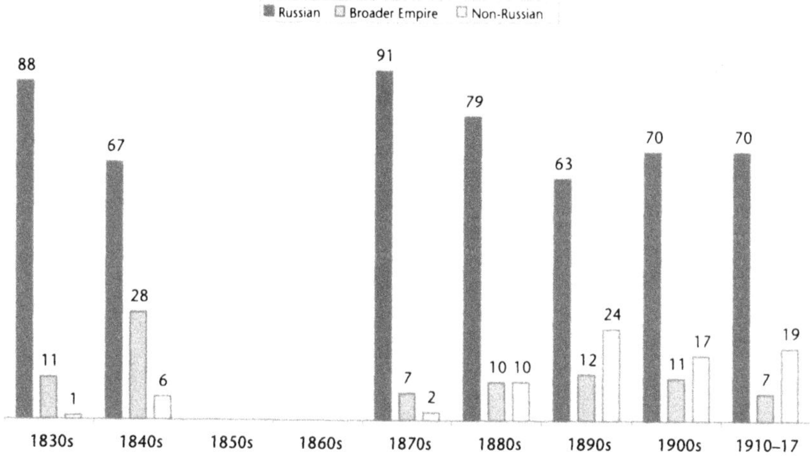

TABLE 2. Thematic Distribution within Russian Subjects

	1830s		1840s		1870s		1880s		1890s		1900s		1910–17	
	titles	%	titles	%	titles	%	titles	%	titles	%	titles	%	titles	%
Early Russian	10	14	1	4			3	3	4	4	12	10	4	5
"Gathering of Lands"	10	14	1	4	3	8	4	4	10	10	9	7	2	2
Ivan the Terrible	7	10	3	12	3	8	2	2	6	6	10	8	4	5
Time of Troubles	8	11	5	21	2	5	4	4	15	14	15	12	12	15
First Romanovs	2	3	2	8	4	10	12	13	5	5	13	11	6	7
Peter the Great	6	9	5	21	6	15	10	11	8	8	16	13	6	7
Age of Empresses	15	21	5	21	14	35	33	36	20	19	21	17	15	18
Paul I					3	8	3	3	7	7	9	7	7	8
1812	10	14	2	8	2	5	3	3	8	8	3	2	11	13
Balance of 19th cen.					1	3	16	17	13	13	12	10	7	8
Miscellaneous Russian	3	4			2	5	2	2	8	8	3	2	9	11
TOTAL RUSSIAN	71		24		40		92		104		123		83	

NOTE: The 1850s and 1860s have been omitted as statistically unrepresentative.

Appendix B

Annotated List of Authors

Anonymous authors. In the 1830s and 1840s a number of novels were published either anonymously or under pseudonyms. Some of them remain unidentified. Normally anonymity served as a refuge for hacks or beginners. However, other considerations might also be involved. After all, the father of the genre, Sir Walter Scott, hid for a long time under the mask of the Great Unknown.

Abaza, Viktor Afanas'evich (1833–1898). The author of historical compilations and a prose writer. In 1887 he published a tale covering the period from the French Revolution to the Empire.

Alekseev, Nikolai Nikolaevich (pseud. N. A. Alekseev-Kungurtsev) (1871–1905). From 1896 until his suicide in 1905 he published over a dozen tales set in medieval and eighteenth-century Russia.

Altaev, Al. (pseud. of Margarita Vladimirovna Iamshchikova) (1872–1959). Children's writer whose literary career spanned six decades. In the 1900s and 1910s she published several dozen historical novels and tales (many of them in the genre of "biographie romancée") for young readers. While some of Altaev's works treat traditional native subjects (e.g., early Rus, Ivan the Terrible), her main specialty was the European Renaissance and Reformation. In the 1920s and 1930s she wrote novels about the history of revolutionary movements. In the 1950s she returned to writing biographies, focusing on the great artists of the Italian Renaissance.

Andreev, A. (dates unknown). In the mid-1830s he published two novels, both of them involving the history of Pskov.

Anichkova, Idaliia Mechislavovna (1843–after 1917). Wrote mostly on contemporary topics but also published the single "historical" novel *Ringil'da* (1896), set in twelfth-century northern Europe. This work stands out as pure chivalric romance devoid of any attempt to reflect historical or social realia.

Arsen'ev, Aleksandr Vasil'evich (1854–1896). Writer and bibliographer. In the 1890s he published several historical novels and tales on Russian subjects.

Avenarius, Vasilii Petrovich (1839–1923). A mediocre anti-nihilist of the 1860s, he reinvented himself as a successful children's author. Starting in 1885, he published numerous historical novels and tales. Especially widely read were his works in the genre of "biographie romancée": a two-part study of Pushkin's youth (1885–87) and the trilogy *Uchenicheskie gody Gogolia* (Gogol's Student Years, 1895–97).

Averkiev, Dmitrii Vasil'evich (1836–1905). A prolific critic, journalist, and writer whose best works in the historical genre include plays dealing with seventeenth-century Russia. His *Khmelevaia noch'* (An Intoxicating Night, 1871) was among the first novels of the second wave. Like the two subsequent novels on medieval Russian life, it is notable for its attention to the details of everyday life. When republishing his historical prose fiction in an 1898 edition of his collected works, he appended the subtitle *povesti iz starinnogo byta.*

Balashevich, Iulii (dates unknown). In 1852 he published the historical novel *Iezuity. V nachale XVII stoletiia* (Jesuits: At the Beginning of the Seventeenth Century) in Riga.

Bantysh-Kamenskii, Dmitrii Nikolaevich (1778–1850). A high-ranking government official and prominent historian, he is best remembered for his pioneering dictionary of Russian biography (1836). Although belonging to an older generation, he paid tribute to the popular genre by anonymously publishing the short novel *Kniazhna Menshikova* (Princess Menshikov, 1833), dealing with the fall of Peter the Great's powerful favorite and the sad fate of his daughter.

Bebutova, Princess Ol'ga Mikhailovna (or Georgievna) (1879–1952). An actress with a taste for scandal and mystification and a proclivity to marry titled aristocrats (her first husband was Prince Bebutov and her second was Count Sollogub), Bebutova supplemented her theatrical career (under the stage name Gurielli) by composing melodramatic novels drawn from contemporary life. Her only historical novel, *Dekabristy* (The Decembrists, 1906), combines sympathy for the failed revolt with "soap opera" situations, gypsy interludes, and mystical visions.

Beliaev, Ivan Stepanovich (1860–1918). Historian and paleographer. His sole historical novel *Iskushenie* (Temptation, 1898) deals with the horrors of Peter I's secret police (*Tainaia kantseliariia*).

Bezobrazov, Pavel Vladimirovich (1859–1918). An expert in Byzantine history and culture, he is the only Russian novelist who specialized in Byzantine subjects. His fictional works include two novels and two tales, published in the early 1890s, drawn from various periods of Byzantine history. Bezobrazov's fascination with Byzantium did not prevent him from adopting liberal Western socio-political views.

Bogoslovskii, Nikolai Gavrilovich (1824–1892). A priest who was also active as a historiographer of the Novgorod province, Bogoslovskii pioneered the "Arakcheev" theme in Russian historical fiction. Assigned to the church at General Arakcheev's former estate of Gruzinovo, Bogoslovskii collected local lore related to the late general and also received access to his private archive, which served as the basis for sketches and stories published in the mid-1860s. In 1880 he wrote the tale *Starye poriadki* (The Old Order of Things), which culminates in the bloody mutiny in Staraia Rusa. In 1882 Bogoslovskii republished both fictional and nonfictional pieces on Arakcheev in the collection *Arakcheevshchina.*

Bogrov, Grigorii Isaakovich (1825–1885). A Russian Jewish writer of some note, Bogrov published one historical novel, *Evreiskii manuskript* (A Jewish Manuscript, 1876), set in mid-seventeenth-century Ukraine.

Briusov, Valerii Iakovlevich (1873–1924). A founding father of Russian symbolism, he made major contributions to historical fiction with his novels *Ognennyi angel* (The Fiery Angel, 1907), set in sixteenth-century Germany, and *Altar' Pobedy* (The Altar of Victory, 1911–12), set in fourth-century Rome.

Brusianin, Vasilii Vasil'evich (1867–1919). A journalist and editor connected with both the Mensheviks and the Bolsheviks, Brusianin was also a prose writer who documented the repercussions of turn-of-the-century social upheavals. In the 1910s he was close to Leonid Andreev, whose influence can be seen in a number of his works, including the historical trilogy *Tragediia Mikhailovskogo zamka* (Tragedy of the Mikhailovskii Castle, 1914–17), which is permeated by Expressionist overtones.

Bulgarin, Faddei Venediktovich (1789–1859). Branded as an unscrupulous hack, secret police informer and enemy of Pushkin, he nonetheless played a significant role in Russian culture, as he contributed to the rise of mass readership. An accomplished journalist and the editor of the most popular newspaper of his day, *Severnaia pchela* (The Northern Bee), he also authored one of the first genuinely popular Russian novels (*Ivan Vyzhigin*, 1829). In addition, Bulgarin vied for the laurels of the first Russian historical novelist, but his *Dimitrii Samozvanets* (Dmitry the Impostor), 1830, was pre-empted by the publication of Zagoskin's *Iurii Miloslavskii* (1829). His other historical novels include *Mazepa* (1833–34) and *Petr Ivanovich Vyzhigin* (1831), a sequel to *Ivan Vyzhigin* set against the backdrop of the War of 1812 (in which Bulgarin fought on Napoleon's side). Although successful in their own right, Bulgarin's historical novels fell short of the popularity of *Ivan Vyzhigin* and could not rival the acclaim of Zagoskin's work.

Bulkin. *See* Ladyzhenskii, Sergei Aleksandrovich

Bykov, A. A. (dates unknown). The author of *Sedaia starina. Original'nyi roman iz drevneegipetskoi zhizni* (Hoary Antiquity: An Original Novel from Ancient Egyptian Life [*Nabliudatel'* 1890:7–12]). Bykov's piece is sharply polemical with respect to Vera Kryzhanovskaia's novel *Le pharaon Mernephta, roman de l'ancienne Égypte* (1888), which deals with the same episodes from Jewish and ancient Egyptian history. Nevertheless, both novels reflect the mystical rendering of history. Whereas Kryzhanovskaia claims to be a medium for the spirit of a seventeenth-century English aristocrat, Bykov's narrator purports to be a reincarnated dignitary of Mernephta who is commanded by his reincarnated ex-ruler to set the historical record straight.

Chaev, Nikolai Aleksandrovich (1824–1914). A playwright in Ostrovskii's circle, Chaev was most famous for his historical dramas. In 1872 he published *Bogatyri*

(Mighty Warriors), set during the reign of Paul I. The title refers both to Suvorov and his soldiers, who confronted the French in Italy, and, more generally, to the mighty Russian *narod.* The novel is filled with digressions—including tirades against liberalism and declarations in the spirit of late Slavophilism and pan-Slavism—that have little to do with the plot.

Charskaya (Churilova), Lidiia Alekseevna (1875–1937). A phenomenally popular author of adolescent literature during the pre–World War I decade, Charskaya wrote several historical tales on topics ranging from medieval Muscovy to Shamil's struggle against the Russian Empire. Her historical fiction displays an extremely superficial acquaintance with the given epoch. Here she follows the sure-fire formula of her other works, centered the action around the adventures of a young heroine with a somewhat hysterical temperament, with tension often the result of unrealized and unarticulated sexual impulses. The prototypical work in this respect is *Smelaia zhizn'. Podvigi zagadochnogo geroia* (A Bold Life: Feats of a Mysterious Hero, 1908), which relates the story of the famous "cavalry maiden" Nadezhda Durova.

Chmyrev, Nikolai Andreevich (1852–1886). A productive historical novelist of the 1880s, all of whose novels deal with Russian subjects.

Danilevskii, Grigorii Petrovich (1829–1990). One of the preeminent historical novelists of the 1870s and 1880s, his *Mirovich* (1875; published in 1879), *Kniazhna Tarakanova* (Princess Tarakanova, 1883), and *Sozzhennaia Moskva* (Moscow Destroyed by Fire, 1886) are among the most popular and solid realistic works of the genre. His *Chernyi god* (The Black Year, 1888), dealing with the Pugachev uprising, is interesting in connection with *The Captain's Daughter.* On the one hand, Danilevskii pays homage to Pushkin, while, on the other, he unintentionally subverts his portrait of Pugachev by presenting Pushkin's fascinating pathfinder through a realistic narrative prism.

Danilevskii, Mikhail Grigor'evich (dates unknown). The son of Grigorii Petrovich. A minor writer, he published a historical novel dealing with the Crimean War entitled *Rassvet. Istoricheskii roman (1853–1856). Po neizdannym istochnikam* (The Dawn: A Historical Novel [1853–1856]; Based on Unpublished Sources, 1908), which is presented as a prologue to the Great Reforms.

De Sanglen, Iakov Ivanovich (1776–1864). Wrote on subjects taken from military history and the history of European literature. His sole novel, *Rytsarskaia kliatva na grobe* (A Knight's Oath on a Sepulcher, 1834), set in fifteenth-century Livonia, is dedicated to the citizens of Reval (Tallinn), where the author spent his youth.

Dmitrevskii, Mikhail Ivanovich (1812–after 1839). In 1839 he published his only historical novel, *Ivan Susanin, ili Smert' za tsaria* (Ivan Susanin, or Death for the Tsar), which is set during the Time of Troubles.

Dmitriev, Dmitry Savvatievich (1848–1915). A prolific writer, beginning in the late 1880s he published over twenty historical novels and tales on various subjects drawn from Russian history. Simple yet engaging, his works are among the more attractive manifestations of popular historical fiction of the late nineteenth century.

Dmitriev, K. (dates unknown). Author of an adventure novel, *Ne v sile Bog, a v pravde* (God Is Not in Might, but in Truth, 1890), set during the reign of Ivan III.

Dobrov (pseud. of Frants Vikent'evich Dombrovskii) (1851–1909). Translator into Russian of works by Boleslaw Prus, Henryk Sienkiewicz, and other Polish writers. In 1888 he published a novel commemorating the nine-hundredth anniversary of the Baptism of Rus.

Dubrovina, Ekaterina Oskarovna (1845/46–1913). One of the first professional female writers, she had ties to political radicals and was an opium addict. Dubrovina wrote several rather unremarkable historical novels and tales (published 1880s–1890s) dealing with various Russian subjects.

Engel'gardt, Nikolai Aleksandrovich (1867–ca. 1942). Writer, publicist, and critic famous for his history of Russian literature and monograph on the evolution of censorship. He wrote three historical novels. *Okrovavlennyi tron* (The Blood-Stained Throne, 1907) is set during the rule of Paul I. *Graf Feniks* (Count Phoenix, 1909) describes Cagliostro's visit to Saint Petersburg in 1779. Engelgardt's attention to Cagliostro and other great mystagogues of the epoch stems from his interest in the doings of members of the world's powerful "underground" (masons, Illuminati, Rosicrucians et al.), whom he sees as the forefathers of nihilism and revolutionary ideologies. *Ognennaia kupel'* (The Font of Fire, 1916) deals with Napoleon's invasion of Russia. Describing how the predatory genius of Europe failed when confronted with the Russian propensity for self-sacrifice, the novel clearly implies parallels with World War I, which was then raging.

Ertel', Vasilii Andreevich (1793–1847). A minor writer and compiler of Russian and German literature readers and dictionaries. He wrote one historical novel—*Garal'd i Elizaveta* (Harald and Elizabeth, 1831)—set during the reign of Ivan the Terrible and dealing, among other things, with the Livonian War, Kurbsky's epistle, and the execution of Vasilii Shibanov. As Russian was not Ertel's native language, the novel was edited by Konstantin Masal'skii.

Erzin, Mikhail. *See* Teben'kov, Mikhail Mikhailovich

Eval'd, Arkadii Vasil'evich (1836–1898). A military engineer by training, Eval'd resigned his commission after the Crimean War, becoming a writer and journalist. His sole historical novel was entitled *Imperator Vizantii. Istoricheskii roman epokhi tsarstvovaniia imp. Aleksandra I* (The Emperor of Byzantium: A Historical Novel from the epoch of Alexander I's reign, 1881). The title refers to a fictional character, an alleged descendant of the Paleolog dynasty residing in Russia, who is prepared to claim the Greek throne if the anti-Turkish rebellion succeeds. Properly historical elements in the novel are minimal.

Fedorov, Boris Mikhailovich (1798–1875). An author belonging to Pushkin's generation. Although the first chapters of his novel *Prince Kurbsky* appeared in 1825, the book was not completed until 1843.

Fedorov-Davydov, Aleksandr Aleksandrovich (1873–1936). A prolific children's writer, he published a number of historical tales in the 1910s.

Filippov, Mikhail Abramovich (1828–1886). A lawyer and publicist, Filippov also paid tribute to belles lettres. His most significant work of historical fiction is the lengthy seventeenth-century saga *Patriarkh Nikon* (Patriarch Nikon, 1885), which represents an honest if not particularly inspiring attempt at popular history.

Filippov, Mikhail Mikhailovich (1858–1903). The son of Mikhail Abramovich. A positivist philosopher with Marxist leanings, journalist, public figure, mathematician, and physicist (he died while experimenting with explosives), Filippov also acted as a literary critic and prose writer. Inter alia, he wrote two historical tales, *Dvorianskaia chest'* (Nobleman's Honor, 1898), whose plot echoes that of Pushkin's *Dubrovskii*, and *Ostap* (1887), which attempts to refute the negative picture of Ukrainian Cossacks portrayed by Henryk Sienkiewicz. His most significant work in the genre is *Osazhdennyi Sevastopol'* (The Besieged Sevastopol, 1888), which appears to be the first Russian historical novel to deal with the Crimean War. This novel won praise from none other then Lev Tolstoi.

Fomin, N. (dates unknown). Author of the first Russian novel on Stenka Razin (1836).

Furman, Petr Romanovich (1809–1856). A Russian pioneer of the "biographie romancée," he authored numerous works (late 1840s–early 1850s) for children and adolescents that mainly dealt with eighteenth-century subjects. Frequently republished in the 1890s and 1910s, they were often edited by Vasilii Avenarius, another master of the genre.

Geintse, Nikolai Eduardovich (1852–1913). A prolific turn-of-the-century writer, he specialized in chronicles about crime and novels based on Russian history. Although his historical novels were criticized for their omnium-gatherum nature—Geintse was even accused of plagiarism—they were popular among less discerning readers and usually went through several printings.

Genkel', German Germanovich (1865–1941). Professor specializing in ancient history. In 1910 he published the tale *Pod nebom Ellady* (Under the Sky of Hellas), which is a rare example of ancient Greek subject matter in Russian historical fiction.

Gessel', Nikolai Petrovich (dates unknown). A lowbrow author of the late 1840s and 1860s. In addition to two novels dealing with the conquest of the northern Caucasus, he published a historical novel entitled *Mstislavlev, ili Sdacha goroda Mogilev* (Mstislavlev, or the Surrender of the City of Mogilev, 1846), which concerns an episode from the Russo-Polish War during the reign of Aleksei Mikhailovich.

Glukharev, Ivan Nikitich (1809–after 1840). A purveyor of pulp fiction in various genres, Glukharev stands out as a master of mimicry. His first "historical" novels, *Ol'ga Miloslavskaia* (1831) and *Grafinia Roslavleva* (Countess Roslavlev, 1832), echo the titles of the more famous works by Zagoskin, though they have no connection whatsoever to the latter and contain little or no historical background.

Gogol', Nikolai Vasil'evich (1809–1852). Although Gogol's ambition to write a comprehensive history of his native Ukraine remained unrealized, it contributed to the creation of *Taras Bulba* (1835), which glorifies the struggle of Ukrainian Cossacks against Polish oppression. It stands out for its combination of historical novel and epic (especially in the revised edition of 1842). A canonical work, it remains one of the most widely read works of Russian historical fiction.

Golitsyn, Prince Sergii Vladimirovich (1823–1879). His sole historical novel, *Byloe vremechko* (These Good Old Times, 1876), concerns the illustrious but unfortunate branch of the Golitsyn family, specifically Prince Vasilii Vasil'evich, Sofia's favorite, and his grandson, Prince Mikhail Alekseevich, who converted to Catholicism during his study abroad and, upon returning to Russia, became a buffoon at the court of Empress Anna Ioannovna. Since the second printed part of the book ends with the Sorbonne years of Prince Mikhail, one can assume that the novel was never finished.

Golota, Petr Ivanovich (1811–after 1857). Writing in the early 1830s, he was a leading purveyor of Little Russian novels dealing with the struggle of the Ukrainian people against Polish oppression in the sixteenth and seventeenth centuries. Although a secondary writer, thematically Golota's works anticipate Gogol's *Taras Bulba.* Also noteworthy is his extensive use of Ukrainian dialogue, with Russian translations.

Gorbachevskii, Ivan Danilovich (dates unknown). Vitebsk-based, he wrote the tale *Starina starodavniaia* (Hoary Antiquity, 1897), which deals with the struggle of the Drevliane tribe against Kiev in the tenth century. It contains detailed descriptions of pagan rituals and the mythology of the early Slavs.

Grebenka, Evgenii Petrovich (1812–1848). Russian-Ukrainian poet and writer. He published one novel (*Chaikovskii,* 1843) dealing with the history of Ukrainian Cossacks.

Griboedov, I. (dates unknown). Author of the novel *Sof'ia Kuchko, ili Liubov' i mshchenie* (Sofia Kuchko, or Love and Vengeance, 1836).

Grinev, Sergei Apollonovich (1856–1914). A colonel of the guards and a military historian, Grinev comes from the gentry family whose name was chosen by Pushkin for his protagonist in *The Captain's Daughter.* In 1894 he published the novel *Povstantsy* (Rebels), which deals with Polish events in 1863.

Gur'ianov, Ivan Gavrilovich (1791–1854). A prolific "writer of the flea market" who openly imitated Bulgarin, he characterized his novel *Marina Mnishekh* (1831) as a "supplement" to Bulgarin's *Impostor.*

Iablochkova, Elizaveta Nikitichna (1771–1843). In 1834 she published anonymously the historical novel *Shigony,* which boasts the longest subtitle in the history of the genre in Russian literature.

Iakimov, V. L. (dates unknown). The author of at least two works (published in 1903 and 1914) dealing with the reign of Aleksei Mikhailovich.

Iarosh, Kiprian Nikolaevich (1854–?). A professor of history of law from Kharkov. In 1901 he published a historical tale dealing with the Time of Troubles.

Il'ina-Pozharskaia, Elena Dmitrievna (1851–1916). The author of historical tales for children published in the early 1910s.

Ivin, Ivan Semenovich (pseud. Kassirov) (1886 or 1868–1918/19). One of the most popular *lubok* writers, he turned to the historical genre in the 1890s, producing remakes of A. K. Tolstoi's *Kniaz' Serebrianyi*, Moskvichin's *Iapancha*, Lazhechnikov's *Ledianoi dom and Basurman*, the latter called *Strashnaia smert' bez viny* (A Terrible Death without Guilt, 1892), among others. He even lists as a historical tale a rewrite of Gogol's *Strashnaia mest'* (Terrible Vengeance), which bears the characteristically altered title *Strashnaia bitva kolduna s mertvetsami* (A Terrible Battle of a Sorcerer against Cadavers).

Kalashnikov, Ivan Trofimovich (1797–1863). Pioneered the Siberian theme in two of his novels—*Doch' kuptsa Zholobova* (The Daughter of Merchant Zholobov, 1831) and *Kamchadalka* (A Girl from Kamchatka, 1833)—and the tale *Izgnanniki* (Exiles, 1834). Despite their vague eighteenth-century background and didactic plots, these works earned praise from contemporary critics for their ethnographic value in providing vivid descriptions of Russia's immense eastern frontier.

Kamenskii, Vasilii Vasil'evich (1884–1961). An artist, writer, and founding father of Russian futurism. He was the author of the only futurist historical novel, *Sten'ka Razin* (1915), a fascinating work that draws on the panoply of futurist poetics (e.g., mosaic composition, linguistic experimentation, "primitivism") within a wider context of early modernism (e.g., search for archetypes, stylistic polyphony, "bio-aesthetics," pan-theatricality). The brutal leader of the Cossack rebellion is portrayed as the Russian Orpheus.

Karasev, A. A. (dates unknown). The author of the historical tale *Polkovnik Gruzinov* (Colonel Gruzinov, 1896), concerning a bizarre and grim episode from the reign of Paul I that involved the execution of the Gruzinov brothers, one of whom (the Cossack colonel Evgraf Gruzinov) was once the emperor's favorite.

Karatygin, Petr Petrovich (1832–1888). A scion of a famous theatrical family, he earned his living by writing fiction and omnium-gatherum histories. Karatygin also authored a number of articles on various subjects drawn from Saint Petersburg's past. His expertise in this area provided the background for several historical novels, published in the 1880s, covering the period from the late eighteenth century to the Decembrist uprising. Among other things, his novels are of interest because they combine echoes of exposé literature with the nascent interest in mysticism.

Karnovich, Evgenii Petrovich (1823–1885). A renowned expert on the history of Russian culture, daily life, and the "secret history" of the eighteenth century, Karnovich turned to historical fiction out of financial necessity. He published eight novels, most of which deal with mid- to late-eighteenth-century Russia. Although of modest artistic value, his works stand out for their solid historical background.

Kassirov. *See* Ivin, Ivan Semenovich

Kazantsev, Nikolai Vladimirovich (1849–1904). Under the influence of Mamin-Sibiriak, he wrote stories and sketches dealing with the Urals region. Although Vengerov identified him as the author of *Protiv techeniia. Istoricheskii roman vremen Sten'ki Razina* (Against the Current: A Historical Novel from the Times of Stenka Razin, 1881), this identification has been questioned in *Russkie pisateli*.

Kel'siev, Vasilii Ivanovich (1835–1872). Best known as a prominent "nihilist" and revolutionary émigré who repented and returned to Russia. Three of his historical novels, written shortly before his death, are of interest mainly because they are among the very first works of the "second wave." Perhaps reflecting Kel'siev's own evolution, his novel *Moskva i Tver'* (Moscow and Tver, 1870) presents the idea that uprisings against the Tatar domination were futile and even detrimental, whereas historical truth guided the strategy of Alexander Nevsky and rulers of the Moscow dynasty, who understood that the eventual deliverance of Rus could only come about through stoic obedience to the powers that be.

Khitrov, Mikhail Ivanovich (1851–1899). An archpriest and spiritual writer, he was the author of a tale about an early Roman saint, published in 1888, that went through many editions.

Khovanskii, M. A. (dates unknown). The author of a novel about the German wife of Tsarevich Aleksei, *Nevestka Petra Velikogo* (Peter the Great's Daughter-in-Law, 1889).

Khrushchov-Sokol'nikov, Gavriil Aleksandrovich (1845–1890). A fiction writer and journalist, in the 1880s he published several historical novels, most of which were serialized in the newspaper *Svet*.

Kislov, Aleksandr Stepanovich (1808–1866). His only historical novel appeared in 1836 and deals with the Time of Troubles.

Kisnemskii, Semen Petrovich (1859–1906). A prolific fiction writer, in 1905 he published a historical novel set in medieval Muscovy.

Kondrat'ev, Ivan Kuz'mich (1849–1904). A popular writer at the lower end of the Russian literary spectrum, from the late 1870s to the late 1890s he published at least six historical novels and tales on various subjects drawn from Russian history. In terms of subject matter, the most interesting of these is *Gunny* (The Huns, 1878), which is set during the period of the great migrations. Following Aleksandr Vel'tman, Kondrat'ev considers the Huns to be Slavs.

Konshin, Nikolai Mikhailovich (1793–1859). A poet within Evgenii Baratynskii's circle, Konshin experimented with writing prose by publishing the 1834 novel *Graf Obianskii, ili Smolensk v 1812 g.* (Count Oboianskii, or Smolensk in 1812), in which he partly draws on his own wartime experiences.

Korenevskii, Vasilii (dates unknown). In 1846 he published a novel set in seventeenth-century Ukraine.

Korf, Baron Fedor Fedorovich (1803–1853). Among his works in various genres, the sole historical novel *Sud v Revel'skom magistrate* (A Trial in the Magistracy of Reval, 1841) is set in sixteenth-century Estland, the ancestral land of the Korfs.

Kornilovich, Aleksandr Osipovich (1800–1834). An author who published his first historical tale in 1825 and continued writing even after being imprisoned for his involvement in the Decembrist revolt. He anonymously published two tales and a short novel, *Andrei Bezymianyi* (1832). Unremarkable for their artistic merits, these works stand out because of the historical erudition of their author, who was an expert on the Petrine epoch. Historical realia were borrowed from Kornilovich by a number of authors, including Pushkin.

Kostomarov, Nikolai Ivanovich (1817–1885). A founding father of modern Ukrainian nationalism and an influential historian, Kostomarov wrote three historical tales and one novel, all of which present the Russian past in an extremely negative light. Kostomarov's main target is pre-Petrine Russia: Ivan the Terrible's reign in the novel *Kudeiar* (1875), Razin's rebellion in *Syn* (The Son, 1865), and Muscovite administration in seventeenth-century Ukraine in *Chernigovka* (A Girl from Chernigov, 1881). In *Kholui* (The Lackey, 1878) Kostomarov extends his criticism to the Petersburgian period, presenting the base mores of both aristocratic masters and their serfs in the eighteenth century. His historical fiction displays strong Russophobic elements: unlike the typical "nihilists" of the day, who tend to concentrate on social evils, Kostomarov points to major defects in the Russian national psyche.

Kostomarova, Aleksandra Koronatovna (1868–?). The author of prose tales, poems, and plays published in the decade prior to World War I, her novel *Muraveinik* (The Anthill, 1914) is perhaps the first work of Russian literature devoted to the Russo-Japanese War and the Revolution of 1905 that identifies itself as a historical novel.

Kostritskii, Mikhail Dmitrievich (pseud. Ordyntsev) (1887–ca. 1941). Although he specialized in fantasy and adventure stories, in the 1910s Kostritskii published a number of historical novels and tales.

Krasnitsky, Aleksandr Ivanovich (pseud. Lavintsev, Lavrov, among others) (1866–1917). An extremely prolific author who published roughly one hundred novels and tales on various topics. His historical collection consists of some twenty titles, including a loosely connected trilogy set in the early days of Russia: *V tumane tysiacheletiia* (In the Mist of a Millennium, 1895), *Groza Vizantii* (The Scourge of Byzantium, 1898), and *V dali vekov* (In the Distance of Centuries, 1901). Set mostly in Byzantium, *Groza Vizantii* deals with the confrontation between Kiev and Constantinople under Emperors Michael and Basil the Macedonian. Other novels by Krasnitsky stand out for their subject matter, if not for their artistic merits. *Belyi general. Povest'-khronika iz zhizni gen. M. D. Skobeleva* (The White General: Chronicle Tale from the Life of General M. D. Skobelev, 1904) is one of the few novels devoted to Mikhail Skobelev, an earlier example of which can be found only in the work of A. A. Sokolov. *Poslednie orly* (Last Eagles, 1912), which deals with the Russian intervention in Hungary during the Revolution of 1848–49, appears to be the only Russian novel on this subject.

Krasnov, Petr Nikolaevich (1869–1947). World War I general, leader of the Don Cossacks during the civil war, and Hitler's ally during World War II, Krasnov reached the zenith of his literary fame as an émigré writer. His literary career, however, began long before the Revolution. Inter alia, he wrote the historical novel *Ataman Platov* (1896), about a fellow Cossack and the hero of the Napoleonic Wars.

Krestovskii, Vsevolod Vladimirovich (1839–1895). The author of the scandalously famous *Peterburgskie trushchoby* (Petersburgian Slums, 1864–66), he worked in a wide variety of genres. His historical tale *Dedy* (The Grandfathers, 1875) emerged as a by-product of his monograph on the history of the Uhlans of the Guard, which was commissioned by the emperor. (At the time Krestovskii was an Uhlan officer.) This work is remarkable in that it represents one of the first attempts at a positive reevaluation of Paul I's reign.

Krylov. Ivan Zakharovich (1816–1869). His historical fiction includes *Iurii, poslednii velikii kniaz' Smolenskii* (Iurii, the Last Great Prince of Smolensk, 1840), a novel in dramatic form, and the popular *lubok* tale *Predanie o tom, kak soldat spas Petra Velikogo ot smerti* (A Legend about a Soldier Who Saved Peter the Great from Death, 1843).

Kryzhanovskaia, Vera Ivanovna (pseud. Rochester) (1857–1924). She occupies a singular place in Russian literature as the preeminent author of occult novels. A practicing medium, Kryzhanovskaia claimed that her works were dictated to her by the spirit of a seventeenth-century English mystic. Some of her novels were first published in French and subsequently appeared in Russian translation. Her historical fiction deals with medieval subjects, Rome, and, above all, ancient Egypt. History is usually relegated to the frame narrative, with the main text often revolving around occult themes (e.g., magic, mediums, clairvoyance, reincarnation) and the author's belief that God is the same irrespective of the various names and features ascribed to Him by different civilizations. In terms of the historiosophic scheme, her most ambitious novel is *Le Pharaon Mernephta* (The Pharaoh Mernephta, 1888; Russian trans. 1906), which contains a revisionist picture of Moses, who is portrayed as an unscrupulous, power-hungry egotist who perverted the true face of the Deity by leading the Jews astray and creating the image of the vengeful, blood-thirsty God of the Old Testament. A hybrid between the occult and historical novel is found in *Dva sfinksa* (Two Sphinxes, 1901), whose heroes are placed into a state of suspended animation in ancient Egypt and subsequently wake up in the first and nineteenth centuries A.D.

Kukel'. *See* Lunin, Viktor Alekseevich

Kukol'nik, Nestor Vasil'evich (1809–1868). His historical novels, which were published in the early 1840s, appeared at the time of the genre's eclipse and could not rival the popularity of his dramas. They are also generally considered inferior to his short stories. Two out of four of his novels deal with non-Russian topics, including fourteenth-century Lithuania (*Al'f i Al'dona*, 1842) and France under Louis XIII (*Evelina de Val'erol'*, 1841).

Kulish, Panteleimon Aleksandrovich (1819–1897). A Ukrainian writer who, in the 1840s and early 1860s, published several historical novels dealing with Little Russian subjects. The publication of his most significant novel, *Chernaia rada* (The Black Council), began in 1845 but was halted because of the author's arrest in connection with his nationalistic activities. The complete novel appeared in 1857 in both Russian and Ukrainian editions. In contrast to Gogol and other earlier authors, Kulish demythologizes the Cossacks, portraying them as a destructive force that contributed to the downfall of the Ukraine.

Kurbatov, A. D. (dates unknown). In 1833 he published anonymously *Poslednii god vlasti gertsoga Birona. Povest', vziataia iz starinnoi arkhivy moego dedushki* (The Last Year of Duke Biron's Power: A Tale Taken from the Old Archive of My Grandfather).

Kuryshev, I. (dates unknown). He published anonymously two novels dealing with medieval Russian subjects, *Maliuta Skuratov* (1833) and *Osnovanie Moskvy* (The Founding of Moscow, 1835).

Kuz'mich, Aleksandr Petrovich (1807?–after 1868). Published two novels dealing with the history of his native Ukraine: *Kazaki* (The Cossacks, 1842), set during the times of Mazepa, and the lengthy *Zinovii-Bogdan Khmel'nitskii* (1846).

Ladyzhenskii, Sergei Aleksandrovich (pseud. Bulkin) (1830–1877). Active during the era of the Great Reforms, he wrote the historical tale *Syshchiki* (Detectives, 1870), reintroducing the theme of Anna Ioannovna's reign into Russian historical fiction.

Lapin, Vasilii Innokent'evich (1823–1886). A writer who continued the work of A. E. Razin following the latter's death.

Lavintsev, A. I. *See* Krasnitskii, Aleksandr Ivanovich

Lavrov, A. I. *See* Krasnitskii, Aleksandr Ivanovich

Lazhechnikov, Ivan Ivanovich (1792–1869). A leading novelist of the 1830s, he was Zagoskin's competitor for the title of the Russian Walter Scott, although Lazhechnikov was perhaps more indebted to the French romantics. His three completed novels—*Poslednii novik* (The Last Page, 1831–33), *Ledianoi dom* (The Ice Palace, 1835), and *Basurman* (The Infidel, 1838)—are among the best works in the historical genre, *The Ice Palace* being one of the most frequently reprinted historical novels.

Lebedev, Mikhail Nikolaevich (1877–1951). In the late 1890s and early 1900s he published several historical tales, two of which dealt with his native region of Perm.

Lebedev, Vladimir Petrovich (1869–1939). A poet and prose writer, in the 1900s and early 1910s he published a dozen historical tales that mostly dealt with medieval Russian subjects, one notable exception being *V boiakh 12-go goda* (In the Battles of the Year 1812), which celebrated the centennial of Napoleon's expulsion.

Leskov, Nikolai Semenovich (1831–1895). In the mid-to-late 1880s he wrote several stylized tales based on *Prolog*, a medieval Russian collection of Byzantine hagiographic legends. *Zenon-zlatokuznets* (Zenon, the Goldsmith, 1888), one of the longer pieces, was banned by the church censors and only reappeared in 1890 under the title *Gora* (The Mountain), now reclassified as a historical novel. Although in terms of volume historical fiction represents only a small part of Leskov's enormous output, it bears the unmistakable imprint of his idiosyncratic genius and is important in anticipating the tendency toward stylization in turn-of-the-century literature.

Levitskii, M. (dates unknown). Wrote at least one tale about Peter the Great that was published in 1904.

Likharev, Nikolai Osipovich (pseud. N. Streshnev) (dates unknown). In the 1900s he published half a dozen tales drawn from Russian church history in the supplement to *Russkii palomnik* (The Russian Pilgrim).

Liubetskii, Sergei Mikhailovich (1808/10–1881). One of the most interesting lowbrow authors of the first wave. In the early 1830s he published four historical novels anonymously, one of which—*Sokol'niki, ili Pokolebanie vladychestva tatar nad Rossieiu* (Sokol'niki, or The Shaking of Tatar Power over Russia, 1832)—was reprinted throughout the nineteenth century.

Liubich-Koshurov, Iosaf Arianovich (1872–1934/37). In the decade prior to the Revolution he published several historical tales that represent the least interesting aspect of his prolific output.

Lunin, Viktor Alekseevich (pseud. Kukel') (1838–after 1914). A prolific *lubok* writer, many—if not all—of his historical tales published at the turn of the century are remakes of works by other authors, including A. K. Tolstoi's *Kniaz' Serebrianyi*, R. M. Zotov's *Tainstvennyi monakh*, and A. A. Pavlov's *Iapancha*.

L'vov, Vladimir Vladimirovich (1805–1856). His writings for children include one historical tale dealing with events in 1812—*Seryi armiak, ili Ispolnennoe obeshchanie* (A Grey Armyak, or A Promise Fulfilled, 1836)—which went through several editions.

L'vova, L. P. (dates unknown). In 1903 he published a historical tale dealing with Erofei Khabarov, the seventeenth-century explorer of the Far East, who is usually overshadowed by his conquistador predecessor Ermak Timofeevich in Russian narratives of the eastern frontier.

Makarova, Sof'ia Markovna (1834–1887). A popular children's writer, she was the author of several historical short stories and two longer tales, *Groznaia tucha* (A Menacing Cloud, 1886), which dealt with Napoleon's invasion, and *Sueta suet* (Vanity of Vanities, 1887), which related the downfall of Aleksandr Menshikov.

Mamin-Sibiriak, Dmitrii Narkisovich (1852–1912). The preeminent Siberian writer, his prolific output includes one long historical tale, *Okhoniny brovi* (Okhonia's Eyebrows, 1892), dealing with Emel'ian Pugachev's insurrection in the Urals.

Markov, Evgenii l'vovich (1835–1903). Brother of Vladislav Markov. He wrote one historical novel with a vague eighteenth-century chronotope, *Razboinitsa Orlikha* (Brigandess Orlikha, 1891), which represents the least interesting aspect of his literary legacy.

Markov, Vladislav l'vovich (1831–1905). Working in various genres, he published three historical novels. *Kurskie porubezhniki* (Frontiersmen of Kursk, 1873) and *Likholet'e* (Troubled Years, 1882) both deal with the Time of Troubles. *Predki v trudnoe vremia* (Ancestors during Hard Times, 1903) is set during the regency of Sofia.

Masal'skii, Konstantin Petrovich (1802–1861). The author of several historical tales and novels, including *Borodoliubie* (The Love of Beards, 1837), one of the few Russian "novels in dramatic scenes" inspired by the genre of Ludovic Vitet's historical scenes. Masal'skii's reputation largely rests on his first novel *Strel'tsy* (The Strelets, 1832), which was reprinted several times (it was a favorite of the young Dostoevskii). Masal'skii's last novel, *Leitenant i poruchik* (Lieutenant and Poruchik), completed in the mid-1840s, was perceived as the work of a writer who had outlived his age.

Maurin, Evgenii Ivanovich (?–1925). In the 1910s he published several adventure novels, most of which are set in France during the late seventeenth and eighteenth centuries.

Mech, Ivan Nikolaevich (pseud. I. Nikolaevich) (dates unknown). A lowbrow author of the 1850s, he published several historical novels, among them *Brilliantovaia luna* (A Diamond Moon, 1854), which deals with the rare subject of Genoese colonies in the Crimea.

Merder, Nadezhda Ivanovna (pseud. Severin) (1839–1906). More famous for works about matrimonial discord in contemporary life, Merder wrote approximately ten historical novels and tales that were published in the 1890s and 1900s. Perhaps reflecting her family background (although impoverished, she was of old noble stock), her favorite genre was the family chronicle set within a vague historical frame, such as *Vorotyntsevy* (The Vorotynsevs, 1891), including its sequel. Some of her works, however, are embedded in specific historical events, such as *Zvezda tsesarevny* (The Star of a Princess, 1906), which deals with the formative years of Elizabeth, Peter I's daughter and the future empress.

Merezhkovskii, Dmitrii Sergeevich (1865–1941). One of the founding fathers of Russian symbolism, he was also a pioneer of early modernist historical fiction. The latter is represented by his trilogy *Khristos i Antikhrist* (Christ and Antichrist, 1895–1905), a "neomythological" piece, replete with eschatological premonitions, that centers on the struggle between paganism and Christianity. It spans the fourth century A.D. to the 1710s, with the action set in the late Roman Empire, Renaissance Italy, and Petrine Russia. Constituting his magnum opus, the trilogy was among the most widely read prose works of the time and gained international recognition thanks to translations in the major European languages. Merezhkovskii further developed his historiosophic scheme in his second trilogy, *Tsarstvo zveria* (Kingdom of the Beast, 1908–1918), which is set in Russia during the first quarter of the nineteenth century, and later in Egyptian novels, which he wrote in the 1920s while in emigration.

Merkli, Mikhail Markovich (1817/18–1846). A minor romantic poet of some note. In 1837 he published anonymously the novel *Boris Godunov i Rossiia v XVII stoletii* (Boris Godunov and Russia in the Seventeenth Century), which is described as *poluistoricheskii* (semihistorical) since the action is centered around the fictional hero Prince Sitskii.

Mikhailov, A. *See* Sheller, A. K.

Mikheev, Vasilii Mikhailovich (1859–1908). A prolific writer and the author of two tales, published in the late 1890s, set during the Time of Troubles.

Miliukov, Aleksandr Petrovich (1817–1897). Having entered the literary scene in the late 1840s as a Westernizer, in his later years he leaned toward Slavophilism. Miliukov's only historical tale *Tsarskaia svad'ba. Bylina o gosudare Ivane Vasil'eviche Groznom* (The Tsar's Wedding: A Song of Tsar Ivan Vasil'evich the

Terrible, 1872) is noteworthy for its intended aim of reproducing the "acutely naive" spirit of folklore and *lubok* prints, although the end result is a mediocre realistic narrative.

Mintslov, Sergei Rudol'fovich (1870–1933). A prominent literary figure and bibliographer. In the 1900s he published several historical novels and tales dealing with various Russian and Lithuanian subjects. Most original in terms of historical conception is *Na zare XVII veka* (At the Dawn of the Seventeenth Century, 1901), which sympathizes with certain actions of the False Dmitrii and portrays Shuiskii as the main villain behind the Time of Troubles. Mintslov continued writing historical novels in emigration.

Mordovtsev, Daniil Lukich (1830–1905). A Russo-Ukrainian writer and amateur historian of note. One of the most prolific authors of the historical genre, his productivity borders on graphomania. Beginning in the mid-1870s, he wrote some forty historical novels and longer tales. Mordovtsev stands out for his pronounced Ukrainian nationalism, Russophobic tendencies (inherited from his mentor and friend Kostomarov), and general populist sympathy for the "centrifugal" forces of history. Although Mordovtsev covered a wide range of topics (including the fashionable Egyptian and Roman subjects during the later stages of his career), his main specialty remained Russo-Ukrainian interaction and the Russian Schism. Perhaps his most enduring and significant work is *Idealisty i realisty* (Idealists and Realists, 1876), which laid the foundation for the negative representation of Peter I in Russian historical fiction.

Moskvichin, Alexei. *See* Pavlov, Aleksei Andreevich

Nashchekina, V. (dates unknown). In 1898 he published a novel covering the reign of Aleksei Mikhailovich.

Nazar'eva, Kapitolina Valer'ianovna (1847–1900). A prolific fiction writer who cultivated various genres. Her historical novel covering the reign of Catherine the Great appeared posthumously in 1902.

Nemirovich-Danchenko, Vasily Ivanovich (1844–1936). The elder brother of the cofounder of the Moscow Art Theater, Vladimir Ivanovich. He was a famous cultural figure in his own right. He rose to prominence in the 1870s and remained popular for many decades, ending his life in emigration as one of the patriarchs of Russian literature. Although extremely prolific as a novelist, Nemirovich-Danchenko is remembered mainly for his travelogues and military journalism. Half a dozen of his historical novels, published from the late 1890s through the early 1910s, reintroduced the theme of the conquest of the Caucasus. They are partially based on his family legacy: his father, a Russian officer of Ukrainian descent, was a veteran of the Caucasian wars, while his mother was an ethnic Armenian. Reflecting his admiration for the natural beauty of the region, his novels glorify the brazen courage of the highlanders, the unassuming heroism of Russians soldiers, and the colorful eccentricities of the Caucasian conquistadors (including such forgotten figures as Baron Zass).

Nikolaev, N. (dates unknown). In 1889 he published *Raby vrazhdy* (Slaves of Animosity), a novel about the Polish uprising of 1863.

Nikolaeva, E. (dates unknown). A fiction writer active in the 1880s and 1890s. In 1889 he published the lengthy novel *Ermak* about the conqueror of Siberia.

Nikolaevich, I. *See* Mech, Ivan Nikolaevich

Nikol'skii, Mikhail Erastovich (1878–?). The author of several rather lowbrow novels, including anniversary pieces for the centennial in 1912 of Napoleon's defeat and the Romanov tercentenary in 1913.

Novosil'tseva, Ekaterina Vladimirovna (pseud. Tamara Tolycheva) (1820–1885). Although descended from an ancient aristocratic family, her writings were mostly aimed at a less well educated readership. In addition to interesting collections of oral history devoted to the War of 1812 and the defense of Sevastopol, in the 1870s and 1880s she published a number of edifying short stories and tales drawn from various periods of Russian history.

Okreits, Stanislav Stanislavovich (1834/36–after 1921). A prolific writer and journalist, in the 1910s he published three novels on subjects taken from Russian history.

Oks, Viktor Borisovich (1879–?). In the 1900s he published several historical tales intended for young readers.

Opochnin, Evgenii Nikolaevich (1858–1928). Best remembered as a historian of Russian theater and an archivist, in the late 1900s and 1910s he also produced a number of historical novels that were serialized in the newspaper *Moskovskii listok* (Moscow Leaflet).

Ordyntsev. *See* Kostritskii, Mikhail Dmitrievich

Orlovskii, S. N. *See* Shil', Sof'ia Nikolaevna

Osetrov, Zakhar Borisovich (dates unknown). A playwright whose tale *Shut Balakirev* (The Jester Balakirev), written to celebrate Saint Petersburg's bicentennial in 1903, is a remake of his earlier historical drama.

Osipov, Andrei Andreevich (1868–1910). The author of several novels and longer tales dealing with various Russian subjects, spanning the dawn of Rus to the late eighteenth century, that adhere to the then fashionable trend of historical stylization. Following the example of various "stone-age" narratives, his tale *Variag* (A Varangian, 1902) presents the world through the eyes of pagan Slavs. The tale *Tri stroki* (Three Lines, 1908), set in the early 1760s, is marked by linguistic stylization. Although it closely parallels *The Captain's Daughter* in several respects, it consciously avoids the tragic aspects of Pushkin's masterpiece.

Pavlov, Aleksei Andreevich (pseud. Aleksei Moskvichin) (1815–after 1849). A prolific lowbrow writer. In the 1830s he wrote half a dozen novels, the most popular of which remains *Iapancha, tatarskii naezdnik, ili Zavoevanie Kazani tsarem Ioannom Groznym* (Iapancha, the Tartar Horseman, or The Conquest of Kazan by Tsar Ivan the Terrible, 1834), which was reprinted numerous times by *lubok* presses and served as the basis for remakes and adaptations.

Pavlov, A. P. (dates unknown). The author of several novels on various Russian subjects that appeared in the early 1900s.

Pavlov, Nikolai Mikhailovich (1835–1906). A writer, publicist, and historian, he was one of the most prominent figures of late Slavophilism. Dismayed by

Kostomarov's negativism in *Syn* (The Son, 1865), Pavlov presented his own vision of Aleksei Mikhailovich's epoch in the tale *Tsarskii sokol'nik* (The Tsar's Falconer, 1870), which emphasizes the harmonious beauty of the old Russian way of life.

Pazukhin, Aleksei Mikhailovich (1851–1919). A prolific author quite popular among less well educated readers. In the 1880s and 1890s he published several historical tales.

Pazukhin, Nikolai Mikhailovich (1857–1898). The brother of A. M. Pazukhin. A purveyor of *lubok* literature, in the 1880s wrote several historical novels and tales, some of which are remakes of works by A. K. Tolstoi, Lermontov, and others.

Petrov, Petr Nikolaevich (1827–1891). An art historian and journalist. In the 1870s and 1880s he published half a dozen historical novels on Russian subjects, one of which, *Ioann III* (1872), grew out of N. V. Kukol'nik's unfinished work.

Pinchuk, Vasilii Andreevich (dates unknown). Active in the 1900s, he published the historical novel *Gore pobezhdennym* (Vae victis, 1904) and the tale *Za krest i veru* (For the Cross and Faith, 1902, coauthored with A. I. Krasnitskii). The latter work deals with Georgian history at the turn of the seventeenth century and early contacts between Russia and Georgia—a rare subject in historical fiction.

Pisemskii, Aleksei Feofilaktovich (1820/21–1881). A major literary figure of the age of Tolstoi and Dostoevskii, he turned to historical fiction at the very end of his career. His last, rather unsuccessful, novel *Masony* (The Masons, 1880) is set during the decline of Russian freemasonry in the 1830s. The properly historical element in the novel is minimal, Pisemskii's main idea being to contrast the selfless idealists of yore with the predators of the capitalist era.

Polevoi, Ksenofont Alekseevich (1801–1867). A collaborator with his brother Nikolai on the journal *Moskovskii telegraf* (The Moscow Telegraph). In 1836 he published *Lomonosov* (1836), which appears to be the first Russian "biographie romancée." (In the late nineteenth century it was reprinted with the subtitle "novel.")

Polevoi, Nikolai Alekseevich (1796–1846). A leading Russian theoretician and critic of the historical novel, he had a pronounced preference for the French romantics over Scott. Polevoi was also one of the genre's precursors, publishing the long tale *Simeon Kirdiapa* in 1828. His magnum opus remains the programmatic novel *Kliatva pri grobe Gospodnem* (An Oath at the Holy Sepulcher, 1832), among the most significant works of the decade. In his subsequent novel *Ioann Tsimiskhii* (John Tzimisces, 1841) Polevoi pioneered the Byzantine theme in Russian historical fiction.

Polevoi, Petr Nikolaevich (1839–1902). The son of Nikolai Alekseevich Polevoi. A professor of Russian literature at the University of Warsaw, he abandoned an academic career in 1871 in order to become a freelance writer and journalist. He is the author of the acclaimed *History of Russian Literature in Sketches and Biographies* as well as several studies on various subjects drawn from Russian history. Starting in 1888, he also published a number of historical novels and tales dealing with Russia during the seventeenth and eighteenth centuries.

Polezhaev, Petr Vasil'evich (pseud. Shubarskii) (dates unknown). A lawyer by profession, he wrote several works on the history of Russian law as well as a historical sketch of the principality of Moscow. In 1878–80 Polezhaev served as the editor and publisher of the journal *Istoricheskaia biblioteka* (Historical Library), where he published his first novel *Prestol i monastyr'* (The Throne and Monastery, 1878), which deals with the conflict between Peter I and his half-sister Sofia. In the following decade he wrote four other historical novels set in eighteenth-century Russia.

Politkovskaia, M. E. (dates unknown). The wife of V. Politkovskii. In 1880 she published the tale *Ivon Moldavskii* (Ivon of Moldavia), which deals with the political turmoil in the principality of Moldavia in the 1570s, specifically the attempts by some Moldavian factions and their Ukrainian allies to secure help from Poland and Russia in their struggle against the Turks. This appears to be the only work in Russian historical fiction whose primary focus is on Moldavian history.

Politkovskii, V. (dates unknown). In 1879–80 he published two historical tales on medieval Russian subjects in *Istoricheskaia biblioteka.*

Pospelov, Aleksei (dates unknown). The author of a popular story about Grishka Otrep'ev. He also published the single novel *Matiushka Verevkin* (1846), which is also set during the Time of Troubles.

Potapenko, Ignatii Nikolaevich (1856–1929). A prolific turn-of-the-century writer. In 1898 he published a novel about Peter the Great's reign.

Potapov, Vasilii Fedorovich (dates unknown). A *lubok* author active during the mid-1840s and 1850s. He wrote several historical novels, the most popular being *Andrei Besstrashnyi, invalid Petra Velikogo* (Andrei the Fearless, a Veteran of Peter the Great, 1851), which went through ten editions.

Protopopov, Aleksandr Pavlovich (pseud. Slavin) (1814–1867). In the mid-1830s and early 1840s he published several lowbrow quasi-historical and historical novels, one of which, *Smert' Napoleona* (Napoleon's Death, 1836), was written in dramatic form.

Pushkin, Aleksandr Sergeevich (1799–1837). His first attempt to emulate Scott—the fragment "Arap Petra Velikogo" (Blackamoor of Peter the Great, 1828), dealing with his own maternal great grandfather—remained unfinished. His subsequent plans for a tale about a *strelets* went unrealized. Pushkin's only completed historical novel, *Kapitanskaia dochka* (The Captain's Daughter, 1836), became a fictional counterpart to his *Istoriia Pugacheva* (A History of Pugachev, 1833). The novel remained largely unnoticed by his contemporaries; it appeared at a time when Pushkin's popularity was beginning to wane and the market was flooded with Russian imitations of Scott. The situation changed after Pushkin's posthumous "canonization." However, even today *Kapitanskaia dochka* is largely perceived as children's literature, this despite the fact that it was written at the height of Pushkin's creative maturity and in many ways represents his "final word." Deceivingly simple, *Kapitanskaia dochka* is one of Pushkin's most complex works and arguably the most perfect Russian historical novel ever written.

Radich, Vasilii Andreevich (1860–1904). A turn-of-the-twentieth-century author. He specialized in Ukrainian subjects drawn from the seventeenth and eighteenth centuries, describing resistance to Polish oppression as well as mutual atrocities committed in the course of this struggle.

Razin, Aleksei Egorovich (1823–1875). In the late 1860s and 1870s he wrote dozens of stories and tales in the series *Russkaia istoriia v povestiakh*. Following his death, his work was continued by V. I. Lapin.

Rochester. *See* Kryzhanovskaia, Vera Ivanovna

Rogova, Ol'ga Il'inichna (also published under the name Shmidt-Moskvitinova) (1851–?). The author of several historical novels and tales, based upon the Ukrainian and Russian past, intended for adolescents. This children's writer was active beginning in the 1880s.

Rossiev, Pavel Amplievich (dates unknown). In the 1900s he published several tales, drawn from the history of the Russian church, which appeared in the supplement to *Russkii palomnik* (The Russian Pilgrim).

Rubakin, Nikolai Aleksandrovich (1862–1946). A prominent bibliographer who advocated the pedagogical use of the historical novel. He wrote several tales drawn from western European medieval and Renaissance history.

Rudnevskii (dates unknown). The author of the lowbrow novel *David Igorevich* (1834), set in eleventh-century Russia.

Ryskin, S. F. (dates unknown). In 1893 he published a historical novel dealing with the history of the Russian schismatics.

Sadovskoi, Boris Aleksandrovich (1881–1952). He wrote stylized short stories that appeared in two collections bearing characteristically Petersburgian and acmeist titles: *Uzor chugunnyi* (The Cast Iron Pattern, 1911) and *Admiralteiskaia igla* (The Admiralty Spire, 1915). Sadovskoi also wrote one longer tale, *Dvukhglavyi orel* (Double-Headed Eagle, 1911), which deals with the youth of Grigorii Potemkin.

Salias de Turnemir, Count Evgenii Andreevich (1840–1908). Often dubbed the Russian Dumas, he was among the most popular and prolific historical novelists of his time, writing upwards of forty novels. He began his career in the genre with the quasi-Tolstoian epic *Pugachevtsy* (The Men of Pugachev, 1873), recounting the Pugachev rebellion. He subsequently displayed a growing predilection for piquant anecdotes and romantic adventures set in high society. His favorite period remained the Russian eighteenth and early nineteenth centuries.

Salmanov, Petr Andreevich (1817–82). In 1839 he published (under a pseudonym) the novel *Chernoe vremia, ili Stseny iz zhizni Emel'ki Pugacheva* (Dark Time, or Scenes from the Life of Emelka Pugachev), a lowbrow piece that was reprinted several times. Perhaps most remarkable is its apparent unawareness of Pushkin's *Kapitanskaia dochka*. The announced sequel to the novel, entitled *Mstitel'* (Avenger), most likely remained unrealized. Salmanov's next historical novel, *Kniaz' Boris Shegliatev* (Prince Boris Shegliatev), set during Batu's Khan's invasion, appeared in 1881. His first and subsequent historical novels thus span more than four decades, which makes Salmanov unique in the history of the genre in Russia.

Savinov, V. N. (dates unknown). In 1854 he published *Znakhari* (Witch Doctors), a lowbrow novel about the Pugachev rebellion that opens with an inept imitation of the snowstorm scene in Pushkin's *Kapitanskaia dochka.*

Sementovskii, Nikolai Maksimovich (1819–1879). A specialist in Ukrainian history and archaeology. His historical fiction is likewise devoted to Little Russian subjects and includes the novels *Kochubei* (1845) and *Potemkin kak kozak Voiska zaporozhskogo* (Potemkin as a Cossack of the Zaporozhian Army, 1851).

Sergievskii, Nikolai Nikolaevich (1873–1918). The author of works in various genres, including biographical sketches of Mikhail Lomonosov, Pushkin, and K. R. As his contribution to the stream of anniversary literature during the Romanov tercentenary, he wrote the historical novel *Na zare tsarstva* (At the Dawn of the Tsardom, 1913). In 1914–17 Sergievskii served as editor of the journal *Nasha Starina* (Our Antiquity), a cheaper version of *Istoricheskii vestnik.*

Severin. *See* Merder, Nadezhda Ivanovna

Severtsev-Polilov (Polilov), Georgii Tikhonovich (1859–1915). A prolific turn-of-the-century author. His historical tales and short stories appeared in the 1900s and 1910s.

Shakhovskaia, Princess Liudmila Dmitrievna (dates unknown). The only Russian historical novelist whose specialty was ancient Rome. An indefatigable graphomaniac, from the early 1880s to the mid-1900s Shakhovskaia wrote over twenty works dealing with various periods of Roman history, from its dawn to the first centuries of Christianity. Works that tended to be lengthy and maintained a consistent story line were termed novels (some ran between five hundred and a thousand pages), while shorter and more loosely organized works were called *bytovye kartiny* (pictures of daily life). Most of her historical fiction was collected under the title *Rimskaia istoriia v belletristicheskom izlozhenii Liudmily Shakhovskoi* (Roman History in the Belletristic Rendering of Liudmila Shakhovskaia), the only exception being *Lev pobeditel'. Pervyi v russkoi literature i. r. iz abissinskoi zhizni* (Lion the Victor: The First Novel about Abyssinian Life in Russian Literature, 1898), which is set in the sixth century A.D. Those of her novels published after 1900 were supplied with her own illustrations, which either qualify her as the grandmother of Russian primitivism or put her sanity in doubt.

Shardin, A. *See* Sukhonin, Petr Petrovich

Shchepkina, Aleksandra Vasil'evna (dates unknown). The author of numerous *rasskazy iz russkogo byta* (stories from Russian daily life). Active in the 1880s and 1890s, Schepkina published at least two historical novels: *Na zare* (At Dawn, 1886), set in mid-eighteenth-century Russia, and *Boiare Starodubskie* (The Boyars Starodubskii, 1897), set during the reign of Aleksei Mikhailovich.

Sheller, A. K. (pseud. A. Mikhailov) (1838–1900). A popular topical writer of "progressive" convictions who began his literary career during the Great Reforms, Mikhailov also paid tribute to historical fiction by publishing two solid yet somewhat insipid novels: *Iz-za vlasti* (For the Sake of Power, 1889), dealing with the Time of Troubles, and *Dvorets i monastyr'* (The Palace and the Convent, 1890), set during the reigns of Vasilii III and Ivan IV.

Shelonskii, N. N. (dates unknown). Active in the 1890s and early 1900s. He wrote at least two historical novels, both of which are based upon nineteenth-century subjects: *Za krest i rodinu. Roman iz epokhi bor'by za osvobozhdenie Gretsii* (For the Cross and Motherland: A Novel from the Epoch of Struggle for the Liberation of Greece, 1893) and *Sevastopol' v osade* (Sevastopol under Siege, 1898).

Shil', Sof'ia Nikolaevna (pseud. S. N. Orlovskii) (1863–1928). Children's author. Her tale *Ziriab* is perhaps the only Russian historical novel dealing with the history of Arabs.

Shishkina, Olimpiada Petrovna (1791–1854). The empress's lady-in-waiting, who harbored literary proclivities. Her major works include two lengthy novels set during the Time of Troubles: *Kniaz' Skopin-Shuiskii* (Prince Skopin-Shuiiskii, 1835) and *Prokopii Liapunov* (1845).

Shmitanovskii, Vasilii Iakovlevich (dates unknown). A *lubok* writer of the 1850s and 1860s. He published the historical tale *Ermak, ili Pokorenie Sibirskogo tsarstva* (Ermak, or The Conquest of Siberian Tsardom, 1858).

Shreknik, Evgenii Fedorovich (dates unknown). Author of several nonfictional and fictional works on the early day of polygraphy. These include two tales and a novel on Gutenberg (1894). He also wrote a novel about the Time of Troubles (1892) and another on the discovery of America by Christopher Columbus (1893).

Shteven, Ivan Petrovich (dates unknown). In the late 1830s he published three quasi-historical novels set against a vague eighteenth-century backdrop.

Shubarskii. *See* Polezhaev, Petr Vasil'evich

Sizova, Aleksandra Konstantinovna (?–1910). Author active around the turn of the twentieth century. She wrote numerous historical tales and stories for children.

Skal'kovskii, Apollon Aleksandrovich (1808–1898). A local historian (he was a resident of Odessa) and the author of numerous works on current affairs in southern Russia. Several of his longer tales published in the late 1840s are set in the eighteenth century and deal with the history of his home region.

Slavin. *See* Protopopov, A. P.

Smirnov, Aleksei (dates unknown). A Petersburgian author of the 1900s. His historical tale *Sklirena* (1901), set in Constantinople during the mid-eleventh century, is one of the few Russian works involving Byzantine subject matter.

Sokolov, Aleksandr Alekseevich (1840–1913). An actor by training, he became an extremely prolific writer and journalist. Beginning in 1879, he published over a dozen historical novels and tales dealing with various Russian and Ukrainian subjects. Thematically his most interesting work is *Belyi general* (The White General, 1889), the first historical novel devoted to General Skobelev, who liberated the Balkans and conquered Central Asia (both subjects rarely treated in Russian historical fiction). The novel was accompanied by the publication of Sokolov's nonfictional book *Belyi general—russkii narodnyi geroi Mikhail Dmitrievich Skobelev 2-i. Ego zhizn', podvigi, khrabrost' i dobrodushie. S prilzoheniem anekdotov i stikhotvorenii* (The White General: The Russian National Hero Mikhail

Dmitrievich Skobelev II; His Life, Heroic Deeds, Bravery, and Good-naturedness; plus Anecdotes and Poems, 1888).

Sokolova, Aleksandra Ivanovna (pseud. Sinee Domino) (1836–1914). Author of numerous works based on contemporary life, including crime novels. In the 1910s she wrote half a dozen historical novels that spanned the period from Anna Ioannovna to Nicholas I. They appeared in the series *Intimnaia zhizn' monarkhov* (The Intimate Life of Monarchs).

Solov'ev, Vsevolod Sergeevich (1849–1903). The eldest son of the historian Sergei Mikhailovich Solov'ev. A major historical novelist active during the 1870s and 1880s, he wrote fourteen novels, the most famous being the five-part *Khronika chetyrekh pokolenii* (A Chronicle of Four Generations, 1881–86), which relates the history of the fictional Gorbatov family from the rule of Catherine the Great to the mid-nineteenth century.

Solov'ev-Nesmelov, N. A. (dates unknown). In 1902 he published a tale about Gutenberg called *Mirnyi zavoevatel'* (A Peaceful Conqueror).

Staniukovich, Konstantin Mikhailovich (1843–1903). Russia's preeminent writer on navel subjects. He published a single historical tale entitled *Sevastopol'skii mal'chik* (A Boy from Sebastopol, 1903).

Staryts'kyi, Mikhail, and Liudmila Staritskaia (father and daughter). In 1899 they jointly published a novel about Bogdan Khmel'nitskii.

Streshnev, N. *See* Likharev, Nikolai Osipovich

Stroev-Pollin, I. A. (pseudonym of Ippolit Alekseevich Nestroev) (1874–?). A minor writer active during the early twentieth century. He wrote a single historical novel entitled *Dekabrist. Istoricheskii roman iz pervoi poloviny nikolaevskikh vremen* (A Decembrist: An Historical Novel from the First Half of the Reign of Nicholas I, 1903).

Sukhonin, Petr Petrovich (pseud. A. Shardin) (1821–1884). A journalist, playwright, and prose writer. In the early 1880s he published three novels spanning the period from Anna Ioannovna to the end of Catherine the Great's reign.

Svetlov (Ivchenko), Valerian Iakovlevich (1860–1935). A turn-of-the-century writer and ballet critic. He published several historical novels, the most notable being *Dar slez* (The Gift of Tears, 1900), purportedly based upon monastic literature of the first centuries A.D. However, it is vastly inferior both to its proclaimed literary model (Anatole France's *Thais*) and to the powerful Byzantine stylizations of Leskov.

Svin'in, Pavel Petrovich (1788–1839). A notable cultural figure and journalist. His two historical novels, *Shemiakin sud* (Shemiaka's Justice, 1832) and *Ermak* (1834), did not enjoy much success. *Shemiakin sud* is devoted to the same episode in Muscovy's domestic feud as Nikolai Polevoi's *Kliatva*, which also appeared in 1832. These novels differ greatly in their interpretation of Prince Shemiaka. They were conceived independently and thus cannot be considered polemical with respect to each other.

Sysoeva, Ekaterina Alekseevna (1829–1893). A writer of works for children. In 1884 she published a tale drawn from Greco-Roman life.

Teben'kov, Mikhail Mikhailovich (pseudonym Mikhail Erzin) (dates unknown). A historian and fiction writer. He is the author of a Byzantine tale published in 1910.

Timofeev, V. I. (dates unknown). In 1915–16 he published two tales set in late eighteenth-century Russia.

Tiumenev, Il'ia Fedorovich (1855–1927). A successful librettist who collaborated with Rimskii-Korsakov and also adapted Wagner for the Russian stage. Tiumenev cultivated various genres. Inter alia, he wrote one historical tale set in fifteenth-century Novgorod (1893).

Tiutchev, Fedor Fedorovich (1860–1916). An author who specialized in military subjects and stories drawn from the life of border guards. He published a historical tale about Russia's war against Shamil (1903).

Tolstoi, Count Aleksei Konstantinovich (1817–1875). A. K. Tolstoi tackled historical themes in drama and verse. In 1862 he published *Kniaz' Serebrianyi* (Prince Serebrianyi), a novel dealing with the reign of Ivan the Terrible. Although it appeared during the heyday of realism, *Kniaz' Serebrianyi* is the last and perhaps the most successful Russian adaptation of the Scottian model. Republished numerous times, it is enshrined in the Russian "junior canon."

Tolstoi, Count Lev Nikolaevich (1828–1910). His *Voina i mir* (War and Peace, 1867–69) is by far the most famous and most ambitious Russian historical novel. It revitalized the historical novel as a serious genre and paved the way for its subsequent popularity. In the 1870s he contemplated writing a novel set in the Petrine era but eventually abandoned the idea. Tolstoi's last completed work of fiction, the tale *Khadzhi Murat* (Hadji-Murad, 1904), also belongs to the historical genre since it is set during the final stages of the conquest of the Caucasus and involves numerous historical characters.

Tolycheva, Tamara. *See* Novosil'tseva, Ekaterina Vladimirovna

Vasil'ev, P. S. (dates unknown). The author of two historical novels, *Van'ka-Kain* (1893) and *Suvorov* (1900).

Veidemeier, Aleksandr Ivanovich (1789–1852). A historian who specialized in the post-Petrine eighteenth century. In 1837 he published (using the initials A. V.) the historical tale *Epizod iz vladychestva Bironova* (An Episode from Biron's Rule), which is set during his favorite period.

Vel'tman, Aleksandr Fomich (1800–1870). An author whose *Koshchei Bessmertnyi* (Koshchei the Deathless, 1833) is one of the most eccentric historical novels, combining medieval history, Russian folk motifs, Indo-European mythology, and Sternian narrative pranks. His second work in the historical genre—*Svetoslavich, vrazhii pitomets* (Svetoslavich, the Fiend's Nursling, 1835), about a werewolf involved in the feuds of Kievan princes—is written in a similar vein. Vel'tman's later novel *Raina, korolevna bolgarskaia* (Raina, Princess of Bulgaria, 1843) is more conventional and contains pan-Slavic overtones, portraying the Russian Prince Sviatoslav as a friend of the Bulgarians in their struggle for national liberation.

Vel'tman, Elena Ivanovna (1816–1868). The wife of Aleksandr Vel'tman. She began her literary activities in the 1840s. Her most significant work is the novel

Prikliucheniia korolevicha Gustava Irikovicha, zhenikha tsarevny Ksenii Goduovoi (The Adventures of Prince Gustav, Son of Eric, the Groom of Tsarevna Ksenia Godunov, 1867), which was first conceived in the 1840s. The novel traces the life of a disinherited Swedish prince and his failed marriage to the daughter of the Russian tsar. Although based on a thorough study of historical sources, Vel't-man's work contains factual inconsistencies characteristic of romantic novels.

Volkonskii, Prince Mikhail Nikolaevich (1860–1917). The scion of an ancient but impoverished family and the nephew of E. P. Karnovich. Volkonskii earned his living by doing literary work. Although best remembered as the author of theatrical parodies, he was also a prolific historical novelist of the turn of the century and in many ways the successor to Count Salias. He published roughly twenty novels, mostly dealing with the secret history of the eighteenth and early nineteenth centuries, where his strong interest in the mystical and the occult is in evidence.

Volkova, E. F. (dates unknown). The author of historical tales and sketches published in the 1900s and 1910s.

Zagoskin, Mikhail Nikolaevich (1789–1852). The Russian Walter Scott. He is the author of the first and—for a long time—the most popular Russian historical novel: *Iurii Miloslavskii* (1829). His second novel, *Roslavlev* (1831), pioneered the theme of the War of 1812. Zagoskin's third novel, *Askol'dova mogila* (Askold's Grave, 1833), set during the reign of Vladimir, was much less successful. It later became the basis for the libretto to Aleksei Verstovskii's famous opera of the same name (1835). Zagoskin returned to the historical genre in the 1840s, producing three more novels.

Zaguliaev, Mikhail Andreevich (1834–1900). A prominent journalist, he also wrote prose fiction, including the novel *Strannaia istoriia* (A Strange Story, 1883), supposedly based on the diary of a Russian aristocrat who joined the Jacobins during the French Revolution.

Zarin, Andrei Efimovich (1862–1929). A prolific author who cultivated historical fiction, among other genres, publishing a dozen novels and tales in the 1900s and 1910s.

Zarin, Fedor Efimovich (pseud. Zarin-Nesvitskii) (1870–ca. 1935). Like his brother Andrei Efimovich, he was a prolific author who also turned to historical fiction, contributing to *Istoricheskii vestnik* and *Istoricheskaia letopis'*.

Zarin-Nesvitskii. *See* Zarin, Fedor Efimovich

Zarnitsyn, Mikhail (dates unknown). An author whose *Sten'ka Razin* (1837) is one of the first Russian novels devoted to Razin's rebellion.

Zenchenko, Mikhail Vasil'evich (1851–?). A political officer of yore who wrote brochures on military history, manuals for the edification of enlisted men, and moralistic short stories drawn from army life. His only historical novel, *Poteshnye, ili Ozorniki i koniukhi Velikogo Petra* ("Toy Soldiers," or Pranksters and Grooms of the Great Peter, 1901), continues the theme of martial edification. Published by the presses of the Wilna Military District, the novel is accompanied by battle plans and patriotic verses of the author's own invention.

Zhdanov, Lev Grigor'evich (pseudonym of Leon Germanovich Gel'man) (1864–1951). Abandoning an acting and directing career in the late 1890s, he became a prolific playwright and was also active in other genres, including the historical novel. From 1904 to the Revolution he authored two-dozen "chronicles" replete with scandalous details and "revelations" from the private lives of Russian monarchs. Typical are *Venchannye zatvornitsy* (Crowned Prisoners, 1907), about the wives of Ivan the Terrible, and *Poslednii favorit* (The Last Favorite, 1911), about Catherine the Great and Platou Zubov.

Zotov, Rafail Mikhailovich (1794/96–1871). One of the leading novelists of the 1830s and a preeminent author of historical adventure novels. His most popular novels include *Leonid, ili Nekotorye cherty iz zhizni Napoleona* (Leonid, or Some Traits from Napoleon's Life, 1832) and *Tainstvennyi monakh, ili Nekotorye cherty iz zhizni Petra I* (A Mysterious Monk, or Some Traits from the Life of Peter I, 1834). He holds the distinction of having remained active in the historical genre for almost four decades. He also seems to have been the first to write a novel about Paul I: *Tainstvennye sily, ili Nekotorye cherty iz tsarstvovania imperatora Pavla I* (Mysterious Forces, or Some Traits from the Reign of Emperor Paul I, 1859). Altogether, he wrote over a dozen novels, the last of which, *Poslednii potomok Chingis-khana* (The Last Descendant of Genghis Khan), published posthumously in 1872, deals with the colorful life of his father, who was the son of the last Crimean khan.

Zriakhov, Nikolai Il'ich (1782/86–late 1840s). A popular *lubok* writer. From the late 1830s to the 1840s he published several quasi-historical novels.

Zubov, Platon Pavlovich (1796–after 1857). An indefatigable adventurer (he was exiled to the southern army for committing fraud) and a lowbrow writer. He specialized in Trans-Caucasian and Persian themes, publishing, among other things, three historical novels. Unlike most Russian Caucasian works dealing with the conquest of the region by the Empire, two of Zubov's novels—*Karabakhskii astrolog* (The Astrologer of Karabakh, 1834) and *Prekrasnaia gruzinka* (A Beautiful Georgian Maiden, 1834)—are set in the pre-Russian period.

Notes

Introduction

1. The only general overview is S. M. Petrov's book dating from the mid-1960s, *Russkii istoricheskii roman XIX veka.* It is, unfortunately, of little worth because of its primitive ideological filters, limited scope, and numerous factual inaccuracies. The most thoroughly studied period is the 1830s. The pioneer in this area is the critic Aleksandr Skabichevsky, whose survey "Nash istoricheskii roman v ego proshlom i nastoiashchem" was produced in the 1880s. Although Skabichevsky provides valuable factual information, his methodological approach is not particularly appealing. Extolling Pushkin and Gogol, Skabichevsky dismisses and ridicules their lesser colleagues. A. Pinchuk's study "Russskii istoricheskii roman (do 50-kh godov XIX v.)," published on the eve of World War I, introduces an even wider range of sources. However, it resorts to a simplistic form of classification, dividing the authors in question into those who faithfully follow historical truth and those who distort it. The most thorough Soviet work on the subject is I. P. Scheblykin's monograph "Russkii istoricheskii roman 30-kh godov XIX veka," which has a rather nondescript methodology but provides a good overview of the contemporary critical response. A number of valuable observations can also be found in Ia. L. Levkovich's article "Printsipy dokumental'nogo povestvovaniia v istoricheskoi proze pushkinskoi pory." More recent contributions include Mark Al'tshuller's monograph *Epokha Val'tera Skotta v Rossii,* which contains an in-depth analysis of numerous texts and also provides a definitive study of Scott's influence on Russian belles lettres. The only drawback of this erudite and insightful book is that it tends to treat deviations from Scott as distortions of the "correct" model. Damiano Rebecchini's article "Russkie istoricheskie romany 30-kh godov XIX veka" contains the most complete bibliographical information for the period and also has interesting thoughts on the nature of the genre. Aside from works on individual authors, which are too numerous to be listed in this note, mention should be made of the following academic editions, which are indispensable for the student of the historical novel: N. G. Ilinskaya's commentary

to Lazhechnikov; A. Peskov's commentary to Zagoskin; M. L. Gasparov's commentary to Briusov; and Z. G. Mints's commentary to Merezhkovsky.

2. Gallie, "*Philosophy and the Historical Understanding*; Danto, *Analytical Philosophy of History*; White, *Foundations of Historical Knowledge*; Nye, "History and Literature: Branches of the Same Tree." For a discussion of the "narrativist" debate, see Dray, 164–90; Gearhart, 3–28; Braudy, 5.

3. See Danto, 362; White, *Metahistory*, 6 n. 5.

4. The ethical issues of narratological relativism are raised in the collection edited by Saul Friedlander entitled *Probing the Limits of Representation: Nazism and the "Final Solution*; see especially the essays by Amos Funkenstein, Perry Anderson, and Hayden White. For a more general discussion of the debate, see the studies by Carr and Gossman.

5. On this point see Lotman, "Problema istoricheskogo fakta."

1. An Overview of the Romantic Era

1. Scott's reception in Russia is well documented. See Zamotin, 339–45; Levin; and especially Dolinin (*Istoriia, odetaia v roman*) and Al'tshuller.

2. For a detailed analysis of Scott's formula, see Al'tshuller, 11–29.

3. A number of scholars tend to exclude Scott from the romantic tradition, regarding him as the founder of the "realistic historical novel." This opinion, which can be traced back to Lukács (63), was repeated by many Soviet scholars (Orlov, 445; Petrov, 120; Mann, *Poetika*, 331) and occasionally by their Western colleagues (D. Brown, 279–80). Such an interpretation stems either from a narrow definition of romanticism, which is tied to the presence of the Byronic protagonist, or from a broad approach to realism, where reflection of certain sociohistorical realia and descriptive verisimilitude are mistaken for realism.

4. For a review of eighteenth- and early-nineteenth-century "historical" prose fiction in Russia, see Pinchuk; Belozerskaia, 58–61; Sipovskii, 1:464–75; Schamschula, 15–67.

5. The male protagonists in both works have rather similar last names (Liuboslavsky/Miloslavsky). Like Karamzin's hero, Yury falls in love with a maiden he sees in church. At the end of Karamzin's tale the narrator stumbles across a dilapidated tombstone that marks his heroes' grave; there is also a tombstone scene at the conclusion of Zagoskin's novel. These rather transparent allusions may testify to the fact that the fiercely patriotic Zagoskin wanted to claim as his literary ancestors not only the foreigner Scott but also the Russian Karamzin.

6. For a detailed overview of the historical tales of the period, see Al'tshuller, 30–58. Bestuzhev's tales are analyzed in Lauren Leighton's excellent monograph *Aleksander Bestuzhev-Marlinsky* (69–76).

7. One could add to this list a completed piece, dating from 1827, that carries the subtitle "historical novel": *Gosnitsky: A Historical Novel with Descriptions of Mores and Customs of the Zaporozhians (Gosnitskii. Istoricheskii roman s opisaniem nravov i obychaev zaporozhtsev)*, by Iv. T . . . [Ivan Telepnev], which is set during the

reign of Basil Shuisky. Abram Reitblat, who identified this work, even considers it to be the first Russian Scottian novel (see Rebekkini, 418). This is an exaggeration, however, since the historical background is extremely vague and the book does not make good its promise to describe the customs and mores of the epoch. Nevertheless, *Gosnitsky* is no less "historical" than many of the lowbrow novels of the 1830s.

8. For the treatment of the complex dynamics between the universal and individual (or, rather, universal, national, and personal), see Zamotin, the academic validity of whose monograph has not faded despite its age.

9. Precedents of Pogodin's dithyramb to Russia's immense diversity are found in Karamzin's introduction to his *History* and in Somov's essay "On Romantic Poetry." For earlier examples of thematic catalogues, see Mikhail Lomonosov's "Idei dlia zhivopisnykh kartin iz russkoi istorii" (Ideas for Paintings from Russian History), which was written in 1764 but only published in 1868, and Karamzin's "O sluchaiakh i kharakterakh v rossiiskoi istorii, kotorye mogut byt' predmetom khudozhestv" (On Episodes and Characters in Russian History That Can Serve as a Subject for Art, 1802).

10. See Reitblat, *Kak Pushkin vyshel v genii.*

11. It is highly probable that Bulgarin, in his capacity as a "loyal" literary expert, reviewed Pushkin's manuscript for Nicholas I. However, Pushkin did not know that the review was rather favorable and could not have accounted for the ban of his drama. Furthermore, Bulgarin's historical concept was so different from Pushkin's that one must speak not of plagiarism but rather of polemics, which still makes the situation highly dubious from an ethical standpoint. For a detailed analysis of this controversy, see Al'tshuller, 108–26.

12. The publisher Stepanov paid Zagoskin 40,000 rubles in assignations for the exclusive right to print 4,800 copies of *Roslavlev* in the course of three years, which was an astronomical sum for an author's honorarium. On the economy of the historical novel, see Rebekkini, 418, 423–28. It is noteworthy that the popularity of Scott began to subside as his Russian followers conquered the market. Scott's Russian translations peaked in 1829, their number steadily diminishing thereafter; see Dolinin, *Istoriia, odetaia v roman,* 166.

13. Although it became canonized as a defining event of national history in the 1830s, the campaign of Minin and Pozharsky, with the ensuing election of Michael Romanov, had previously come to prominence during the first decade of the century; see Zorin, 157–86. For the mythological potential of the Time of Troubles, see Caryl Emerson's classic study *Boris Godunov: Transpositions of a Russian Theme.*

14. For a detailed analysis of Vigny's influence in Polevoi's *Oath,* see Koz'min, 88–115.

15. For an extensive discussion of this issue, see Al'tshuller.

2. Fact and Fiction in the Romantic Novel

1. It should be noted, however, that the historical novel is not more formulaic than other popular genres of the period (e.g., the Byronic narrative poem).

2. For a summary of the debate surrounding the notion of Russian romanticism, see Leighton, "On a Discrimination of Russian Romanticism," and Mann, *Dinamika russkogo romantizma*.

3. See E. W. Brown, 173–94, and Dolinin, *Istoriia, odetaia v roman*, 200–204. The device per se is older and can be traced back to the preromantic period. For example, it can be found in Karamzin's "Natalya" and "Martha," as well as in Kheraskov's *Cadmus and Harmonia* (1789) and *Numa, or Flourishing Rome* (1768). Much scholarly attention has also been paid to the relationship between the main text of Karamzin's *History* and his potentially subversive notes (see Emerson, 39; Kozlov, "Primechaniia," 553; Rubinshtein, 177; Wachtel, 63). Here I will refrain from discussing these instances of self-invalidation since they involve different contexts.

4. For variations in the semantics of subtitles, see Rebekkini, 417.

5. I am aware of only two works that belong to the genre of "historical scenes": Protopopov's *Death of Napoleon* (1836) and Masalsky's *The Love of Beards* (1837). In my bibliographic apparatus I list them alongside novels, although their genre designation is disputable.

6. Here Polevoi paraphrases Vitet: "I pictured to myself that I was strolling through Paris in May of 1588 during the tumultuous events of the day, that I was in the palace, or in church, or in the home of a citizen, or at an inn, and recorded everything of interest I could see or hear" (quoted in Masa'skii, *Borodoliubie*, 4:231).

7. Rebbekini sees in this device the influence of Vitet (420), while Al'tshuller points to possible links with Scott's extensive use of dialogue (26–28, 167).

8. As Zagoskin put it his collection *Moscow and Muscovites:* "When many characters are talking, then a narrative is certainly out of place. All those explanatory words like 'so-and-so said,' 'so-and-so answered,' 'such-and-such objected,' 'he interrupted, she butted in' only disconcert and confuse the reader, so allow me to use the usual dramatic form" (2:92).

9. "Walter Scott's novel belongs properly to neither epic, nor lyric, nor dramatic poetry, but is the sum of them all" (Nadezhdin, Review of *Roslavlev*, 90).

10. For the image of the author as *Puppenmeister* in western European literature, see Dolinin, *Istoriia, odetaia v roman*, 190; see also Reizov, 545–46.

11. Victor Cousin, a French popularizer of German philosophy who influenced Vigny, uses "le réel" and "le vrai" to distinguish between these two truths; see Reizov, 162–65.

12. "Volynsky, a man in his fifties, makes mischief like a youth," comments the reviewer of *The Son of the Fatherland* (Anon., Review of *Ledianoidom*, 69). The reviewer was most likely Nikolai Polevoi, which is highly ironic given his own record of poetic license.

13. See, e.g., Odoevskii, *Russkie nochi*, 7; Bestuzhev-Marlinskii, *Sochineniia*, 2:465.

14. My description of romantic contradictions and romantic irony is largely based on the work of Lydia Ginzburg and Alexander Dolinin.

15. For literary reminiscences in *Askold's Grave*, see Al'tshuller, 100–107.

16. His Sternian playfulness notwithstanding, Veltman is often paradoxically quite serious in following the flights of his own imagination, which tends to undermine the validity of his scholarly essays.

17. For a classic analysis of these literary subterfuges, see Dolinin, *Istoriia, odetaia v roman.*

3. The Changing and the Unchanged

1. Aside from the historical novel, the traditional standard of beauty, cast in a most negative light, may be seen in Mikhail Pogodin's tale "Chernaia nemoch'" (Black Sickness, 1829). The protagonist, a lofty young man horrified by the materialistic world of his abusive merchant father, passionately desires an education, but his parents treat his wish as a strange malady that will soon be cured by marrying him to the daughter of a fellow merchant. She is described as a short, fat girl of thirteen, with puffy cheeks and a heavily painted face, who is decked out in gold, silver, and numerous precious stones. Seeing no other alternative, the frustrated young man commits suicide.

2. For a detailed case-by-case examination of this issue, see Al'tshuller.

3. It is important to remember that Zagoskin wrote this in 1831, whereas Sergei Uvarov's famous memorandum was issued in 1833. Thus, the triad was not merely Uvarov's brainchild but emerged from the nationalistic discourse of the era.

4. This idiom may indeed have a pre-Christian origin (*sviatoi*/holy being derived from *svet*/light; thus the land of light, as opposed to foreign "darkness"), but it is very unlikely that Zagoskin was aware of this etymology.

5. The romantic underpinnings of Uvarov's triad—including its connections with German romanticism in general and Schlegel in particular—have been pointed out by Gustav Shpet. For an excellent analysis of Uvarov's philosophical and ideological background, see Zorin, 337–74.

4. Masterpieces in Context

1. This type, as well as many other hackneyed formulas of the epoch's historical novel, can be traced back to the tradition of the gothic novel, which was assimilated by the fashionable frenetic school; see Vatsuro, 465–87.

2. The most extensive use of Ukrainian is found in the historical novels of Petr Golota, which contain dialogue in Ukrainian that is translated into Russian in the endnotes.

3. Here Gogol actually contradicts his sources (e.g., Guillaume Beauplan's *Description of the Ukraine*, which provided many details for *Bulba*); he writes that Cossacks strictly followed the rules of fasting (*Pss*, 9:81).

4. The theme of romantic rebellion, which is here intertwined with Gogol's "positional philosophy," is paralleled in the protagonist's "rebellion" in "The Diary of a Madman."

5. For an excellent overview of the Cossack myth and the image of Russianness, see Kornblatt.

6. Conversely, Gavriel' Shapiro—who has conducted an extensive analysis of Gogol's pseudonyms and various "signatures" embedded in the texts—takes the epithet "proud" (used to describe the goldeneye) at face value, seeing it as Gogol's assertion of his supreme position in Russian literature (153–54).

7. There is an extensive body of scholarly literature on Pushkin's adaptation of Scottian motifs. See, e.g., Dolinin, *Istoriia, odetaia v roman;* Frazier; and Al'tshuller.

8. With respect to the poetic qualities of *The Captain's Daughter,* see Davydov and Schmid.

9. See Dolinin, "Swerving from Walter Scott."

10. For a detailed comparison between *Miloslavsky* and *The Captain's Daughter,* see Petrunina, "Pushkin i Zagoskin."

11. The economy of gift giving and its implications in *The Captain's Daughter* are thoroughly analyzed by Bethea in "Slavic Gift-Giving."

12. As Alexander Dolinin has convincingly demonstrated in several articles, *The Captain's Daughter* can be viewed as a proto-Slavophile work. Already in his *History of Pugachev* Pushkin distances himself from French romantic historiography, with its notion of historical progress, by implying the otherness of Russian history, where a hidden providential design exists behind a seemingly meaningless series of events; see Dolinin, "Historicism or Providentialism?" *The Captain's Daughter,* while rooted in the Scottian tradition, ultimately departs from it, abandoning the European historical dimension in favor of Russian "metahistory," where the horror of history is overcome by the Russian version of the Christian caritative ethos; see Dolinin, "Swerving from Walter Scott."

13. The creators of a Russian cinematic version of *The Captain's Daughter* entitled *A Russian Rebellion* tried to solve the problem by "correcting" Pushkin. The offscreen voice of Petrusha Grinyov informs us: "my father, Andrei Petrovich Grinyov, resigned his commission immediately after the death of Emperor Petr Fedorovich. I recall this very vividly, for at this time I was already five years of age" (*Russkii bunt*). Thus, although the implicit contradiction of Pushkin's text is eliminated, so is the complexity of its associations.

14. Other fascinating "odd ends" in the implied biography of Grinyov senior are discussed in Ospovat, "Istoricheskii material," 40–55.

15. Among these critics one can name Blok, Bliumenfel'd, and Mal'tsev.

16. See the following for early versions of this view: Viazemskii, *Pss,* 2:377; Katkov, quoted in "*Kapitanskaia dochka* v kritike," 244; and Kliuchevskii, 7:147.

17. Tsvetaeva's strong opinions notwithstanding, her essay contains a number of valuable ideas. In comparing the novel and the history, she mentions Pushkin's poem "Hero," stresses the popular truth reflected in *The Captain's Daughter,* and describes fairy-tale elements in the novel.

18. On this point see, e.g., Shklovskii, *Gamburgskii schet,* 32.

19. See Annenkov, quoted in "*Kapitanskaia dochka* v kritike," 243; Cherniaev, 61.

20. A good analysis of Pushkin's "Hero" can be found in Mikkelson, "Pushkin's 'Geroj'"; see also Evdokimova, 74–84. On Pushkin and Vigny, see Ungurianu, "Kontseptsiia dvukh pravd."

21. On the Kharlova connection and other instances of amplified violence in the novel through references to the *History*, see Dolinin, "Eshche raz o khronologii," 53–54.

22. On violence in *The Captain's Daughter*, see Shklovskii, *Zametki o proze Pushkina*, 109; Lavretskaia, 141–42; and Debreczeny, 257.

23. Aleksandr Ospovat has drawn attention to another pessimistic historical theme based on subtle allusions and inconspicuous anachronisms scattered throughout the text; see his essays "Iz nabliudenii nad tsarskoesl'skim toposom" and "Iz kommentariia k *Kapitanskoi dochke*. This theme involves Russia's perennial war waged somewhere in the "East," with endless attempts to gain control over this or that fortress. Thus, the military developments of the *pugachevshchina* can be viewed as a continuation of this historical delirium.

5. Tolstoy's "Book" and a New Kind of Historical Novel

1. For additional observations on A. K. Tolstoy and Scott, see Al'tshuller, 270–73.

2. Although "Lozhechnikov" was an accepted variant spelling of Lazhechnikov's name in the 1830s (cf. Plaksin, 349), the stress was on the "e" (hence the o/a alteration). In stressing the "o" Shchedrin may be implying that the writer's name is derived from the term *lozhechnik* (a folk musician who uses a pair of wooden spoons to produce clicking sounds), thus relegating Lazhechnikov's writing to the realm of the lowbrow *lubok* literature.

3. Cf. Melnikov-Pechersky's tale "The Olden Years" (1857).

4. Nikolai Pavlov criticized *The Son* in the newspaper *Day*, while *The Contemporary* came to Kostomarov's defense, accusing Pavlov of naiveté and childish notions of history. In 1870 Pavlov offered his own vision of the Russian seventeenth century in the tale "The Tsar's Falconer" (see chapter 6).

5. For a good description of Tolstoy's polemical technique, see Shklovskii, *Mater'ial i stil'*, 71–72.

6. Vladimir Alexandrov has introduced the apt term "hermeneutic indices" in connection with a general theory of reading—and *Anna Karenina* in particular. This term refers to "built-in" indicators present in a work of art that delimit the range of possible interpretations. Although several of the indicators I consider are found not in the text per se but rather in the cultural context, the idea is nevertheless very similar, namely, to exclude the arbitrariness of interpretation.

7. Certain contradictions in Vyazemsky's criticism were already noticed in 1869 by N. Solovyov, the reviewer for *Severnaia pchela* (The Northern Bee); see Gusev, 831.

8. This kind of gingerbread originated in the city of Vyazmy, which was once ruled by the ancestors of Vyazemsky; hence his family name. In 1830 a similar

connection was made by Vyazemsky's literary foe Faddei Bulgarin, who ridiculed him as a P. Kovryzhkin ("Mr. Gingerbread"). Page 192 in this volume of *Russkii arkhiv* is followed by pages 01–015, after which normal pagination resumes.

9. One can hardly speak of Tolstoy influencing Vyazemsky or vice versa. Vyazemsky wrote his memoirs after reading Tolstoy's description of Borodino, but, given his aversion to *War and Peace,* it is unlikely that he was somehow unconsciously influenced by Tolstoy. The latter was not familiar with details of Vyazemsky's exploits at the time he composed the Borodino chapters, although he was probably aware of Vyazemsky's peculiar role during the battle. Among Tolstoy's sources there is a private letter dating from 1812, which states that Prince Vyazemsky "had the audacity to participate in the Battle of Borodino as a spectator" (quoted in Gusev, 762). However, it would be too farfetched to conclude that Vyazemsky served as a prototype for Pierre. Experiencing events through the eyes of "unattached" spectators is a part of Tolstoy's technique of estrangement (cf. Olenin observing the battle between Cossacks and Chechens in *The Cossacks*). Western European literature also provides a famous example of an innocent at the battlefield in the figure of Fabrice del Dongo at Waterloo in Stendhal's *Charterhouse of Parma.*

10. Cf. the following passage from Tolstoy: "He reported that his regiment had been attacked by French cavalry and that, though the attack had been repulsed, he had lost more than half his men. He said the attack had been repulsed, employing this military term to describe what had occurred to his regiment, but in reality he did not himself know what had happened during that half-hour to the troops entrusted to him, and could not say with certainty whether the attack had been repulsed or his regiment had been broken up" (*War and Peace,* 157–58).

11. A separate issue concerns how well informed Tolstoy was in matters of contemporary historiography. Several critics have correctly noted that he used as his polemical target obsolete or second-rate histories; see Vitmer, 6–7; Lachinov, 121; Kareev, 128–29).

12. The translation is by Duffield White of Eikhenbaum, *Tolstoi in the Sixties,* 236.

13. An essay based on the book appeared in 1891 in the journal *The Russian Thought.* The book itself was not published until 1911–12. Although Leontiev speaks only about Norov, his conclusions also apply to Vyazemsky and Demenkov as well.

14. Tolstoy invokes providence several times in War *and Peace.* However, his providence is not a transcendental force but rather a synonym for the complex, immanent "laws" governing history; on this point see Bocharov, 111.

15. Vyazemsky's criticism must have been especially painful for Tolstoy since both he and the old prince ultimately belonged to the same camp of aristocratic frondeurs resisting the onslaught of "progress." In *War and Peace,* with its loving depiction of the life of the landed gentry, Tolstoy also emphatically objected to the exposés of serfdom prevalent in the "nihilistic" literature of the 1860s. For this he was labeled a reactionary by "democratic" critics. On the double-pronged attack against *War and Peace* from the left and the right, see Eikhenbaum, *Lev Tolstoi,* 392–94.

16. For a classic description of the realistic paradigm, see Ginzburg, *O literaturnom geroe.*

17. As Eikhenbaum puts it, *War and Peace* is the result of "interbreeding between scholarly and literary forms" (*Lev Tolstoi,* 226).

18. For a thought-provoking criticism of Morson's theoretical premises, see Grodetskaia, "Vozvrashchenie k diskussii o zhanre *Voiny i mira.*"

19. Morson terms this map "dialogic" (138). However, in stretching the notion of "dialogue" that far, one would have to recognize that, for example, a student's test covered in the instructor's red ink is a dialogic document as well. In his "dialogue" with historians Tolstoy constantly ridicules and dismisses his opponents. Polemics in which one side is annihilated can hardly be called a "dialogue" in the Bakhtinian sense.

6. The Age of Positivism

1. This had already been noted by contemporary reviewers. See Skabichevskii, "Literaturnye protivorechiia," 35–37, 40; idem, *Istoriia noveishei russkoi literatury,* 347; Mikhailovskii, 5:451; Borozdin, 613–14; and Garshin, 131–34.

2. Cf. Eikhenbaum, *Lev Tolstoi,* 226.

3. In addition to Skabichevskii and Mikhailovskii, see Shelgunov; Sokolov; S. S.; and N. N.

4. In the final quarter of the nineteenth century most novels were initially serialized in journals. This guaranteed wider circulation and higher honoraria for authors. According to Reitblat, who provides an excellent analysis of the literary market of the epoch, publication in a popular journal was on average ten times more profitable than a book format; see *Ot Bovy k Bal'montu,* 91.

5. Negative fallout from Salias's popularity is still evident in the late 1920s. In *The Twelve Chairs* by Ilya Ilf and Evgeny Petrov he is mentioned as the epitome of outmoded bourgeois taste (see Shcheglov, 1:128–30). In terms of his royalties, in the 1880s Salias belonged to the most elite group of Russian authors, averaging 300 rubles per printer's sheet in thick journals, which put him in the same category as Dostoevsky and Leskov. Only Turgenev earned more, averaging 350 rubles per sheet; see Reitblat, *Ot Bovy k Bal'montu,* 88.

6. For a rebuttal of Mordovtsev's portrayal of Peter, see Bulgakov; Mikhailovskii, 6:251–78; and Sokolov.

7. Even the positive portrayal of Peter had Russophobic connotations: in this case Peter was presented as the enemy of the stagnant conservatism and ritualistic fanaticism of old Muscovy.

8. This fictional defector is not entirely without historical precedent: a Kostomarov was sent to study in England by Boris Godunov and never returned.

9. If Kostomarov's *Son* can be seen as a negative take on *The Captain's Daughter,* the Razin episode in *The Tsar's Falconer* develops the situation in a positive direction. At the time of the rebellion, the heroine's father is a provinical *voivode.* Although he bravely defends the city, it falls and the *voivode* is captured (cf. the

situation with the Belogorskaya Fortress). The family nanny tries to intercede on behalf the *voivode* and is murdered by the rebels (cf. the murder of Vasilisa Egorovna). The *voivode*'s daughter, like Masha Mironova, escapes capture by changing into simple attire. Events also develop differently from Pushkin's novel: the *voivode* escapes death, being freed by his own daughter, and there are no suspicious dealings with the rebels or treason on the part of a nobleman.

10. Pavlov's lyrical and nostalgic intonations in his narrative about "forgotten" Muscovy presage the nostalgic mood of *Anno Domini*, by Ivan Shmelev, who reminisces about the vanished traditional Russia of his childhood.

11. Yury Bartenev, son of the famous archivist Petr Bartenev, makes the following observation in Pavlov's obituary: "*The Tsar's Falconer* bridged the gap between the imperial period in Russian life and pre-Petrine Russia. This is its significance for the history of the Russian national consciousness" (645). However, it appears that Bartenev exaggerates the impact of his mentor's work. *The Tsar's Falconer* received little notice, while Kostomarov's exposés were backed by his celebrity status in Russian intellectual circles. While conducting research in the Slavonic Library at the University of Helsinki (which was known as the Aleksandrovskii Universitet v Gelsingforse during the imperial period), I came across a sui generis postscript in the Kostomarov-versus-Pavlov debate. The final page of *The Son* contains an epic commentary that is jarringly out of sync with the rest of the tale: "Everything calmed down. The rightful authority prevailed and the revolt was thwarted. [. . .] In June the chief rebel himself, Stenka Razin, received his well-deserved punishment. [. . .] Peace returned to Rus" (*Syn*, 205). In the library copy of the book a reader of yore—perhaps a budding radical of the revolutionary era—has crossed out the adjectives in the phrases "rightful authority" and "well-deserved punishment." The pages of the 1904 edition of Pavlov's *Falconer* were still uncut when I checked the book out in the summer of 2002.

12. For a listing of foreign authors translated into Russian, see Mezier.

13. The eighteenth century provided ample material for developing the contrasting image of Russianness, the foundations of which were laid during the romantic period (see chapter 3). The paradigmatic Russian hero is Potemkin, the "splendid prince of Tauride." Beneath his insatiable lust for power, luxury, and carnal pleasure there is relentless thought about God and truth and "a sense of disgust for all earthly pleasures" (*Sochineniia*, 1:398). The latter is very much akin to Tolstoy's description of "that vague and quite Russian feeling of contempt for everything conventional, artificial, and human—for everything the majority of men regard as the greatest good in the world" (*War and Peace*, 800). It is not surprising that Potemkin is featured in a number of novels during the late nineteenth century. Curiously, he resurfaces as the quintessential embodiment of Russianness in the novel *Belaia tserkov'* (The White Church, 1982), by the prominent Moldavian writer Ion Drutse. In the stage version of the novel, Potemkin's paradoxical Russian breadth was emphasized in the brilliant performance of Vladimir Soshalsky. The original production of the play, under the title *Obretenie* (Ye Shall Find) was banned soon after its premiere in 1984 and reappeared in 1988, during Glasnost, under the

Pushkin-inspired title *Imia strannogo Potemkina* (The Name of the Strange Potemkin). The play, directed by Ion Ungurianu, was performed by the Central Academic Theater of the Soviet Army.

14. See, e.g., Solovyov's *Sergei Gorbatov*. The found-manuscript device is most consistently implemented in the first part of Danilevsky's *Princess Tarakanova* and—less adroitly—in his *Black Year* (11).

15. A lengthy dramatic dialogue suddenly appears in the middle of Filippov's *Patriarch Nikon* (295–306).

16. There are numerous Ukrainian songs in Mordovtsev's *Idealists and Realists*.

17. A reference to the legend of Kudeyar closes Kostomarov's novel; see also the ending of Pushkin's *History of Pugachev;* Lazhechnikov's *Ice Palace;* and Lyubetsky's *Tanka*.

18. See the opening of Mordovtsev's *Lord Novgorod the Great*.

19. E.g., in *The Lackey* Kostomarov recalls Gogol's Nozdrev ("Kholui," 71). Sergiy Golitsyn in his *Good Old Times* refers to various authors, including Dostoevsky, in connection with the psychology of crime. His comment concerning *The Devils* and *The Idiot* is rather odd: "Two of Dostoevsky's (not so great) novels" (149).

20. See the long descriptions of "anti-liberal" escapades—only tangentially related to the plot—in *Mighty Warriors* by Nikolai Chaev; occasional reference to "our hero" in Kostomarov's *Lackey;* comments inserted into the text by Golitsyn; and frequent lyrical and judgmental digressions by Mordovtsev.

21. In several footnotes in *Love & Crown* Karnovich deliberates over his choice of linguistic stylization in a character's speech (138). The most extended instance of metadescription in the main text of a novel is found in Pyotr Karatygin's *Deeds of Yore,* where he gives ironic advice to young authors on how to bulk out their manuscripts—and their honoraria—by supplying culinary details (93).

22. I am aware of only one instance of an open admission of anachronism. Describing a notorious double duel involving Zavadsky, Griboedov, Sheremetev, and Yakubovich, Karatygin admits that he changed the date and place of the first encounter (59).

23. In Tolstoy's *War and Peace* there are two or three footnotes. Other instances are found in Filippov's *Patriarch Nikon,* as well as in novels by Karnovich.

24. On occasion the use of older novelistic conventions create comic effects. For example, in one of his Egyptian novels Mordovtsev—the most "archaic" author of the second wave—includes an episode that dates back to Karamzin and Zagoskin: in the epilogue the narrator supposedly stumbles upon the grave of his heroine. Mordovtsev gives this time-honored ending a positivist archaeological spin: the reader sees not just a tomb but also the mummy of the heroine, which is discovered by the author at a museum. The authenticity of his discovery is certified by the museum's curator (*Zamurovannaia tsaritsa,* 147).

25. Even when practitioners of the genre emphasized the difference between the novel and history, they would still routinely confuse the two. This was the case with Princess Shakhovskaya, a prolific graphomaniac who produced numerous Roman novels. In the preface to one of her creations she makes the following statement:

"The novel is never more than a novel [. . .] a more or less successful attempt to join in one whole disparate fragments of surviving historical notes of facts and their causes" (*Sivilla*, unpag.)

26. Publication of feuilleton novels in daily newspapers also placed works of historical fiction into a documentary context; see Reitblat, 114.

27. One antiromantic tirade can be traced directly to Bazarov, the arch-nihilist of Turgenev's *Fathers and Sons*. In Karatygin's novel *The Sorcerers*, which is set at the very beginning of the nineteenth century, the hero, a young scientist and student of medicine, reasons about love in the following fashion: "Heavenly creature? You must have forgotten your physiology and anatomy lessons, my young man. Your deity is a woman like all the rest. [. . .] Just like all the others your nymph eats and drinks and engages in all the biological functions. She also suffers from those fated, inescapable days when she is paler than usual and complains of pain in the lower back. [. . .] Your beauty is well formed, but her pelvic bones are poorly developed, and this bodes ill for future childbirth. Imagine this heavenly creature during pregnancy! On her white-marble brow and her dainty cheeks appear brown freckles; episodes of hysterics [. . .] nausea, even . . . vomiting! And her walk, which now is light and graceful, will then remind you of a lame duck waddling from side to side! And as for crooked legs, remember how you were enchanted by the sight of her small, delicate foot shod in an elegant slipper. [. . .] Look at her unshod and you will hardly like her toes, perhaps, crooked and made even uglier by calluses!" (*Chernoknizhniki*, 140).

28. When the grateful Grinev offers the Pathfinder a glass of tea at the inn, the latter replies that this is not a Cossack drink and asks instead for vodka, which he—having crossed himself—swallows in one gulp. This passage contains a historical detail that underscores the differing lifestyles of the nobility and the common people (tea at this time was indeed an upper-class drink) and also foreshadows the maximalism of Pugachev, who does everything "bottoms up." Two other instances involve descriptions of Pugachev feasting with his chieftains. There the "orgiastic" element is combined with the culinary simplicity of Pugachev's "court," which is content with basic Cossack fare.

7. The End of Progress

1. In the 1870s and 1880s the share of foreign subjects was 2 and 10 percent, respectively. The figure for the 1880s was somewhat inflated: out of a total of eleven novels devoted to foreign subjects, seven were written by Princess Lyudmila Shakhovskaya, a prolific graphomaniac specializing in Roman history whose work made little impact on the broader literary process. Aleksandr Amfiteatrov explicitly dismisses her role in pioneering the Roman theme; according to him, the first noteworthy Russian novel dealing with ancient Rome was Merezhkovsky's *Julian the Apostate* (151).

2. European antecedents include Flaubert's *Salammbô* (1862), numerous works by Georg Ebers (1870s), and Anatole France's *Thaïs* (1890). Similar trends may

also be found in Polish literature. The most prominent historical novels of the period include: Boleslaw Prus's *Pharaoh* (1895), the quasi-populist tale of a well-meaning ruler who was confronted and defeated by the powerful priestly caste; and Henryk Sienkiewicz's *Quo Vadis?* (1895), a Christian melodrama played out against lavish archaeological settings. The latter enjoyed enormous popularity and was awarded the Nobel Prize in literature in 1905.

3. After the Revolution, the series was revived under the auspices of Maxim Gorky. It prospered during Soviet times and still remains a recognizable brand on the Russian book market.

4. Similar guides also appeared in western Europe; see Bowen, Bock and Weitzel.

5. The use of realistic narrative clichés sometimes creates a dissonance with the mystical content of such works. This is especially conspicuous in historical tales about saints that appeared in the supplement to *The Russian Pilgrim*, representing a curious offshoot of the biographical tale, or "hagiographie romancée," if one may be permitted such a coinage.

6. An almost comical example of how deeply ingrained the notion of progress was is found in *The Two Sphinxes*, by Vera Kryzhanovskaya (Rochester) (1901), an occult novel whose action spans almost three millennia. In such a work the idea of progress might not seem particularly appropriate. However, this is not the case. One of Kryzhanovskaya's protagonists, a great Egyptian sculptor who was placed in a state of hibernation in the eighth century B.C., wakes up during Roman times. Awed by the perfection of Greco-Roman sculpture, he exclaims: "What progress your art has made! [. . .] I can see that before I take up my craft again I will have to study under one of your sculptors since I don't want to appear outmoded" (*Dva sfinksa*, 60). This sounds like a caricature of the positivist view of artistic evolution assailed by Pavel Florensky in his treatise *On Reverse Perspective*.

7. The term "metahistory" was popularized in Anglo-American critical discourse by Hayden White in the 1970s in connection with the narratological approach to history. Its Russian usage can be traced back to the 1930s, specifically to the prominent émigré critic Pyotr Bitsilli, who contrasts the atemporal plane of metahistory to the delirium of empirical history; see Dolinin, "Clio Laughs Last." I use the term primarily as a synonym for a neomythological approach to history, as described by Yeleazar Meletinsky in his study on the poetics of the myth: "The thrust of the 20th-century mythologism [. . .] lies in revealing certain constant, eternal principles, both positive and negative, that shine through the flow of empirical existence and historical change. This mythologism entails going beyond socio-historical boundaries, as well as the boundaries of space and time" (295–96).

8. According to Zara Mints, the origins of the twentieth-century "neomythologism"—usually associated with the novels of James Joyce, Thomas Mann, Franz Kafka, and D. H. Lawrence dating from the 1920s and 1930s—can be traced back to the Russian symbolist movement and, in particular, to Merezhkovsky's trilogy; see her article "O nekotorykh neomifologicheskikh tekstakh." In this respect, it is appropriate to label the symbolists as modernists, although some scholars may

prefer to treat them as protomodernists. Besides, the term "modernism" was regularly used in critical discourse of the 1900s and 1910s. On this point see Gurevich, "Dal'nozorkie," 144; Kogan, *Ocherki*, 105; Belyi, Review of *Ognennyi angel*.

9. Merezhkovsky's dualism can be traced to Nietzsche's famous differentiation between the Apollonian and Dionysian, while the idea of synthesis has clear parallels with Solovyov's all-unity (*vseedinstvo*). Merezhkovsky's wife, Zinaida Gippius, expressly denies any direct influence of Solovyov on her husband, claiming that they developed their respective theories independently (266–67). One can also point to less highbrow proponents of religious synthesis, including Kryzhanovskaya (Rochester). Here, for example, is how she interprets Julian the Apostate in her novel *In hoc signo vinces!* of 1893: "Christianity viewed him as an enemy and labeled him an apostate; however, this great mind desired only to unite the idea of Christ with ancient science, with the understanding that there is one God who exists in His absolute perfection" (*Sim pobedishi!*, 326).

10. See Mints, "O nekotorykh 'neomifologicheskikh' tekstakh," 100–101; idem, "O trilogii," 25.

11. Having said that, one should not ignore shifts in Merezhkovsky's views, which he himself acknowledges (cf. *Pss*, 1:vi–vii). This can account for certain discrepancies between the books of his first trilogy; on this point see Christensen. In her memoirs Zinaida Gippius warns against reducing Merezhkovsky's philosophy to the two proverbial abysses. However, the main framework of his thought remains unchanged. As Vladislav Khodasevich summarizes Merezhkovsky's idée fixe: "Christianity before Christ and paganism after the pagans . . . these were to remain for Merezhkovsky the themes of his entire life" (*Koleblemyi trenozhnik*, 538).

12. For a discussion of cyclization in Merezhkovsky's works, see Kolobaeva, 446.

13. Trotsky's article on Merezhkovsky appeared in the journal *Kievan Thought* in May 1911. For an analysis, see Mikhailova, "L.Trotskii o Merezhkovskom."

14. See Amfiteatrov's review of *Julian the Apostate* and Sadovskoy's rebuttal of *Alexander I*. For more on this issue see Ponomareva.

15. At this time Stoker was not widely known in his home country either. Thus, the 1911 edition of the *Encyclopaedia Britannica* contains an article on Corelli, but there is no entry on Stoker.

16. Russian literary antecedents include A. K. Tolstoy's stories "Upyr'" and "Sem'ia vurdalaka." The latter appeared posthumously in 1884 in *Russkii vestnik*.

17. These phenomena have been well researched. The most important studies include those by Henryk Baran and Mikhail Odessky.

18. A wider background for the dreams of earthly immortality in Russian culture of the period is sketched by Irene Masing-Delic in her excellent study *Abolishing Death*.

19. Such a paradoxical linkage is characteristically Merezhkovskian. Conversely, in his anniversary article on Tolstoy (1908) Aleksandr Blok compares the great writer to the sun, which causes vampires to flee.

20. As a by-product of this preparation, he wrote several nonfiction pieces, including articles on the controversial medieval scholar-adventurer Agrippa von

Nettesheim (the principal historical character in *The Fiery Angel*) and an unpublished book of sketches on fourth-century Rome.

21. Vsevolod Setchkareff carries Kuzmin's verdict a step further, describing *The Fiery Angel* as "one of the best historical novels in world literature" (254).

22. Endnotes appeared in the second editions of both novels (1909 and 1913, resp.). The "found manuscript" device in the second edition of *The Altar of Victory* is less consistent. In the preface Bryusov unequivocally refers to the tale as if it were one of his own creations and also includes a bibliography listing primary and secondary sources.

23. At least one German reader appears to have been taken in and asked the publisher to provide him with the name of the person who owned the original manuscript; see Iasinskaia, 106.

24. See Solov'ev, 29; Godin, 125; Gurevich, 150.

25. Other examples of historical stylizations (in a very broad sense) at the turn of the century include: Idalia Anichkova's chivalry romance *Ringilda* (1896); Valerian Svetlov's *The Gift of Tears* (1900), openly modeled on France's *Thais* both in genre and theme; Andrei Osipov's tale *Three Lines* (1908), which represents a take on *The Captain's Daughter*. Osipov's tale *The Varangian* (1902) portrays the world through the eyes of pagan Slavs. Such attempts at reproducing primitive, premodern or even pre-historical consciousness, which has several precedents in European literature of the time, can also be considered a *sui generis* version of stylization. Stylizations appearing in the 1910s acquire a distinct acmeist flavor (cf. Boris Sadovskoi's tales and short stories; Kuzmin's quasi-historical and historical prose; and also short stories by Kuzmin's nephew Sergei Auslender.)

26. Merezhkovsky's own critical weapons were often turned against him, his novelistic art being labeled "dead" and "lifeless."

27. The following are some of the most conspicuous examples of such allusions. First, in *The Fiery Angel* there is a situational parallelism with Gogol's *Vii* in the scene where the hero, in search of lodging for the night, insists on gaining access to a locked dwelling without suspecting that he will encounter a witch there who, figuratively speaking, will ride him for the rest of the tale. Gogolian allusions are further enhanced by the drawing of the magic circle in the sorcery scene. Second, departing from Agrippa's house in Bonn, Ruprecht remarks: "I [. . .] left the room [. . .] hardly expecting that I would encounter the great magician, and under such strange circumstances!" (4:132). This Pushkinian turn of phrase is reminiscent of several passages in *The Captain's Daughter* and resonates with Pushkin's concept of fate. Third, on one occasion Renata sounds very much like Dostoevsky's *Underground Man:* "Perhaps I am not amazed at all. Perhaps I am even glad that Heinrich hates me" (5:138). In the novel Doctor Faustus also expresses Dostoevsky's favorite ideas about the paradoxes of the free will: "Man can seek sorrow, and suffering, and death itself" (232). Fourth, the brotherhood of "new men" mentioned several times by Count von Wellen clearly brings to mind the proverbial "new men" of Nikolai Chernyshevsky's *What Is to Be Done?* The following are several examples from *The Altar of Victory*. First, travelers cannot convince a stubborn stationmaster to change

their horses, recalling a topos familiar to Russian readers from the literature of Pushkin's era (5:104–5). Second, Iunius's self-doubt ("No, I'm not a Roman, I'm a Christian" [220]) recalls Raskolnikov's painful introspection in *Crime and Punishment.* Third, the council of Rea's adepts is strikingly reminiscent of the members of Pugachev's council in *The Captain's Daughter* (321). Fourth, battle scenes bear the clear imprint of *War and Peace* (356–58), while Little Namia displays an uncanny similarity to Natasha Rostova. Lastly, the following are examples drawn from *Jupiter Overthrown.* First, the protagonist, pondering how he has brought misfortune, death, and destruction to people he has encountered, sounds very much like Lermontov's Pechorin. Second, the promiscuous teenager Sylvia is strongly reminiscent of Liza Kokhlakova in Dostoevksy's *Brothers Karamazov.*

28. Bryusov paid tribute to the mysticism of his epoch, actively studying magic and practicing spiritism, which is reflected in *The Fiery Angel.* In his contemporary review of *The Fiery Angel* Andrei Bely even labels it a work that is "outwardly historical [. . .] but inwardly occult" (Review of *Ognennyi Angel,* 93). In retrospect, however, Bely characterizes Bryusov as a curious agnostic and describes his creed as follows: "There's a forty percent chance that God exists, a forty percent chance that there is no God, and the decisive twenty go to skepticism" (*Nachalo veka,* 306). Whereas for Merezhkovsky Christianity and paganism are absolutes, this is not the case for Bryusov. In his view Christianity represents a higher truth during a given historical epoch, but in time it will be replaced by another truth, as Father Nikolai prophesizes in the unfinished novel *Jupiter Overthrown* (*Iupiter poverzhennyi,* 5:525).

29. For a classic description of this tortured relationship and its context, see Khodasevich's essay "The End of Renata" in his *Necropolis.*

30. For more on *zhiznetvorchestvo,* see Bethea, *Khodasevich,* 44.

31. As a contemporary reviewer put it, "*The Altar of Victory,* as everyone could see quite clearly, was a continuation and almost a repetition of *The Fiery Angel*" (Chudovskii). See also Gasparov, "Bryusov i antichnost'," 545–46.

32. The fourth century had been a favorite period among the French decadents, first in the 1830s and then in the 1890s, when the fin-de-siècle mood was identified with the atmosphere of the late empire. However, what interests Bryusov (and Merezhkovsky in *Julian the Apostate*) is not decadence per se but rather the clash between Christianity and paganism and the threat of imminent change of civilizations.

33. For a detailed discussion of the theme of the apocalypse during the symbolist period, see Bethea, *The Shape of Apocalypse,* 105–44.

34. Thus, Kamensky's historical digression on the abuses of the Muscovite state contains verbatim quotations from Kostomarov without identifying the source (cf. Kamenskii, 21–25; Kostomarov, "Bunt Sten'ki Razina," 302–3). Kamensky even makes some elementary mistakes while copying Kostomarov's data.

35. The following are some of the major factual distortions and dubious inventions found in the novel. First, according to several foreign sources whose validity is questioned by Solovyov, Razin's elder brother was executed by Muscovite authorities, which helps explain his animosity toward the state. Kamensky goes even

further and sends to the gallows Razin's father, while Razin and his younger brother, Frol, look on. Second, whereas in the novel Frol is executed together with his brother, according to historical sources he was so frightened of death that he announced he had additional important information to disclose, which rescued him from imminent execution. His ultimate fate remains unknown. Third, according to historical sources Vaska Us, Razin's savage chieftain, died from some horrible disease after being eaten alive by worms. In the novel Us drowns in the Volga. Fourth, there is the highly unusual description of the legendary episode where Razin drowns the Persian princess. According to the novel, the princess was not captured by force but rather joined Razin of her own free will. Madly in love with the ataman, the princess asked him to throw her into the river upon realizing that he would return to his wife. Fifth, following the same melodramatic thread, in the novel Razin was betrayed to the authorities by his own wife, who was duped into believing that the princess was still alive and that Razin might return to her.

36. For obvious reasons Kamensky moved precisely in this direction in his postrevolutionary recycling of *Stenka Razin,* which included a play, a poem, and a revised version of the novel (1929). In the latter Razin addresses the masses from the scaffold, prophesying a victorious revolution. Kamensky also removed nationalistic digressions and expanded the theme of class rivalry (inter alia, he adds an episode depicting the tsar and his boyars plotting to defeat Razin.) On Kamensky's reworkings of *Stenka Razin,* see Vladimir Markov, 327, 332.

37. This particular passage can be traced, in part, to Solovyov's musings about Razin's miraculous transformations: "Razin was a true Cossack, one of those Russian people of old, those mighty warriors identified in the popular imagination with the Cossacks, whose surplus of strength kept them from sitting at home and turned them into free Cossacks who would roam the vast expanse of the steppes or set out for other wide-open spaces, the sea, for example, or at least the Mother Volga. We have already seen what sort of a man Razin was. He would go on a diplomatic mission to the Kalmyks in the spring and in the autumn was already prepared to make a pilgrimage to the opposite end of the land, to the Solovki islands. 'I have murdered and looted enough; now is the time to save my soul.' Razin returned from his pilgrimage to the Don, where things were as cramped as in a cage" (11:289).

38. On the futurists' indebtedness to symbolism, see Vladimir Markov, 2–3, 327.

39. A comparison of Razin to Orpheus is found in T. L. Nikolskaya's entry on Kamensky, see *Russkie pisateli,* 2:457. Partially identifying himself with Razin/Orpheus, Kamensky could also enjoy an etymological pun involving his own last name. Instead of choosing the common etymology (*kamen',* stone), one can derive it from *kameny* (Camenae, or the Muses), which makes him a kinsman to Orpheus, the son of a muse.

40. While the Ivanov connection is pure conjecture, Evreinov undoubtedly exerted a considerable influence over Kamensky, who was close to him during the novel's composition and subsequently published an apologetic book about his friend.

In Lieu of a Conclusion

1. Here is how Bely describes the dialectics of the subjective and objective in Merezhkovsky's trilogy: "The depth of the soul and the surface of history are like two mirrors placed opposite each other, only between them the labyrinthine abyss of mystery reveals itself. Is it not all the same which of these two mirrors is turned toward the other, the mirror of the soul or the mirror of history? No mystery will be reflected in either if taken separately" ("Trilogiia," 420).

2. For a description of the canon and attributes of the Petersburgian text, see the classic studies of Antsyferov; Toporov; Lotman, "Simvolika Peterburga"; and Mints, "O trilogii."

3. Lazhechnikov began working on his novel no later than January 1833. It was published in 1834–35 (first in excerpted form and then in full), shortly after the appearance of Pushkin's *Queen of Spades* (1834) and the completion of *The Bronze Horseman* (1833). Moreover, *The Ice Palace* reached reading audiences earlier than Pushkin's poem, which was only published in 1837. Gogol's *Arabesques* appeared in the spring of 1835, following published excerpts from *The Ice Palace*. "The Nose" was published in 1836, while "The Overcoat" only appeared in 1842. For more on the reception of Lazhechnikov's novel and its place in the Petersburgian tradition, see my article "*Ledianoi dom* Lazhechnikova i peterburgskii kanon."

4. This is an obvious allusion to Karl Bryullov's famous painting *The Last Day of Pompeii*, which was exhibited at the Hermitage in August 1834, around the time of the novel's creation. Such references to contemporary art are typical of Lazhechnikov (see chapter 2).

5. Tolstoy briefly mentions the white nights in the episode where Pierre, breaking his promise to Prince Andrew, heads for a night of debauchery at Anatol's. Among other things, Pierre understands that on a night like that he will not be able to sleep. Thus, the Petersburgian climate contributes to the "fall" of a character, albeit in a rather physiological fashion.

6. See, in particular, *Peterburgskoe deistvo*, 182–85. Salias also underscores how alien Saint Petersburg is to the rest of Russia (a recurrent motif throughout the Petersburgian text), to which he gives a characteristic conservative Muscovite twist: "Somewhere at land's end, in some swamps, there where the Russian world ends and Finland begins [. . .] some dragoons [. . .] and grenadiers perform amazing feats and do impossible things, but these feats [. . .] are not of any interest outside [. . .] Petersburg's city line. [. . .] [The Russian people] live in hunger and cold but piously and patiently put all their hopes not in Petersburg's Germans and half-Germans, but in the Lord God and His holy saints" (221–22).

7. This also creates a stylistic dissonance within the text that the symbolists attempt to avoid in their stylizations. For example, although Mordovtsev renders linguistic peculiarities of parables told by a "God's fool," he accompanies them with the following commentary: "The God's fools of yore were a remarkable type. [. . .] The God's fool is the first example of satire. Fomushka was such a God's fool. [. . .] He was a hardened propagandist of the anti-Petrine trend" (168–69).

8. This is most likely a reference to Dostoevsky's recently published novel *The Raw Youth* (1875). Generally speaking, allusions of that type are not characteristic of realistic fiction. They do occur occasionally, but do not represent any kind of system. The novel's protagonist is based on an actual historical figure who was executed in 1721 for denouncing Peter as the Antichrist. There is no connection between him and Konstantin Levin of Tolstoy's *Anna Karenina*, which was still being written when *The Idealists* was published. The virtually simultaneous appearance of two Levins on the Russian literary scene is nothing more than an amusing coincidence.

9. Another instance of Petersburgian mythology that can arguably be traced to Dostoevsky is found in Prince Sergiy Golitsyn's *Good Old Times*, which also appeared in 1876. In an episode that takes place around 1700, a gypsy fortuneteller predicts that the main characters will meet again under strange circumstances in a big city (viz. the not-yet-built Petersburg). When asked where this city is located, she responds with the following perplexing riddle: "Nowhere! In the forest, on the swamp . . . there is no city!" (2:399).

10. Despite obvious conceptual differences between Mordovtsev and Merezhkovsky, similarities between their novels can be found on many levels: (1) historical background, including the affair of Tsarevich Alexei; (2) an emphasis on the widespread opposition to Peter's reforms and the popular perception of the tsar as the Antichrist; (3) the graphic portrayal of Peter's cruelty and episodes where protagonists stumble upon the gruesome remains of mass executions; (4) "God-seeking" protagonists; (5) a brief mention of Captain Vasily Levin in *Peter and Alexis*, which can be viewed as a "footnote" referring to Mordovtsev; (6) the introduction of contrasting musical divertimentos (Ukrainian vs. Russian songs in Mordovtsev; Italian vs. Russian songs in Merezhkovsky); (7) "statuesque" epithets in the description of Mary Hamilton; and (8) a marked strangeness in the appearance of Alexei's beautiful mistress Afroska.

11. The link to *The Idiot* is further strengthened by the fact that both Prince Lev Myshkin and Prince Tikhon Zalessky are naive youngsters arriving in the "New Babylon," are descended from ancient but impoverished aristocratic families, and suffer from epilepsy.

12. Having been exiled to the children's room, like most of the historical novels dating from the 1830s, *The Ice Palace* was hardly taken as a serious literary subtext during the symbolist era. However, Lazhechnikov's novel remained popular throughout the imperial period. In addition to the examples previously mentioned in chapter 1, one can add epigraphs from Lazhechnikov in Danilevsky's *Mirovich*, which was among the most widely read novels of the second wave, and also—closer to Merezhkovsky's times—the operatic version of *The Ice Palace* (with music by Arseny Koreshchenko and a libretto by M. I. Tschaikovsky) which was staged in 1900 in the Bolshoi Theater, with Fyodor Chaliapin singing the part of Duke Biron (see Il'inskaia, 2:645). While most potential allusions to Lazhechnikov in *Peter and Alexis* may be of a polygenetic nature, Merezhkovsky's Summer Garden episode bears an uncanny resemblance to Lazhechnikov's description of the Summer

Garden during the happy days under Peter: "The alleys burgeoned and clamored with activity. Couples petted on the benches; kisses could be heard in the grotto, quaintly decorated with seashells; the fountains gurgled and the marble statues themselves seemed to move among the groups, running to and fro" (*Ledianoi dom*, 29).

13. Tynyanov's novel, whose organizing metaphor is a pendulum, suggests clear parallels between the post-Decembrist era and nascent Stalinism; see Brintlinger on this point.

14. For an excellent discussion of Nabokov in the context of the émigré historical imagination, see Dolinin, "Clio Laughs Last."

Works Cited

Anon. Review of *Ledianoi dom*, by I. I. Lazhechnikov. *Syn Otechestva* 5.4 (1838): 69–70.

———. Review of *Pugachevtsy*, by Count E. A. Salias. *Russkii vestnik* 110, no. 4 (1874): 865–94.

———. Review of *Volkhvy*, by Vsevolod Solov'ev. *Russkii vestnik* 212, no. 1 (1891): 331–36.

Aksakov, S. T. *Sobranie sochinenii*. Vol. 3. Moscow: Khudozhestvennaia literatura, 1986.

Alexandrov, Vladimir E. *Limits to Interpretation: The Meanings of* Anna Karenina. Madison: University of Wisconsin Press, 2004.

Altaev, Al. *Apostol istiny. Istoricheskaia povest' o zhizni odnogo iz velikikh geroev nauki.* St. Petersburg and Moscow: M. O. Vol'f, [1908].

———. *Svetochi pravdy. Ocherki iz zhizni velikikh liudei.* 2nd ed. St. Petersburg: O. N. Popova, 1903.

Al'tshuller, Mark. *Epokha Val'tera Skotta v Rossii. Istoricheskii roman 1830-kh godov.* St. Petersburg: Akademicheskii proekt, 1996.

Amfiteatrov, A. "Russkii literator i rimskii imperator." In his *Literaturnyi al'bom*, 2nd rev. ed., 150–87. St. Petersburg: Obshchestvennaia pol'za, 1907.

Anderson, Perry. "On Emplotment: Two Kinds of Ruin." In *Probing the Limits of Representation: Nazism and the "Final Solution,"* ed. Saul Friedlander, 54–65. Cambridge, Mass.: Harvard University Press, 1992.

Antsiferov, N. P. *Dusha Peterburga* (1922). Rpt. Paris: YMCA-Press, 1978.

Apostolov, N. N. (Ardens). *Lev Tolstoi nad stranitsami istorii.* Moscow: Komissiia po oznamenovaniiu stoletiia so dnia rozhdeniia L. N. Tolstogo, 1928.

Ardens, N. N. (Apostolov). *Tvorcheskii put' L. N. Tolstogo.* Moscow: AN SSSR, 1962.

Avenarius, V. P. *Iunosheskie gody Pushkina. Biograficheskaia povest'.* St. Petersburg: Izd. zhurnala *Rodni*, 1888.

Baran, Kh. "Nekotorye reministsentsii u Bloka: Vampirizm i ego istochniki." In his *Poetika russkoi literatury nachala XX veka,* 264–83. Moscow: Progress-Univers, 1993.

Bareetenev, Iurii. "Nikolai Mikhailovich Pavlov (Nekrologicheskaia stat'ia)." *Russkii arkhiv* 1 (1906): 640–48.

Bartenev, P. I. Introduction to "Zametki veterana 1812 goda," by P. S. Demenkov. *Russkii arkhiv* 49, no. 3 (1911): 385.

Barthes, Roland. "Historical Discourse." In *Introduction to Structuralism,* ed. Michael Lane, 145–55. New York: Basic Books, 1970.

Belinskii, V. G. *Polnoe sobranie sochinenii.* 13 vols. Moscow: AN SSSR, 1953–59.

Belozerskaia, N. *Vasilii Trofimovich Narezhnyi. Istoriko-literaturnyi ocherk.* 2nd rev. ed. St. Petersburg: Izd. L. F. Panteleeva, 1896.

Belyi, Andrei. "Merezhkovskii." In his *Lug zelenyi. Kniga statei* (1910), 134–51. Rpt. New York: Johnson Reprint, 1967.

———. *Nachalo veka.* Moscow: STD SSR, 1990.

———. Review of *Ognennyi angel,* by V. Briusov. *Vesy* 9 (1909): 91–93.

———. "Trilogiia." In his *Arabeski* (1911), 415–29. Rpt. Munich: Wilhelm Fink, 1969.

Bestuzhev-Marlinskii, A. A. "Ob"iavlenie ot obshchestva prisposobleniia tochnykh nauk k slovesnosti." In his *Polnoe sobranie sochinenii.* 12 vols. St. Petersburg: Tip. III Otdeleniia sobstvennoi E. I. V. Kantseliarii, 1835–39.

———. *Sochineniia.* 2 vols. Moscow: Khudozhestvennaia literatura, 1981.

Bethea, David M. *Khodasevich: His Life and Art.* Princeton, N.J.: Princeton University Press, 1983.

———. *The Shape of Apocalypse in Modern Russian Fiction.* Princeton, N.J.: Princeton University Press, 1989.

———. "Slavic Gift-Giving, the Poet in History, and Pushkin's *The Captain's Daughter.*" In *Russian Subjects: Empire, Nation, and the Culture,* ed. Monika Greenleaf and Stephen Moeller-Sally, 259–73. Evanston, Ill.: Northwestern University Press, 1998.

Bliumenfel'd, V. "Khudozhnechiskie elementy v *Istorii pugachevskogo bunta* Pushkina." *Voprosy literatury* 1 (1968): 154–74.

Blok, G. *Pushkin v rabote nad istoricheskimi istochnikami.* Moscow and Leningrad: AN SSSR, 1949.

Bloom, Harold. *The Western Canon: The Books and School of the Ages.* New York: Harcourt Brace & Co., 1994.

Bocharov, Sergei. *Roman L. Tolstogo "Voina i mir."* Moscow: GIKhL, 1963.

Bock, Hermann, and Karl Weitzel. *Der historische Roman als Begleiter der Weltgeschichte: Ein Fuehrer durch das Gebiet der historischen Romane und Novellen.* Leipzig: Hachmeister & Thal, n.d.

Bogdanovich, A. I. [A. B.]. Review of *Petr i Aleksei,* by D. S. Merezhkovskii. *Mir Bozhii* 3 (1904): sec. 2:7–10; 7 (1905): sec. 2:1–5.

Borozdin, A. K. "Tridtsatipiatiletie literaturnoi deiatel'nosti Grafa E. A. Saliasa." *Istoricheskii vestnik* 75 (1899): 608–16.

Bowen, Herbert Courthope. *Descriptive Catalogue of Historical Novels & Tales: For the Use of School Libraries and Teachers of History*. London: Stanford, 1882.

Braudy, Leo. *Narrative Form in History and Fiction: Hume, Fielding and Gibbon*. Princeton, N.J.: Princeton University Press, 1970.

Brintlinger, Angela. "Fact and Fiction in Tynjanov's *Smert' Vazir-Muchtara:* Paradoxes of a 'Scientific Novel.'" *Russian Literature* [Amsterdam] 34 (1996): 273–302.

Briusov, V. *Altar' Pobedy*. Vol. 5 of his *Sobranie sochinenii*. Moscow: Khudozhestvennaia literatura, 1975.

———. *Iupiter poverzhennyi*. Vol. 5 of his *Sobranie sochinenii*. Moscow: Khudozhestvennaia literatura, 1975.

———. *Ognennyi angel*. Vol. 4 of his *Sobranie sochinenii*. Moscow: Khudozhestvennaia literatura, 1974.

———. *Ognennyi angel. Povest' v XVI glavakh*. 2nd ed. Moscow: Skorpion, 1909.

Brown, David. *Walter Scott and the Historical Imagination*. London: Routledge & Kegan Paul, 1979.

Brown, Edward William. *A History of Russian Literature of the Romantic Period*. Vol. 2. Ann Arbor, Mich.: Ardis, 1986.

Bulgakov, F. I. "V zashchitu istorii v istoricheskom romane (Pis'mo v redaktsiiu)." *Istoricheskii vestnik* 6 (1881): 835–37.

Bulgarin, F. V. *Dimitrii Samozvanets. Istoricheskii roman*. 4 vols. St. Petersburg: V tipografii A. Smirdina, 1830.

———. *Mazepa*. In his *Sochineniia*, 367–634. Moscow: Sovremennik, 1990.

———. *Petr Ivanovich Vyzhigin. Naravoopisatel'nyi istoricheskii roman XIX veka*. 4 vols. St. Petersburg: V tip. A. Pliushara, 1831.

Carr, David. *Time, History, Narrative*. Bloomington: Indiana University Press, 1986.

Chaadaev, P. Ia. *Stat'i i pis'ma*. Moscow: Sovremennik, 1989.

Cherniaev, N. I. *"Kapitanskaiia dochka" Pushkina*. Moscow: Universitetskaia tipografiia, 1897.

Christensen, Peter G. "*Christ and Antichrist* as Historical Novel." *Modern Language Studies* 20, no. 3 (summer 1990): 67–77.

Chudetskaiia, E. "*Ognennyi angel*. Istoria sozdaniia I pechati." In *Sobranie sochinenii*, by V. Briusov, 4:340–49. Moscow: Khudozhestvennaia literatura, 1974.

Chudovskii, V. "*Russkaia mysl'* i romany V. Briusova, Z. Gippius, D. Merezhkovskogo." *Apollon* 2 (1913): 72–77.

Collingwood, R. G. *The Idea of History*. New York: Oxford University Press, 1956.

Danilevskii, G. P. *Chernyi god (Pugachovshchina). Istoricheskii roman*. St. Petersburg: Tip. V. V. Komarova, 1892.

———. "Istoriki-ochevidtsy." In *Roman L. N. Tolstogo "Voina i mir" v russkoi kritike*, ed. I. N. Sukhikh, 333–35. Leningrad: Izd-vo Leningradskogo un-ta, 1989.

——— *Mirovich*. In his *Mirovich. Kniazhna Tarakanova. Sozzhennaia Moskva*, ed. B. Iakovlev, 5–410. Moscow: Izvestiia, 1961.

———. *Sozhzhennaia Moskva. Istoricheskii roman*. In his *Mirovich. Kniazhna Tarakanova. Sozhzhennaia Moskva*, ed. B. Iakovlev, 533–766. Moscow: Izvestiia, 1961.

Danto, Arthur. *Analytical Philosophy of History*. Cambridge: Cambridge University Press, 1965.

Davydov, Sergei. "The Sound and Theme in the Prose of A. S. Pushkin: A Logo-Semantic Study of Paronomasia." *Slavic and East European Journal* 27, no. 1 (1983): 1–18.

Debreczeny, Paul. *The Other Pushkin: A Study of Alexander Pushkin's Prose Fiction*. Stanford, Calif.: Stanford University Press, 1983.

Demenkov, P. S. "Zametki veterana 1812 goda." *Russkii arkhiv* 49, no. 3 (1911): 385–466.

De-Pule, M. F. "Voina iz-za *Voiny i mira*." In *Roman L. N. Tolstogo "Voina i mir" v russkoi kritike*, ed. I. N. Sukhikh, 326–32. Leningrad: Izd-vo Leningradskogo un-ta, 1989.

Dolgopolov, L. *Na rubezhe vekov. O russkoi literature kontsa XIX—nachala XX veka*. Leningrad: Sovetskij pisatel', 1977.

Dolinin, Alexander. "Clio Laughs Last: Nabokov's Answer to Historicism." In *Nabokov and His Fiction: New Perspectives*, ed. Julian Connolly, 197–215. Cambridge: Cambridge University Press, 1999.

———. "Eshche raz o khronologii *Kapitanskoi dochki*." In *Pushkin i drugie. Sbornik statei k 60-letiiu professora Sergeia Aleksandrovicha Fomicheva*, ed. V. A. Koshelev, 52–59. Novgorod: NGU, 1997.

———. "Historicism or Providentialism? Pushkin's *History of Pugachev* in the Context of French Romantic Historiography." *Slavic Review* 58, no. 2 (Summer 1999): 291–308.

———. *Istoriia, odetaia v roman. Val'ter Skott i ego chitateli*. Moscow: Kniga, 1988.

———. "Swerving from Walter Scott: *The Captain's Daughter* as a Metahistorical Novel." *Elementa* 4 (2000): 313–29.

Dostoevsky, F. M. *Polnoe sobranie sochinenii*. 30 vols. Leningrad: Nauka, 1972–90.

Dray, William H. *On History and Philosophers of History*. Leiden, The Netherlands: E. J. Brill, 1989.

Eikhenbaum, Boris. *Lev Tolstoi. 60-e gody*. Leningrad and Moscow: GIKhL, 1931.

———. *Tolstoi in the Sixties*. Trans. Duffield White. Ann Arbor, Mich.: Ardis, 1982.

Emerson, Caryl. *Boris Godunov: Transpositions of a Russian Theme*. Bloomington: Indiana University Press, 1986.

Evdokimova, Svetlana. *Pushkin's Historical Imagination*. New Haven, Conn.: Yale University Press, 1999.

Feikhtvanger, L. "O smysle i bessmyslitse istoricheskogo romana." In his *Sobranie sochinenii v dvenadtsati tomakh*, 12:667–74. Moscow: Khudozhestvennaia literatura, 1968.

Feuer, Kathryn B. *Tolstoy and the Genesis of "War and Peace."* Ed. Robin Feuer Miller and Donna Tusssing Orwin. Ithaca, N.Y.: Cornell University Press, 1996.

Filippov, M. A. *Patriarkh Nikon. Istroicheskii roman*. 2 vols. St. Petersburg: Izd. Soikina, 1899.

Frazier, Melissa. "*Kapitanskaia dochka* and the Creativity of Borrowing." *Slavic and East European Journal* 37, no. 4 (1993): 472–89.

Friedlander, Saul, ed. *Probing the Limits of Representation: Nazism and the "Final Solution."* Cambridge, Mass.: Harvard University Press, 1992.

Funkenstein, Amos. "History, Counterhistory, and Narrative." In *Probing the Limits of Representation: Nazism and the "Final Solution,"* ed. Saul Friedlander, 66–81. Cambridge, Mass.: Harvard University Press, 1992.

Gallie, W. B. *Philosophy and the Historical Understanding.* London: Chatto & Windus, 1964.

Garshin, Evgenii. *Kriticheskie etiudy.* St. Petersburg: Tip. I. N. Skorokhodova, 1888.

Gasiorowska, Xenia. *The Image of Peter the Great in Russian Fiction.* Madison: University of Wisconsin Press, 1979.

Gasparov, M. L. "Briusov i antichnost'." In *Sobranie sochinenii,* by V. Briusov, 5:543–56. Moscow: Khudozhestvennaia literatura, 1975.

———. "Briusov i bukvalizm." In *Poetika perevoda,* 29–62. Moscow: Raduga, 1988.

Gearhart, Suzanne. *The Open Boundary of History and Fiction.* Princeton, N.J.: Princeton University Press, 1984.

Gertsen, A. I. *Sobranie sochinenii v tridtsati tomakh.* Moscow: AN SSSR, 1954–65.

Ginzburg, L. M. *O literaturnom geroe.* Leningrad: Sovetskii pisatel', 1979.

———. "Zapisi 1920–1930-kh godov." In her *Chelovek za pis'mennym stolom,* 4–182. Leningrad: Sovetskii pisatel', 1989.

Gippius, Zinaida. *Vospominaniia.* Moscow: Zakharov, 2001.

Godin, Iakov. Review of *Ognennyi angel,* by V. Briusov. *Sovremennyi mir* no. 3, section 2 (1909): 124–26.

Gogol', N. V. *The Collected Tales of Nikolai Gogol.* Trans. Richard Pevear and Larissa Volokhonsky. New York: Vintage, 1999.

———. *Polnoe sobranie sochinenii.* 14 vols. Moscow and Leningrad, 1937–52.

———. *Taras Bul'ba* (1842 ed.). In his *Sobranie sochinenii,* 6 vols., 2:31–152. Moscow: GIKhL, 1952.

———. *Taras Bul'ba* (*Mirgorod* ed.). In his *Sobranie sochinenii,* 6 vols., 2:247–320. Moscow: GIKhL, 1952.

———. *Taras Bulba.* In *Mirgorod,* trans. David Magarshack, 29–174. New York: Farrar, Straus & Cudahy, 1962.

Golitsyn, S. V. *Byloe vremechko. Istoricheskii roman.* Moscow: T. Ris, 1876.

Golota, P. *Nalivaiko, ili Vremena bedstvii Malorossii. Istoricheskii roman XVI veka.* 4 vols. Moscow: V universitetskoi tip., 1833.

Goncourt, Edmond, and Jules de Goncourt. *Germinie Lacerteux.* Trans. Leonard Tancock. New York: Penguin, 1984.

Gossman, Lionel. *Between History and Literature.* Cambridge, Mass.: Harvard University Press, 1990.

Grodetskaia, A. G. "Vozvrashchenie k diskussii o zhanre *Voiny i mira.*" *Russkaia literatura* 3 (1991): 182–86.

Gurevich, L. "Dal'nozorkie." Review of *Ognennyi angel,* by V. Briusov, and *Pervaia kniga rasskazov,* by M. Kuzmin. *Russkaia mysl'* no. 3, section 2 (1910): 143–53.

Gusev, N. N. *Lev Nikolaevich Tolstoi. Materialy k biografii s 1855 po 1869 god.* Moscow: AN SSSR, 1957.

Hugo, Victor. *Notre-Dame de Paris*. Trans. Alban Krailsheimer. Oxford: Oxford University Press, 1993.

Iakubovich, D. P. "'Kapitanskaia dochka' i romany V. Skotta." *Vremennik Pushkinskoi komissii* 4–5 (1939): 165–97.

Iasinskaia, Z. I. "Istoricheskii roman Briusova *Ognennyi angel*." In *Briusovskie chteniia 1963 goda*, ed. K. V. Aivazian, 101–29. Erevan: Aiastan, 1964.

Il'inskaia, N. G. "Kommentarii." In *Sochineniia v dvukh tomakh*, by I. I. Lazhechnikov, 1:513–40; 2:641–83. Moscow: Khudozhestvennaia literatura, 1986.

Ivanov, V. I. "Dve stikhii v sovremennom simvolizme." In his *Po zvezdam. Stat'i i aforizmy*, 247–308. St. Petersburg: Ory, 1909.

———. "O Dionise Orficheskom." *Russkaia mysl'* 11 (1913): 70–98.

———. "O russkoi idee." In his *Po zvezdam. Stat'i i aforizmy*, 309–37. St. Petersburg: Ory, 1909.

Ivanov-Razumnik, R. V. "Mertvoe masterstvo (D. Merezhkovskii)." In his *Tvorchestvo i kritika*, vol. 2. St. Petersburg: Prometei, [1911].

Izmailov, A. *Literaturnyi Olimp. Kharakteristiki, vstrechi, portrety, avtografy*. Moscow: Tip. T-va I. D. Sytina, 1911.

Kamenskii, Vasilii. *Sten'ka Razin. Roman*. Moscow: Kul'tura, 1916.

Kandiev, B. I. *Roman-epopeia L. N. Tolstogo "Voina i mir". Kommentarii*. Moscow: Prosveshchenie, 1967.

"*Kapitanskaia dochka* v kritike i literaturovedenii." In *Kapitanskaia dochka*, by A. S. Pushkin, ed. G. P. Makogonenko, 233–80. Leningrad: Nauka, Literaturnye pamiatniki, 1984.

Karamzin, N. M. *Istoriia gosudarstva Rossiiskogo*. 12 vols. (1842–44). Rpt. Moscow: Kniga, 1989.

———. "Natal'ia, boiarskaia doch'." In his *Russkaia istoricheskaia povest' v dvukh tomakh*, 1:27–59. Moscow: Khudozhestvennaia literatura, 1988.

Karatygin, P. P. *Chernoknizhniki. Roman iz vremen tsarstvovaniia Pavla I*. St. Petersburg: Tip. V. V. Komarova, 1885.

———. *Dela davno minuvshikh dnei. Istoricheskii roman*. St. Petersburg: Tip. V. V. Komarova, 1888.

Kareev, N. I. *Filosofiia istorii v russkoi literature*. St. Petersburg: Prometei, 1912.

Karnovich, E. P. *Liubov' i korona. Paguba*. Stavropol': Kavkazskii krai, 1992.

Khodasevich, V. F. *Koleblemyi trenozhnik. izbrannoe*. Moscow: Sovetskii pisatel', 1991.

——— "Konets Renaty." In his *Nekropol?*, 7–60. Paris: YMCA Press, 1976.

Kireevskii, I. V. *Polnoe sobranie sochinenii*. 2 vols. Ed. M. Gershenzon. Moscow: Put', 1911.

Kliuchevskii, V. O. *Sochineniia v vos'mi tomaka*. 8 vols. Moscow: Izd-vo sotsial'no-ekonomicheskoi literatury, 1956–59.

Kogan, Petr. *Ocherki po istorii noveishei russkoi literatury*. Vol. 3, *Sovremenniki*. Bands 2–3, *Mistiki i bogoiskateli*. Moscow: Zaria, 1901–11.

Kolobaeva, L. A. "Merezhkovskii—romanist." *Izvestiia Akademii Nauk SSSR. Seriia Literatury i Iazyka* 50, no. 5 (September–October 1991): 445–53.

Kornblatt, Judith Deutsch. *The Cossack Hero in Russian Literature*. Madison: University of Wisconsin Press, 1992.

Kostomarov, N. I. "Bunt Sten'ki Razina." *Otechestvennye zapiski* 121 (1858): 11–12.

———. *Kholui. Epizod iz istorichesko-bytovoi russkoi zhizni pervoi poloviny XVIII st.* St. Petersburg: N. A. Lebedev, 1885.

———. "Kudeiar. Istoricheskaia khronika v trekh knigakh." *Vestnik Evropy* 52 (1875): 461–548; 53 (1875): 5–77, 465–548.

———. *Syn. Rasskaz iz vremen XVII veka*. St. Petersburg: E. N. Akhmatova, 1865.

Kozlov, V. P. *"Istoriia gosudarstva rossiiskogo" N. M. Karamzina v otsenkakh sovremennikov*. Moscow: Nauka, 1989.

———. "'Primechaniia' Karamzina k *Istorii gosudarstva Rossiiskogo*." In *Istoriia gosudarstva Rossiiskogo*, by N. M. Karamzin, 1:551–73. Moscow: Nauka, 1989.

Kozmin, N. K. *Ocherki iz istorii russkogo romantizma. N. A. Polevoi kak vyrazitel' literaturnykh napravlenii sovremennoi emu epokhi*. St. Petersburg: Tip. I. N. Skorokhodova, 1903.

Kryzhanovskaya, V. I. (Rochester). *Dva sfinksa*. St. Petersburg: V. V. Komarov, 1901.

———. *Sim pobedishi!* (*Hoc signo vinces!*). St. Petersburg: V. V. Komarov, 1893.

Kucharska, Eugenia. *Rosyjscka powiesc historyczna pierwszego trzydziestolecia XIX w*. Opole: WSP w Opolu, 1976.

Kukol'nik, N. V. *Evelina de Val'erol'*. In his *Sochineniia*, vol. 1, *Romany*. St. Petersburg: V tip. I. Fishona, 1851–52.

Lachinov, N. A. "Po povodu poslednego romana gr. Tolstogo." In *Roman L. N. Tolstogo "Voina i mir" v russkoi kritike*, ed. I. N. Sukhikh, 116–27. Leningrad: Izd-vo Leningradskogo un-ta, 1989.

Lavretskaia, V. *Proizvedeniia A. S. Pushkina na temy russkoi istorii*. Moscow: Uchebno-pedagogicheskoe izdatel'stvo, 1962.

Lazhechnikov, I. I. *Basurman*. In his *Sochineniia v dvukh tomakh*, 2:295–640. Moscow: Khudozhestvennaia literatura, 1986.

———. *Ledianoi dom*. In his *Sochineniia v dvukh tomakh*, 2:5–294. Moscow: Khudozhestvennaia literatura, 1986.

———. *Poslednii novik*. In his *Sochineniia v dvukh tomakh*, 1:27–511. Moscow: Khudozhestvennaia literatura, 1986.

Leighton, Lauren G. *Aleksander Bestuzhev-Marlinsky*. New York: Twayne, 1975.

———. "On a Discrimination of Russian Romanticism." In his *Russian Romanticism: Two Essays*, 1–40. The Hague: Mouton, 1975.

Leont'ev, K. *Analiz, stil' i veianie. O romanakh gr. L. N. Tolstogo*. Providence, R.I.: Brown University Press, 1965.

Levin, Iu. D. "Prizhiznennaia slava Val'tera Skotta v Rossii." In *Epokha romantizma. Iz istorii mezhdunarodnykh sviazei russkoi literatury*, ed. M. P. Alekseev, 5–67. Leningrad: Nauka, 1975.

Levkovich, Ia. L. "Printsipy dokumental'nogo povestvovaniia v istoricheskoi proze pushkinskoi pory." In *Pushkin. Issledovaniia i materialy*, ed. M. P. Alekseev, 6:171–96. Leningrad: Nauka, 1969.

L. N. Tolstoi v russkoi kritike. 2nd. ed. Ed. S. P. Bychkov. Moscow: GIKhL, 1952.

Lotman, Iu. M. "Problema istoricheskogo fakta." In his *Vnutri mysliashchikh mirov*, 301–6. Moscow: Iazyki russkoi kul'tury, 1996.

———. "Simvolika Peterburga i problemy semiotiki goroda." In his *Izbrannye stat'i v trex tomax*, 2:9–21. Tallin: Aleksandra, 1992.

Lukács, Georg. *The Historical Novel*. Trans. Hannah and Stanley Mitchell. London: Merlin, 1965.

Maikov, Valerian. *Kriticheskie opyty (1845–1847)*. St. Petersburg: Izdanie zhurnala "Panteon Literatury," 1891.

Mal'tsev, M. *Tema krest'ianskogo vosstaniia v tvorchestve A. S. Pushkina*. Cheboksary: Chuvashkoe gosizdatel'stvo, 1960.

Mann, Iu. V. *Dinamika russkogo romantizma*. Moscow: Aspekt, 1995.

———. "Fakul'tety Nadezhdina." In *Literaturnaia kritika. Estetika*, by N. I. Nadezhdin, 3–44. Moscow: Khudozhestvennaia literatura, 1972.

———. *Poetika russkogo romantizma*. Moscow: Nauka, 1976.

Manzoni, Alessandro. *On the Historical Novel*. Trans. Sandra Bermann. Lincoln: University of Nebraska Press, 1984.

Markov, Vladimir. *Russian Futurism: A History*. Berkeley: University of California Press, 1968.

Markov, Vladislav. *Kurskie porubezhniki. Istoricheskii roman*. St. Petersburg: Rodina, 1895.

Martem'ianov, T. A. "Iz predanii o Sten'ke Razine." *Istoricheskii vestnik* 109 (1907): 828–61.

Masal'skii, K. P. *Borodoliubie*. In his *Sochineniia*, 1:229–382. St. Petersburg: V tip. K. Zhernakova, 1843.

———. *Strel'tsy. Iistoricheskii roman*. 4 vols. St. Petersburg: Tip. shtaba Otdel'nogo korpusa vnutrennnei strazhi, 1834.

Masing-Delic, Irene. *Abolishing Death: A Salvation Myth of Russian Twentieth-Century Literature*. Stanford, Calif.: Stanford University Press, 1992.

Meletinskii, E. M. *Poetika mifa*. Moscow: Nauka, 1976.

Merezhkovsky, D. S. *Polnoe sobranie sochinenii*. 24 vols. Moscow: Tip. I. D. Sytina, 1914.

Mezhevich, V. Review of *Basurman*, by I. I. Lazhechnikov. *Galateia* 1–2 (1839): 134–60.

Mezier, A. V. *Ukazatel' istoricheskikh romanov, original'nykh i perevodnykh, raspolozhennykh po stranam i epokham*. St. Petersburg: Tip. N. N. Skorokhodova, 1902.

Mikhailova, M. V. "L. Trotskii o Merezhkovskom." In *D. S. Merezhkovskii. Mysl' i slovo*, ed. V. A. Keldysh, I. V. Koretskaia, and M. A. Nikitina, 326–36. Moscow: Nasledie, 1999.

Mikhailovskii, N. K. *Sochineniia*. 6 vols. St. Petersburg: Izdanie zhurnala *Russkoe Bogatstvo*, 1896–97.

Mikkelson, Gerald "Pushkin's 'Geroj': A Verse Dialogue on Truth." *Slavic and East European Journal* 18, no. 4 (Winter 1974): 367–72.

Mints, Z. G. "O nekotorykh 'neomifologicheskikh' tekstakh v tvorchestve russkikh simvolistov." *Tvorchestvo A. A. Bloka i russkaia kul'tura XX veka. Blokovskii sbornik* vol. 3. *Uchenye zapiski Tartuskogo gosudarstvennoko universiteta* 459 (1979): 76–120.

———. "O trilogii Merezhkovskogo *Khristos i Antikhrist.*" In *Khristos i Antikhrist. Trilogiia,* by D. S. Merezhkovskii, 1:5–26; Commentaries: 1:397–415; 2:368–94; 3:402–30; 4:598–636. Moscow: Kniga, 1989–90.

Mordovtsev, D. L. *Gospodin Velikii Novgorod.* In his *Polnoe sobranie istoriheskikh romanov, povestei i rasskazov,* 3:1–189. St. Petersburg: Izd-vo P. P. Sojkina, n.d.

———. *Idealisty i realisty. Istoricheskii roman.* St. Petersburg: Tip. A. Suvorina, 1878.

———. "Kritika i bibliografiia." Review of *Sochineniia,* by G. P. Danilevskii. *Drevniaia i novaia Rossiia* 3 (1878): 267–70.

———. "K slovu ob storicheskom romane i ego kritike (Pis'mo v redaktsiiu)." *Istoricheskii vestnik* 6 (1881): 642–51.

———. *Lzhedmitrii. Istoricheskii roman iz smutnogo vremeni.* In his *Polnoe sobranie istoriheskikh romanov, povestei i rasskazov,* 12:5–246. St. Petersburg: Izd-vo P. P. Sojkina, n.d.

———. *Zamurovannaia tsaritsa. Roman iz zhizni Drevnego Egipta.* In his *Polnoe sobranie istoriheskikh romanov, povestei i rasskazov,* 2:1–147. St. Petersburg: Izd-vo P. P. Sojkina, n.d.

Morson, Gary Saul. *Hidden in Plain View: Narrative and Creative Potentials in "War and Peace."* Stanford, Calif.: Stanford University Press, 1987.

Nadezhdin, N. I. Review of *Roslavlev,* by M. N. Zagoskin. *Teleskop* 4 (1831): 77–93, 216–35.

N. N. "Rossiiskie Val'ter-Skotty." *Delo* 11 (1878): 167–79.

Norov, A. S. "Voina i mir (1805–1812) s istoricheskoi tochki zreniia i po vospominaniiam sovremennika (Po povodu sochineniia grafa L. N. Tolstogo *Voina i mir*)." *Voennyi sbornik* 11 (1868): 189–246.

Nye, Russel B. "History and Literature: Branches of the Same Tree." In *Essays on History and Literature,* ed. Robert H. Bremner, 123–62. Columbus: Ohio State University Press, 1966.

Odesskii, M. P. "Mif o vampire i russkaia sotsial-demokratiia." *Literaturnoe obozrenie* 3 (1995).

Odoevskii, V. F. *Russkie nochi.* Leningrad: Nauka, Literaturnye pamiatniki, 1975.

Oksman, Iu. G. "Pushkin v rabote nad romanom *Kapitanskaia dochka.*" In *Kapitanskaia dochka,* by A. S. Pushkin, 145–99. Moscow: Nauka, Literaturnye pamiatniki, 1984.

Orlov, S. A. *Istoricheskii roman Val'tera Skotta.* Gorkii: Gor'kovskii gos. universitet, 1960.

Orwin, Donna. *Tolstoy's Art and Thought, 1847–1880.* Princeton, N.J.: Princeton University Press, 1993.

Osipov, A. A. *Tri stroki. Istoricheskaia povest'dlia iunoshestva. Iz vremen tsarstvovanii Elizavety Petrovny, Petra III i Ekateriny II.* St. Petersburg: A. F. Devrien, 1908.

Ospovat, A. L. "Istoricheskii material i istoricheskie alliuzii v *Kapitanskoi dochke.*" In *Tynianovskii sbornik,* ed. M. O. Chudakova, 10:40–67. Moscow: OGI, 1998.

———. "Iz kommentariia k *Kapitanskoi dochke:* lubochnye kartinki." In *Pushkinskaia konferentsiia v Stenforde, 1999. Materialy i issledovaniia,* ed. David M Bethea, 357–65. Moscow: OGI, 2001.

———. "Iz nabliudenii nad tsarskosel'skim toposom *Kapitanskoi dochki.*" In *Tynianovskii sbornik,* ed. M. O. Chudakova, 11:199–207. Moscow: OGI, 2002.

Panov, S. I., and A. M. Ranchin, "D. L. Mordovtsev i ego istoricheskaia proza." In *Za ch'i grekhi? Velikii raskol,* by D. L. Mordovtsev, 5–30. Moscow: Pravda, 1990.

Pavlov, N. Review of *Syn,* by N. Kostomarov. In his *Nashe perekhodnoe vremiia,* 18–26. Moscow: T. I. Gagen, 1888.

———. *Tsarskii sokol'nik. Istoricheskaia povest' iz vvremen Alekseia Mikhailovicha.* Moscow: I. N. Kushnerov, 1904.

Petrov, S. M. *Russkii istoricheskii roman XIX veka.* Moscow: Khudozhestvennaia literatura, 1964.

Petrunina, N. N. *Proza Pushkina (Puti evolutsii).* Leningrad: Nauka, 1987.

———. "Pushkin i Zagoskin (*Kapitanskaia dochka* i *Iurii Miloslavskii*)." *Russkaia literatura* 4 (1972): 110–20.

Pinchuk, A. "Russskii istoricheskii roman (do 50-kh godov XIX v.)." *Filologicheskie zapiski* 1–6 (1913); 1–3 (1914).

Plaksin, Vasilii. *Rukovodstvo k poznaniiu istorii literatury.* St. Petersburg: V tip. III Otdeleniia Sobstv. E. I. V. Kantseliarii, 1833.

Pogodin, M. P. "Pis'ma M. P. Pogodina k S. P. Shevyrevu. 1829 god." *Russkii arkhiv* 5 (1882): 67–126.

———. "Pis'mo o russkikh romanakh." In *Severnaia lira na 1827 god,* ed. T. M. Gol'ts and A. L. Grishunin, 133–40. Moscow: Nauka, Literaturnye pamiatniki, 1984.

Pokrovskii, K. V. "Istochniki romana *Voina i mir.*" In *"Voina i mir". Sbornik,* ed. V. P. Obninskii and T. I. Pollner, 113–28. Moscow: Zadruga, 1912.

Polevoi, Ksenofont. *Mikhail Vasil'evich Lomonosov.* 2 vols. Moscow: V tip. Avgusta Semena, 1836.

———. "O russkikh povestiakh i romanakh." *Moskovskii telegraf* 29 (1829): 312–28.

Polevoi, Nikolai. *Istoriia russkogo naroda.* 6 vols. Moscow: V tipografii Avgusta Semena, 1829–33.

———. *Kliatva pri grobe Gospodnem. Russlaia byl' XV veka.* In his *Izbrannaia istoricheskaia proza,* 283–691. Moscow: Pravda, 1990.

———. Review of *Doch' kuptsa Zholobova,* by N. Kalashnikov, and *Poiata, doch' Lezdeiki,* by F. Bernatovich. *Moskovskii telegraf* 43, no. 3 (1832): 391–401.

———. Review of *Ivan Mazepa,* by Petr Golota. *Muskovskii telegraf* 48, no. 24 (1832): 555–57.

———. Review of *Koshchei Bessmertnyi,* by A. Vel'tman. *Moskovskii telegraf* 52 (1833): 612–17.

———. Review of *Russkii Zhil'blaz,* by Aleksandr Sibiriakov, and *Grafinia Roslavleva. Moskovskii telegraf* 45 (1832): 229–33.

———. "O romanakh Viktora Giugo i voobshche o noveishikh romanakh (protiv stat'i g-na Shove)." *Moskovskii telegraf* 43 (1832): 85–105, 211–38, 370–90.

Polevoi, Nikolai, and Ksenofont Polevoi. *Literaturnaia kritika. Stat'i i retsenzii (1825–1842).* Leningrad: Khudozhestvennaia literatura, 1990.

Ponomareva, G. "Zametki o semantike 'pereputannykh tsitat' v istoricheskikh romanakh D. S. Merezhkovskogo." In *Klassitsizm i modernizm. Sbornik statei*, ed. I. V. Abramets, 102–11. Tartu: Tartuskii un-t, 1994.

Protopopov, A. *Chernyi grob, ili Krovavaia zvezda. Pover'e XVII v.* 2 vols. Moscow: V tip. Lazarevykh in-ta vostochnykh iazykov, 1835.

———. *Pan Iagozhinskii, otstupnik i mstitel'. Roman, vziatyi iz drevnikh pol'slikh predanii*. Moscow: V universitetskoi tip., 1836.

Pushkin, A. S. *Eugene Onegin*. Trans. James E. Falen. New York: Oxford University Press, 1998.

———. *Kapitanskaia dochka*. 2nd rev ed. Ed. G. P. Makogonenko. Leningrad: Nauka, Literaturnye pamiatniki, 1984.

———. *Polnoe sobranie sochinenii*. 16 vols. Moscow and Leningrad: AN SSSR, 1937–59.

———. *Pushkin on Literature*. Ed. and trans. Tatiana Wolff. London: Athlone; Stanford, Calif.: Stanford University Press, 1986.

———. *"The Queen of Spades" and Other Stories*. Trans. Alan Myers. New York: Oxford University Press, 1999.

R. B. "Ob istoricheskom romane fo Frantsii i Anglii." *Syn Otechestva* 46 (1834): 537–52, 601–16.

Rebekkini, Damiano. "Russkie istoricheskie romany 30-kh godov XIX veka (Bibliograficheskii ukazatel')." *Novoe literaturnoe obozrenie* 34 (1998): 416–33.

Reitbalt, A. I. *Kak Pushkin vyshel v genii. Istoriko-sotsiologicheskii ocherki*. Moscow: NLO, 2001.

———. *Ot Bovy k Bal'montu. Ocherki po istorii chteniia v Rossii vo vtoroi polovine XIX veka*. Moscow: MPI, 1991.

Reizov, B. G. *Frantsuzskii istoricheskii roman v epokhu romantizma*. Leningrad: GIKhL, 1958.

Riasanovsky, Nicholas V. *The Image of Peter the Great in Russian History and Thought*. New York: Oxford University Press, 1985.

Rozanov, V. V. "Sredi inoiazychnykh (D. S. Merezhkovskii)." *Mir iskusstva* 7–8 (1903): 69–86.

Rubakin, N. A. "Istoricheskie romany i prepodavanie istorii." In *Ukazatel' istoricheskikh romanov, original'nykh i perevodnykh, raspolozhennykh po stranam i epokham*, compiled by A. V. Mezier, 1–29. St. Petersburg: Tip. N. N. Skorokhodova, 1902.

Rubinshtein, N. L. *Russkaia istoriografiia*. Moscow: Gospolitizdat, 1941.

Rudnevskii. *David Igorevich, kniaz' Vladimirskii, ili 1097 god. Istoricheskii roman XI veka*. 4 vols. Moscow: V tip. M. Ponomareva, 1834.

Russkie pisateli (1800–1917). Biograficheskii slovar'. 4 vols. Moscow: Bol'shaia rossiiskaia entsiklopedia-Fianit, 1992–99.

Russkii bunt. Feature film based on Aleksandr Pushkin's novel *The Captain's Daughter*. Directed by Aleksandr Proshkin. Moscow: Kinostudiia NTV-Profit, 1999.

Sadovskoi, Boris. "Oklevetannye teni" (1912). In his *Ledokhod. Stat'i i zamietki*, 130–34. Petrograd: Tipografia Sirius, 1916.

Salias, E. A. *Sobranie sochinenii.* 30 vols. Moscow: A. A. Kartsev, 1894–1904.

———. *Sochineniia.* 2 vols. Moscow: Khudozhestvennaia literatura, 1992.

Saltykov-Shchedrin, M. E. *Polnoe sobranie sochinenii.* 20 vols. Moscow and Leningrad: GIKhL, 1933–41.

Schamschula, Walter. *Der russische historische Roman vom Klassizismus bis zur Romantik.* Meisenheim am Glan: Anton Hain, 1961.

Schmid, W. *Proza Pushkina v poeticheskom prochtenii.* St. Petersburg: Izd-vo Sankt-Peterburgskogo un-ta, 1996.

Scott, Sir Walter. *Ivanhoe.* Vol. 4.of his *Complete Waverley Novels in Twelve Volumes.* Philadelphia: J. B. Lippincott, 1858.

———. *Waverley, or 'Tis Sixty Years Since / Guy Mannering, or The Astrologer.* Boston: Dana Estes, 1902.

Senkovskii O. I. (Baron Brambeus). "Istoricheskii roman." In his *Sobranie sochinenii,* 8:29–59. St. Petersburg: V tip. V. Bezobrazova i Ko, 1858–59.

Setchkareff, V. "Narrative Prose of Brjusov." *International Journal of Slavic Linguistics and Poetics* 1–2 (1959): 237–65.

——— *Severnaia lira na 1827 god.* Ed. T. M. Gol'ts and A. L. Grishunin. Moscow: Nauka, Literaturnye pamiatniki, 1984.

Shakhovskaia, L. *Sivilla. Istoricheskii roman./ Karfagen i Rim. Istoricheskii roman.* Moscow: Tip. E. I. Pogodinoi, 1881.

Shapiro, Gavriel'. "Nikolai Gogol' I gordyi gogol': pisatel' i ego imia." *Russian Language Journal* 144 (1989): 145–59.

Shcheblykin, I. P. "Russkii istoricheskii roman 30-kh godov XLX veka." In *Problemy zhanrovogo razvitiia v russkoi literature XLX veka,* ed. V. V. Shakhov, 3–232. Ryazan: RGPI, 1972.

Shcheglov, Iu. K. *Romany Il'fa i Petrova. Sputnik chitatelia.* 2 vols. Vienna: Wiener Slavistischer Almanach, 1990–91.

Shelgunov, N. "Besplodnaia niva." *Delo* 10 (1880): 41–63.

Shishkina, Olimpiada. *Kniaz' Skopin-Shuiskii, ili Rossiia v nachale XVII stoletiia.* 4 vols. St. Petersbrug: V tip. meditsinskogo departamenta minist. vnutr. del, 1835.

Shklovskii, Victor. *Gamburgskii schet.* Leningrad: Izd-vo pisatelei, 1928.

———. *Material i stil' v romane Tolstogo "Voina i mir."* Moscow: Federatsiia, [1928]. Repr. The Hague: Mouton, 1970.

———. *Zametki o proze Pushkina.* Moscow: Sovetskii pisatel', 1937.

Sipovskii, V. V. *Ocherki iz istorii russkogo romana (XVIII vek).* 2 vols. St. Petersburg: Trud, 1909–10.

Skabichevskii, A. M. *Istoriia noveishei russkoi literatury, 1848–1892 gg.* 3rd rev. ed. St. Petersburg: Izdanie F. Pavlenkova, 1897.

———. "Literaturnye protivorechiia." Review of *Pugachevtsy,* by Count E. A. Salias, and *Bogatyri,* by N. A. Chaev. *Otechestvennye zapiski* 213 (1874 "Sovremennoe obozrenie"): 1–43.

———. "Nash istoricheskii roman v ego proshlom i nastoiashchem." In his *Sochineniia v dvukh tomakh,* 2:653–792. St. Petersburg: Tip. gazety "Novosti," 1890.

Sobolev, A. L. "D. S. Merezhkovskii v rabote nad romanom *Smert' bogov. Iulian Otstupnik.*" In *D. S. Merezhkovskii. Mysl' i slovo,* ed. V. A. Keldysh, I. V. Koretskaia, and M. A. Nikitina, 31–50. Moscow: Nasledie, 1999.

Sokal'skii, P. P. Review of *Mirovich,* by G. P. Danilevskii. *Russkaia mysl'* 11 (1880): sec. 9:10–14.

Sokolov, N. M. "Petr Velikii i Val'ter-Skotty—mogil'shchiki." *Russkaia starina* 2 (1894): 191–209; 3 (1894): 164–92.

Solov'ev, Sergei M. *Istoriia Rossii s drevneishikh vremen.* 15 vols. Moscow: ISEL, 1962–66.

———. Review of *Ognennyi angel,* by V. Briusov. *Russkaia mysl'* no. 2, section 3 (1909): 29–30.

Somov, O. M. "O romanticheskoi poezii." In *Russkie esteticheskie traktaty pervoi treti XIX veka,* ed. Z. A. Kamenskii, 2:545–61. Moscow: Iskusstvo, 1974.

S. S. "Istoriki-romanisty i istoriki-zhurnalisty." *Delo* 12 (1879): 252–73.

Svin'in Pavel. *Shemiakin sud, ili Poslednee mezhduusobie udel'nykh kniazei russkikh. Istoricheskii roman XV stoletiia.* 4 vols. Moscow: V tip. Stepanova, 1832.

Tolstoi, A. K. *Kniaz' Serebrianyi. Povest' vremen Ioanna Groznogo.* Moscow: Baian, 1991.

Tolstoi, Leo. *Polnoe sobranie sochinenii.* 90 vols. Moscow and Leningrad: GIKhL, 1928–59.

———. *War and Peace.* Trans. Aylmer and Louise Maude. Ed. George Gibian. New York: Norton, 1996.

Toporov, V. N. "Peterburg i 'Peterburgskii tekst russkoi literatury' (Vvedenie v temu)." In his *Mif. Ritual. Simvol. Obraz. Issledovaniia iz oblasti mifopeticheskogo. Izbrannoe,* 259–367. Moscow: Progress/Kul'tura, 1995.

Tsvetaeva, M. "Pushkin i Pugachev." In her *Sochineniia v dvukh tomakh.* Vol. 2: *Proza,* 368–98. Moscow: Khudozhestvennaia literatura, 1980.

Turgenev I. S. *Sobranie sochinenii.* 12 vols. Moscow: Khudozhestvennaia literatura, 1953–58.

Tynianov, Iu. N. "O literaturnoi evoliutsii." In his *Poetika—Itoriia literatury—Kino,* 270–81. Moscow: Nauka, 1976.

Ungurianu, Dan. "Kontseptsiia dvukh pravd u Pushkina i Vin'i: Eshche raz k voprosu ob istochnikakh stikhotvoreniia 'Geroi.'" *Revue des études slaves* 70, no. 4 (1998): 815–24.

———. "*Ledianoi dom* Lazhechnikova i peterburgskii kanon (K voprosu o genezise peterburgskogo teksta)." *Russian Literature* 51, no. 4 (May 2002): 471–81.

Vaiskopf, M. *Siuzhet Gogolia. Mifologiia. Ideologiia. Kontekst.* Moscow: Radiks, 1993.

Vatsuro, V. E. *Goticheskii roman v Rossii.* Moscow: Novoe literaturnoe obozrenie, 2002.

Vel'tman, A. F. *Koshchei bessmertnyi. Bylina starogo vremeni.* In his *Romany,* 22–233. Moscow: Sovremennik, 1985.

Vengerov, S. A. "Ivan Ivanovich Lazhechnikov: Kritiko-biograficheskii ocherk." In *Polnoe sobranie sochinenii,* by I. I. Lazhechnikov, 1:i–cxxxi. St. Petersburg: Izd. M. O. Vol'fa, 1900–1901.

Viazemskii, P. A. *Polnoe sobranie sochinenii*. 12 vols. St. Petersburg: Izdanie gr. S. D. Sheremeteva, 1878–96.

———. "Vospominaniia o 1812 gode." *Russkii arkhiv* 1 (1869).

Vigny, Alfred de. *Cinq-Mars*. New York: Current Literature, 1923.

Vitmer, A. *1812 god v "Voine i mire". Po povodu istoricheskikh ukazanii IV toma "Voiny i mira" grafa L. N. Tolstogo*. St. Petersburg: V tip. Dep-ta udelov, 1869.

Vvedenskii, Arsenii. "Graf Evgenii Andreevich Salias." *Istoricheskii vestnik* 61 (1890): 380–99.

Wachtel, Andrew Baruch. *An Obsession with History: Russian Writers Confront the Past*. Stanford, Calif.: Stanford University Press, 1994.

White, Hayden. "Historical Emplotment and the Problem of Truth." In *Probing the Limits of Representation: Nazism and the "Final Solution,"* ed. Saul Friedlander, 37–53. Cambridge, Mass.: Harvard University Press, 1992.

———. *Metahistory: The Historical Imagination in Nineteenth-Century Europe*. Baltimore, Md.: Johns Hopkins University Press, 1973.

White, Morton. *Foundations of Historical Knowledge*. New York: Harper & Row, 1965.

Zagoskin, M. N. *Askol'dova mogila. Romany, povesti*. Moscow: Sovremennik, 1989.

———. *Brynskii les. Istoricheskii roman iz pervykh godov tsarstvovaniia Petra Velikogo*. In his *Polnoe sobranie sochinenii v dvukh tomakh*, 1:237–448. St. Petersburg: Izdanie V. I. Gubinskogo, 1902.

———. *Iurii Miloslavskii, ili Russkie v 1612 godu*. In his *Sochineniia v dvukh tomakh*, ed. A. Peskov, 1:35–286. Moscow: Khudozhestvennaia literatura, 1987.

———. *Kuz'ma Petrovich Miroshev. Russkaia byl' vremen Ekateriny II*. In his *Polnoe sobranie sochinenii v dvukh tomakh*, 1:651–940. St. Petersburg: Izdanie V. I. Gubinskogo, 1902.

———. *Moskva i moskvichi. Zapiski Bogdana Il'icha Bel'skogo*. In his *Polnoe sobranie sochinenii v dvukh tomakh*, 2:65–498. St. Petersburg: Izdanie V. I. Gubinskogo, 1902.

———. *Roslavlev, ili Russkie v 1812 godu*. In his *Sochineniia v dvukh tomakh*, ed. A. Peskov, 1:287–618. Moscow: Khudozhestvennaia literatura, 1987.

———. *Russkie v nachale os'mnadtsatogo stoletiia. Rasskaz iz vremen edinoderzhaviia Petra I*. In his *Sochineniia v dvukh tomakh*, ed. A. Peskov, 2:447–671. Moscow: Khudozhestvennaia literatura, 1987.

———. *Toska po rodine*. In his *Polnoe sobranie sochinenii v dvukh tomakh*, 2:769–924. St. Petersburg: Izdanie V. I. Gubinskogo, 1902.

Zaidenshur, E. E. *"Voina i mir" L. N. Tolstogo. Sozdanie velikoi knigi*. Moscow: Kniga, 1966.

Zamotin, I. I. *Romantizm dvadtsatykh godov XIX stoletiia v russkoi literature*. Vol. 2. 2nd. rev. ed. St. Petersburg and Moscow: Izdanie t-va M. O. Vol'f, 1913.

Zandberg, D. G. *Istoricheskaia belletristika v shkole. Opyt sistematicheskogo kriticheskogo ukazatelia*. Part I: *Vseobshchaia istoriia*, ed. D. N. Egorov. Moscow: A. A. Levenson, 1912.

Zorin, Andrei. *Kormia dvuglavogo orla . . . Literatura i gosudarstvennaia ideologiia v Rossii v poslednei treti XVIII—pervoi treti XIX veka.* Moscow: NLO, 2001.

Zotov, R. M. *Leonid, ili Nekotorye cherty iz zhizni Napoleona.* In his *Sobranie sochinenii v piati tomakh,* 3:5–580. Moscow: Terra, 1996.

———. *Shapka iurodivogo, ili Trilistvennik. Istoricheskii roman iz vremen Elizavety i Ekateriny II.* In his *Sobranie sochinenii v piati tomakh,* 1:13–652. Moscow: Terra, 1996.

Index

Page numbers in bold italics refer to figures.

www.ingramcontent.com/pod-product-compliance
Lightning Source LLC
Chambersburg PA
CBHW070640310726
48982CB00001B/347
9780299225001